Breaking Up

AIMEE FRIEDMAN

ART BY CHRISTINE NORRIE

AN IMPRINT OF

NEW YORK TORONTO LONDON AUCKLAND SYDNEY MEXICO CITY NEW DELHI HONG KONG BUENOS AIRES

For my mother, who predicted it,
and for my father and my sister, who believed her.

With thanks to Craig Walker, David Levithan,
Janna Morishima, and Christine Norrie.
— AF

For chocolate cake and shopping, letters and surprises in the mail, long chats and coffee breaks, and being there for me at the drop of a hat... Kathryn, Sarah, and Janna. Also to Aimee and her terrific manuscript, the fine people at Scholastic, Matt Kindt and John Kuramoto for saving me, the Sexton-Dalzells, Yali Lin, JD, Marion Vitus, Chris Sager, S. Jhoanna Robledo, and my friends from Two Rooms. Lastly, thank you to Andy, Josie, Catherine, and Orwell. My lovely little family who inspire me every single minute of the day.
— CN

Text copyright © 2007 by Aimee Friedman
Art copyright © 2007 by Christine Norrie

ISBN-13: 978-0-439-74867-4
ISBN-10: 0-439-74867-4

10 9 8 7 6 5 4 3 2 1   07 08 09 10

First edition, January 2007
Lettering by Andrew Lis
Edited by David Levithan & Janna Morishima
Book design by Kristina Albertson
Creative Director: David Saylor
Printed in the U.S.A.

Chapter 1: Snapshots

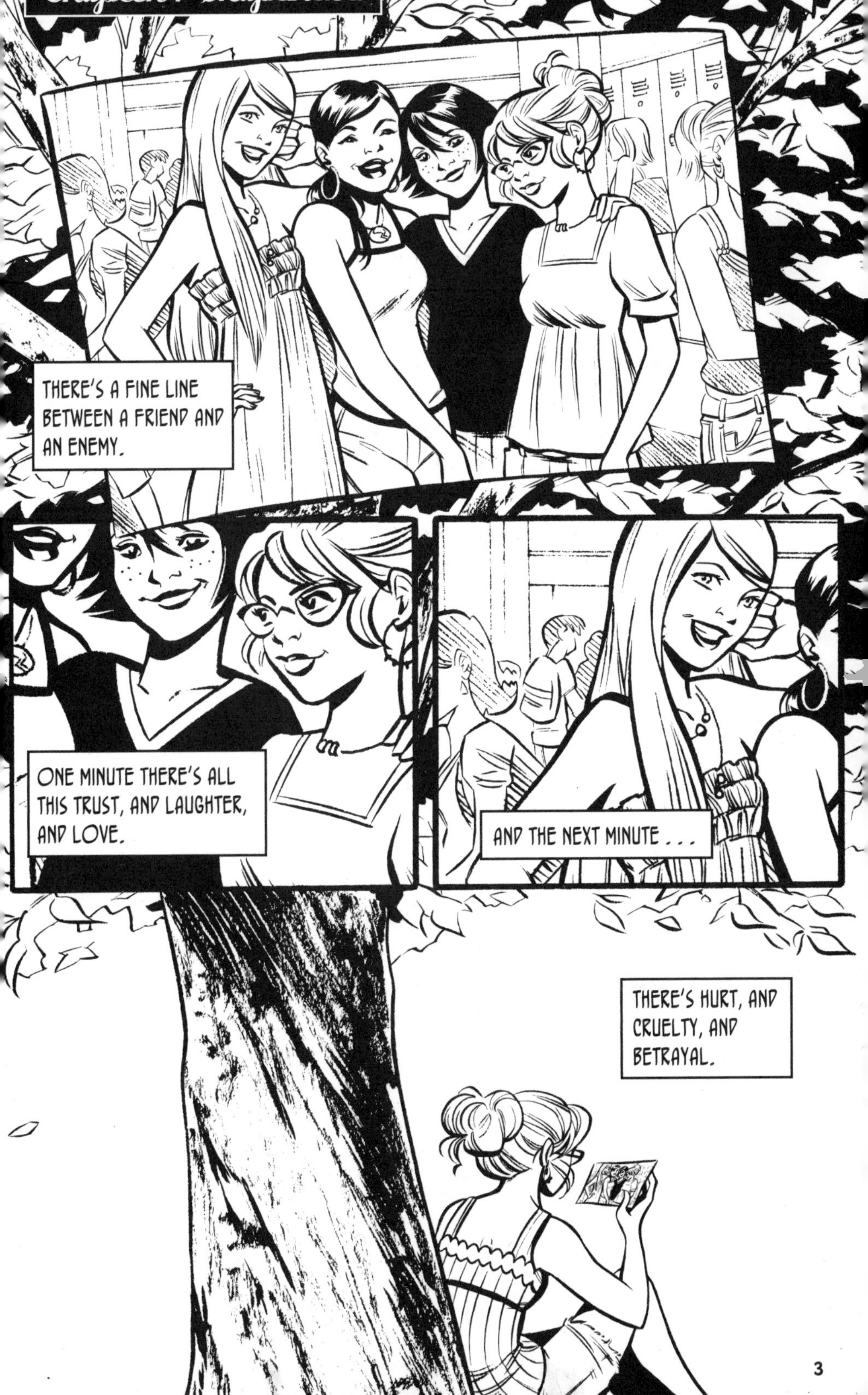
THERE'S A FINE LINE BETWEEN A FRIEND AND AN ENEMY.
ONE MINUTE THERE'S ALL THIS TRUST, AND LAUGHTER, AND LOVE.
AND THE NEXT MINUTE . . .
THERE'S HURT, AND CRUELTY, AND BETRAYAL.

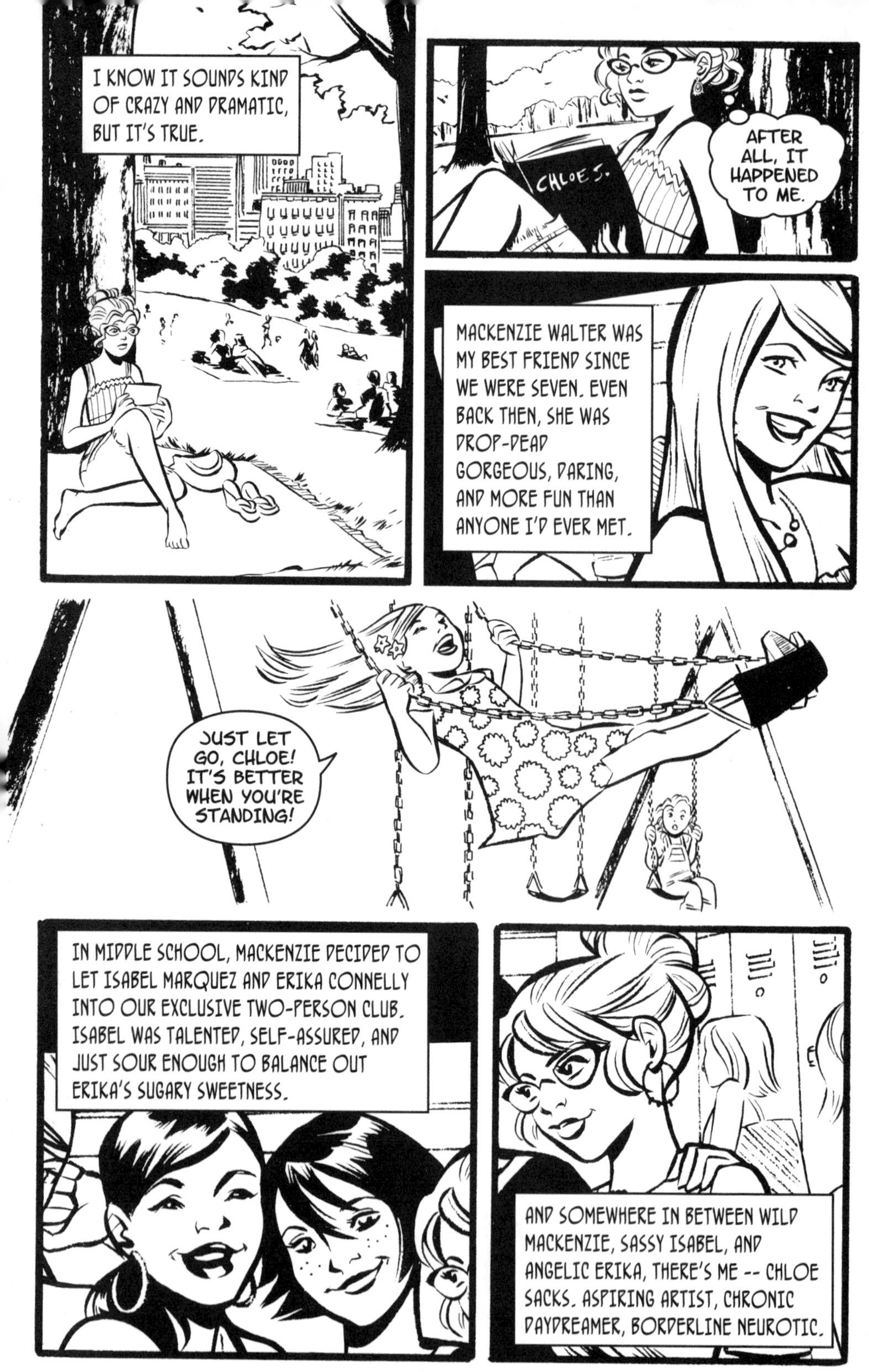
I KNOW IT SOUNDS KIND OF CRAZY AND DRAMATIC, BUT IT'S TRUE.
CHLOE S.
AFTER ALL, IT HAPPENED TO ME.
MACKENZIE WALTER WAS MY BEST FRIEND SINCE WE WERE SEVEN. EVEN BACK THEN, SHE WAS DROP-DEAD GORGEOUS, DARING, AND MORE FUN THAN ANYONE I'D EVER MET.
JUST LET GO, CHLOE! IT'S BETTER WHEN YOU'RE STANDING!
IN MIDDLE SCHOOL, MACKENZIE DECIDED TO LET ISABEL MARQUEZ AND ERIKA CONNELLY INTO OUR EXCLUSIVE TWO-PERSON CLUB. ISABEL WAS TALENTED, SELF-ASSURED, AND JUST SOUR ENOUGH TO BALANCE OUT ERIKA'S SUGARY SWEETNESS.
AND SOMEWHERE IN BETWEEN WILD MACKENZIE, SASSY ISABEL, AND ANGELIC ERIKA, THERE'S ME -- CHLOE SACKS. ASPIRING ARTIST, CHRONIC DAYDREAMER, BORDERLINE NEUROTIC.

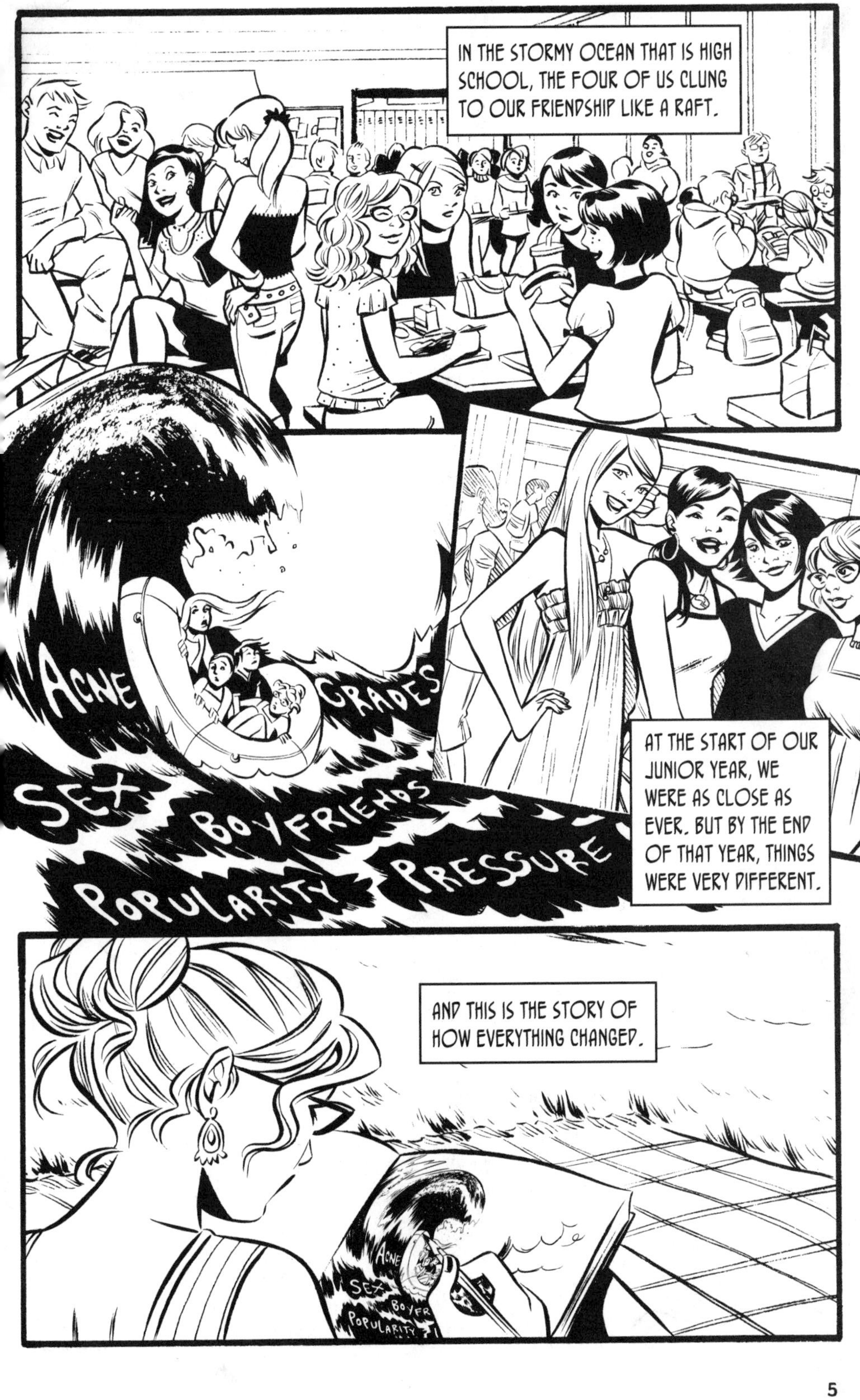
IN THE STORMY OCEAN THAT IS HIGH SCHOOL, THE FOUR OF US CLUNG TO OUR FRIENDSHIP LIKE A RAFT.
ACNE
GRADES
SEX
BOYFRIENDS
POPULARITY
PRESSURE
AT THE START OF OUR JUNIOR YEAR, WE WERE AS CLOSE AS EVER. BUT BY THE END OF THAT YEAR, THINGS WERE VERY DIFFERENT.
AND THIS IS THE STORY OF HOW EVERYTHING CHANGED.

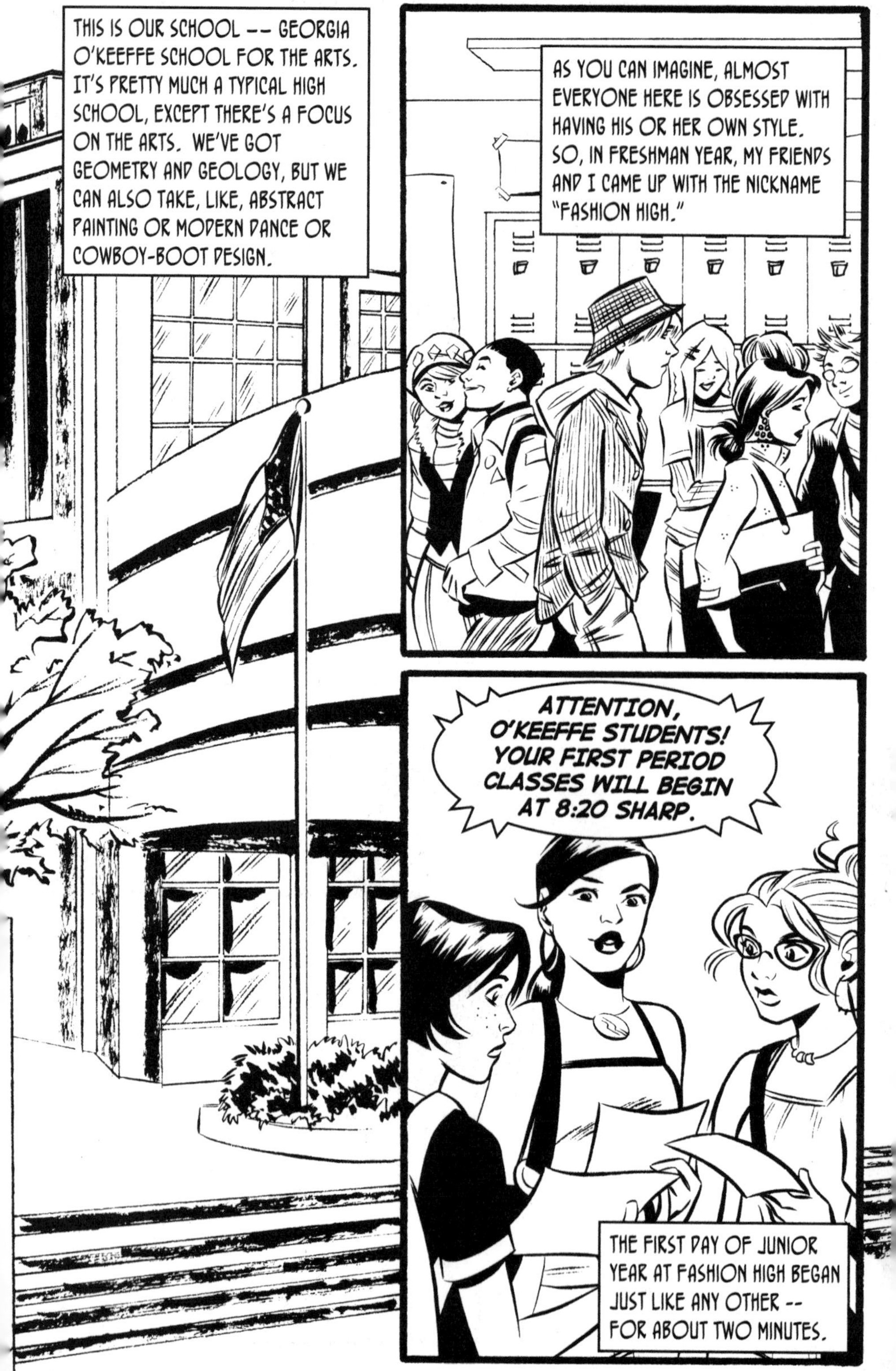
THIS IS OUR SCHOOL -- GEORGIA O'KEEFFE SCHOOL FOR THE ARTS. IT'S PRETTY MUCH A TYPICAL HIGH SCHOOL, EXCEPT THERE'S A FOCUS ON THE ARTS. WE'VE GOT GEOMETRY AND GEOLOGY, BUT WE CAN ALSO TAKE, LIKE, ABSTRACT PAINTING OR MODERN DANCE OR COWBOY-BOOT DESIGN.
AS YOU CAN IMAGINE, ALMOST EVERYONE HERE IS OBSESSED WITH HAVING HIS OR HER OWN STYLE. SO, IN FRESHMAN YEAR, MY FRIENDS AND I CAME UP WITH THE NICKNAME "FASHION HIGH."
ATTENTION, O'KEEFFE STUDENTS! YOUR FIRST PERIOD CLASSES WILL BEGIN AT 8:20 SHARP.
THE FIRST DAY OF JUNIOR YEAR AT FASHION HIGH BEGAN JUST LIKE ANY OTHER -- FOR ABOUT TWO MINUTES.

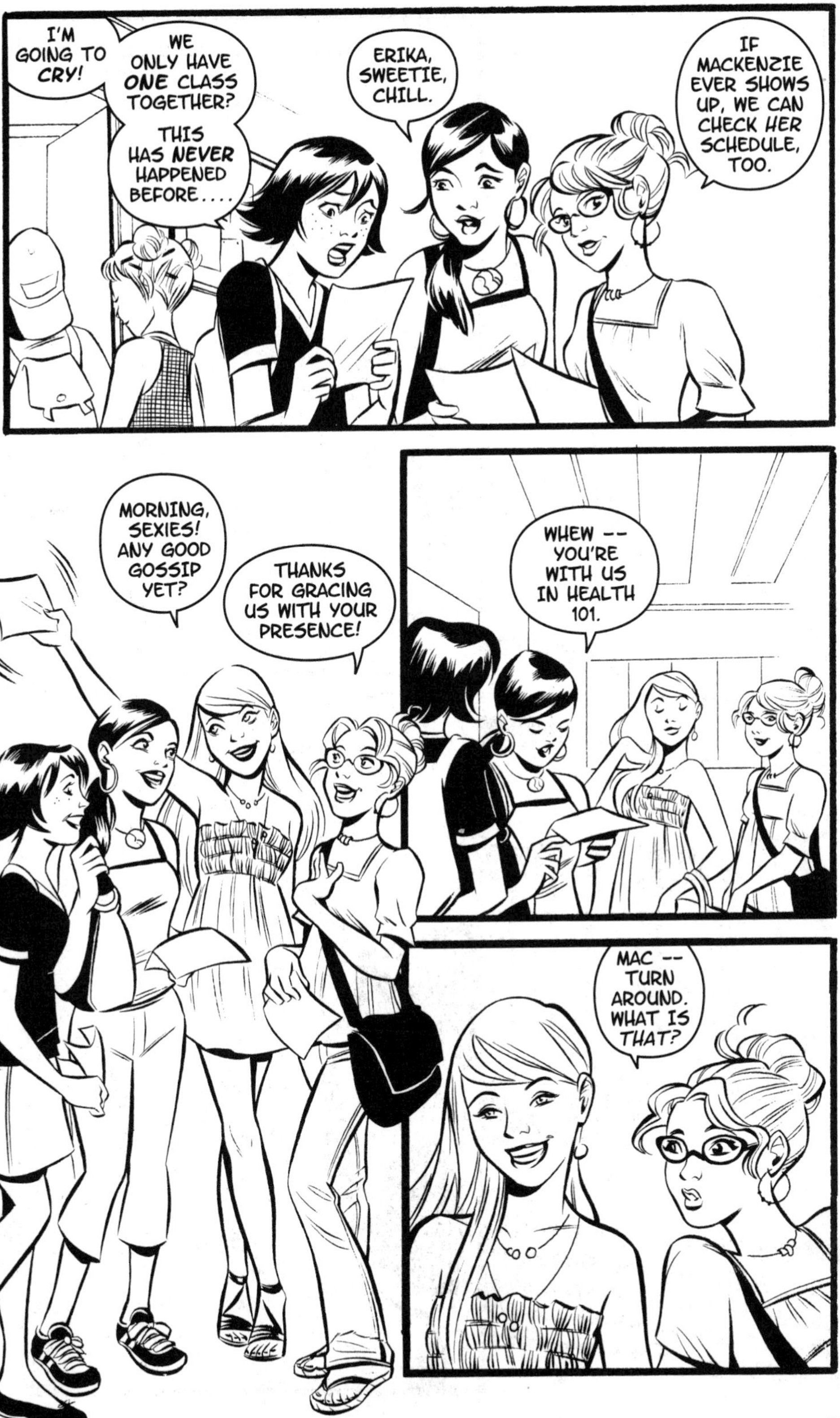
I'M GOING TO CRY!
WE ONLY HAVE ONE CLASS TOGETHER?
THIS HAS NEVER HAPPENED BEFORE....
ERIKA, SWEETIE, CHILL.
IF MACKENZIE EVER SHOWS UP, WE CAN CHECK HER SCHEDULE, TOO.
MORNING, SEXIES! ANY GOOD GOSSIP YET?
THANKS FOR GRACING US WITH YOUR PRESENCE!
WHEW -- YOU'RE WITH US IN HEALTH 101.
MAC -- TURN AROUND. WHAT IS THAT?

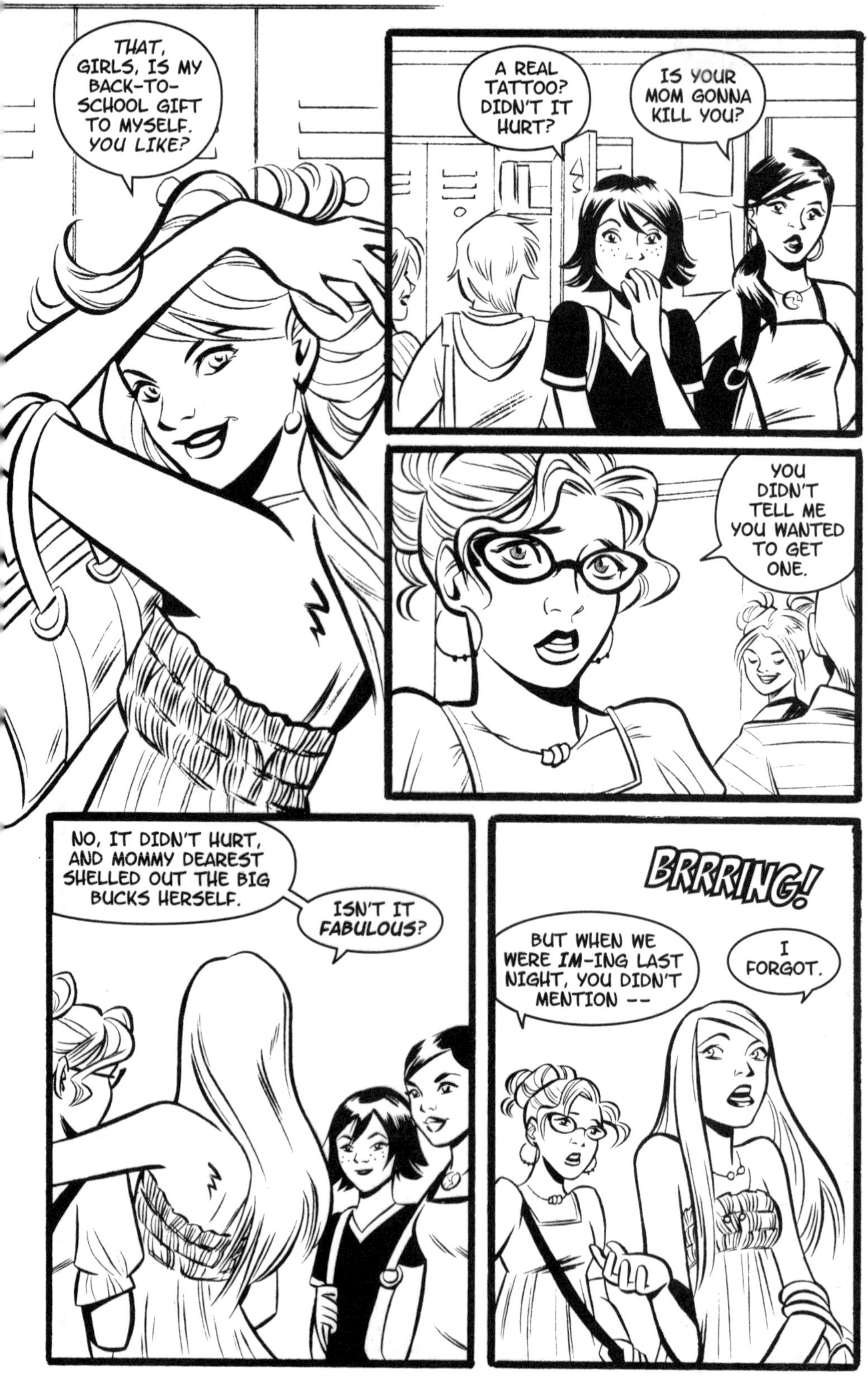
THAT, GIRLS, IS MY BACK-TO-SCHOOL GIFT TO MYSELF. YOU LIKE?
A REAL TATTOO? DIDN'T IT HURT?
IS YOUR MOM GONNA KILL YOU?
YOU DIDN'T TELL ME YOU WANTED TO GET ONE.
NO, IT DIDN'T HURT, AND MOMMY DEAREST SHELLED OUT THE BIG BUCKS HERSELF.
ISN'T IT *FABULOUS*?
BRRRING!
BUT WHEN WE WERE *IM*-ING LAST NIGHT, YOU DIDN'T MENTION --
I FORGOT.

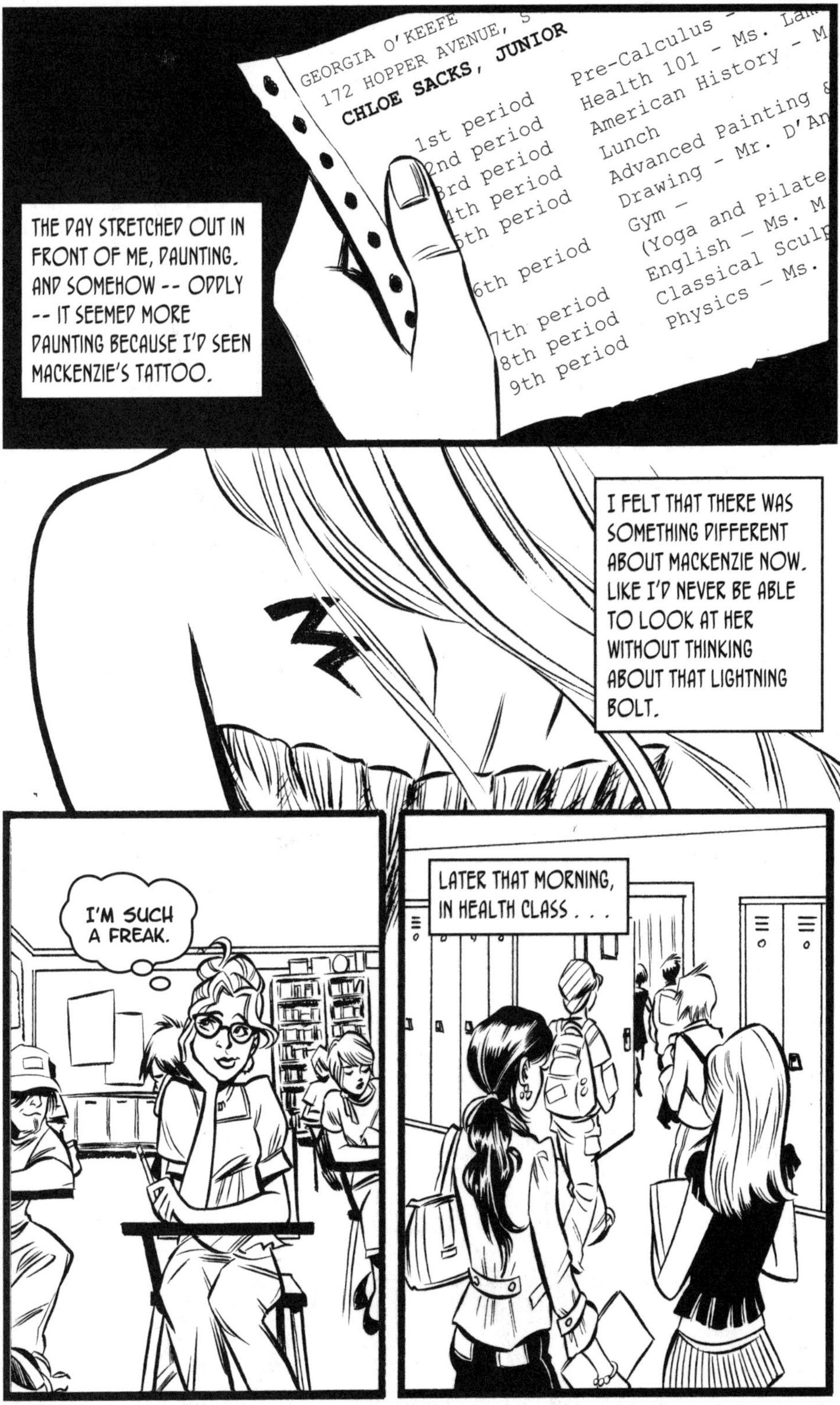
GEORGIA O'KEEFE
172 HOPPER AVENUE,
CHLOE SACKS, JUNIOR
1st period Pre-Calculus
2nd period Health 101 - Ms.
3rd period American History
4th period Lunch
5th period Advanced Painting
Drawing - Mr. D'An
6th period Gym –
(Yoga and Pilate
7th period English – Ms.
8th period Classical Sculp
9th period Physics – Ms.
THE DAY STRETCHED OUT IN FRONT OF ME, DAUNTING. AND SOMEHOW -- ODDLY -- IT SEEMED MORE DAUNTING BECAUSE I'D SEEN MACKENZIE'S TATTOO.
I FELT THAT THERE WAS SOMETHING DIFFERENT ABOUT MACKENZIE NOW. LIKE I'D NEVER BE ABLE TO LOOK AT HER WITHOUT THINKING ABOUT THAT LIGHTNING BOLT.
I'M SUCH A FREAK.
LATER THAT MORNING, IN HEALTH CLASS . . .

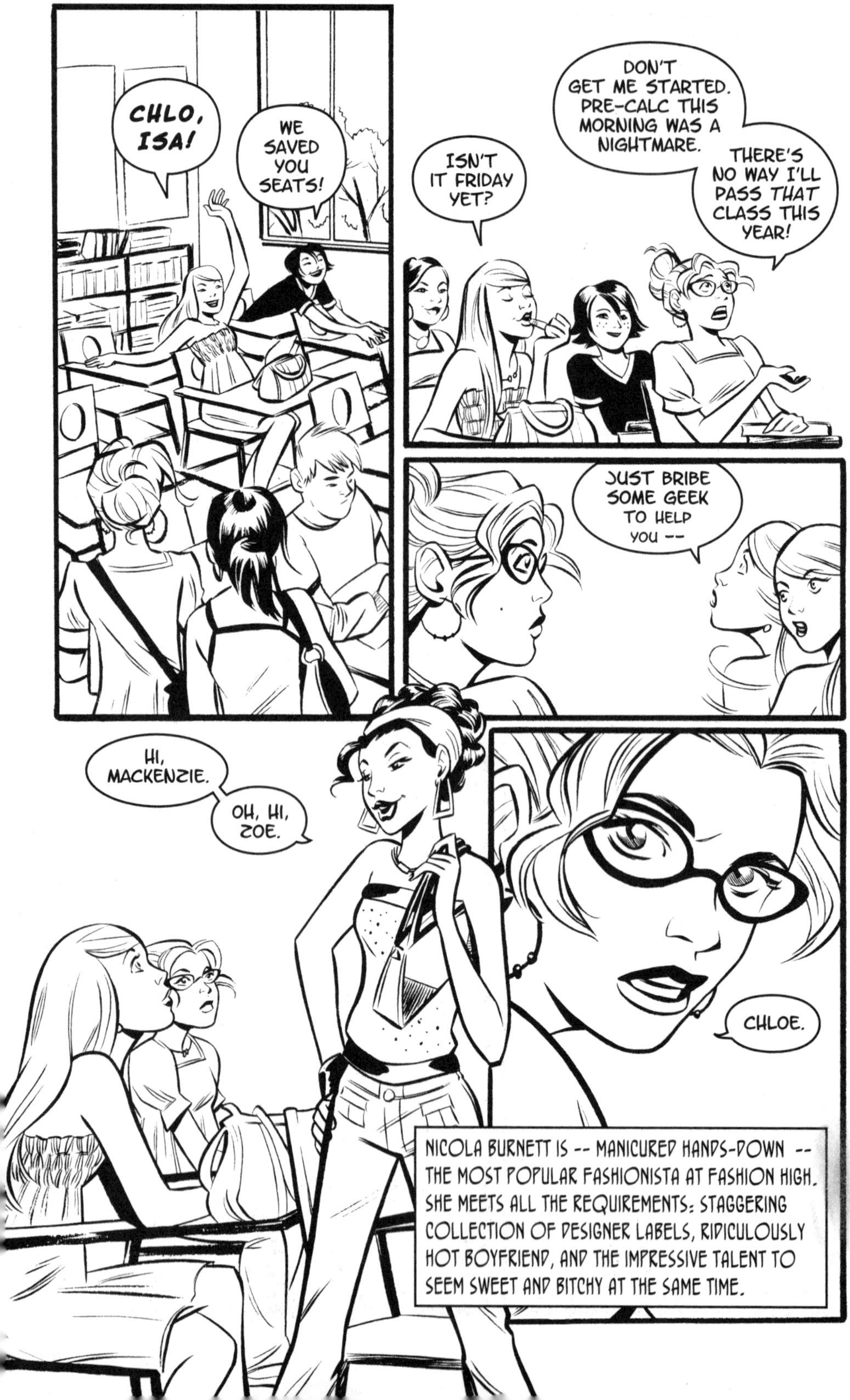
CHLO, ISA!
WE SAVED YOU SEATS!
ISN'T IT FRIDAY YET?
DON'T GET ME STARTED. PRE-CALC THIS MORNING WAS A NIGHTMARE.
THERE'S NO WAY I'LL PASS THAT CLASS THIS YEAR!
JUST BRIBE SOME GEEK TO HELP YOU --
HI, MACKENZIE.
OH, HI, ZOE.
CHLOE.
NICOLA BURNETT IS -- MANICURED HANDS-DOWN -- THE MOST POPULAR FASHIONISTA AT FASHION HIGH. SHE MEETS ALL THE REQUIREMENTS: STAGGERING COLLECTION OF DESIGNER LABELS, RIDICULOUSLY HOT BOYFRIEND, AND THE IMPRESSIVE TALENT TO SEEM SWEET AND BITCHY AT THE SAME TIME.

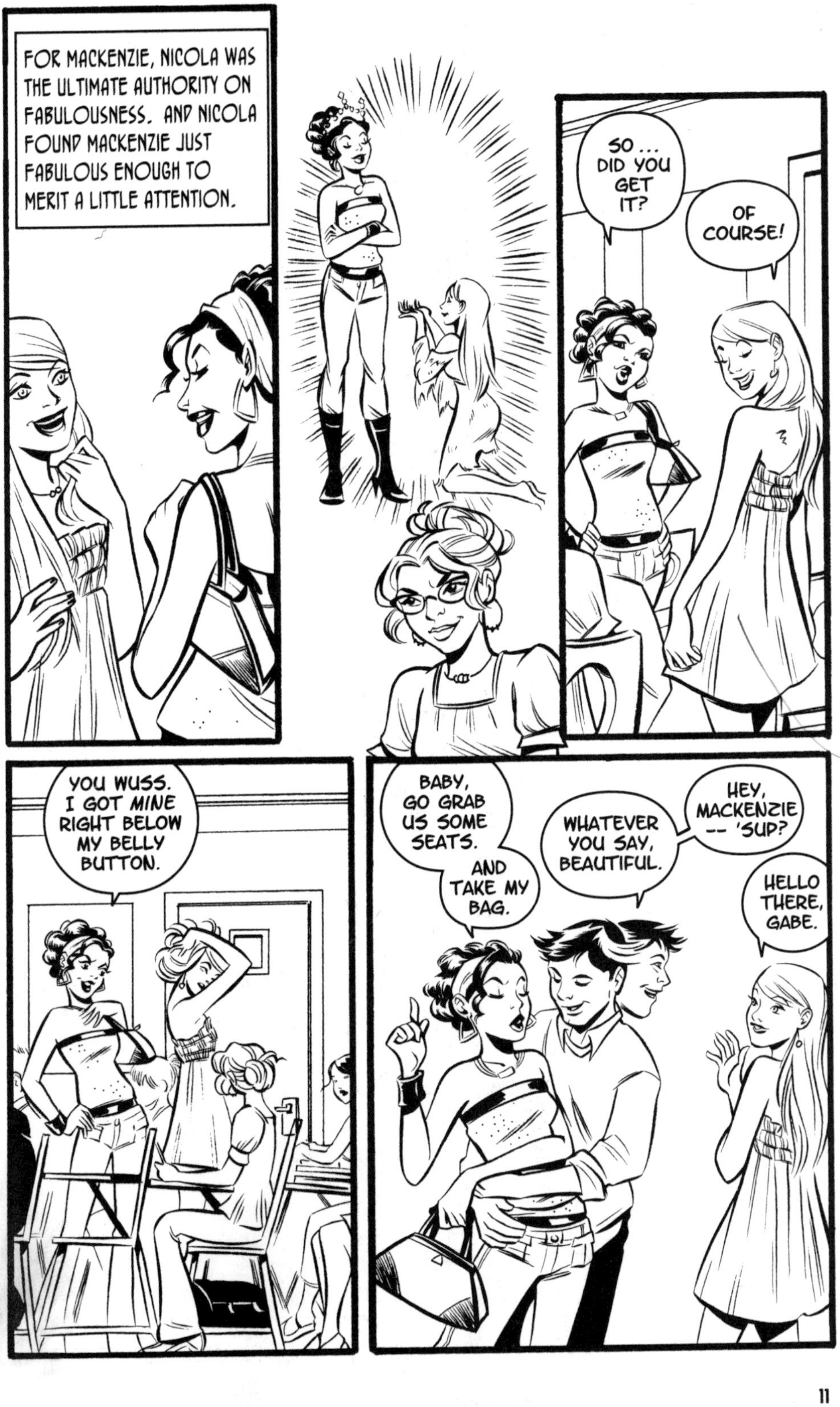
FOR MACKENZIE, NICOLA WAS THE ULTIMATE AUTHORITY ON FABULOUSNESS. AND NICOLA FOUND MACKENZIE JUST FABULOUS ENOUGH TO MERIT A LITTLE ATTENTION.
SO ... DID YOU GET IT?
OF COURSE!
YOU WUSS. I GOT *MINE* RIGHT BELOW MY BELLY BUTTON.
BABY, GO GRAB US SOME SEATS.
AND TAKE MY BAG.
WHATEVER YOU SAY, BEAUTIFUL.
HEY, MACKENZIE -- 'SUP?
HELLO THERE, GABE.

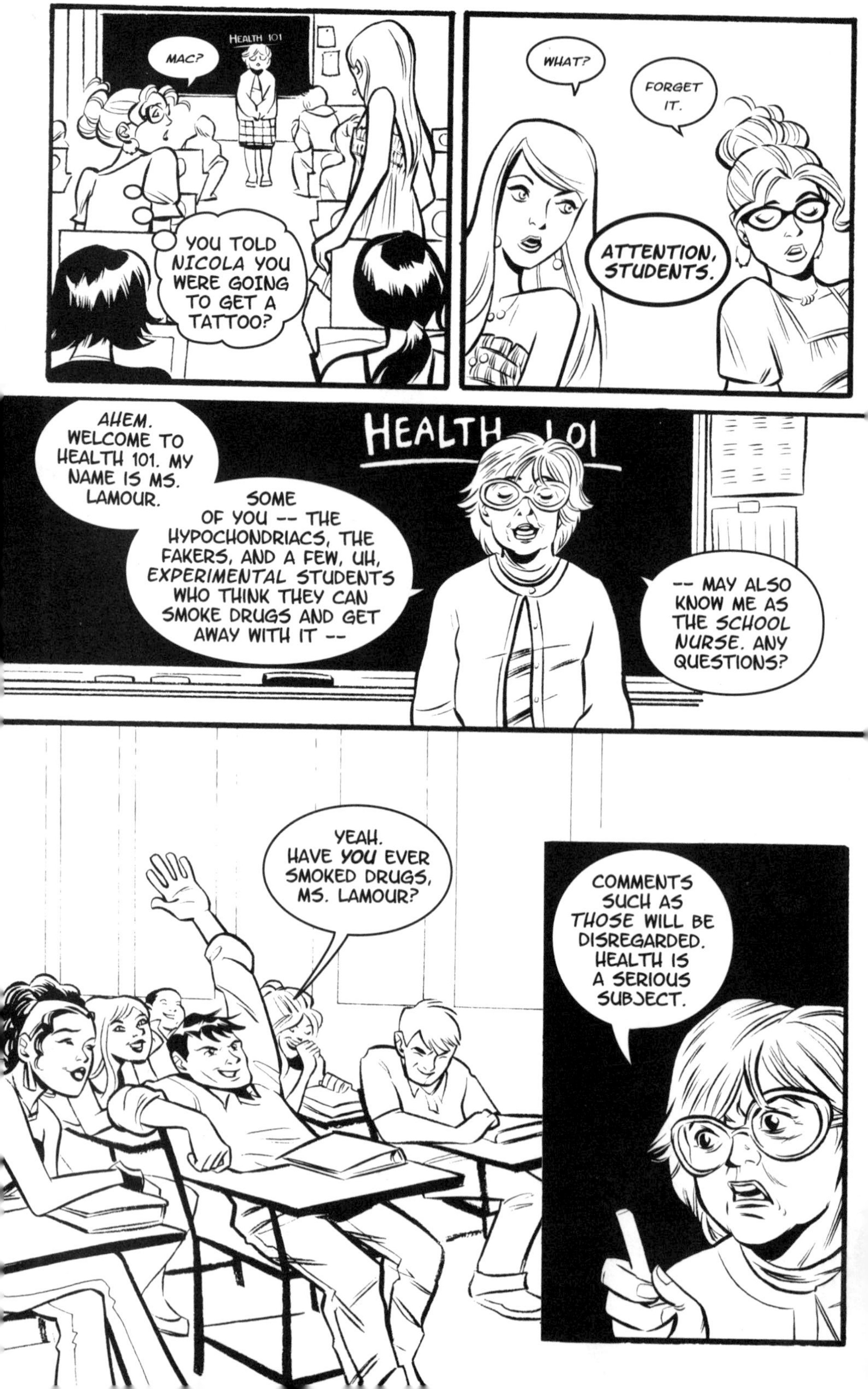
HEALTH 101
MAC?
YOU TOLD NICOLA YOU WERE GOING TO GET A TATTOO?
WHAT?
FORGET IT.
ATTENTION, STUDENTS.
HEALTH 101
AHEM. WELCOME TO HEALTH 101. MY NAME IS MS. LAMOUR.
SOME OF YOU -- THE HYPOCHONDRIACS, THE FAKERS, AND A FEW, UH, EXPERIMENTAL STUDENTS WHO THINK THEY CAN SMOKE DRUGS AND GET AWAY WITH IT --
-- MAY ALSO KNOW ME AS THE SCHOOL NURSE. ANY QUESTIONS?
YEAH. HAVE YOU EVER SMOKED DRUGS, MS. LAMOUR?
COMMENTS SUCH AS THOSE WILL BE DISREGARDED. HEALTH IS A SERIOUS SUBJECT.

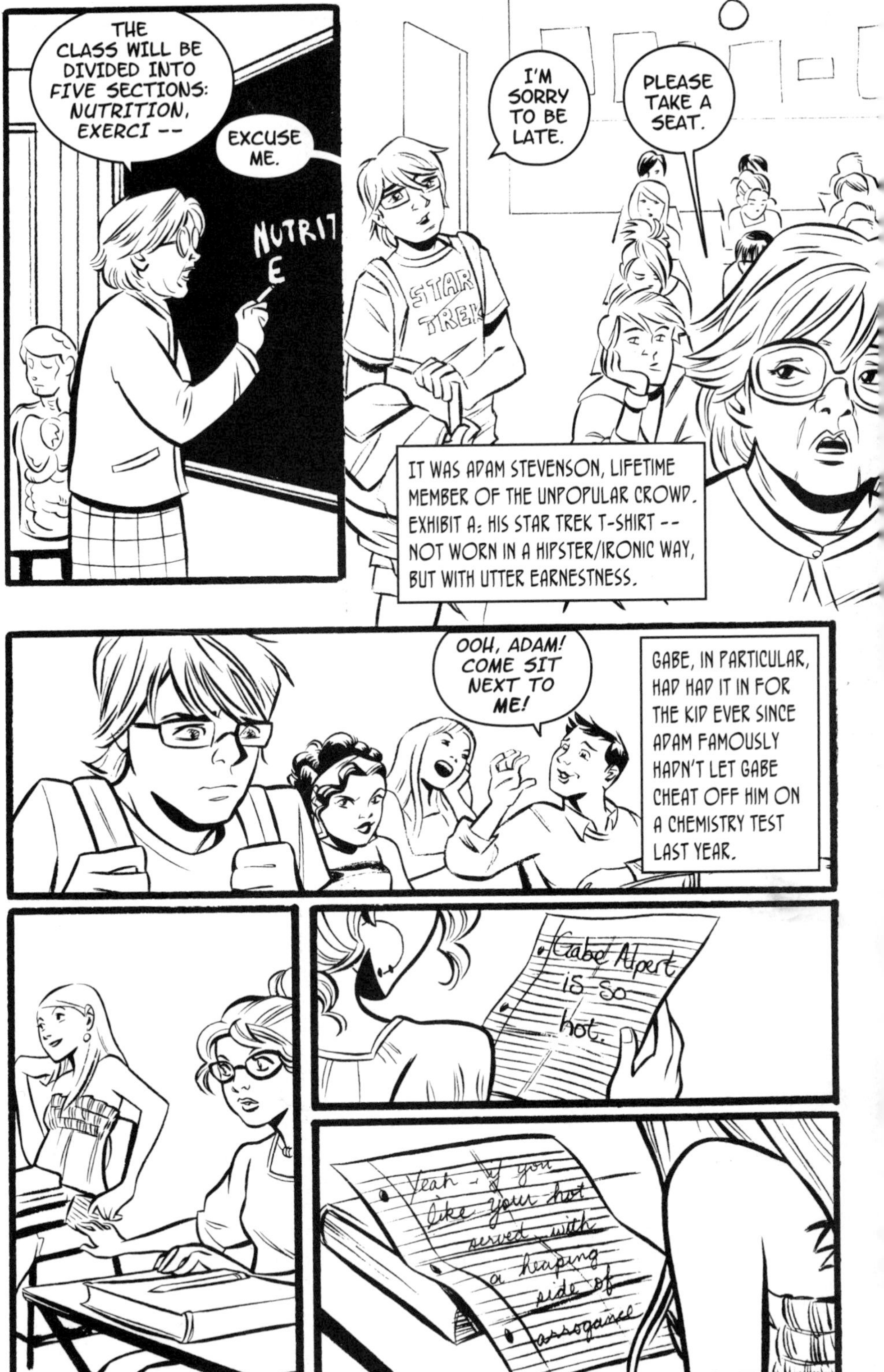
THE CLASS WILL BE DIVIDED INTO FIVE SECTIONS: NUTRITION, EXERCI --
EXCUSE ME.
NUTRIT
E
I'M SORRY TO BE LATE.
PLEASE TAKE A SEAT.
STAR TREK
IT WAS ADAM STEVENSON, LIFETIME MEMBER OF THE UNPOPULAR CROWD. EXHIBIT A: HIS STAR TREK T-SHIRT -- NOT WORN IN A HIPSTER/IRONIC WAY, BUT WITH UTTER EARNESTNESS.
OOH, ADAM! COME SIT NEXT TO ME!
GABE, IN PARTICULAR, HAD HAD IT IN FOR THE KID EVER SINCE ADAM FAMOUSLY HADN'T LET GABE CHEAT OFF HIM ON A CHEMISTRY TEST LAST YEAR.
Gabe Alpert is so hot.
Yeah - if you like your hot served with a heaping side of arrogance

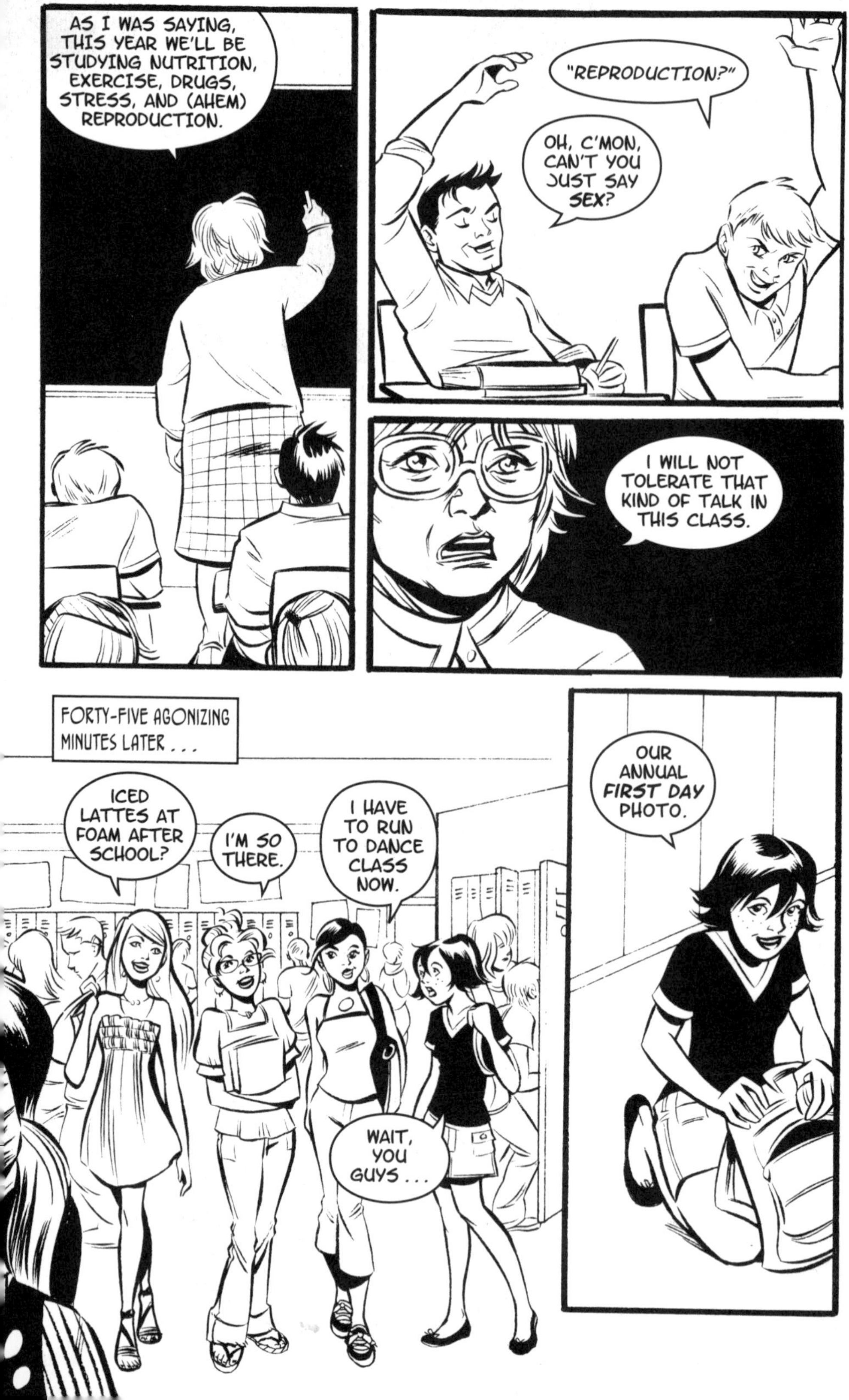
AS I WAS SAYING, THIS YEAR WE'LL BE STUDYING NUTRITION, EXERCISE, DRUGS, STRESS, AND (AHEM) REPRODUCTION.
"REPRODUCTION?"
OH, C'MON, CAN'T YOU JUST SAY SEX?
I WILL NOT TOLERATE THAT KIND OF TALK IN THIS CLASS.
FORTY-FIVE AGONIZING MINUTES LATER . . .
ICED LATTES AT FOAM AFTER SCHOOL?
I'M SO THERE.
I HAVE TO RUN TO DANCE CLASS NOW.
WAIT, YOU GUYS . . .
OUR ANNUAL FIRST DAY PHOTO.

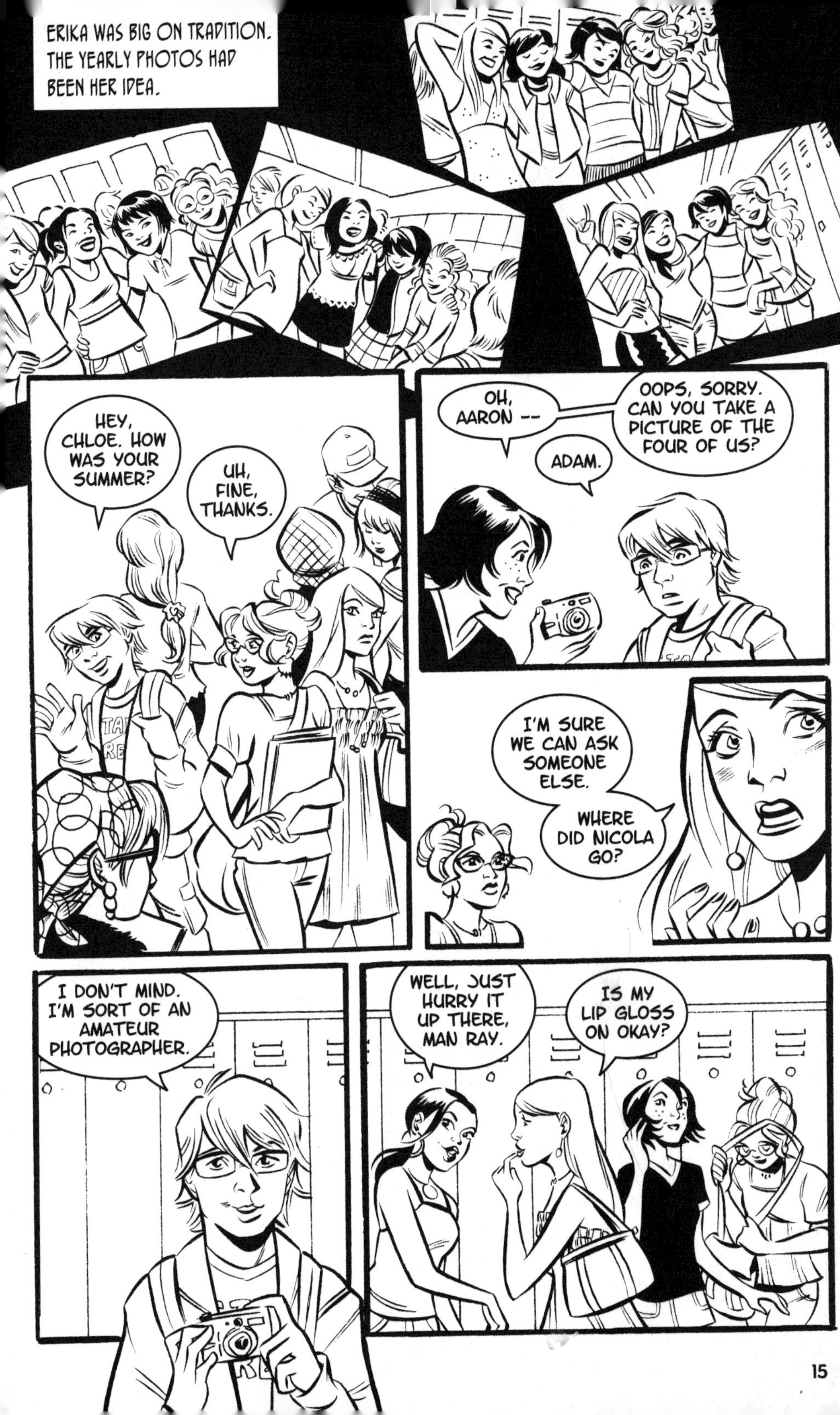
ERIKA WAS BIG ON TRADITION. THE YEARLY PHOTOS HAD BEEN HER IDEA.
HEY, CHLOE. HOW WAS YOUR SUMMER?
UH, FINE, THANKS.
OH, AARON --
ADAM.
OOPS, SORRY. CAN YOU TAKE A PICTURE OF THE FOUR OF US?
I'M SURE WE CAN ASK SOMEONE ELSE.
WHERE DID NICOLA GO?
I DON'T MIND. I'M SORT OF AN AMATEUR PHOTOGRAPHER.
WELL, JUST HURRY IT UP THERE, MAN RAY.
IS MY LIP GLOSS ON OKAY?

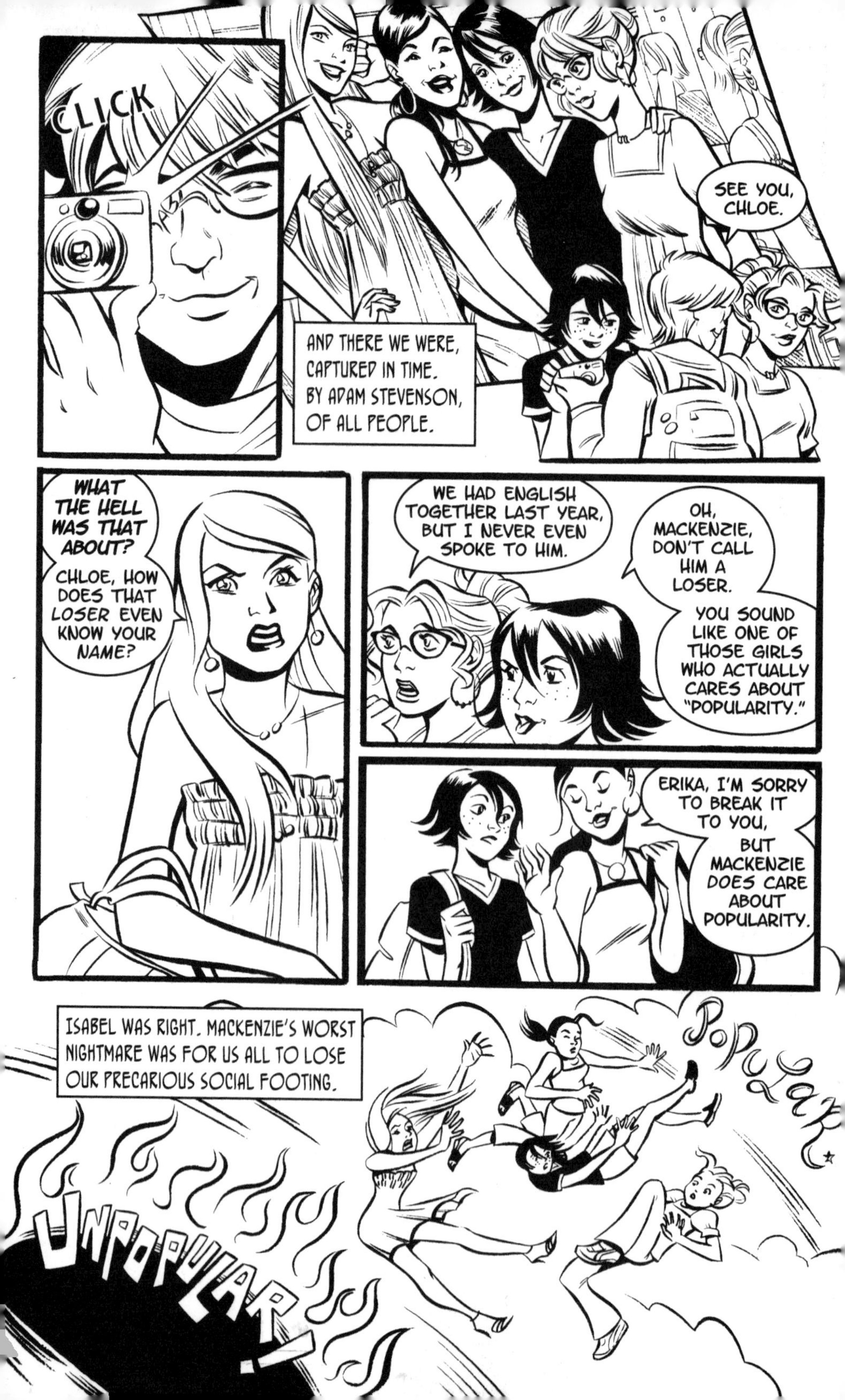
CLICK
SEE YOU, CHLOE.
AND THERE WE WERE, CAPTURED IN TIME. BY ADAM STEVENSON, OF ALL PEOPLE.
WHAT THE HELL WAS THAT ABOUT?
CHLOE, HOW DOES THAT LOSER EVEN KNOW YOUR NAME?
WE HAD ENGLISH TOGETHER LAST YEAR, BUT I NEVER EVEN SPOKE TO HIM.
OH, MACKENZIE, DON'T CALL HIM A LOSER.
YOU SOUND LIKE ONE OF THOSE GIRLS WHO ACTUALLY CARES ABOUT "POPULARITY."
ERIKA, I'M SORRY TO BREAK IT TO YOU,
BUT MACKENZIE DOES CARE ABOUT POPULARITY.
ISABEL WAS RIGHT. MACKENZIE'S WORST NIGHTMARE WAS FOR US ALL TO LOSE OUR PRECARIOUS SOCIAL FOOTING.
POPULAR
UNPOPULAR!

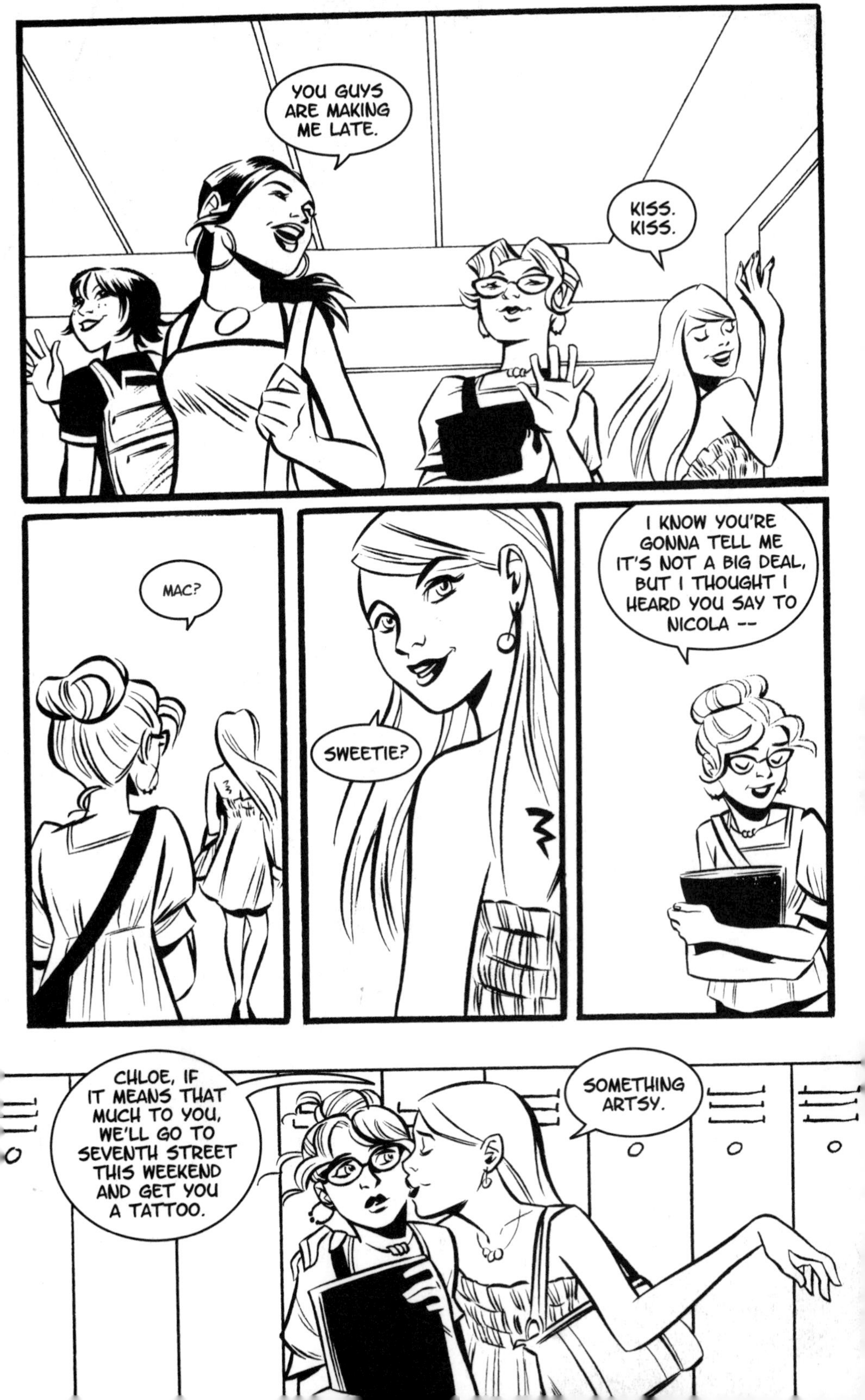
YOU GUYS ARE MAKING ME LATE.
KISS. KISS.
MAC?
SWEETIE?
I KNOW YOU'RE GONNA TELL ME IT'S NOT A BIG DEAL, BUT I THOUGHT I HEARD YOU SAY TO NICOLA --
CHLOE, IF IT MEANS THAT MUCH TO YOU, WE'LL GO TO SEVENTH STREET THIS WEEKEND AND GET YOU A TATTOO.
SOMETHING ARTSY.

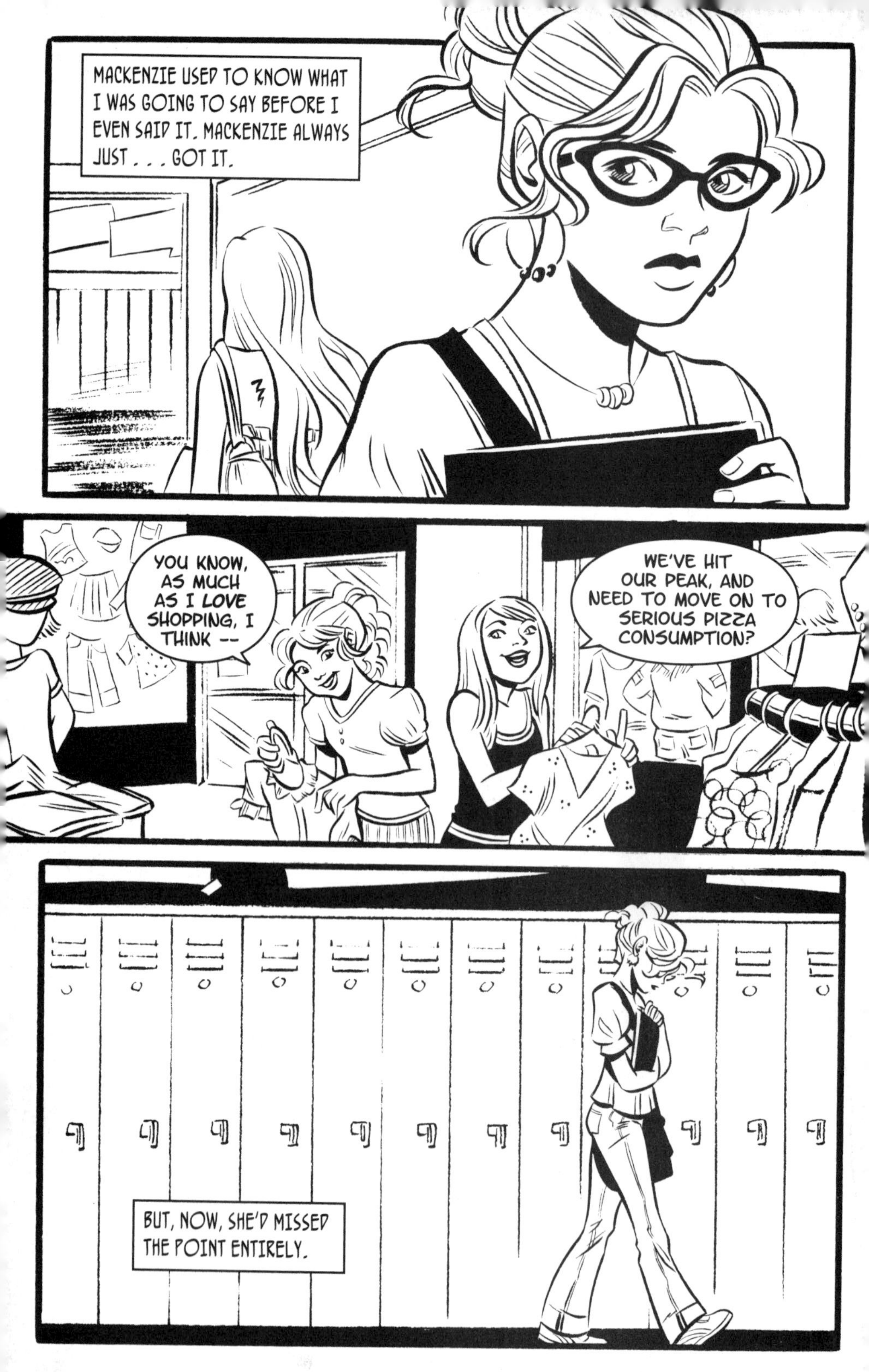
MACKENZIE USED TO KNOW WHAT I WAS GOING TO SAY BEFORE I EVEN SAID IT. MACKENZIE ALWAYS JUST . . . GOT IT.
YOU KNOW, AS MUCH AS I LOVE SHOPPING, I THINK --
WE'VE HIT OUR PEAK, AND NEED TO MOVE ON TO SERIOUS PIZZA CONSUMPTION?
BUT, NOW, SHE'D MISSED THE POINT ENTIRELY.

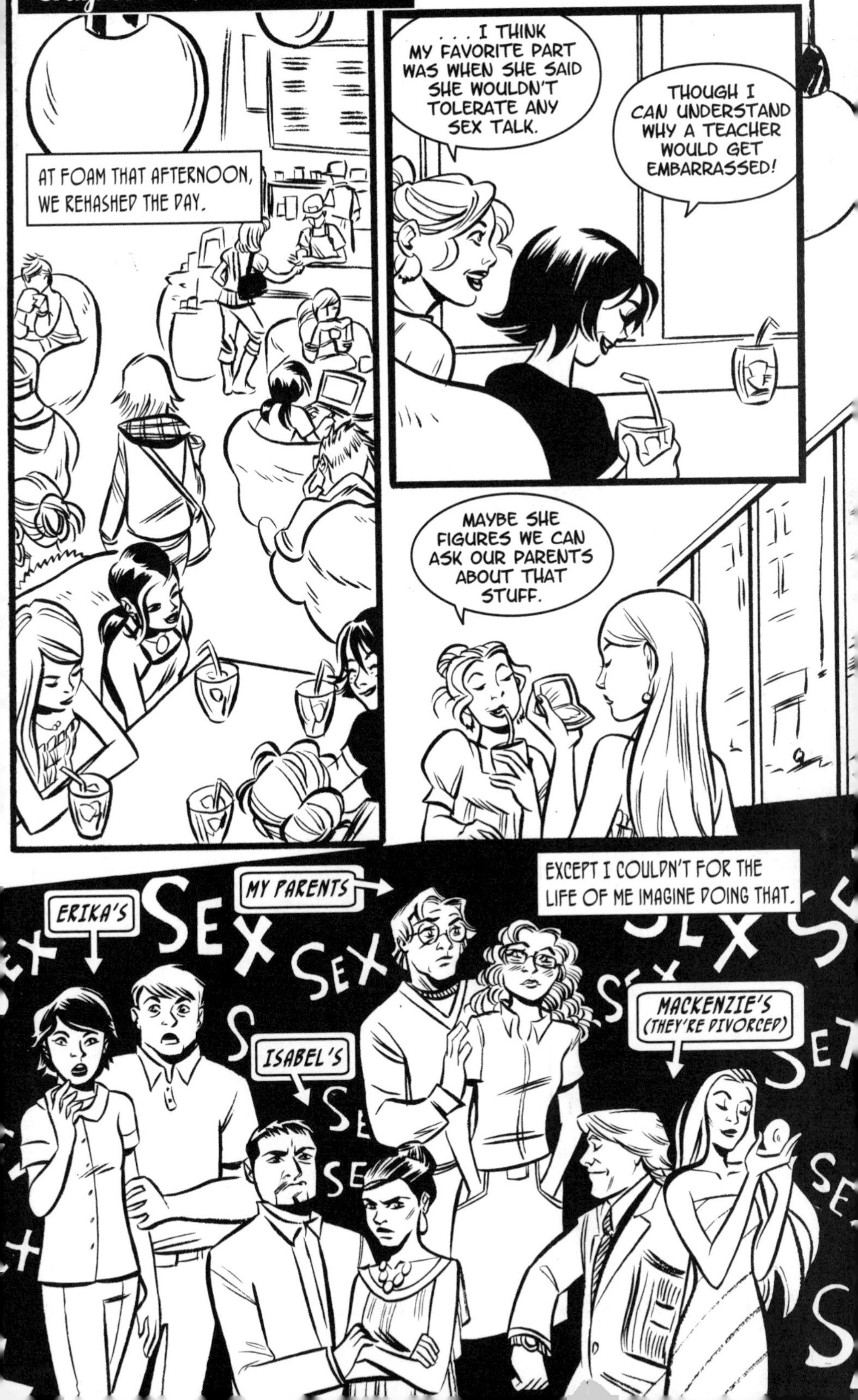
AT FOAM THAT AFTERNOON, WE REHASHED THE DAY.
. . . I THINK MY FAVORITE PART WAS WHEN SHE SAID SHE WOULDN'T TOLERATE ANY SEX TALK.
THOUGH I CAN UNDERSTAND WHY A TEACHER WOULD GET EMBARRASSED!
MAYBE SHE FIGURES WE CAN ASK OUR PARENTS ABOUT THAT STUFF.
EXCEPT I COULDN'T FOR THE LIFE OF ME IMAGINE DOING THAT.
ERIKA'S
MY PARENTS
ISABEL'S
MACKENZIE'S (THEY'RE DIVORCED)
SEX
SEX

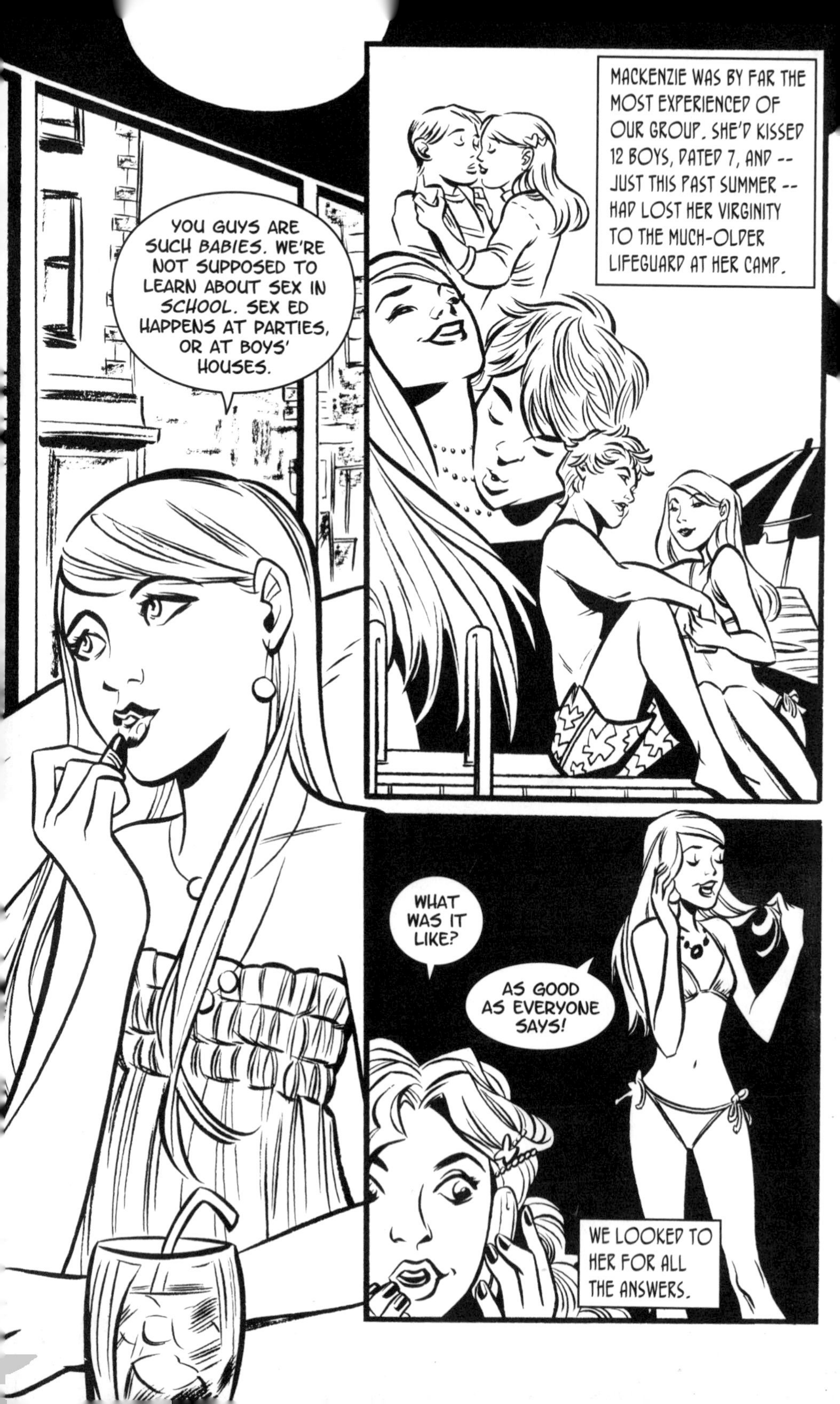
YOU GUYS ARE SUCH BABIES. WE'RE NOT SUPPOSED TO LEARN ABOUT SEX IN SCHOOL. SEX ED HAPPENS AT PARTIES, OR AT BOYS' HOUSES.
MACKENZIE WAS BY FAR THE MOST EXPERIENCED OF OUR GROUP. SHE'D KISSED 12 BOYS, DATED 7, AND -- JUST THIS PAST SUMMER -- HAD LOST HER VIRGINITY TO THE MUCH-OLDER LIFEGUARD AT HER CAMP.
WHAT WAS IT LIKE?
AS GOOD AS EVERYONE SAYS!
WE LOOKED TO HER FOR ALL THE ANSWERS.

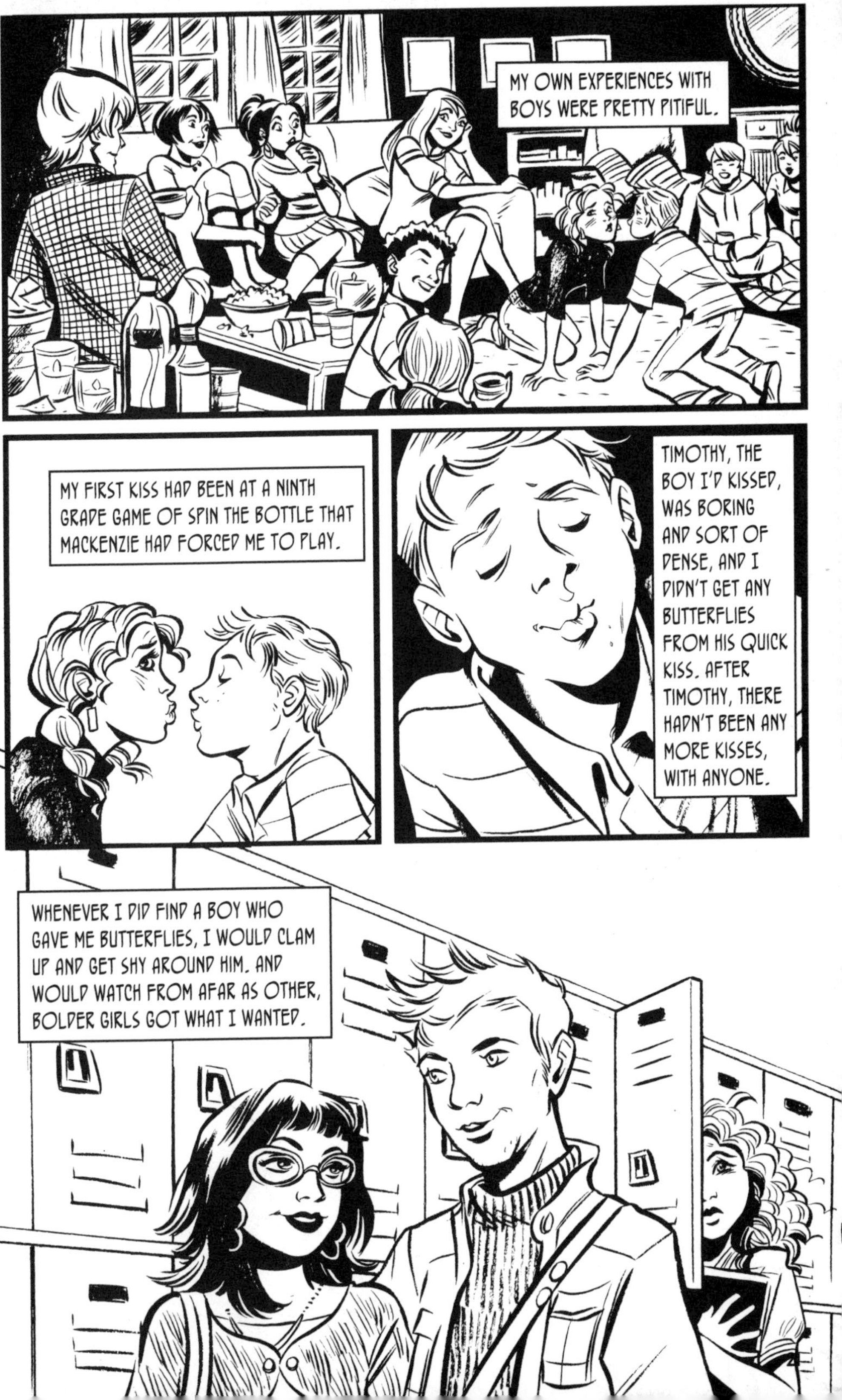
MY OWN EXPERIENCES WITH BOYS WERE PRETTY PITIFUL.
MY FIRST KISS HAD BEEN AT A NINTH GRADE GAME OF SPIN THE BOTTLE THAT MACKENZIE HAD FORCED ME TO PLAY.
TIMOTHY, THE BOY I'D KISSED, WAS BORING AND SORT OF DENSE, AND I DIDN'T GET ANY BUTTERFLIES FROM HIS QUICK KISS. AFTER TIMOTHY, THERE HADN'T BEEN ANY MORE KISSES, WITH ANYONE.
WHENEVER I DID FIND A BOY WHO GAVE ME BUTTERFLIES, I WOULD CLAM UP AND GET SHY AROUND HIM. AND WOULD WATCH FROM AFAR AS OTHER, BOLDER GIRLS GOT WHAT I WANTED.

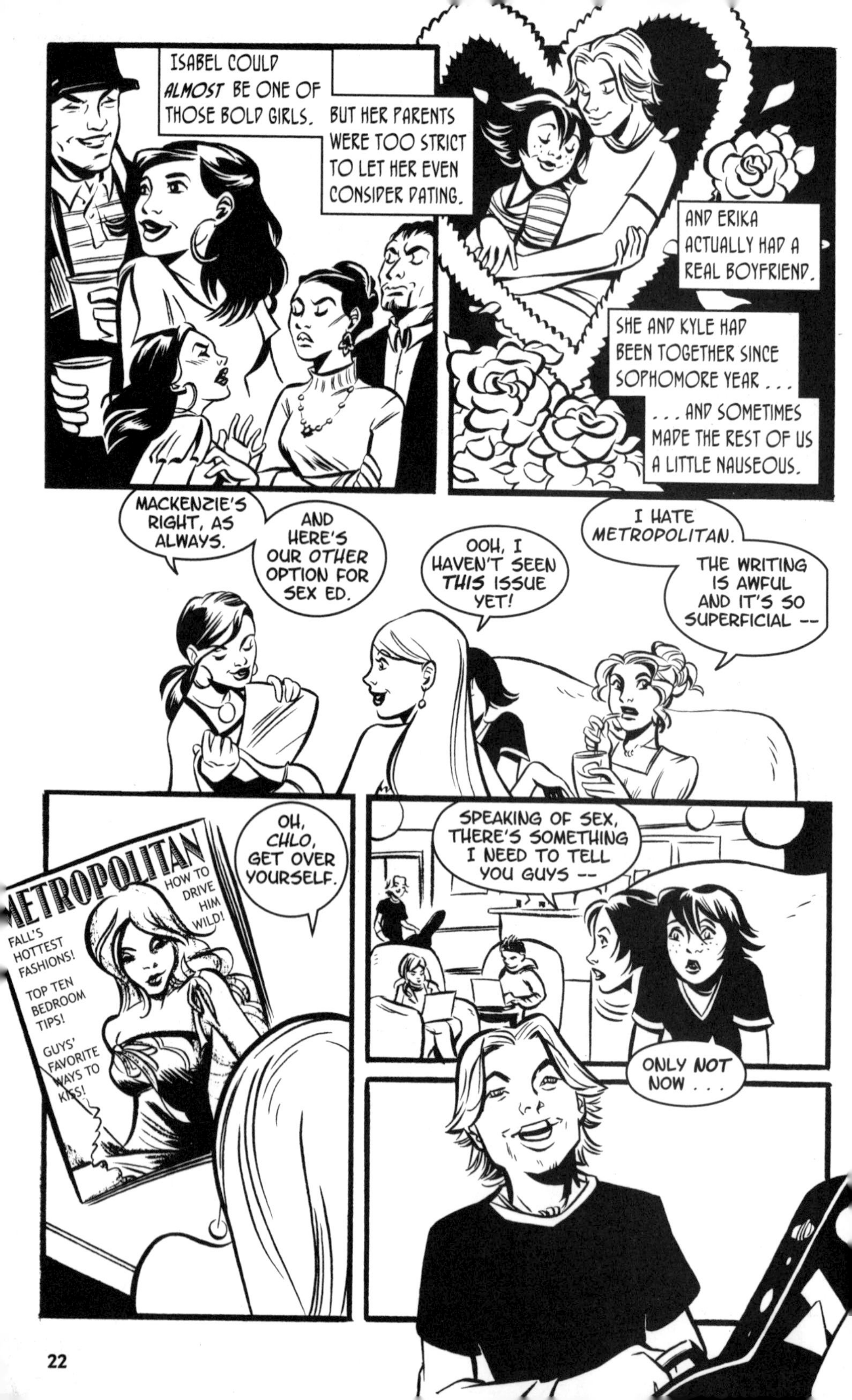
ISABEL COULD ALMOST BE ONE OF THOSE BOLD GIRLS.
BUT HER PARENTS WERE TOO STRICT TO LET HER EVEN CONSIDER DATING.
AND ERIKA ACTUALLY HAD A REAL BOYFRIEND.
SHE AND KYLE HAD BEEN TOGETHER SINCE SOPHOMORE YEAR . . .
. . . AND SOMETIMES MADE THE REST OF US A LITTLE NAUSEOUS.
MACKENZIE'S RIGHT, AS ALWAYS.
AND HERE'S OUR OTHER OPTION FOR SEX ED.
OOH, I HAVEN'T SEEN THIS ISSUE YET!
I HATE METROPOLITAN.
THE WRITING IS AWFUL AND IT'S SO SUPERFICIAL --
METROPOLITAN
HOW TO DRIVE HIM WILD!
FALL'S HOTTEST FASHIONS!
TOP TEN BEDROOM TIPS!
GUYS' FAVORITE WAYS TO KISS!
OH, CHLO, GET OVER YOURSELF.
SPEAKING OF SEX, THERE'S SOMETHING I NEED TO TELL YOU GUYS --
ONLY NOT NOW . . .

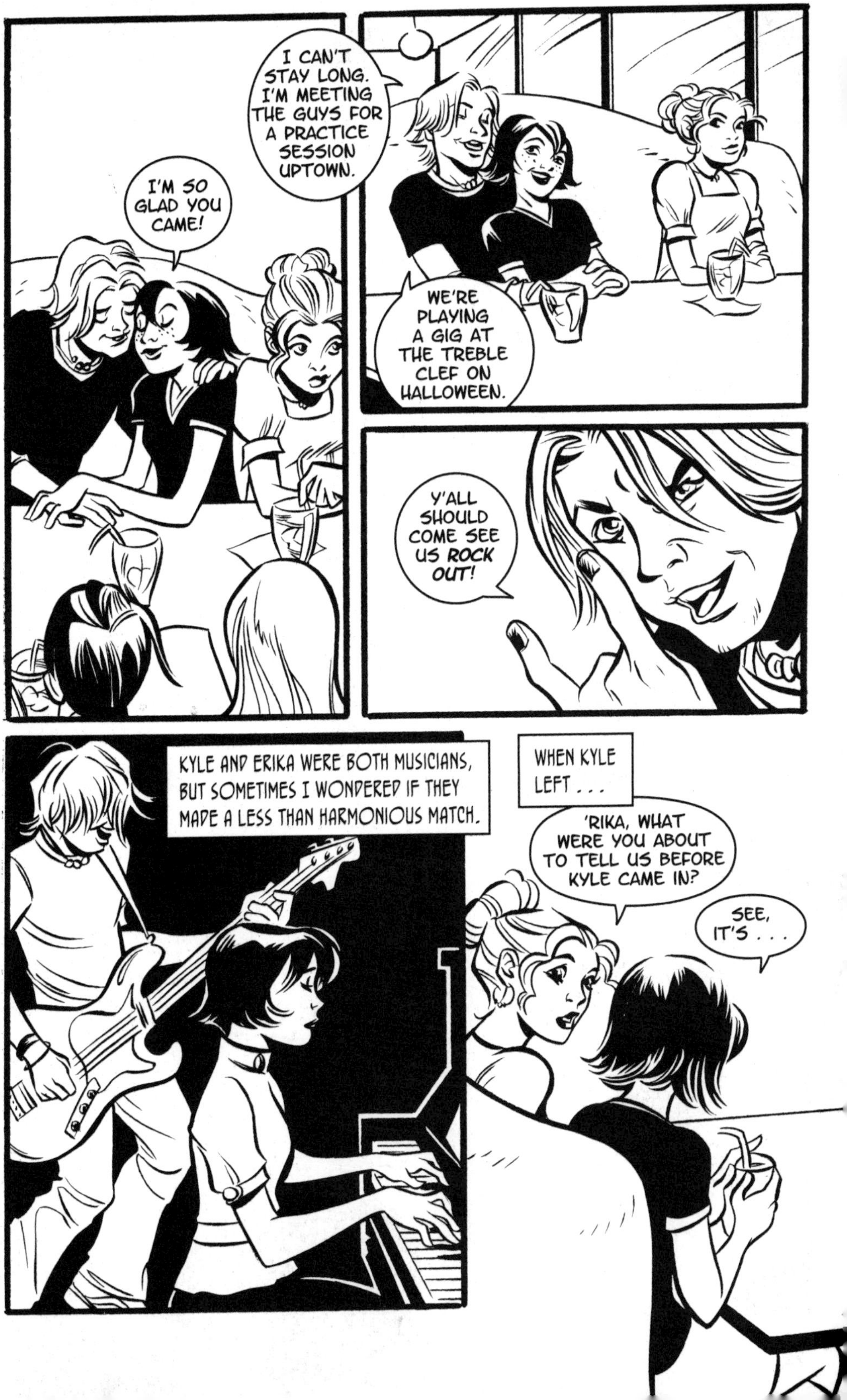
I'M SO GLAD YOU CAME!
I CAN'T STAY LONG. I'M MEETING THE GUYS FOR A PRACTICE SESSION UPTOWN.
WE'RE PLAYING A GIG AT THE TREBLE CLEF ON HALLOWEEN.
Y'ALL SHOULD COME SEE US ROCK OUT!
KYLE AND ERIKA WERE BOTH MUSICIANS, BUT SOMETIMES I WONDERED IF THEY MADE A LESS THAN HARMONIOUS MATCH.
WHEN KYLE LEFT . . .
'RIKA, WHAT WERE YOU ABOUT TO TELL US BEFORE KYLE CAME IN?
SEE, IT'S . . .

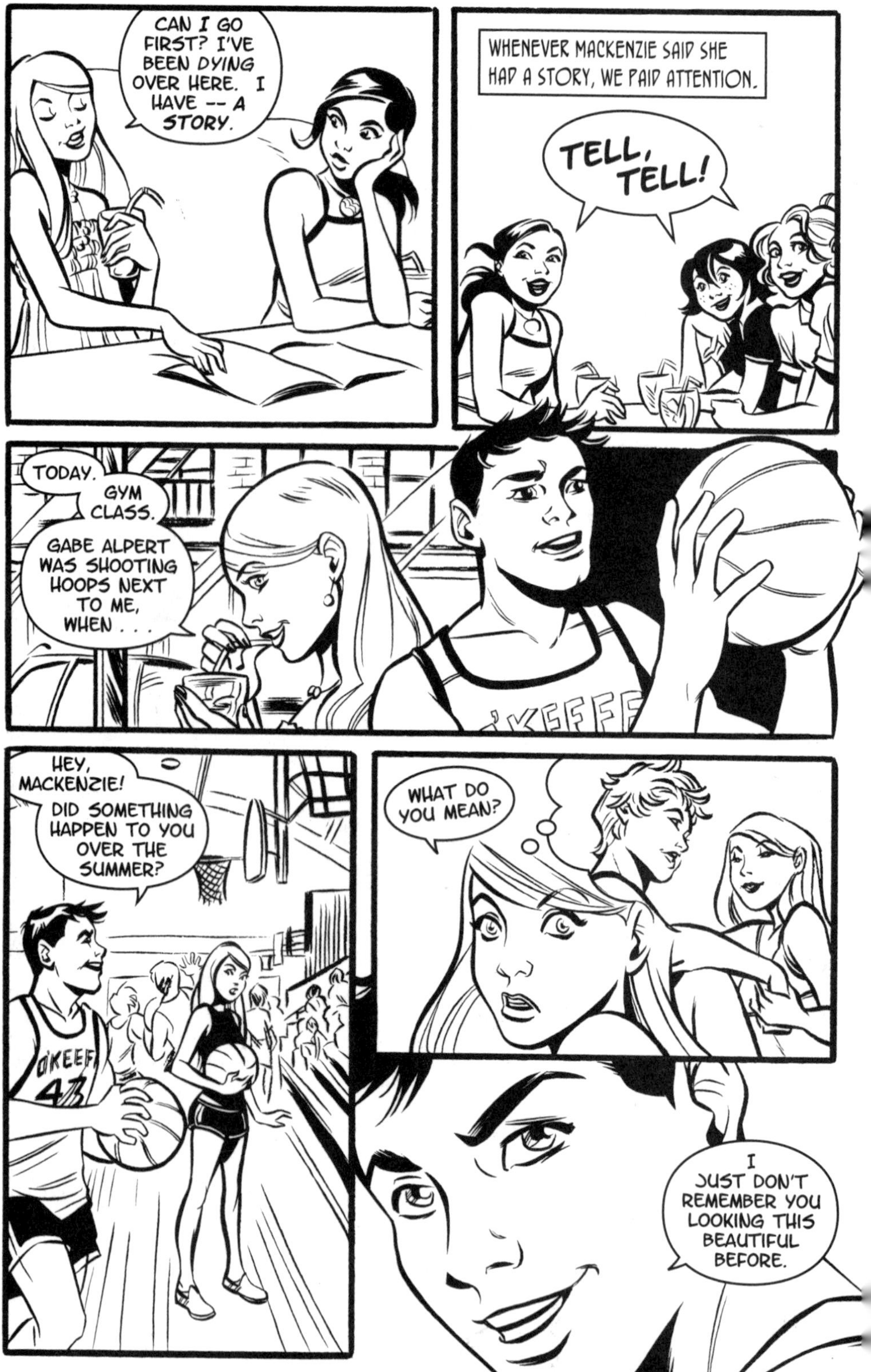
CAN I GO FIRST? I'VE BEEN DYING OVER HERE. I HAVE -- A STORY.
WHENEVER MACKENZIE SAID SHE HAD A STORY, WE PAID ATTENTION.
TELL, TELL!
TODAY.
GYM CLASS.
GABE ALPERT WAS SHOOTING HOOPS NEXT TO ME, WHEN . . .
HEY, MACKENZIE!
DID SOMETHING HAPPEN TO YOU OVER THE SUMMER?
WHAT DO YOU MEAN?
I JUST DON'T REMEMBER YOU LOOKING THIS BEAUTIFUL BEFORE.

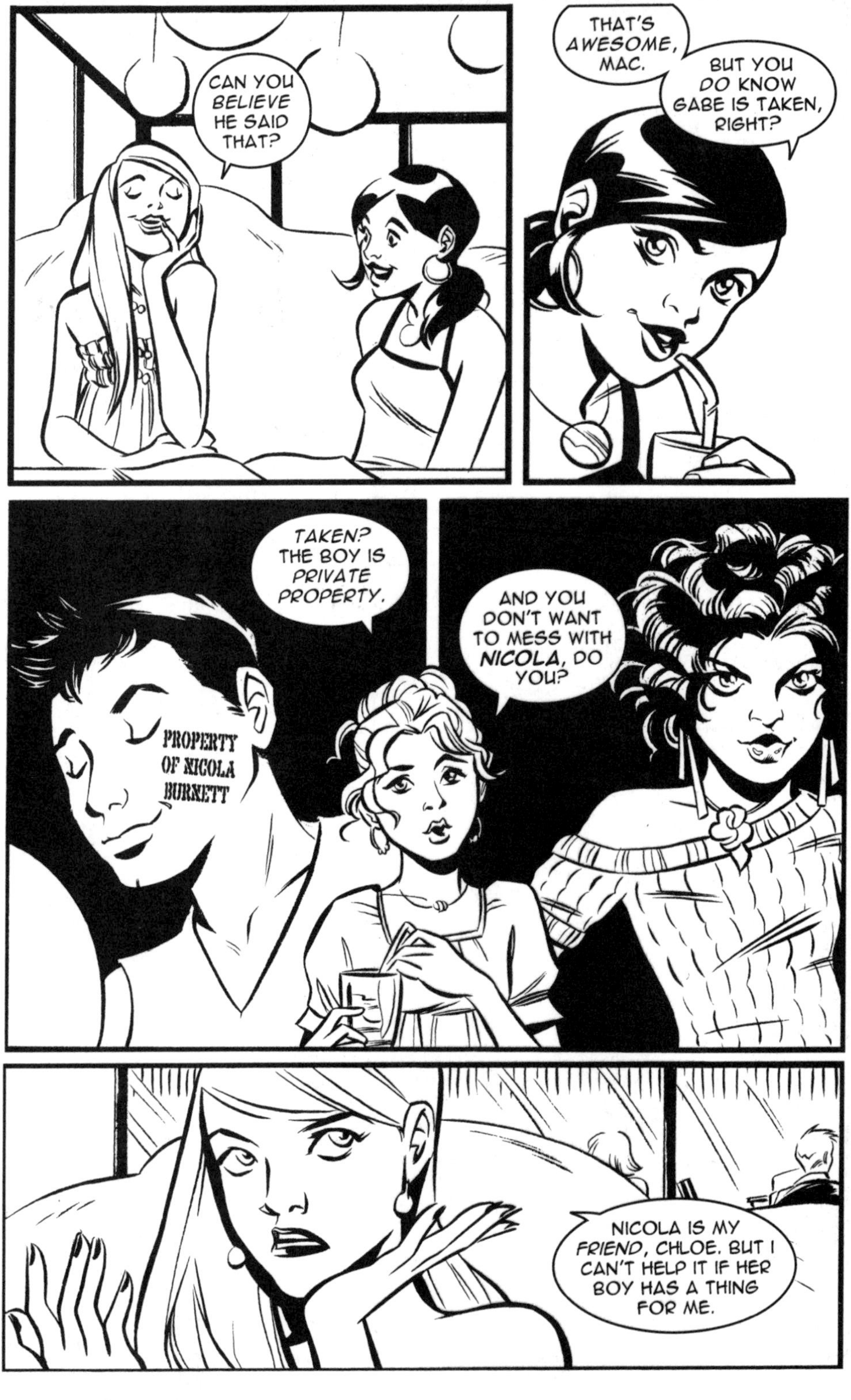
CAN YOU BELIEVE HE SAID THAT?
THAT'S AWESOME, MAC.
BUT YOU DO KNOW GABE IS TAKEN, RIGHT?
TAKEN? THE BOY IS PRIVATE PROPERTY.
PROPERTY OF NICOLA BURNETT
AND YOU DON'T WANT TO MESS WITH NICOLA, DO YOU?
NICOLA IS MY FRIEND, CHLOE. BUT I CAN'T HELP IT IF HER BOY HAS A THING FOR ME.

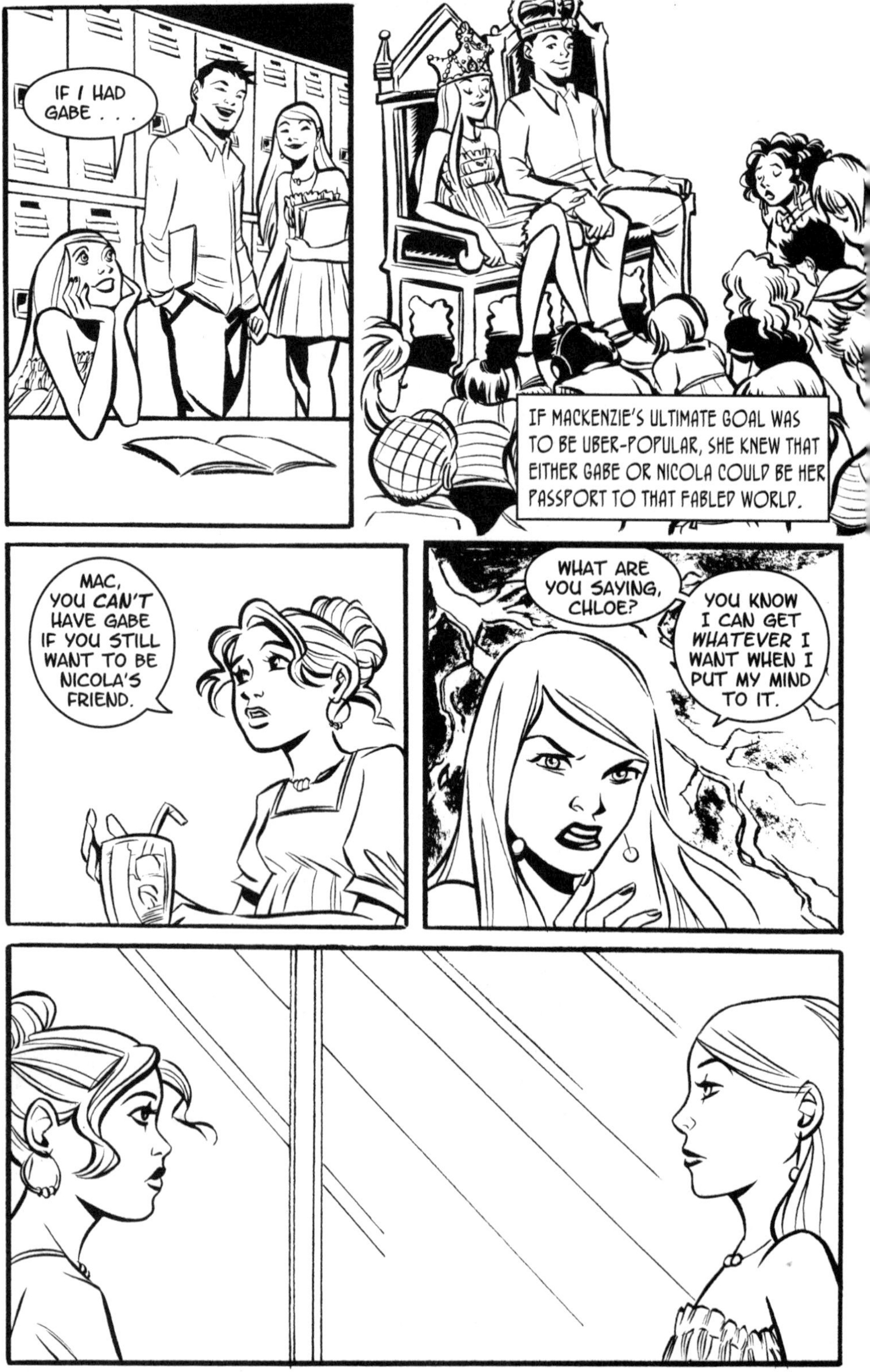
IF I HAD GABE . . .
IF MACKENZIE'S ULTIMATE GOAL WAS TO BE UBER-POPULAR, SHE KNEW THAT EITHER GABE OR NICOLA COULD BE HER PASSPORT TO THAT FABLED WORLD.
MAC, YOU CAN'T HAVE GABE IF YOU STILL WANT TO BE NICOLA'S FRIEND.
WHAT ARE YOU SAYING, CHLOE?
YOU KNOW I CAN GET WHATEVER I WANT WHEN I PUT MY MIND TO IT.

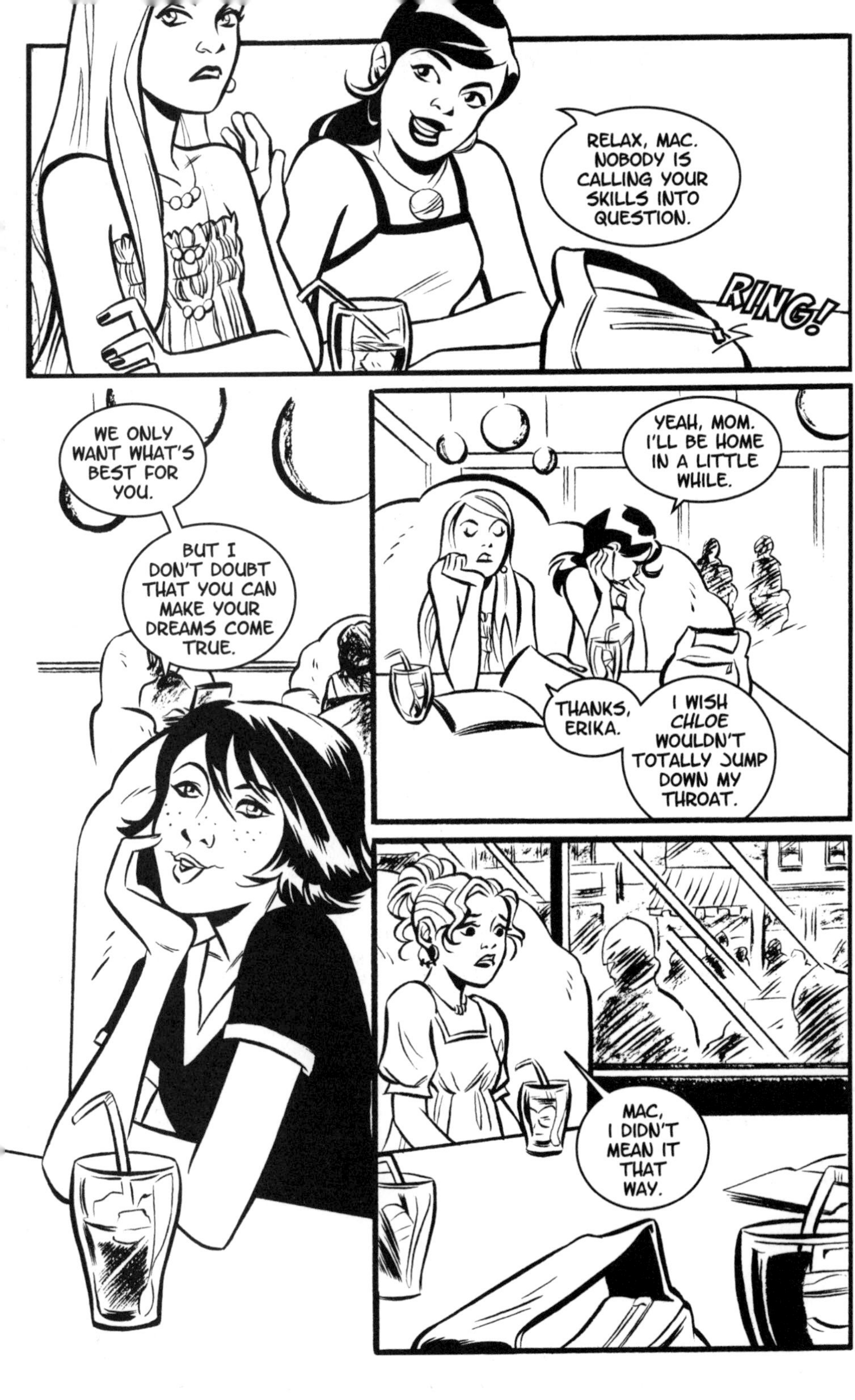
RELAX, MAC. NOBODY IS CALLING YOUR SKILLS INTO QUESTION.
RING!
WE ONLY WANT WHAT'S BEST FOR YOU.
BUT I DON'T DOUBT THAT YOU CAN MAKE YOUR DREAMS COME TRUE.
YEAH, MOM. I'LL BE HOME IN A LITTLE WHILE.
THANKS, ERIKA.
I WISH CHLOE WOULDN'T TOTALLY JUMP DOWN MY THROAT.
MAC, I DIDN'T MEAN IT THAT WAY.

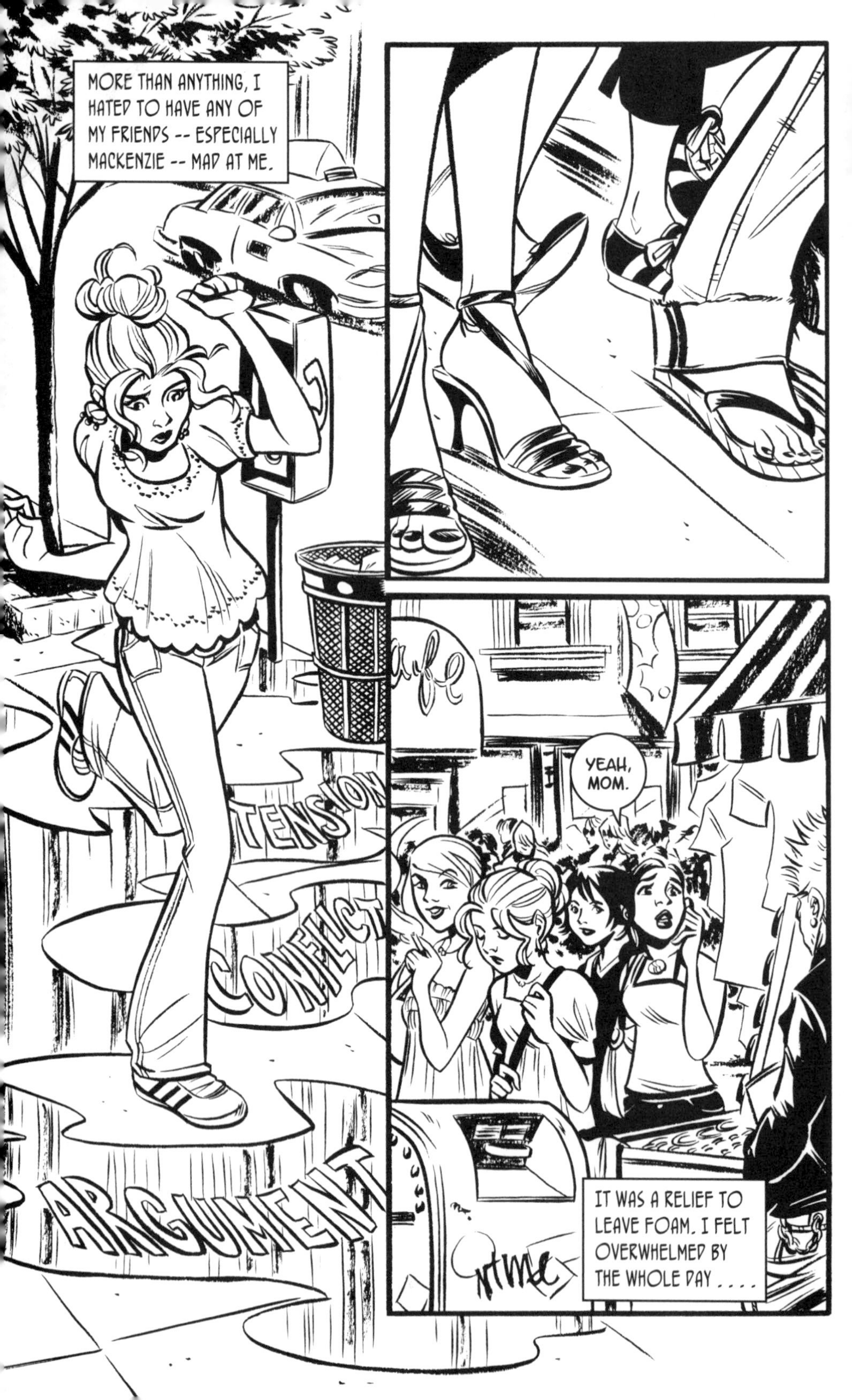
MORE THAN ANYTHING, I HATED TO HAVE ANY OF MY FRIENDS -- ESPECIALLY MACKENZIE -- MAD AT ME.
TENSION
CONFLICT
ARGUMENT
Cafe
YEAH, MOM.
IT WAS A RELIEF TO LEAVE FOAM. I FELT OVERWHELMED BY THE WHOLE DAY . . . .

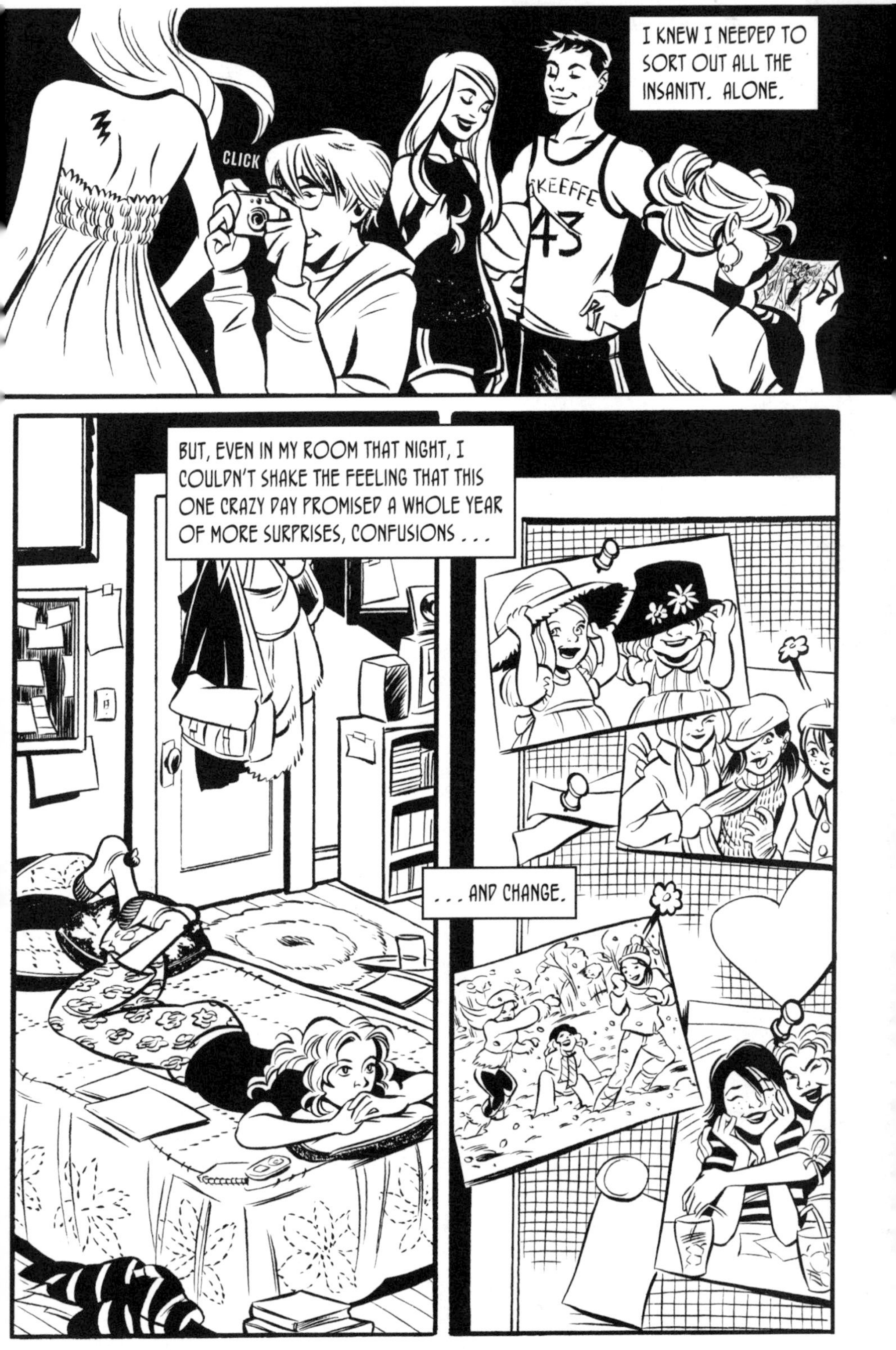
I KNEW I NEEDED TO SORT OUT ALL THE INSANITY. ALONE.
CLICK
BUT, EVEN IN MY ROOM THAT NIGHT, I COULDN'T SHAKE THE FEELING THAT THIS ONE CRAZY DAY PROMISED A WHOLE YEAR OF MORE SURPRISES, CONFUSIONS . . .
. . . AND CHANGE.

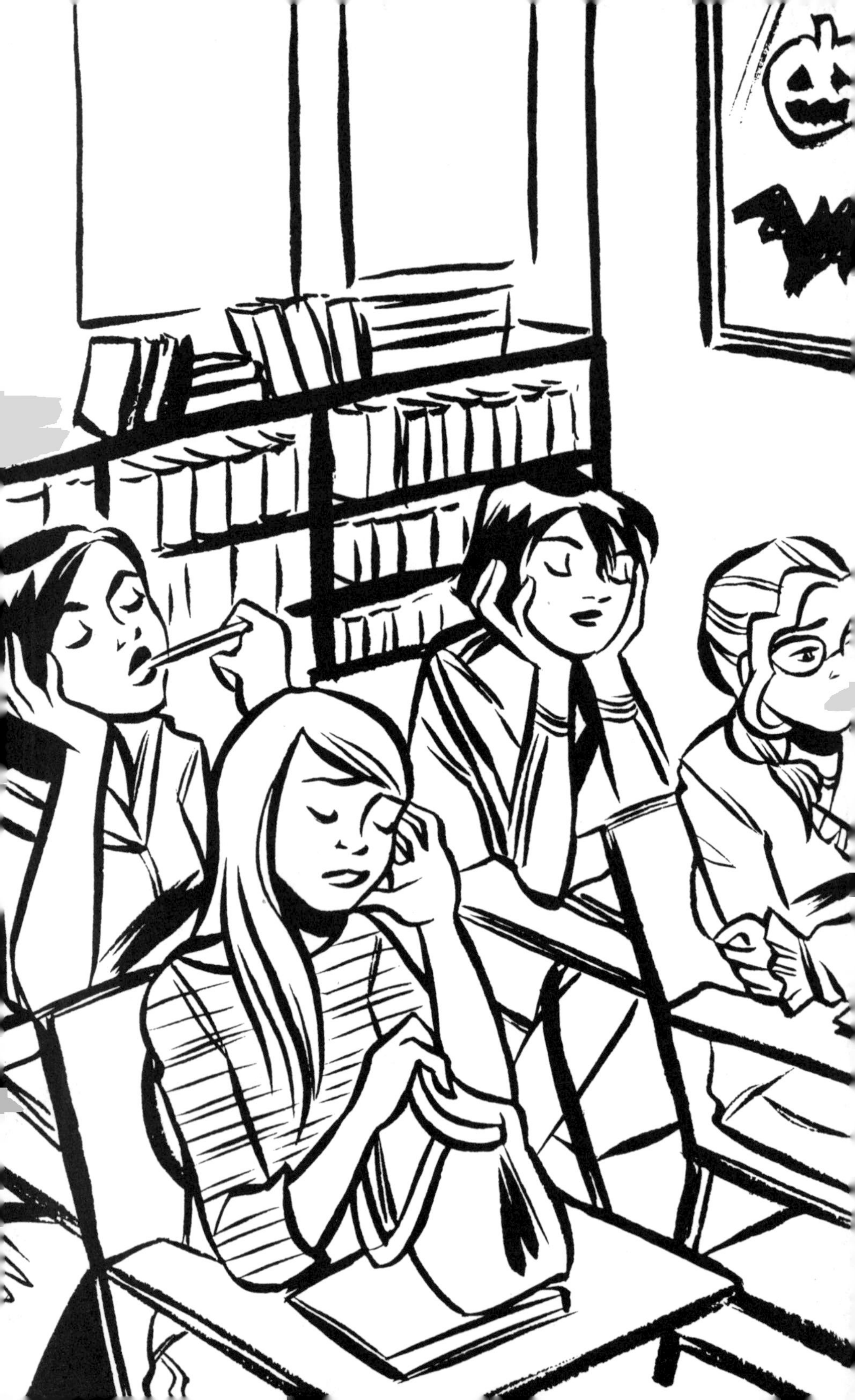

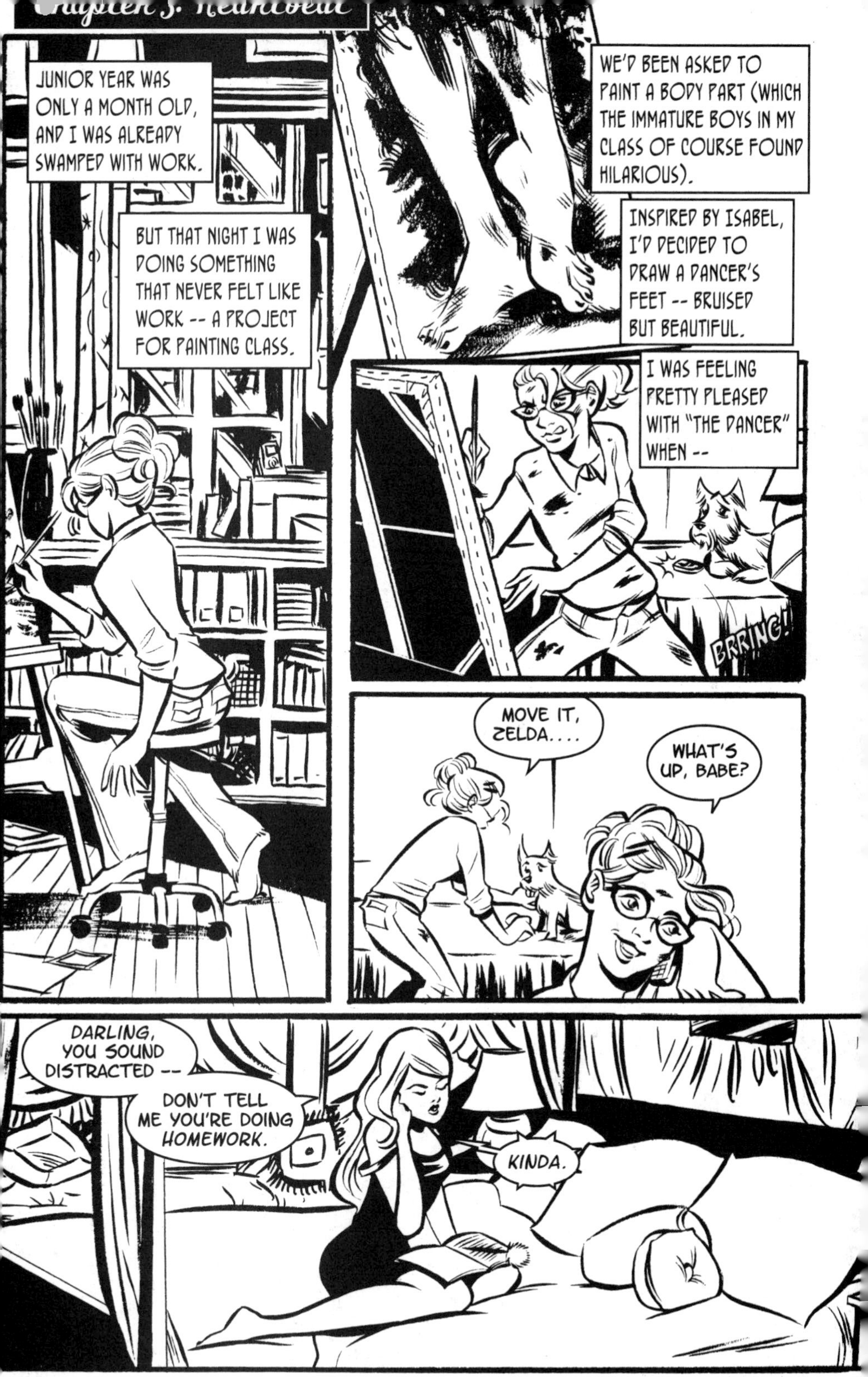
JUNIOR YEAR WAS ONLY A MONTH OLD, AND I WAS ALREADY SWAMPED WITH WORK.
BUT THAT NIGHT I WAS DOING SOMETHING THAT NEVER FELT LIKE WORK -- A PROJECT FOR PAINTING CLASS.
WE'D BEEN ASKED TO PAINT A BODY PART (WHICH THE IMMATURE BOYS IN MY CLASS OF COURSE FOUND HILARIOUS).
INSPIRED BY ISABEL, I'D DECIDED TO DRAW A DANCER'S FEET -- BRUISED BUT BEAUTIFUL.
I WAS FEELING PRETTY PLEASED WITH "THE DANCER" WHEN --
BRRING!
MOVE IT, ZELDA....
WHAT'S UP, BABE?
DARLING, YOU SOUND DISTRACTED --
DON'T TELL ME YOU'RE DOING HOMEWORK.
KINDA.

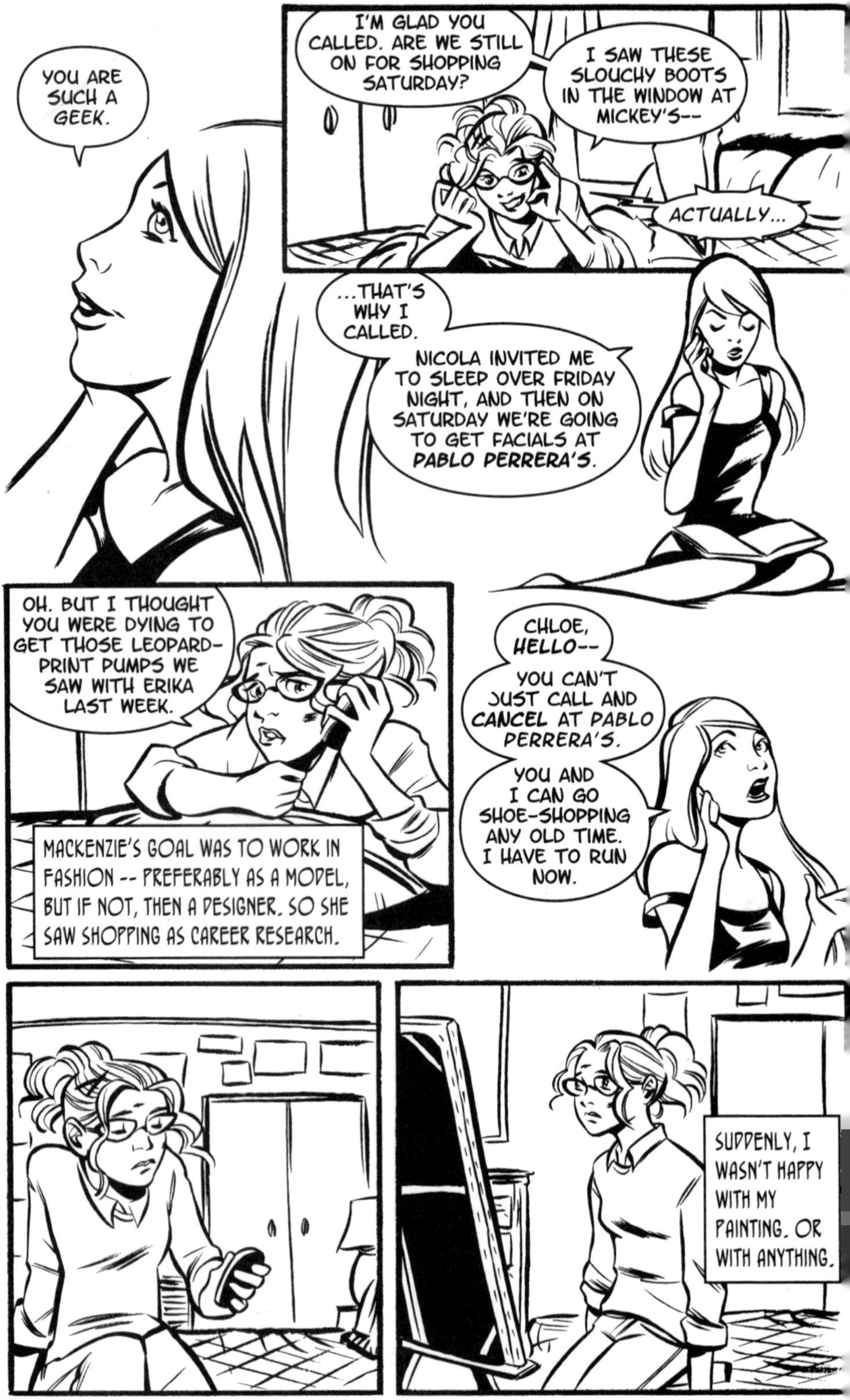

YOU ARE SUCH A GEEK.
I'M GLAD YOU CALLED. ARE WE STILL ON FOR SHOPPING SATURDAY?
I SAW THESE SLOUCHY BOOTS IN THE WINDOW AT MICKEY'S--
ACTUALLY...
...THAT'S WHY I CALLED.
NICOLA INVITED ME TO SLEEP OVER FRIDAY NIGHT, AND THEN ON SATURDAY WE'RE GOING TO GET FACIALS AT PABLO PERRERA'S.
OH. BUT I THOUGHT YOU WERE DYING TO GET THOSE LEOPARD-PRINT PUMPS WE SAW WITH ERIKA LAST WEEK.
MACKENZIE'S GOAL WAS TO WORK IN FASHION -- PREFERABLY AS A MODEL, BUT IF NOT, THEN A DESIGNER. SO SHE SAW SHOPPING AS CAREER RESEARCH.
CHLOE, HELLO--
YOU CAN'T JUST CALL AND CANCEL AT PABLO PERRERA'S.
YOU AND I CAN GO SHOE-SHOPPING ANY OLD TIME. I HAVE TO RUN NOW.
SUDDENLY, I WASN'T HAPPY WITH MY PAINTING. OR WITH ANYTHING.

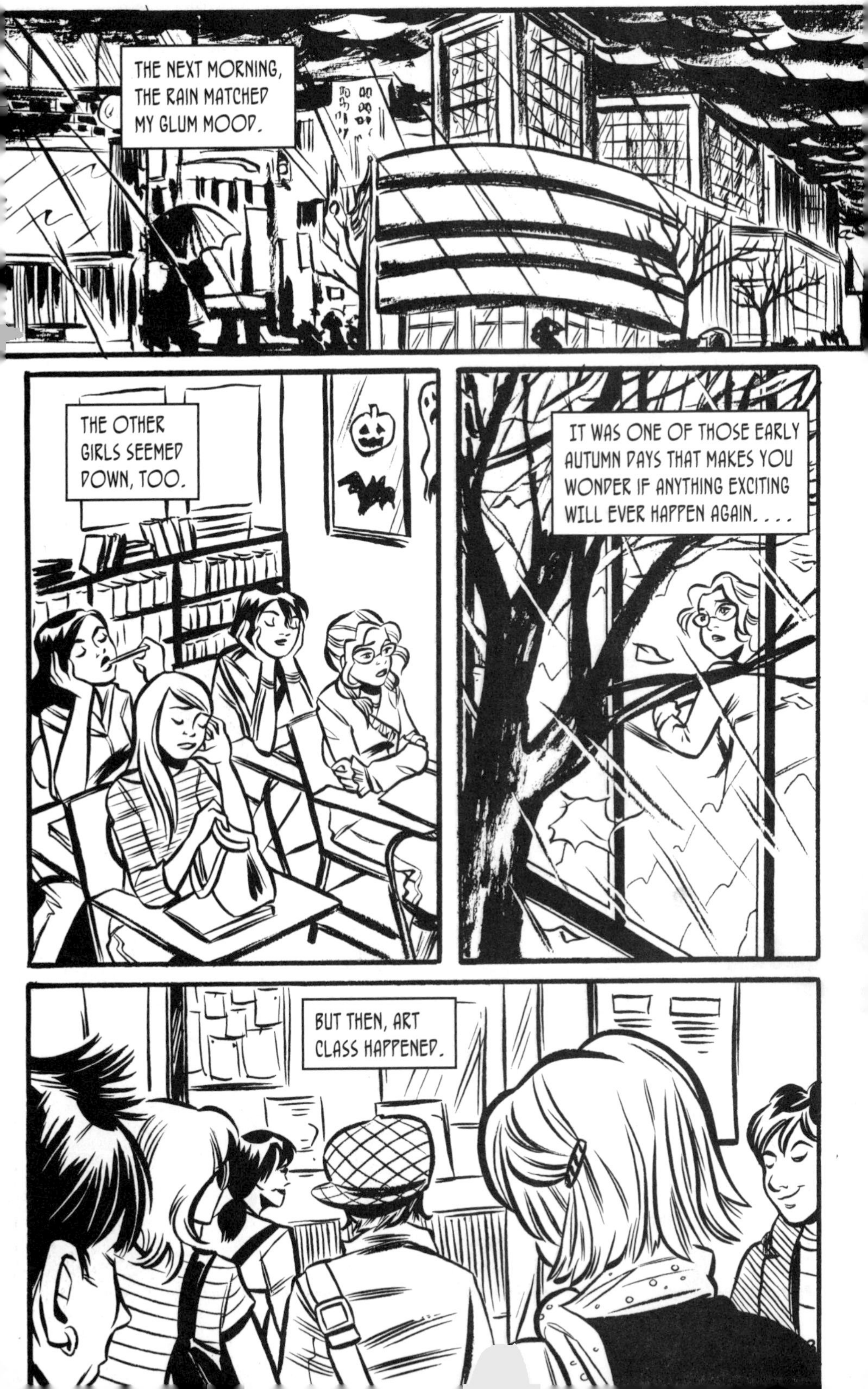
THE NEXT MORNING, THE RAIN MATCHED MY GLUM MOOD.
THE OTHER GIRLS SEEMED DOWN, TOO.
IT WAS ONE OF THOSE EARLY AUTUMN DAYS THAT MAKES YOU WONDER IF ANYTHING EXCITING WILL EVER HAPPEN AGAIN. . . .
BUT THEN, ART CLASS HAPPENED.

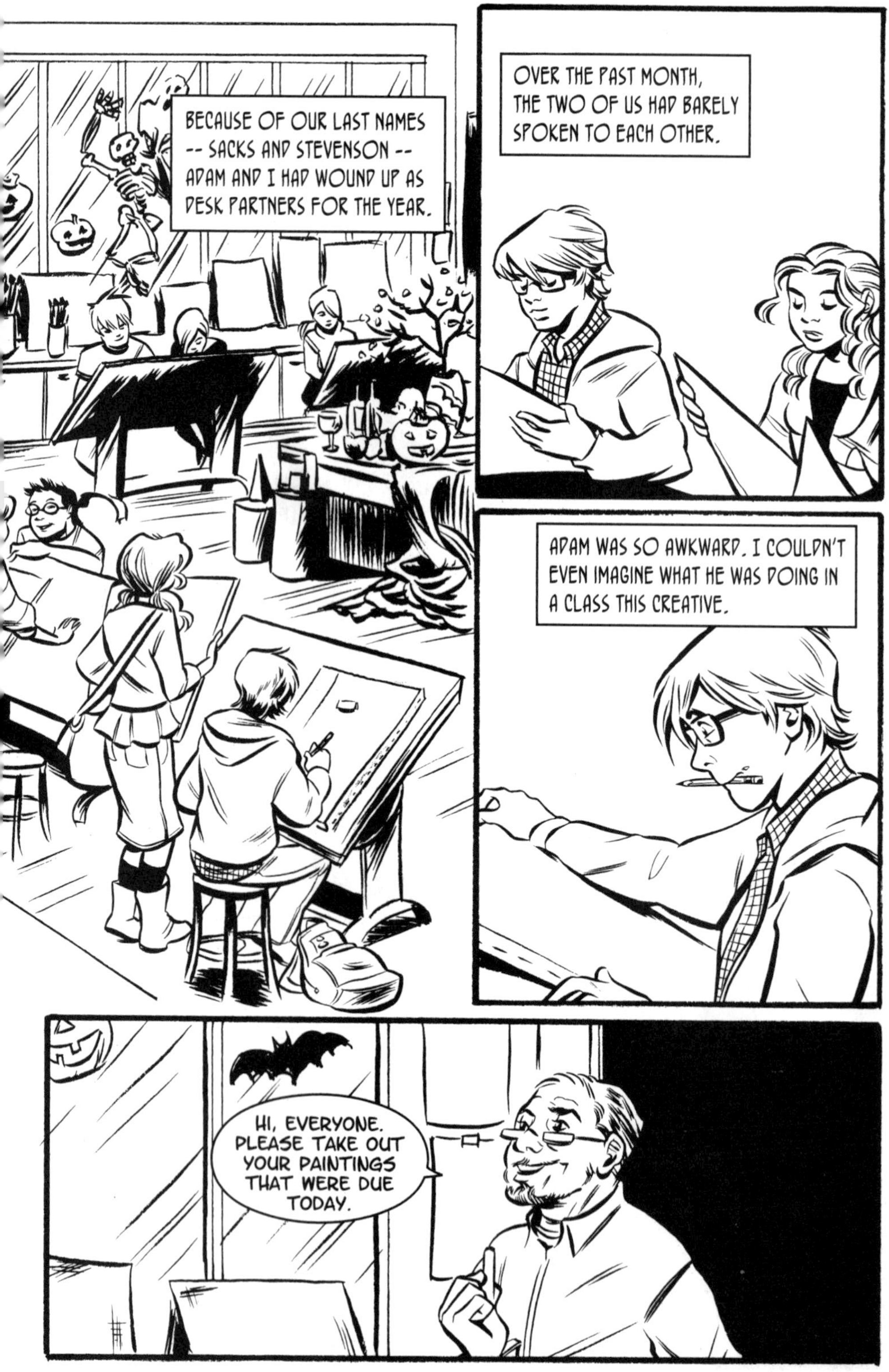
BECAUSE OF OUR LAST NAMES -- SACKS AND STEVENSON -- ADAM AND I HAD WOUND UP AS DESK PARTNERS FOR THE YEAR.
OVER THE PAST MONTH, THE TWO OF US HAD BARELY SPOKEN TO EACH OTHER.
ADAM WAS SO AWKWARD. I COULDN'T EVEN IMAGINE WHAT HE WAS DOING IN A CLASS THIS CREATIVE.
HI, EVERYONE. PLEASE TAKE OUT YOUR PAINTINGS THAT WERE DUE TODAY.

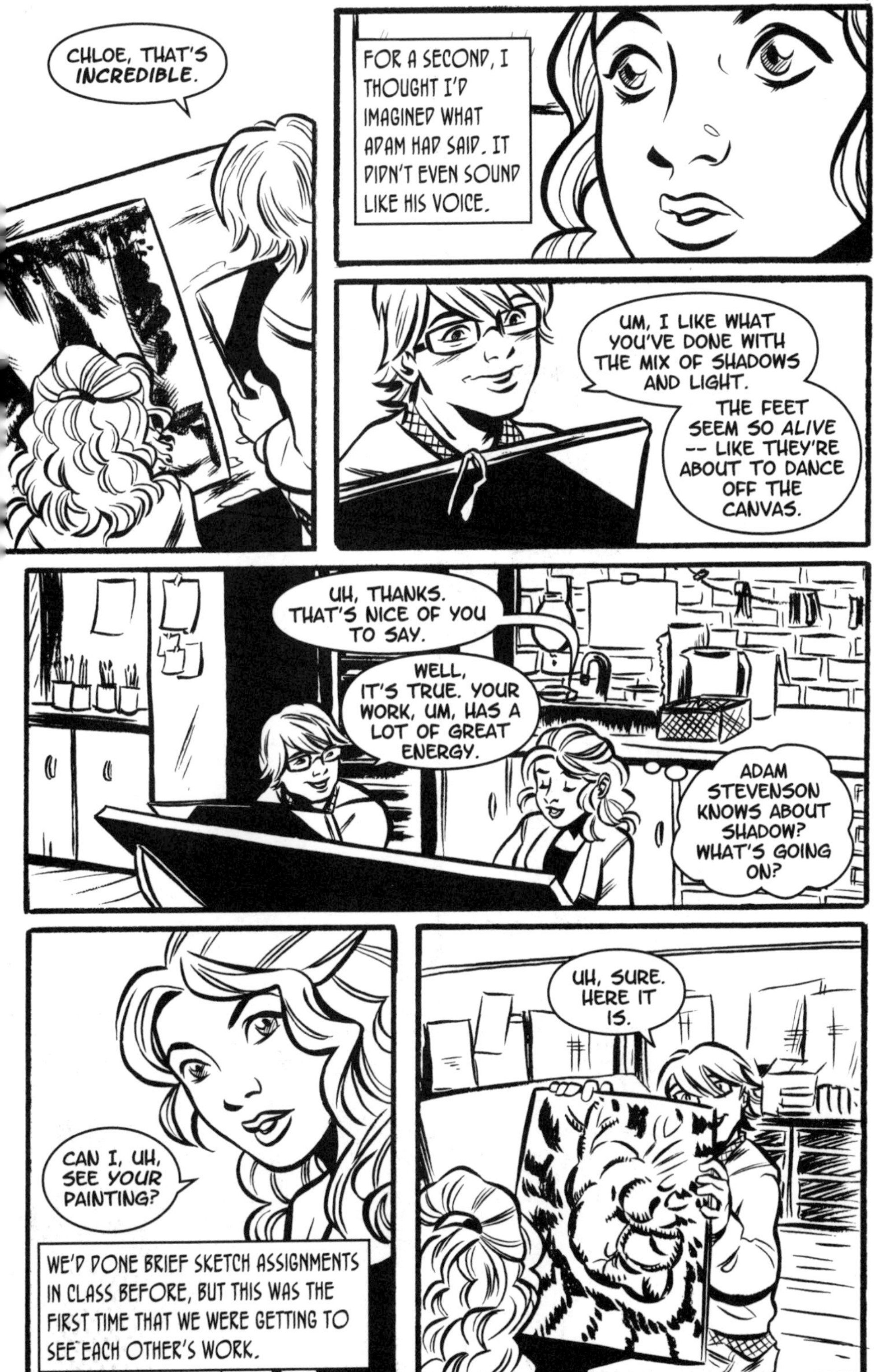
CHLOE, THAT'S INCREDIBLE.
FOR A SECOND, I THOUGHT I'D IMAGINED WHAT ADAM HAD SAID. IT DIDN'T EVEN SOUND LIKE HIS VOICE.
UM, I LIKE WHAT YOU'VE DONE WITH THE MIX OF SHADOWS AND LIGHT.
THE FEET SEEM SO ALIVE -- LIKE THEY'RE ABOUT TO DANCE OFF THE CANVAS.
UH, THANKS. THAT'S NICE OF YOU TO SAY.
WELL, IT'S TRUE. YOUR WORK, UM, HAS A LOT OF GREAT ENERGY.
ADAM STEVENSON KNOWS ABOUT SHADOW? WHAT'S GOING ON?
CAN I, UH, SEE YOUR PAINTING?
WE'D DONE BRIEF SKETCH ASSIGNMENTS IN CLASS BEFORE, BUT THIS WAS THE FIRST TIME THAT WE WERE GETTING TO SEE EACH OTHER'S WORK.
UH, SURE. HERE IT IS.

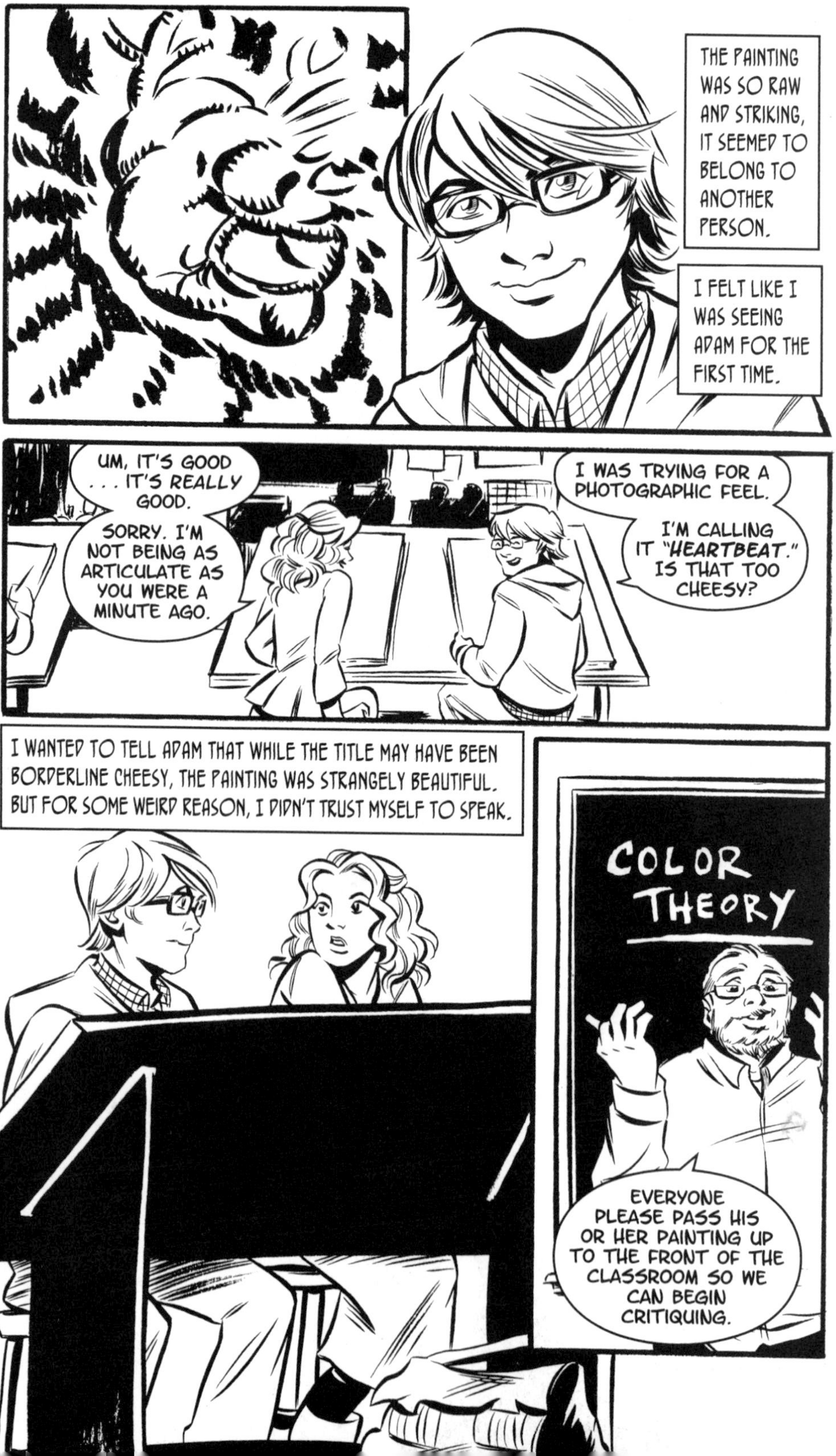
THE PAINTING WAS SO RAW AND STRIKING, IT SEEMED TO BELONG TO ANOTHER PERSON.
I FELT LIKE I WAS SEEING ADAM FOR THE FIRST TIME.
UM, IT'S GOOD . . . IT'S REALLY GOOD.
SORRY. I'M NOT BEING AS ARTICULATE AS YOU WERE A MINUTE AGO.
I WAS TRYING FOR A PHOTOGRAPHIC FEEL.
I'M CALLING IT "HEARTBEAT." IS THAT TOO CHEESY?
I WANTED TO TELL ADAM THAT WHILE THE TITLE MAY HAVE BEEN BORDERLINE CHEESY, THE PAINTING WAS STRANGELY BEAUTIFUL. BUT FOR SOME WEIRD REASON, I DIDN'T TRUST MYSELF TO SPEAK.
COLOR THEORY
EVERYONE PLEASE PASS HIS OR HER PAINTING UP TO THE FRONT OF THE CLASSROOM SO WE CAN BEGIN CRITIQUING.

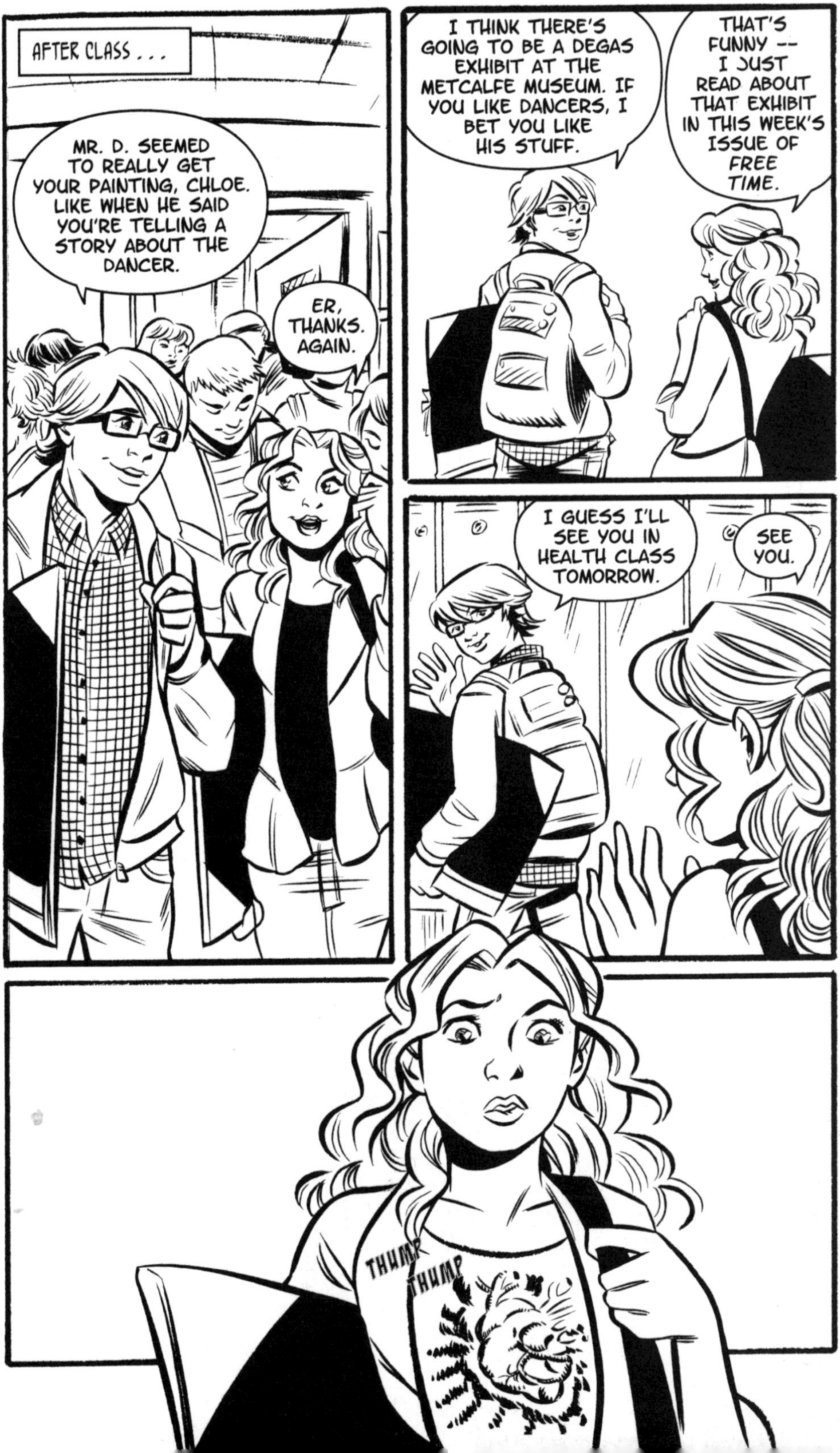
AFTER CLASS . . .
MR. D. SEEMED TO REALLY GET YOUR PAINTING, CHLOE. LIKE WHEN HE SAID YOU'RE TELLING A STORY ABOUT THE DANCER.
ER, THANKS. AGAIN.
I THINK THERE'S GOING TO BE A DEGAS EXHIBIT AT THE METCALFE MUSEUM. IF YOU LIKE DANCERS, I BET YOU LIKE HIS STUFF.
THAT'S FUNNY -- I JUST READ ABOUT THAT EXHIBIT IN THIS WEEK'S ISSUE OF FREE TIME.
I GUESS I'LL SEE YOU IN HEALTH CLASS TOMORROW.
SEE YOU.
THUMP
THUMP

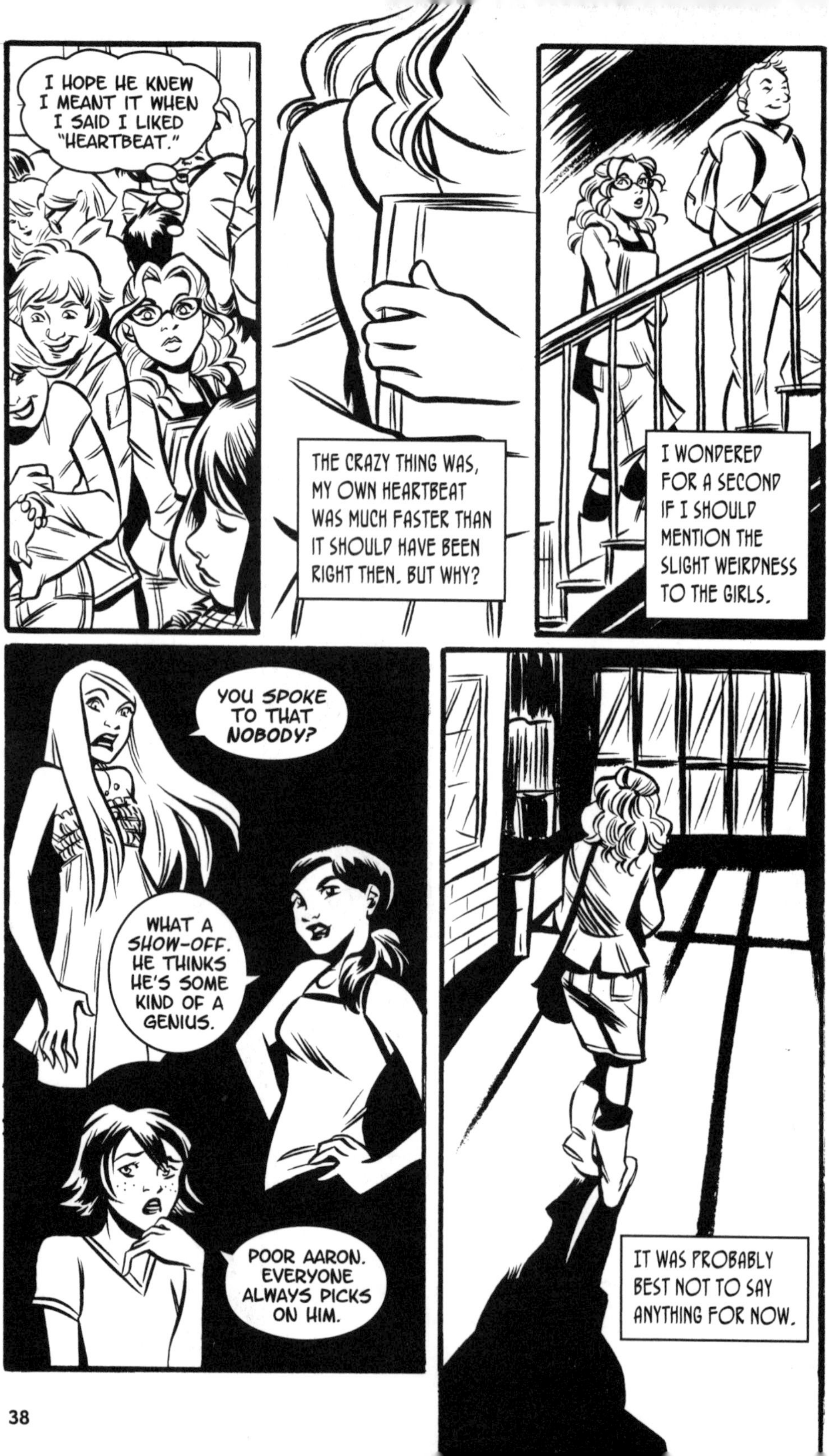
I HOPE HE KNEW I MEANT IT WHEN I SAID I LIKED "HEARTBEAT."
THE CRAZY THING WAS, MY OWN HEARTBEAT WAS MUCH FASTER THAN IT SHOULD HAVE BEEN RIGHT THEN. BUT WHY?
I WONDERED FOR A SECOND IF I SHOULD MENTION THE SLIGHT WEIRDNESS TO THE GIRLS.
YOU SPOKE TO THAT NOBODY?
WHAT A SHOW-OFF. HE THINKS HE'S SOME KIND OF A GENIUS.
POOR AARON. EVERYONE ALWAYS PICKS ON HIM.
IT WAS PROBABLY BEST NOT TO SAY ANYTHING FOR NOW.

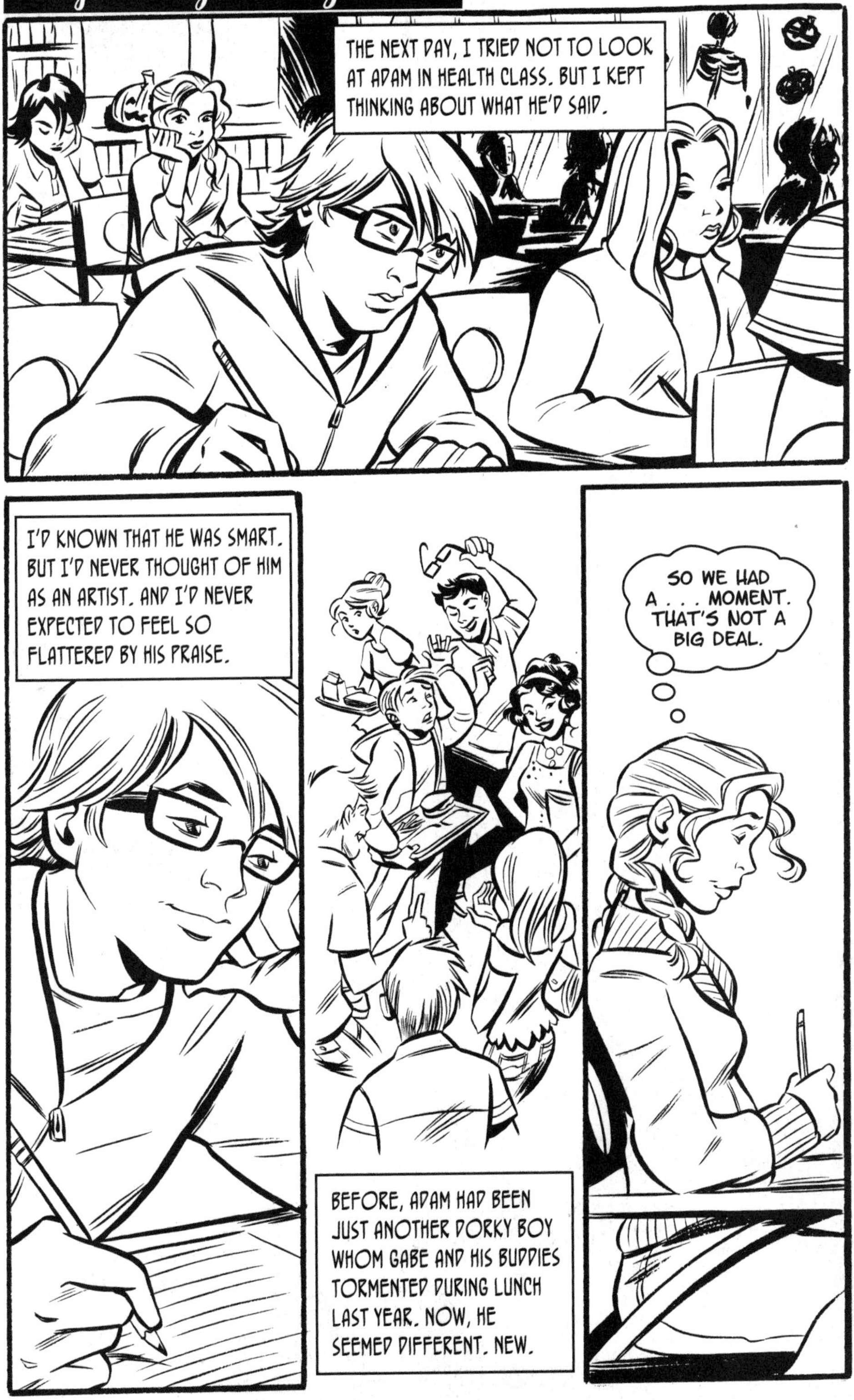
THE NEXT DAY, I TRIED NOT TO LOOK AT ADAM IN HEALTH CLASS. BUT I KEPT THINKING ABOUT WHAT HE'D SAID.
I'D KNOWN THAT HE WAS SMART. BUT I'D NEVER THOUGHT OF HIM AS AN ARTIST. AND I'D NEVER EXPECTED TO FEEL SO FLATTERED BY HIS PRAISE.
BEFORE, ADAM HAD BEEN JUST ANOTHER DORKY BOY WHOM GABE AND HIS BUDDIES TORMENTED DURING LUNCH LAST YEAR. NOW, HE SEEMED DIFFERENT. NEW.
SO WE HAD A . . . MOMENT. THAT'S NOT A BIG DEAL.

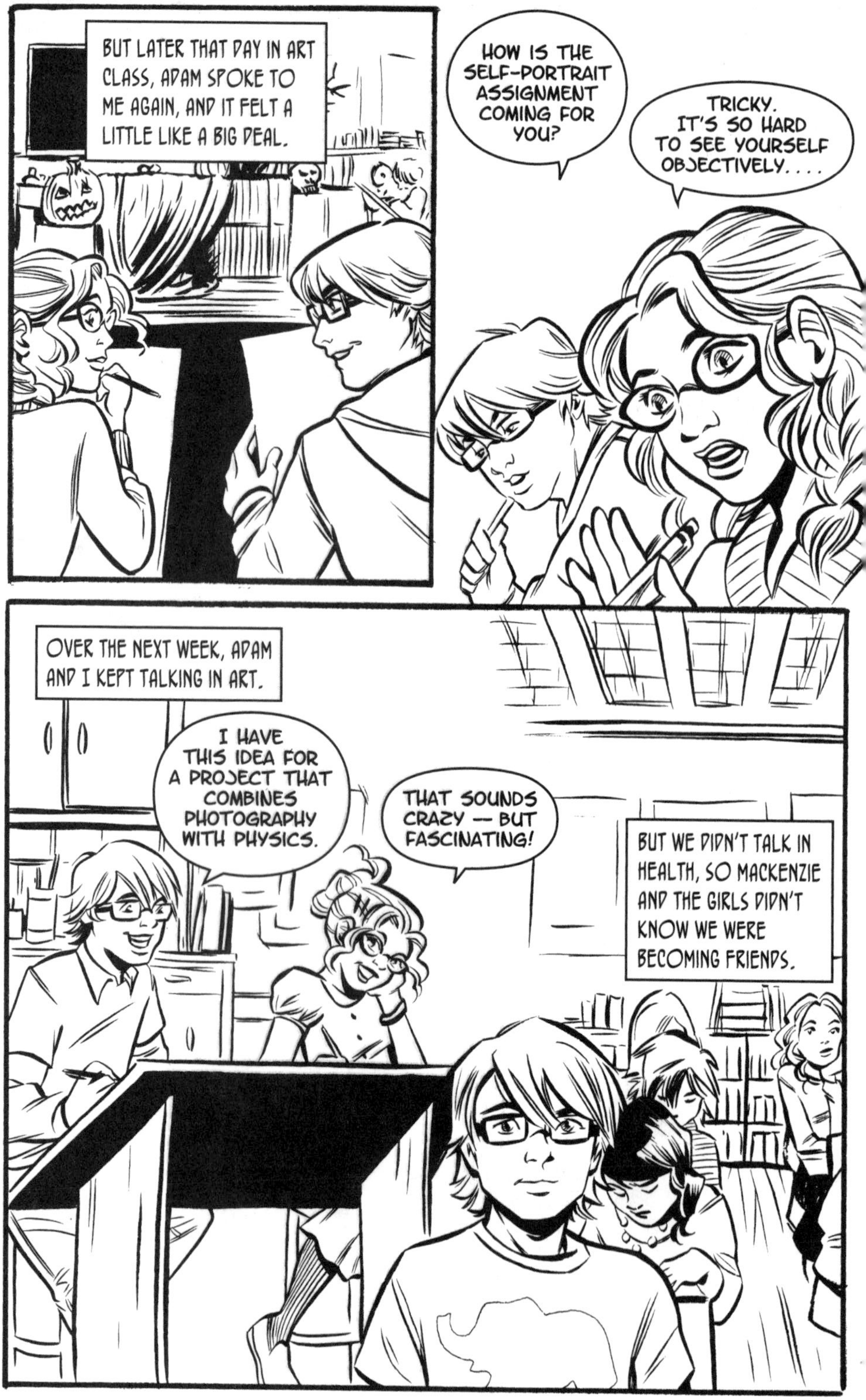

BUT LATER THAT DAY IN ART CLASS, ADAM SPOKE TO ME AGAIN, AND IT FELT A LITTLE LIKE A BIG DEAL.
HOW IS THE SELF-PORTRAIT ASSIGNMENT COMING FOR YOU?
TRICKY. IT'S SO HARD TO SEE YOURSELF OBJECTIVELY. . . .
OVER THE NEXT WEEK, ADAM AND I KEPT TALKING IN ART.
I HAVE THIS IDEA FOR A PROJECT THAT COMBINES PHOTOGRAPHY WITH PHYSICS.
THAT SOUNDS CRAZY -- BUT FASCINATING!
BUT WE DIDN'T TALK IN HEALTH, SO MACKENZIE AND THE GIRLS DIDN'T KNOW WE WERE BECOMING FRIENDS.

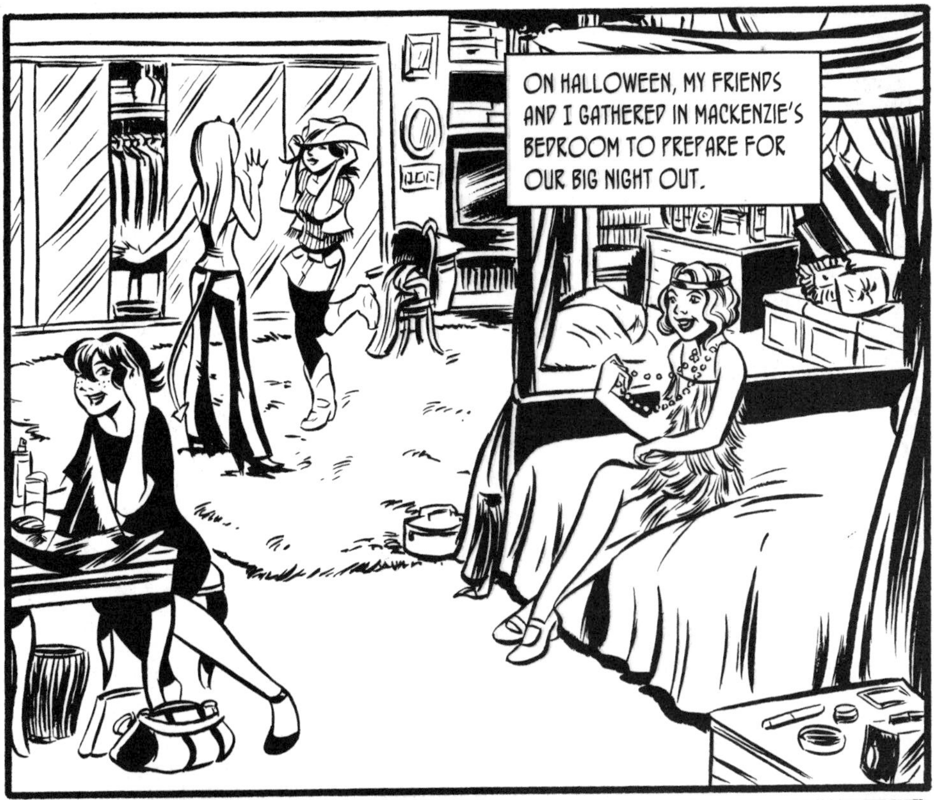
ON HALLOWEEN, MY FRIENDS AND I GATHERED IN MACKENZIE'S BEDROOM TO PREPARE FOR OUR BIG NIGHT OUT.

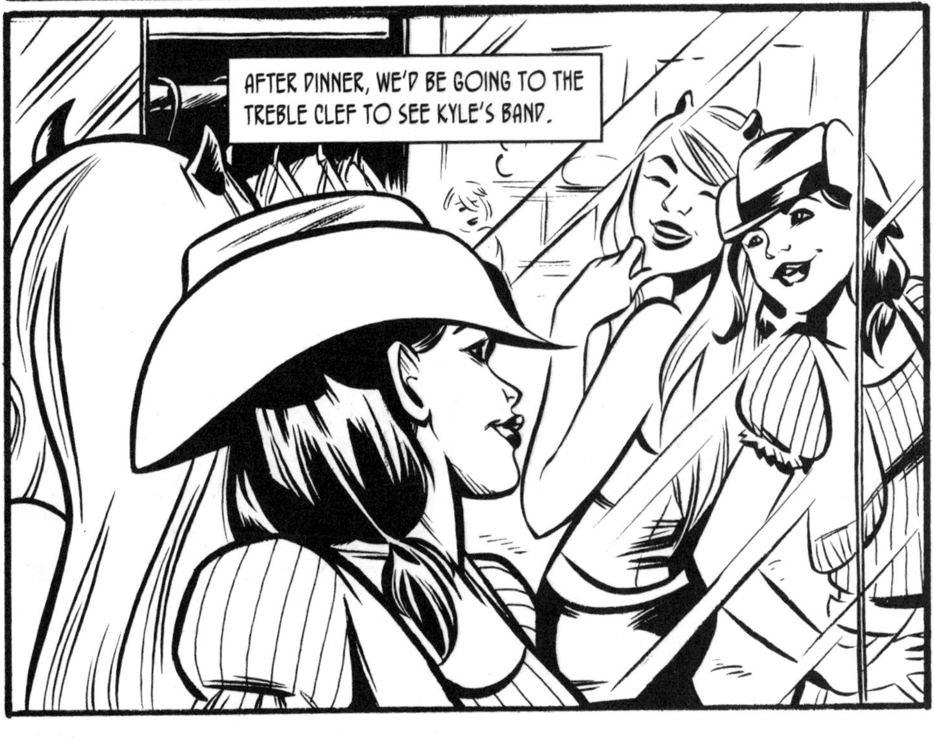
AFTER DINNER, WE'D BE GOING TO THE TREBLE CLEF TO SEE KYLE'S BAND.

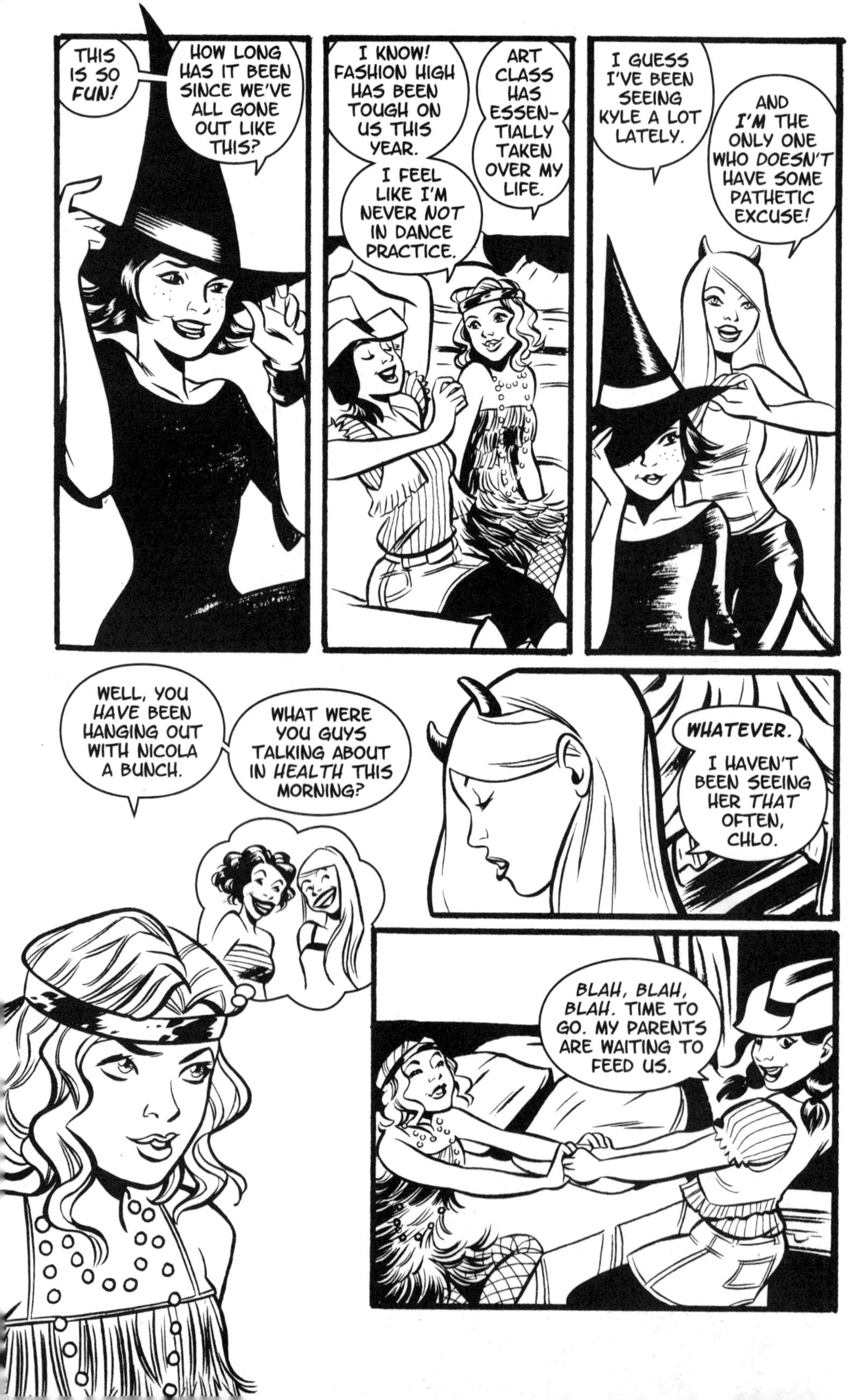
THIS IS SO FUN!
HOW LONG HAS IT BEEN SINCE WE'VE ALL GONE OUT LIKE THIS?
I KNOW! FASHION HIGH HAS BEEN TOUGH ON US THIS YEAR.
I FEEL LIKE I'M NEVER NOT IN DANCE PRACTICE.
ART CLASS HAS ESSEN-TIALLY TAKEN OVER MY LIFE.
I GUESS I'VE BEEN SEEING KYLE A LOT LATELY.
AND I'M THE ONLY ONE WHO DOESN'T HAVE SOME PATHETIC EXCUSE!
WELL, YOU HAVE BEEN HANGING OUT WITH NICOLA A BUNCH.
WHAT WERE YOU GUYS TALKING ABOUT IN HEALTH THIS MORNING?
WHATEVER.
I HAVEN'T BEEN SEEING HER THAT OFTEN, CHLO.
BLAH, BLAH, BLAH. TIME TO GO. MY PARENTS ARE WAITING TO FEED US.

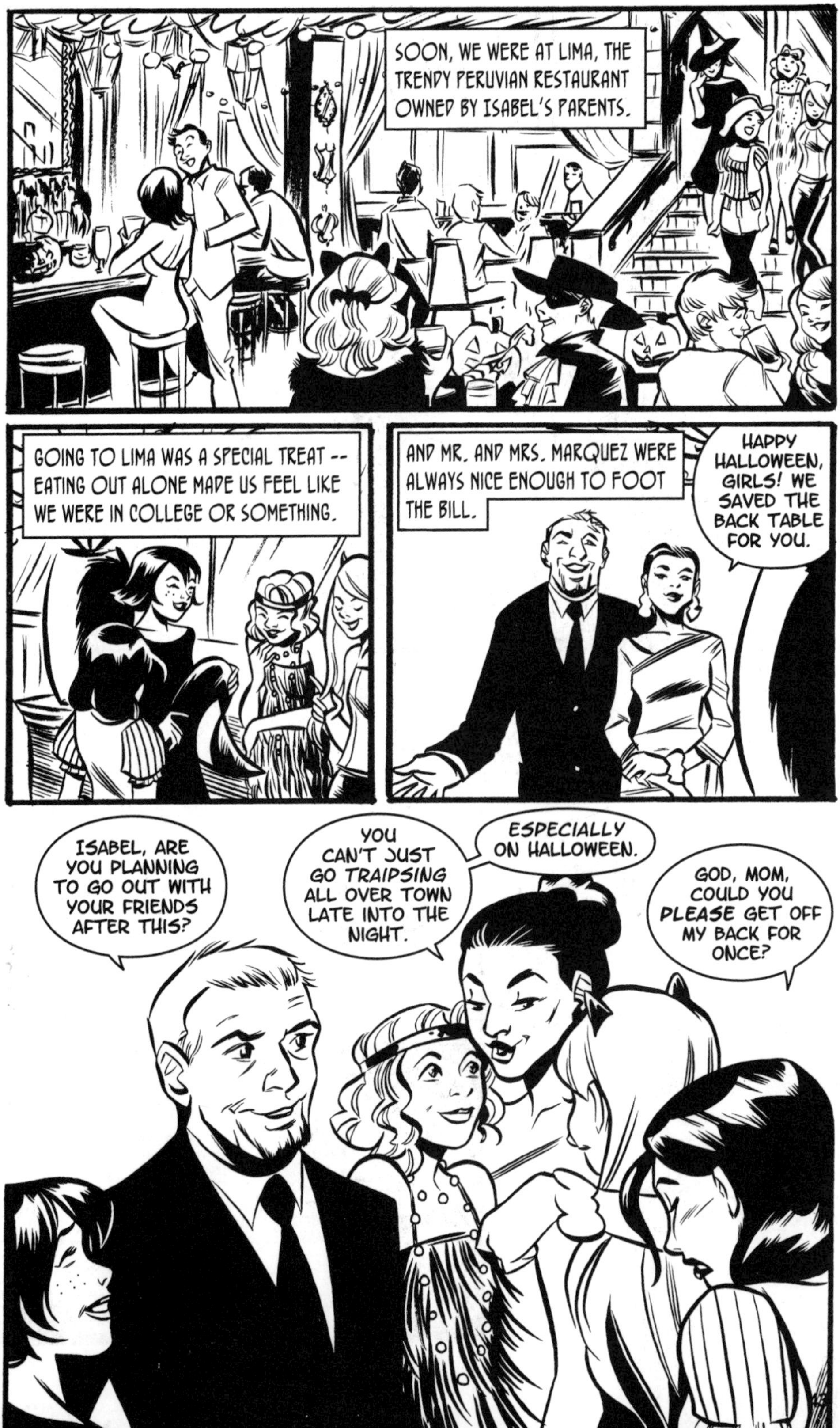
SOON, WE WERE AT LIMA, THE TRENDY PERUVIAN RESTAURANT OWNED BY ISABEL'S PARENTS.
GOING TO LIMA WAS A SPECIAL TREAT -- EATING OUT ALONE MADE US FEEL LIKE WE WERE IN COLLEGE OR SOMETHING.
AND MR. AND MRS. MARQUEZ WERE ALWAYS NICE ENOUGH TO FOOT THE BILL.
HAPPY HALLOWEEN, GIRLS! WE SAVED THE BACK TABLE FOR YOU.
ISABEL, ARE YOU PLANNING TO GO OUT WITH YOUR FRIENDS AFTER THIS?
YOU CAN'T JUST GO *TRAIPSING* ALL OVER TOWN LATE INTO THE NIGHT.
ESPECIALLY ON HALLOWEEN.
GOD, MOM, COULD YOU **PLEASE** GET OFF MY BACK FOR ONCE?

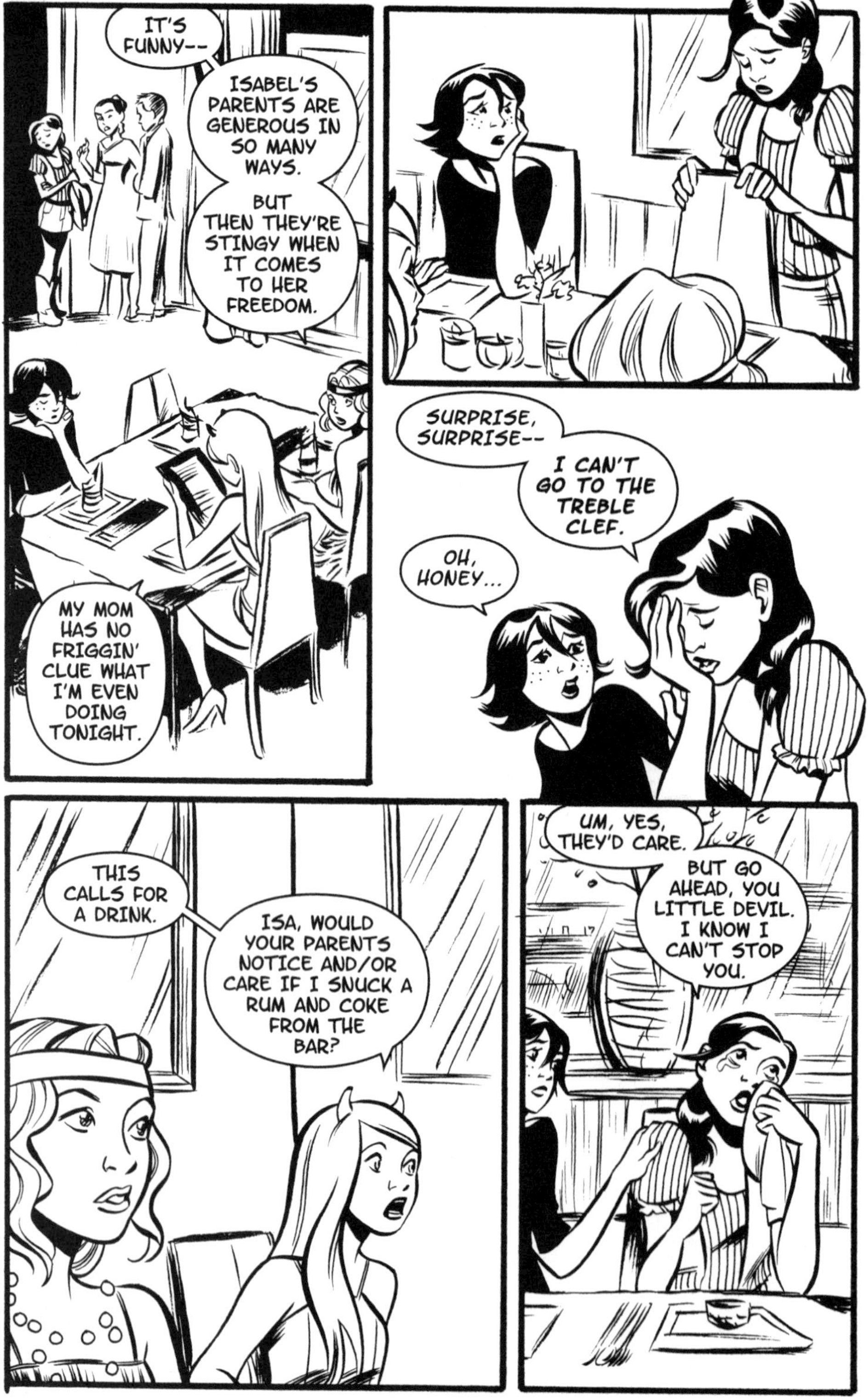
IT'S FUNNY--
ISABEL'S PARENTS ARE GENEROUS IN SO MANY WAYS.
BUT THEN THEY'RE STINGY WHEN IT COMES TO HER FREEDOM.
MY MOM HAS NO FRIGGIN' CLUE WHAT I'M EVEN DOING TONIGHT.
SURPRISE, SURPRISE--
I CAN'T GO TO THE TREBLE CLEF.
OH, HONEY...
THIS CALLS FOR A DRINK.
ISA, WOULD YOUR PARENTS NOTICE AND/OR CARE IF I SNUCK A RUM AND COKE FROM THE BAR?
UM, YES, THEY'D CARE.
BUT GO AHEAD, YOU LITTLE DEVIL. I KNOW I CAN'T STOP YOU.

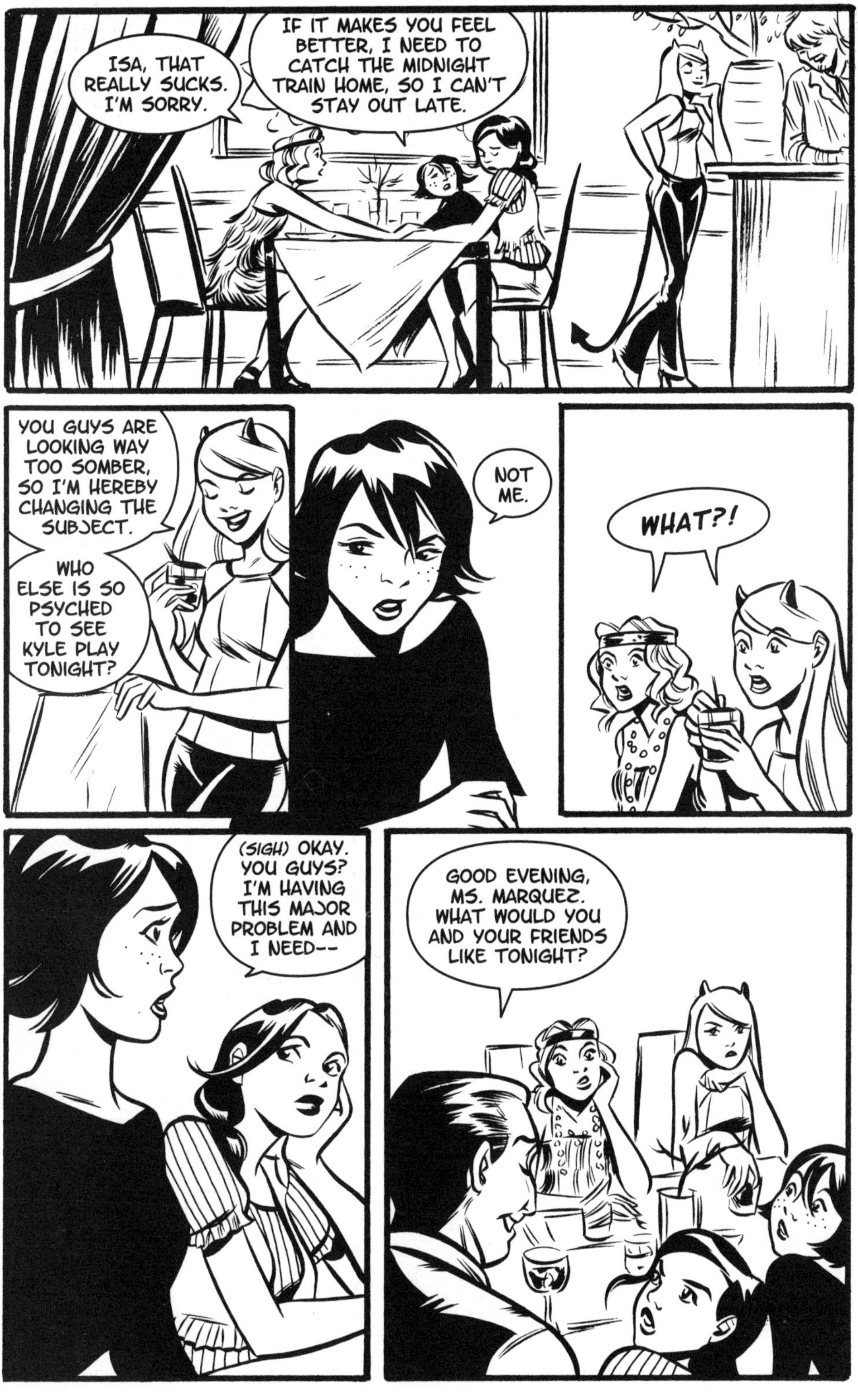
ISA, THAT REALLY SUCKS. I'M SORRY.
IF IT MAKES YOU FEEL BETTER, I NEED TO CATCH THE MIDNIGHT TRAIN HOME, SO I CAN'T STAY OUT LATE.
YOU GUYS ARE LOOKING WAY TOO SOMBER, SO I'M HEREBY CHANGING THE SUBJECT.
WHO ELSE IS SO PSYCHED TO SEE KYLE PLAY TONIGHT?
NOT ME.
WHAT?!
(SIGH) OKAY. YOU GUYS? I'M HAVING THIS MAJOR PROBLEM AND I NEED--
GOOD EVENING, MS. MARQUEZ. WHAT WOULD YOU AND YOUR FRIENDS LIKE TONIGHT?

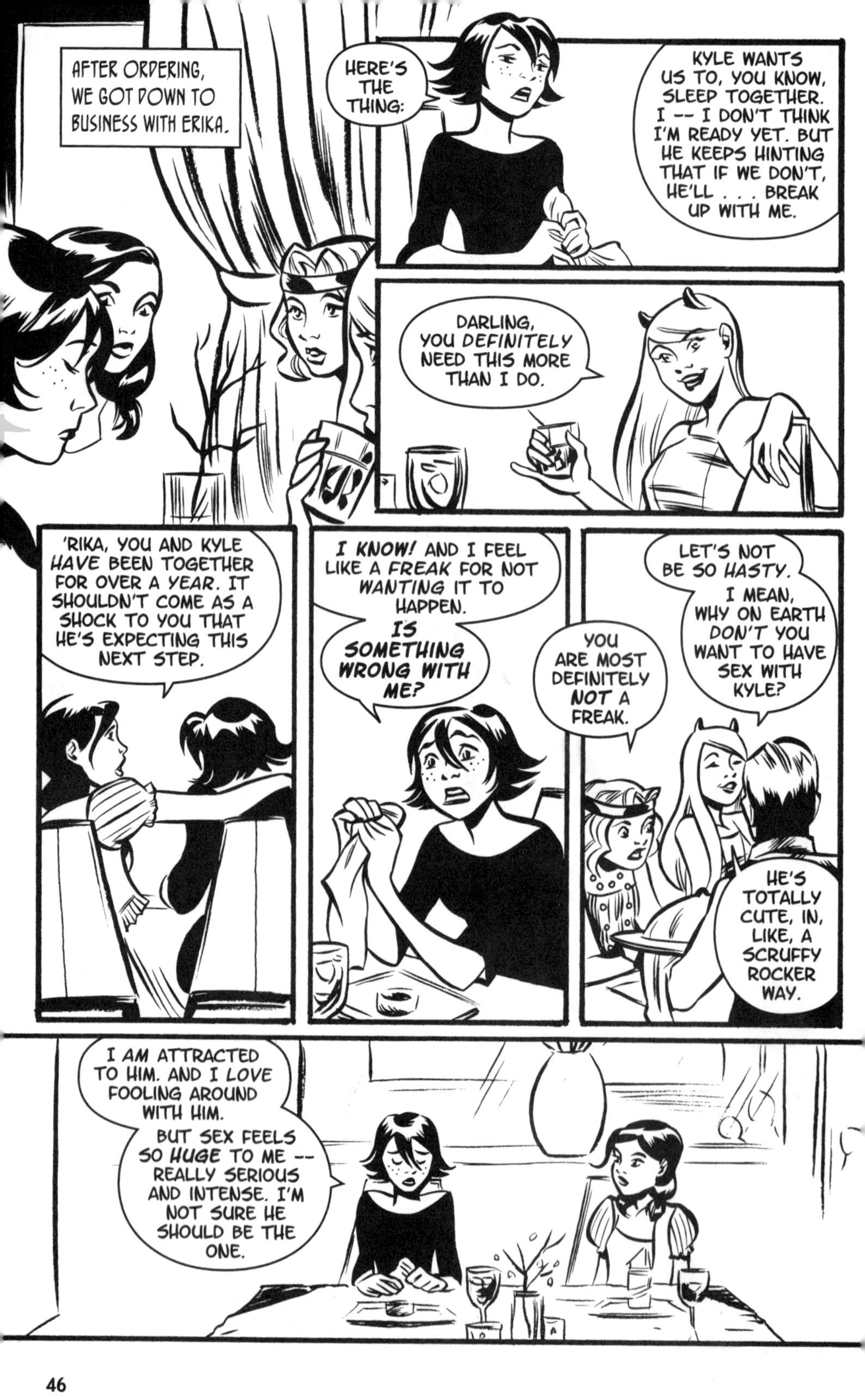

AFTER ORDERING, WE GOT DOWN TO BUSINESS WITH ERIKA.
HERE'S THE THING:
KYLE WANTS US TO, YOU KNOW, SLEEP TOGETHER. I -- I DON'T THINK I'M READY YET. BUT HE KEEPS HINTING THAT IF WE DON'T, HE'LL . . . BREAK UP WITH ME.
DARLING, YOU DEFINITELY NEED THIS MORE THAN I DO.
'RIKA, YOU AND KYLE HAVE BEEN TOGETHER FOR OVER A YEAR. IT SHOULDN'T COME AS A SHOCK TO YOU THAT HE'S EXPECTING THIS NEXT STEP.
I KNOW! AND I FEEL LIKE A FREAK FOR NOT WANTING IT TO HAPPEN.
IS SOMETHING WRONG WITH ME?
YOU ARE MOST DEFINITELY NOT A FREAK.
LET'S NOT BE SO HASTY.
I MEAN, WHY ON EARTH DON'T YOU WANT TO HAVE SEX WITH KYLE?
HE'S TOTALLY CUTE, IN, LIKE, A SCRUFFY ROCKER WAY.
I AM ATTRACTED TO HIM. AND I LOVE FOOLING AROUND WITH HIM.
BUT SEX FEELS SO HUGE TO ME -- REALLY SERIOUS AND INTENSE. I'M NOT SURE HE SHOULD BE THE ONE.

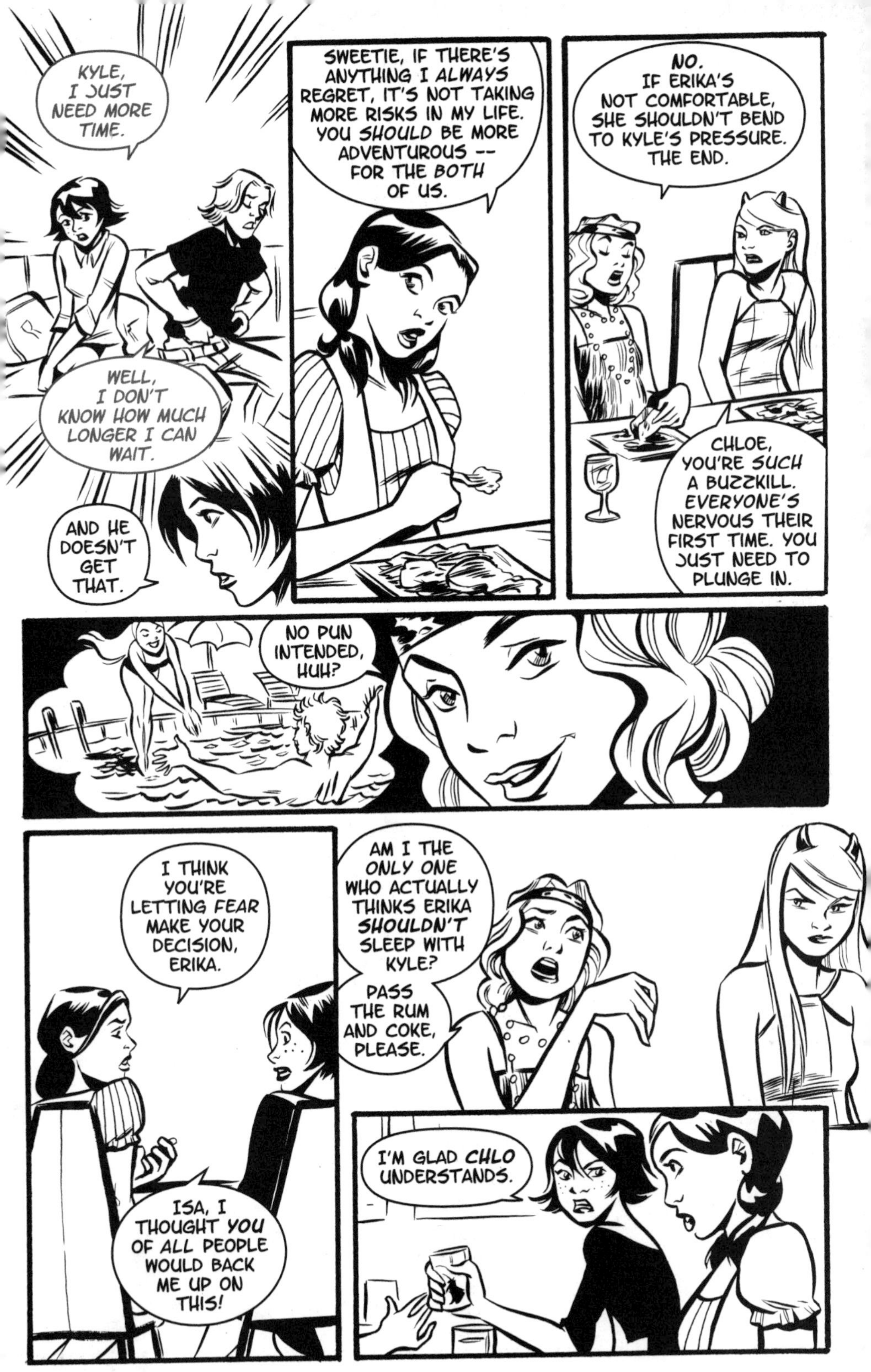
KYLE, I JUST NEED MORE TIME.
WELL, I DON'T KNOW HOW MUCH LONGER I CAN WAIT.
AND HE DOESN'T GET THAT.
SWEETIE, IF THERE'S ANYTHING I ALWAYS REGRET, IT'S NOT TAKING MORE RISKS IN MY LIFE. YOU SHOULD BE MORE ADVENTUROUS -- FOR THE BOTH OF US.
NO. IF ERIKA'S NOT COMFORTABLE, SHE SHOULDN'T BEND TO KYLE'S PRESSURE. THE END.
CHLOE, YOU'RE SUCH A BUZZKILL. EVERYONE'S NERVOUS THEIR FIRST TIME. YOU JUST NEED TO PLUNGE IN.
NO PUN INTENDED, HUH?
I THINK YOU'RE LETTING FEAR MAKE YOUR DECISION, ERIKA.
ISA, I THOUGHT YOU OF ALL PEOPLE WOULD BACK ME UP ON THIS!
AM I THE ONLY ONE WHO ACTUALLY THINKS ERIKA SHOULDN'T SLEEP WITH KYLE?
PASS THE RUM AND COKE, PLEASE.
I'M GLAD CHLO UNDERSTANDS.

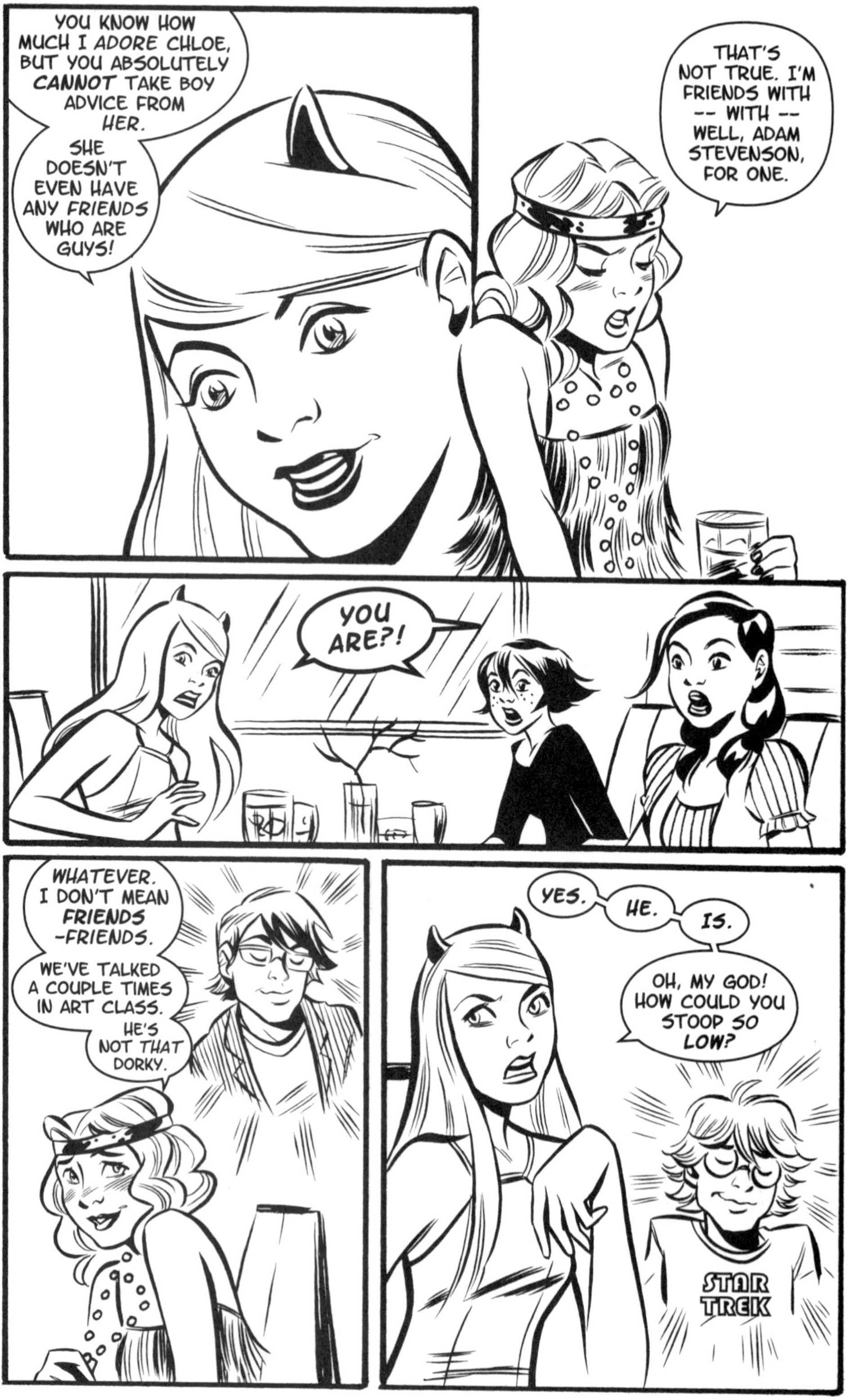
YOU KNOW HOW MUCH I ADORE CHLOE, BUT YOU ABSOLUTELY CANNOT TAKE BOY ADVICE FROM HER.
SHE DOESN'T EVEN HAVE ANY FRIENDS WHO ARE GUYS!
THAT'S NOT TRUE. I'M FRIENDS WITH -- WITH -- WELL, ADAM STEVENSON, FOR ONE.
YOU ARE?!
WHATEVER. I DON'T MEAN FRIENDS -FRIENDS.
WE'VE TALKED A COUPLE TIMES IN ART CLASS.
HE'S NOT THAT DORKY.
YES.
HE.
IS.
OH, MY GOD! HOW COULD YOU STOOP SO LOW?
STAR TREK

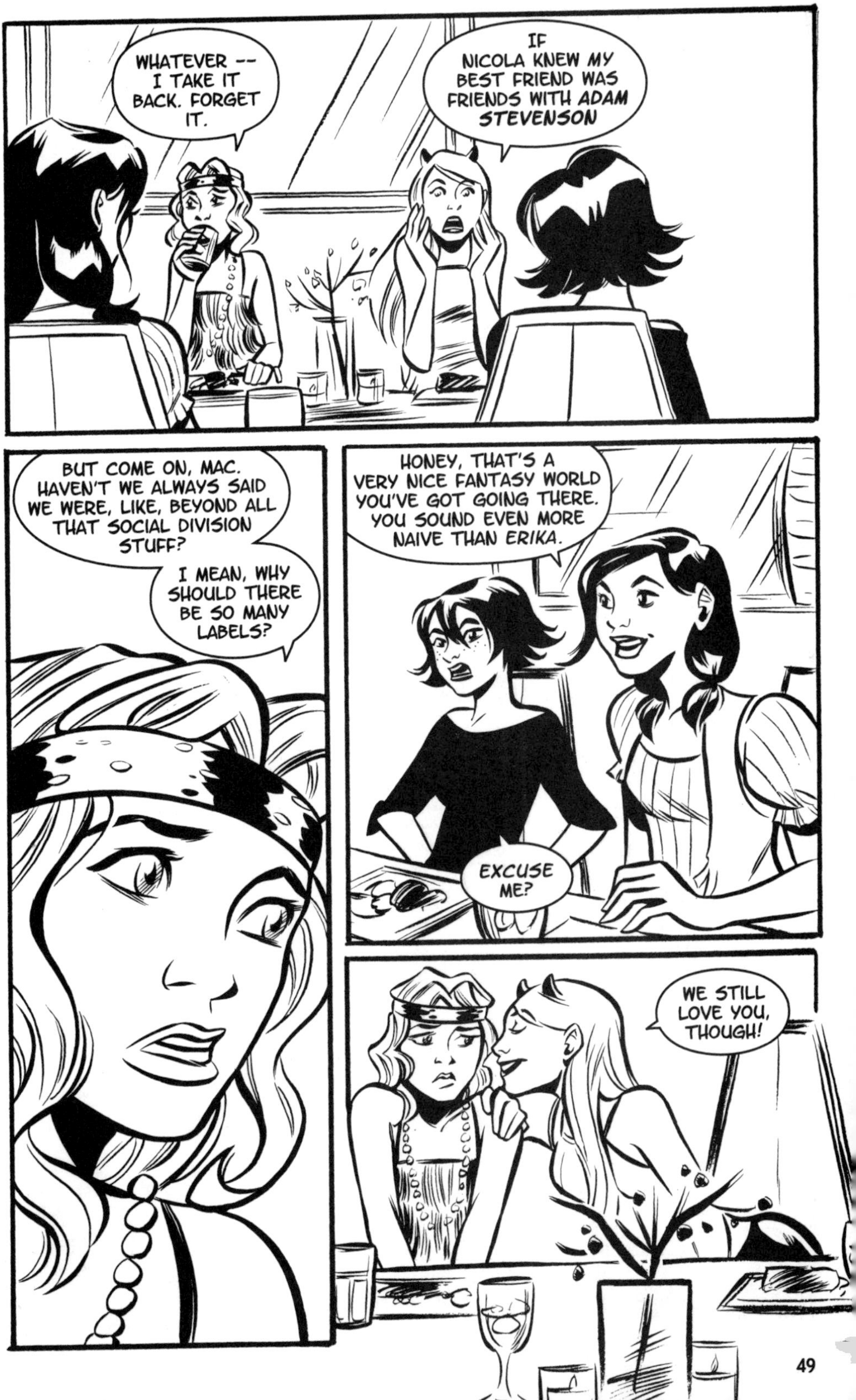

WHATEVER -- I TAKE IT BACK. FORGET IT.
IF NICOLA KNEW MY BEST FRIEND WAS FRIENDS WITH ADAM STEVENSON
BUT COME ON, MAC. HAVEN'T WE ALWAYS SAID WE WERE, LIKE, BEYOND ALL THAT SOCIAL DIVISION STUFF?
I MEAN, WHY SHOULD THERE BE SO MANY LABELS?
HONEY, THAT'S A VERY NICE FANTASY WORLD YOU'VE GOT GOING THERE. YOU SOUND EVEN MORE NAIVE THAN ERIKA.
EXCUSE ME?
WE STILL LOVE YOU, THOUGH!

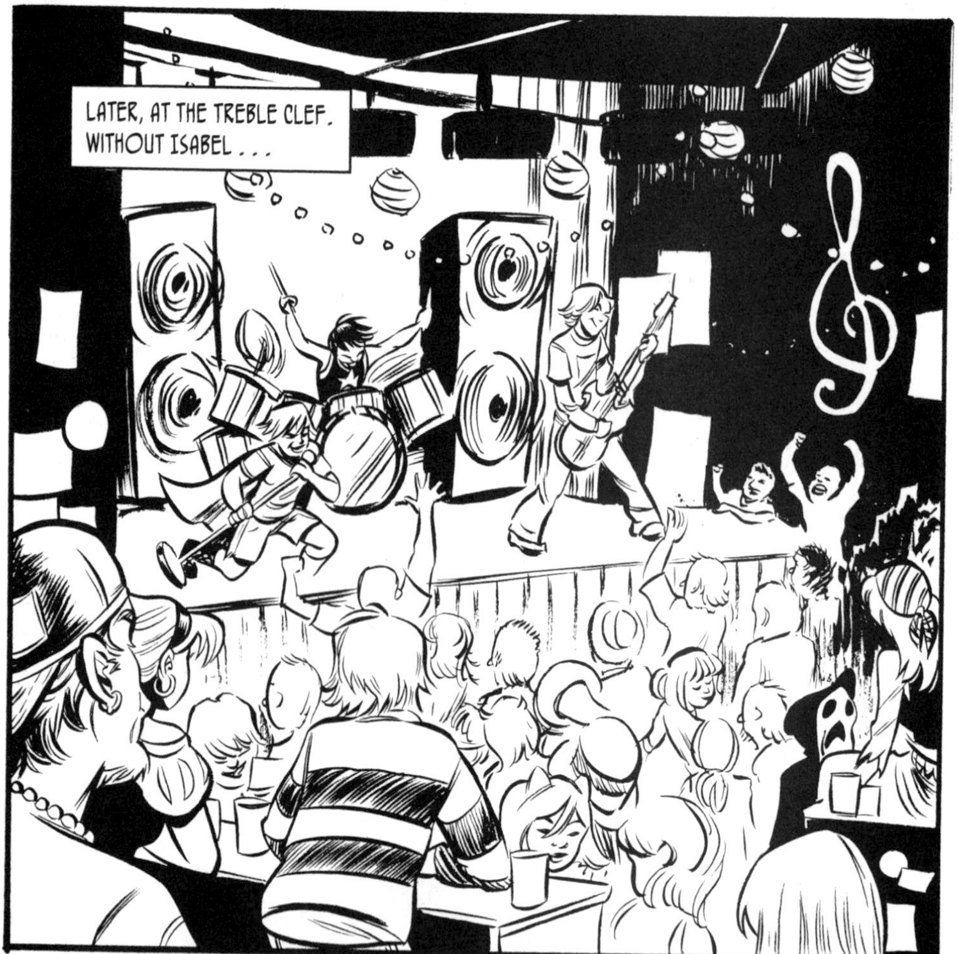
LATER, AT THE TREBLE CLEF. WITHOUT ISABEL . . .

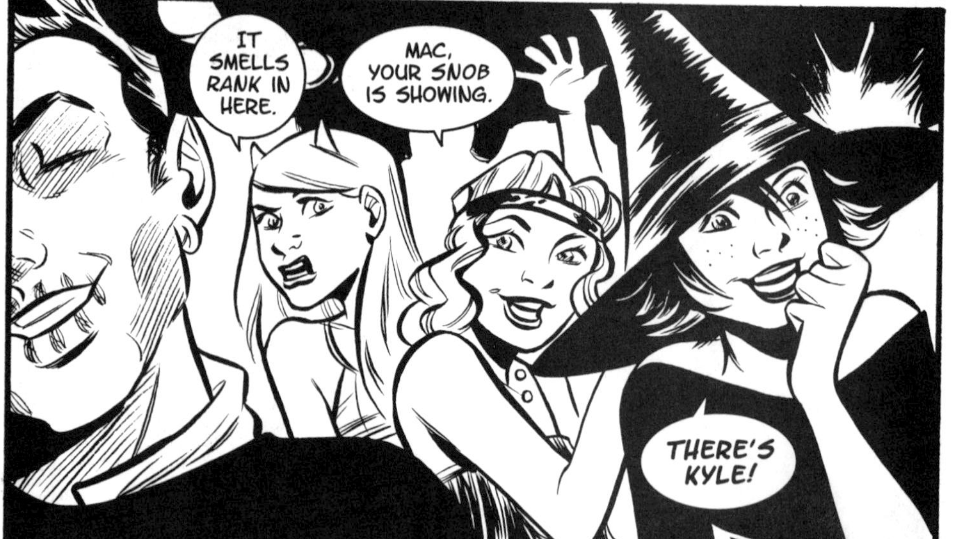
IT SMELLS RANK IN HERE.
MAC, YOUR SNOB IS SHOWING.
THERE'S KYLE!

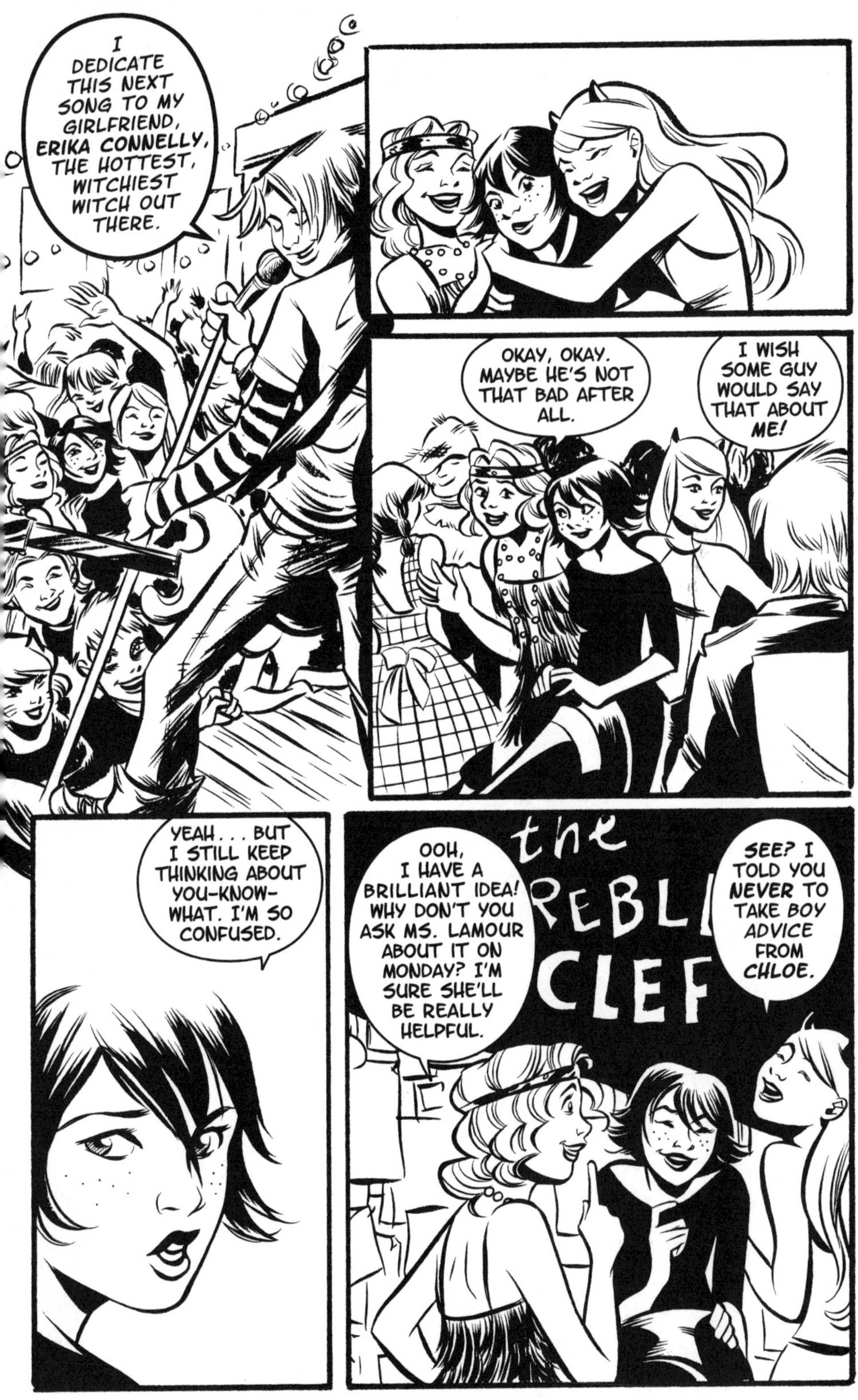
I DEDICATE THIS NEXT SONG TO MY GIRLFRIEND, ERIKA CONNELLY, THE HOTTEST, WITCHIEST WITCH OUT THERE.
OKAY, OKAY. MAYBE HE'S NOT THAT BAD AFTER ALL.
I WISH SOME GUY WOULD SAY THAT ABOUT ME!
YEAH . . . BUT I STILL KEEP THINKING ABOUT YOU-KNOW-WHAT. I'M SO CONFUSED.
the REBL CLEF
OOH, I HAVE A BRILLIANT IDEA! WHY DON'T YOU ASK MS. LAMOUR ABOUT IT ON MONDAY? I'M SURE SHE'LL BE REALLY HELPFUL.
SEE? I TOLD YOU NEVER TO TAKE BOY ADVICE FROM CHLOE.

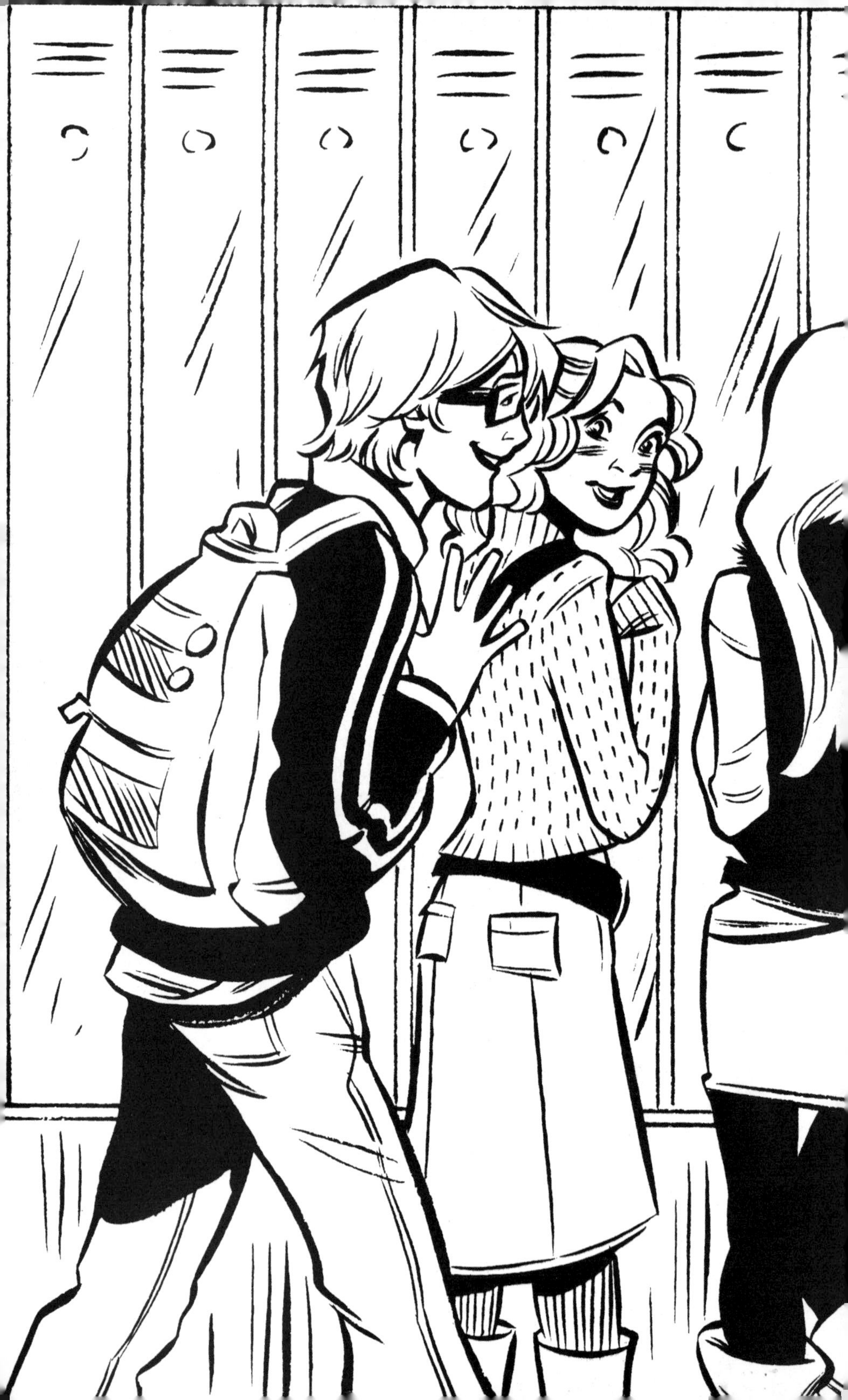

Chapter 5: Invitation Insanity

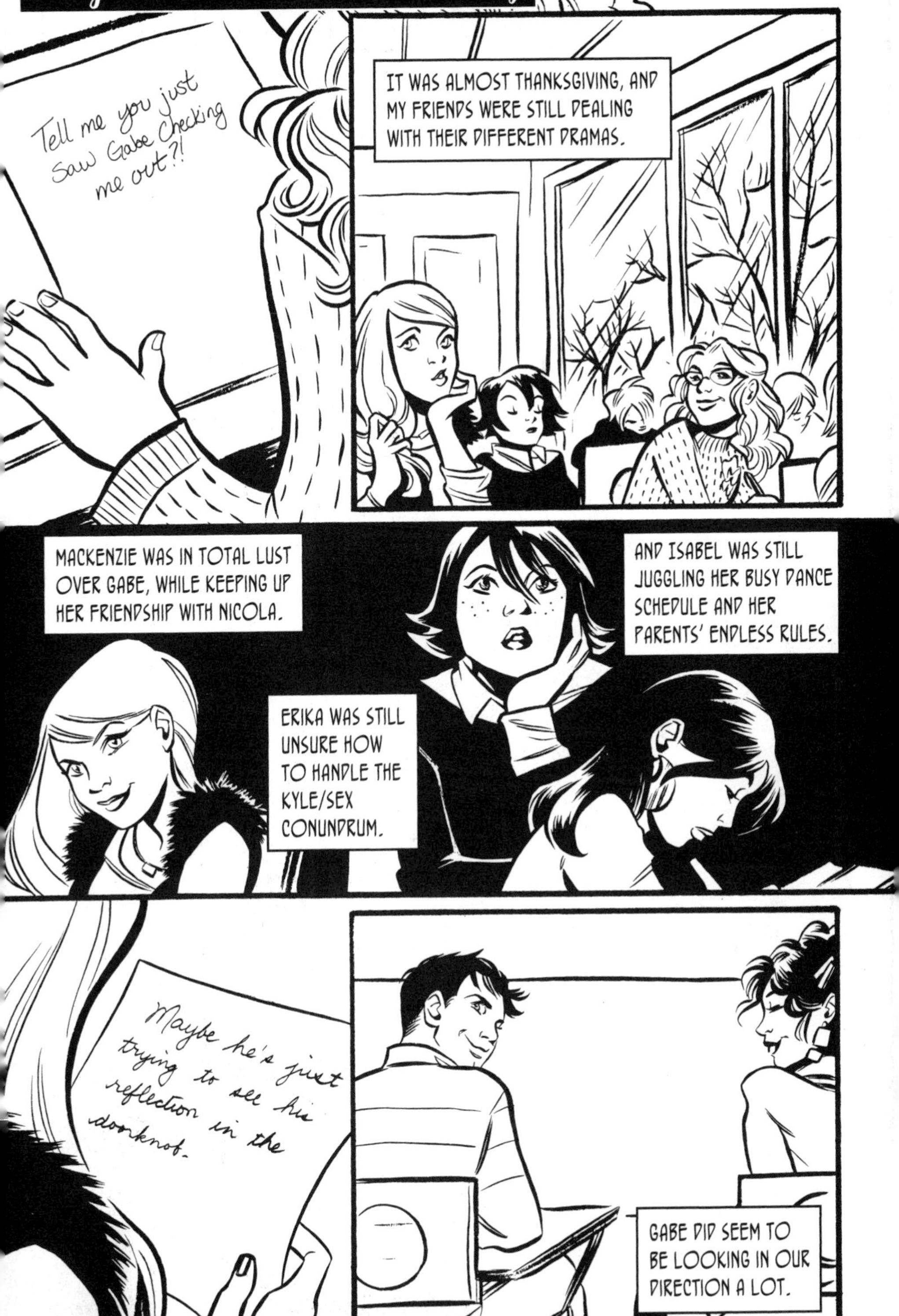
Tell me you just Saw Gabe Checking me out?!
IT WAS ALMOST THANKSGIVING, AND MY FRIENDS WERE STILL DEALING WITH THEIR DIFFERENT DRAMAS.
MACKENZIE WAS IN TOTAL LUST OVER GABE, WHILE KEEPING UP HER FRIENDSHIP WITH NICOLA.
AND ISABEL WAS STILL JUGGLING HER BUSY DANCE SCHEDULE AND HER PARENTS' ENDLESS RULES.
ERIKA WAS STILL UNSURE HOW TO HANDLE THE KYLE/SEX CONUNDRUM.
Maybe he's just trying to see his reflection in the doorknob.
GABE DID SEEM TO BE LOOKING IN OUR DIRECTION A LOT.

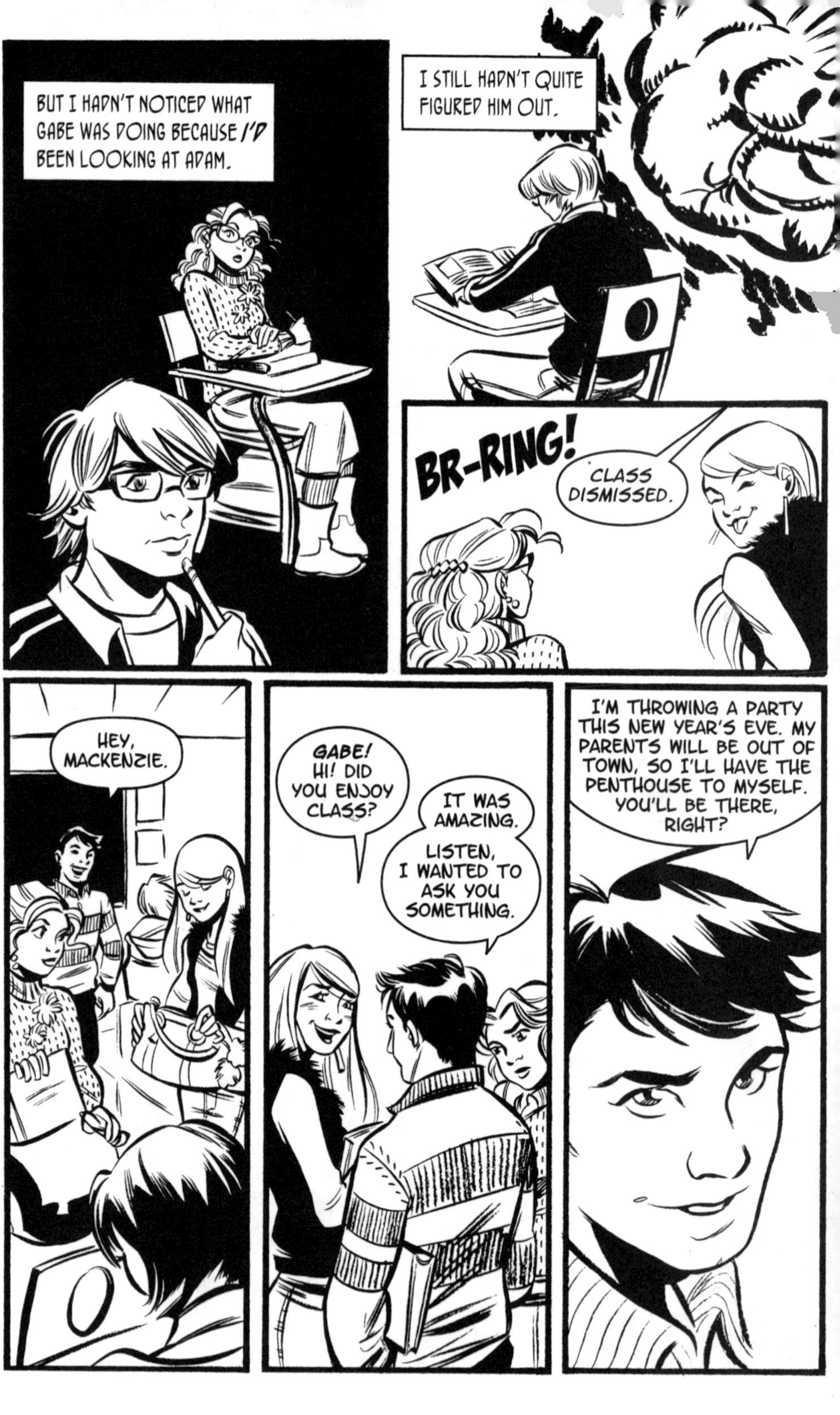
BUT I HADN'T NOTICED WHAT GABE WAS DOING BECAUSE I'D BEEN LOOKING AT ADAM.
I STILL HADN'T QUITE FIGURED HIM OUT.
BR-RING!
CLASS DISMISSED.
HEY, MACKENZIE.
GABE! HI! DID YOU ENJOY CLASS?
IT WAS AMAZING.
LISTEN, I WANTED TO ASK YOU SOMETHING.
I'M THROWING A PARTY THIS NEW YEAR'S EVE. MY PARENTS WILL BE OUT OF TOWN, SO I'LL HAVE THE PENTHOUSE TO MYSELF. YOU'LL BE THERE, RIGHT?

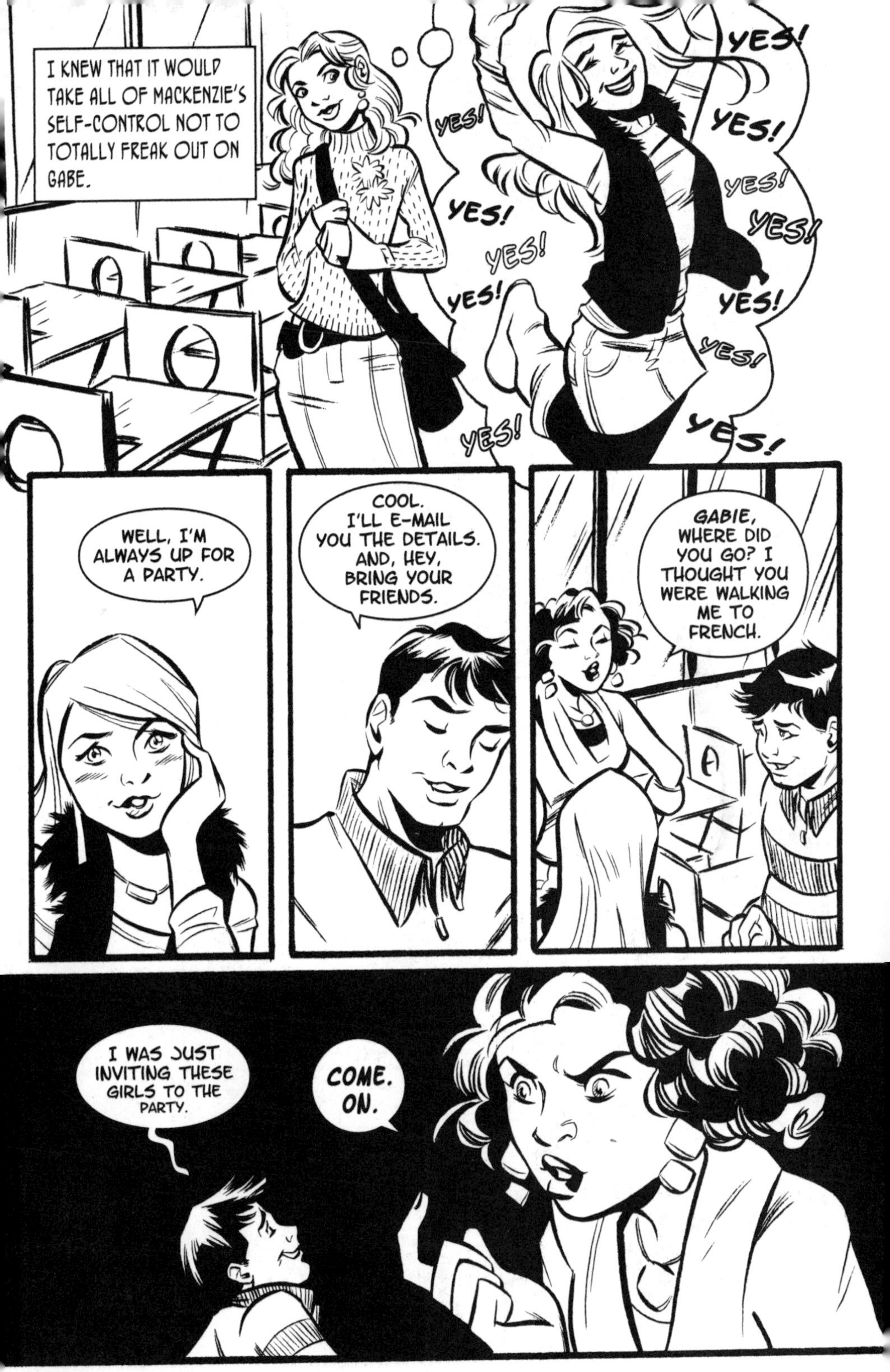

I KNEW THAT IT WOULD TAKE ALL OF MACKENZIE'S SELF-CONTROL NOT TO TOTALLY FREAK OUT ON GABE.
YES!
YES!
YES!
YES!
YES!
YES!
YES!
YES!
YES!
YES!
YES!
YES!
YES!
WELL, I'M ALWAYS UP FOR A PARTY.
COOL. I'LL E-MAIL YOU THE DETAILS. AND, HEY, BRING YOUR FRIENDS.
GABIE, WHERE DID YOU GO? I THOUGHT YOU WERE WALKING ME TO FRENCH.
I WAS JUST INVITING THESE GIRLS TO THE PARTY.
COME. ON.

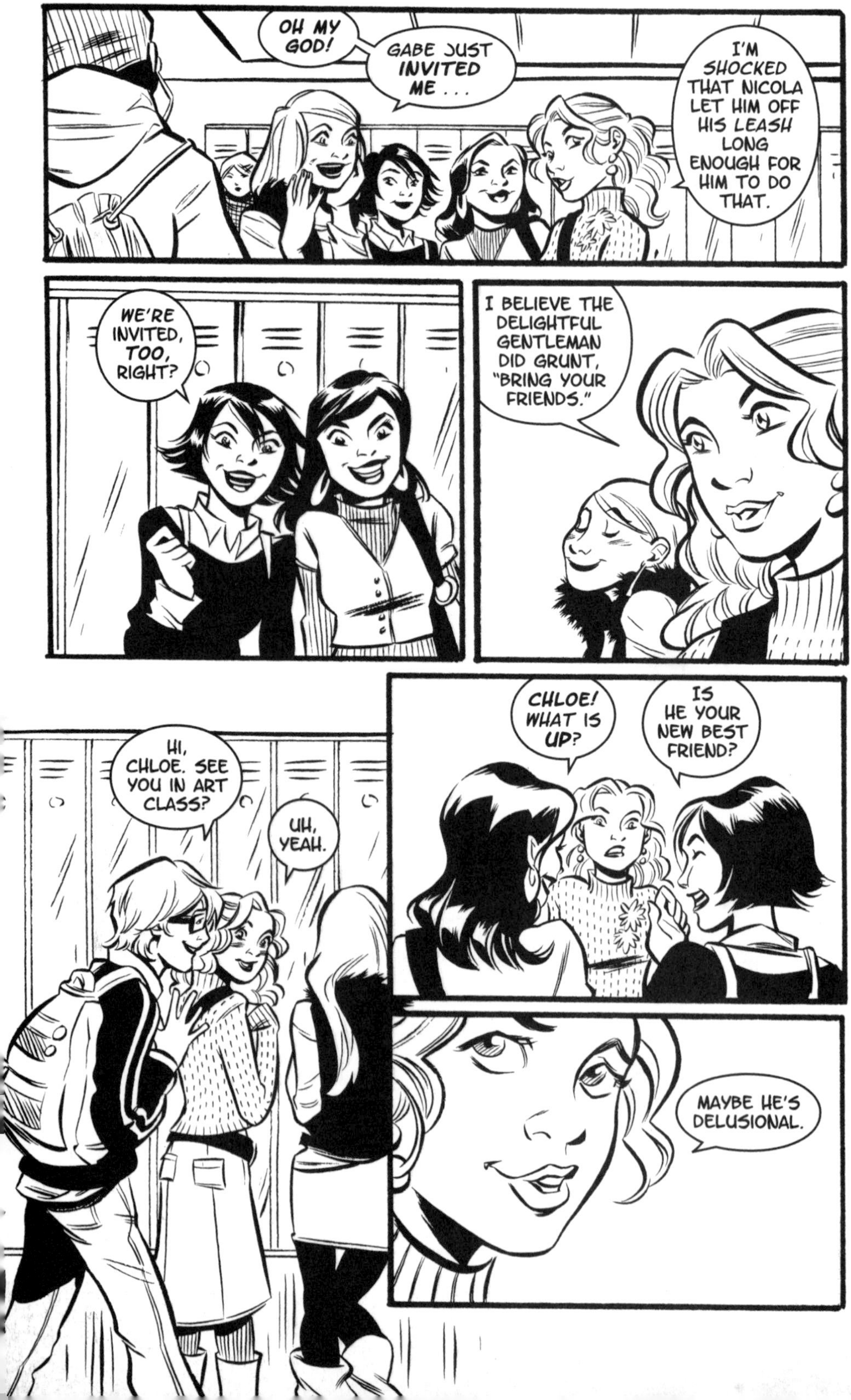

OH MY GOD!
GABE JUST INVITED ME . . .
I'M SHOCKED THAT NICOLA LET HIM OFF HIS LEASH LONG ENOUGH FOR HIM TO DO THAT.
WE'RE INVITED, TOO, RIGHT?
I BELIEVE THE DELIGHTFUL GENTLEMAN DID GRUNT, "BRING YOUR FRIENDS."
HI, CHLOE. SEE YOU IN ART CLASS?
UH, YEAH.
CHLOE! WHAT IS UP?
IS HE YOUR NEW BEST FRIEND?
MAYBE HE'S DELUSIONAL.

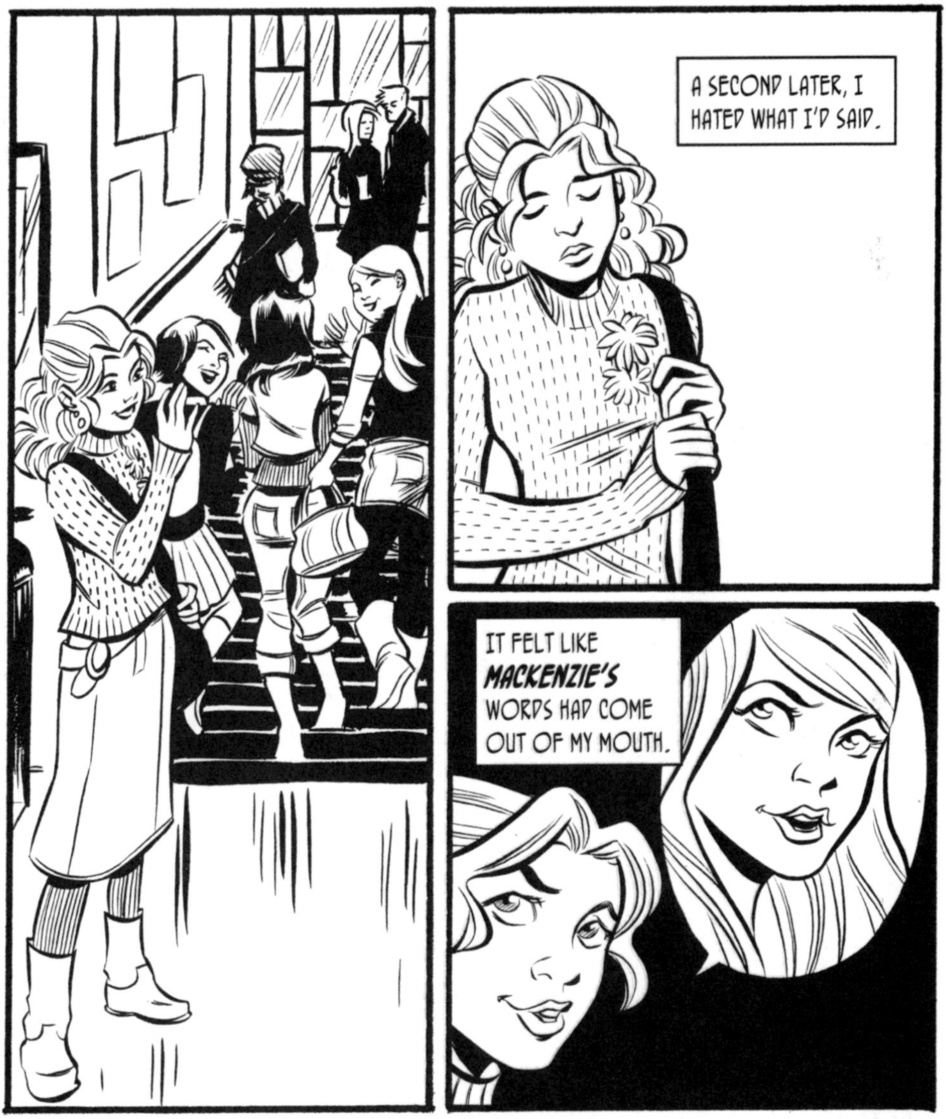
A SECOND LATER, I HATED WHAT I'D SAID.
IT FELT LIKE MACKENZIE'S WORDS HAD COME OUT OF MY MOUTH.

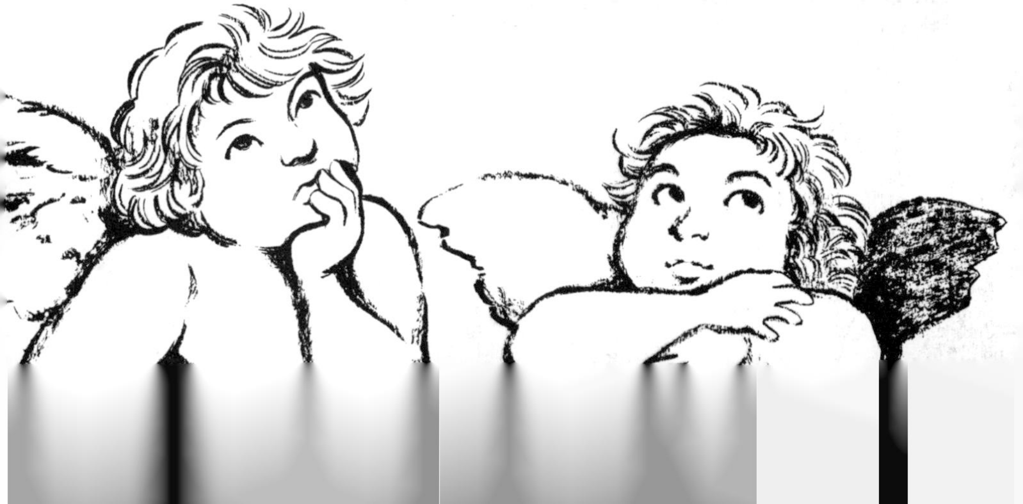

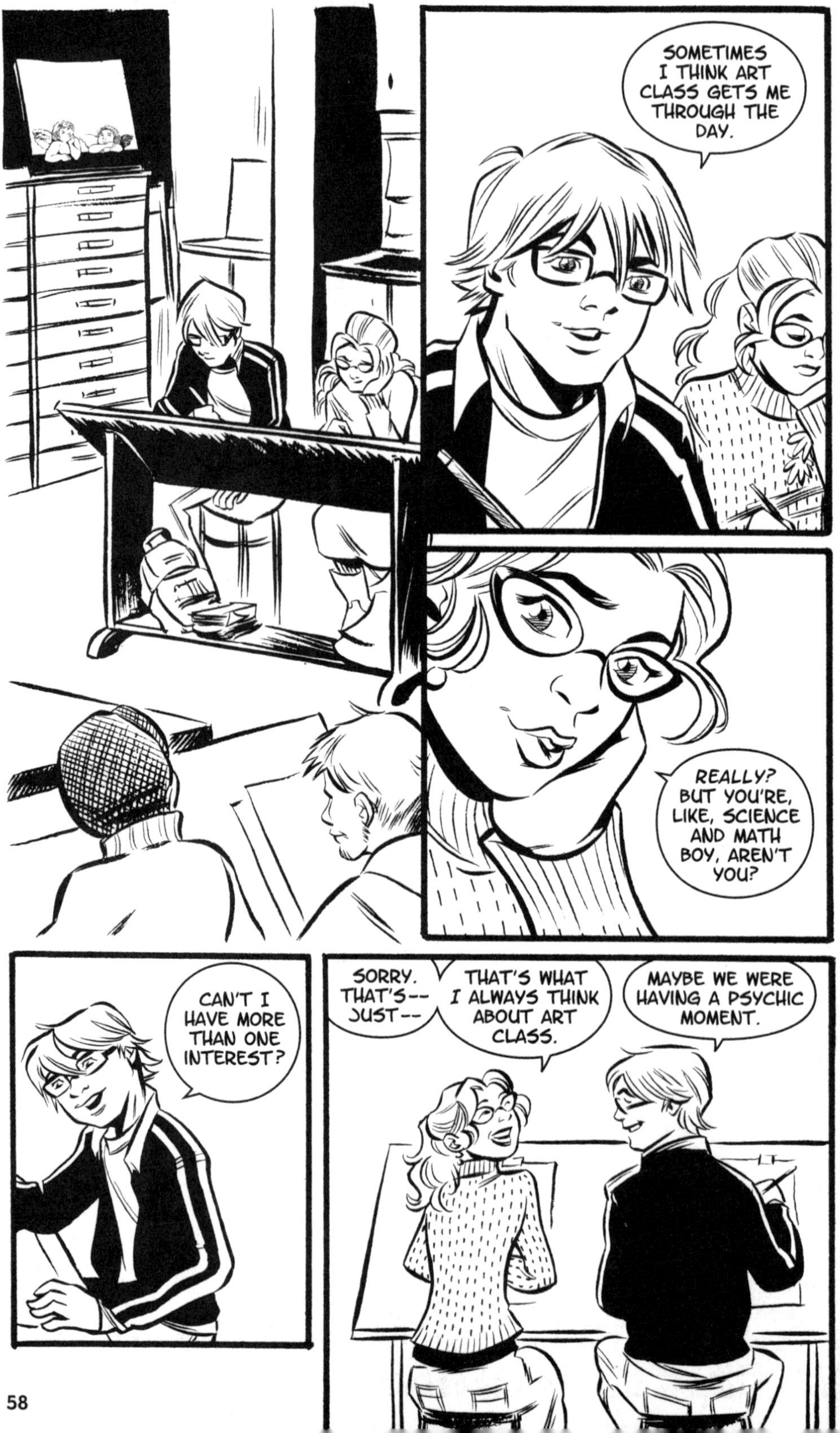
SOMETIMES I THINK ART CLASS GETS ME THROUGH THE DAY.
REALLY? BUT YOU'RE, LIKE, SCIENCE AND MATH BOY, AREN'T YOU?
CAN'T I HAVE MORE THAN ONE INTEREST?
SORRY. THAT'S-- JUST--
THAT'S WHAT I ALWAYS THINK ABOUT ART CLASS.
MAYBE WE WERE HAVING A PSYCHIC MOMENT.

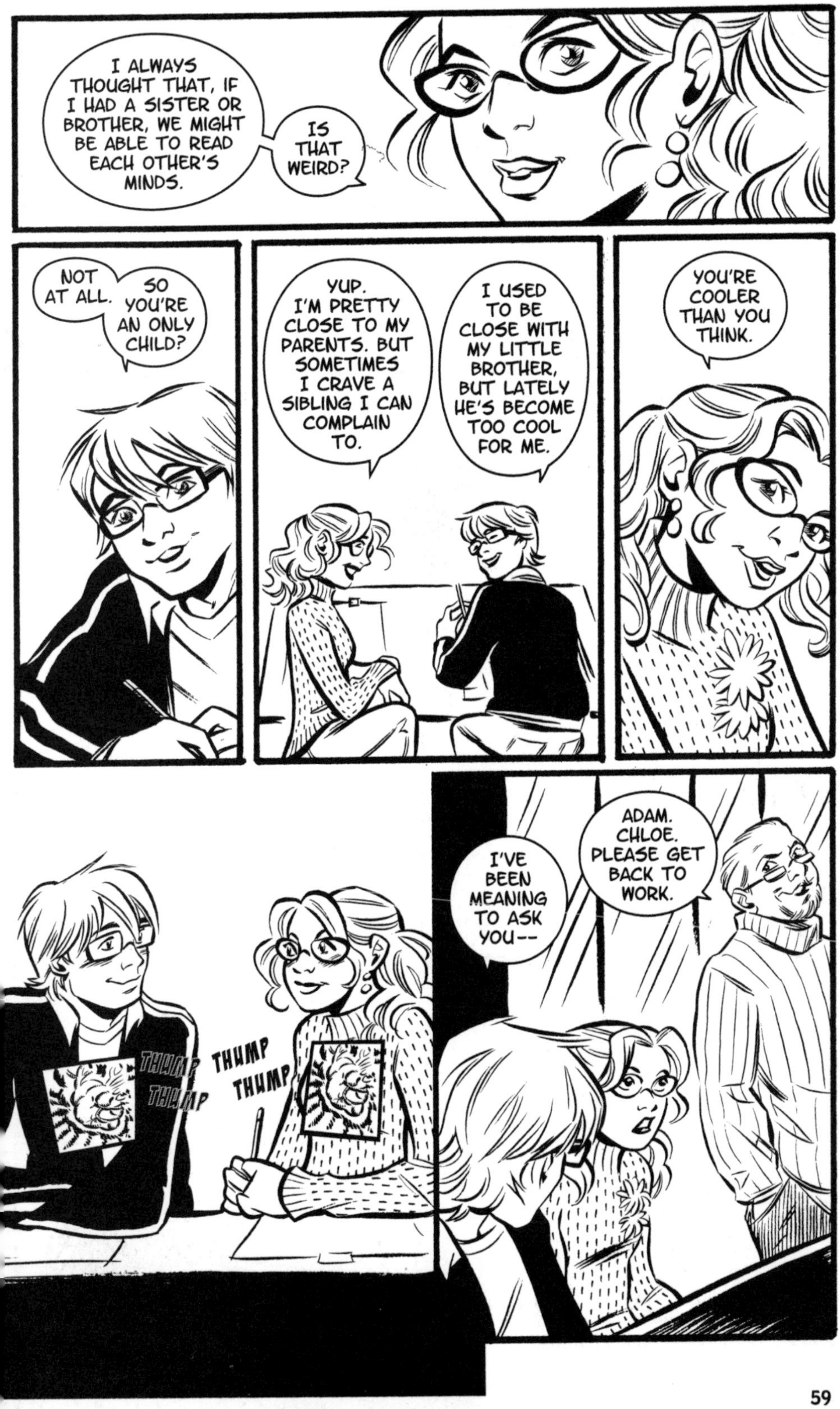
I ALWAYS THOUGHT THAT, IF I HAD A SISTER OR BROTHER, WE MIGHT BE ABLE TO READ EACH OTHER'S MINDS.
IS THAT WEIRD?
NOT AT ALL.
SO YOU'RE AN ONLY CHILD?
YUP. I'M PRETTY CLOSE TO MY PARENTS. BUT SOMETIMES I CRAVE A SIBLING I CAN COMPLAIN TO.
I USED TO BE CLOSE WITH MY LITTLE BROTHER, BUT LATELY HE'S BECOME TOO COOL FOR ME.
YOU'RE COOLER THAN YOU THINK.
THUMP THUMP
THUMP THUMP
I'VE BEEN MEANING TO ASK YOU--
ADAM. CHLOE. PLEASE GET BACK TO WORK.

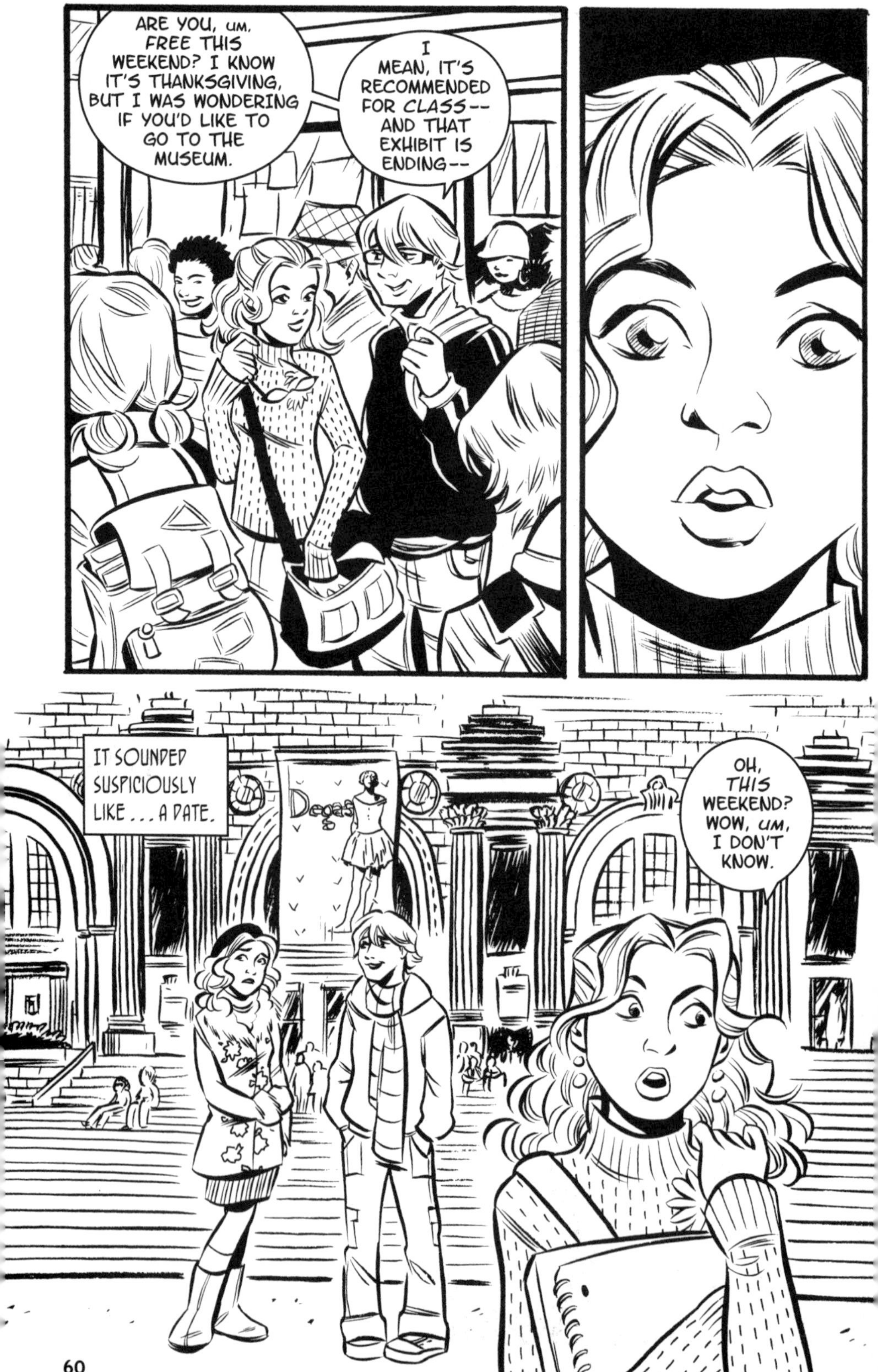
ARE YOU, UM, FREE THIS WEEKEND? I KNOW IT'S THANKSGIVING, BUT I WAS WONDERING IF YOU'D LIKE TO GO TO THE MUSEUM.
I MEAN, IT'S RECOMMENDED FOR CLASS-- AND THAT EXHIBIT IS ENDING--
IT SOUNDED SUSPICIOUSLY LIKE . . . A DATE.
Degas
OH, THIS WEEKEND? WOW, UM, I DON'T KNOW.

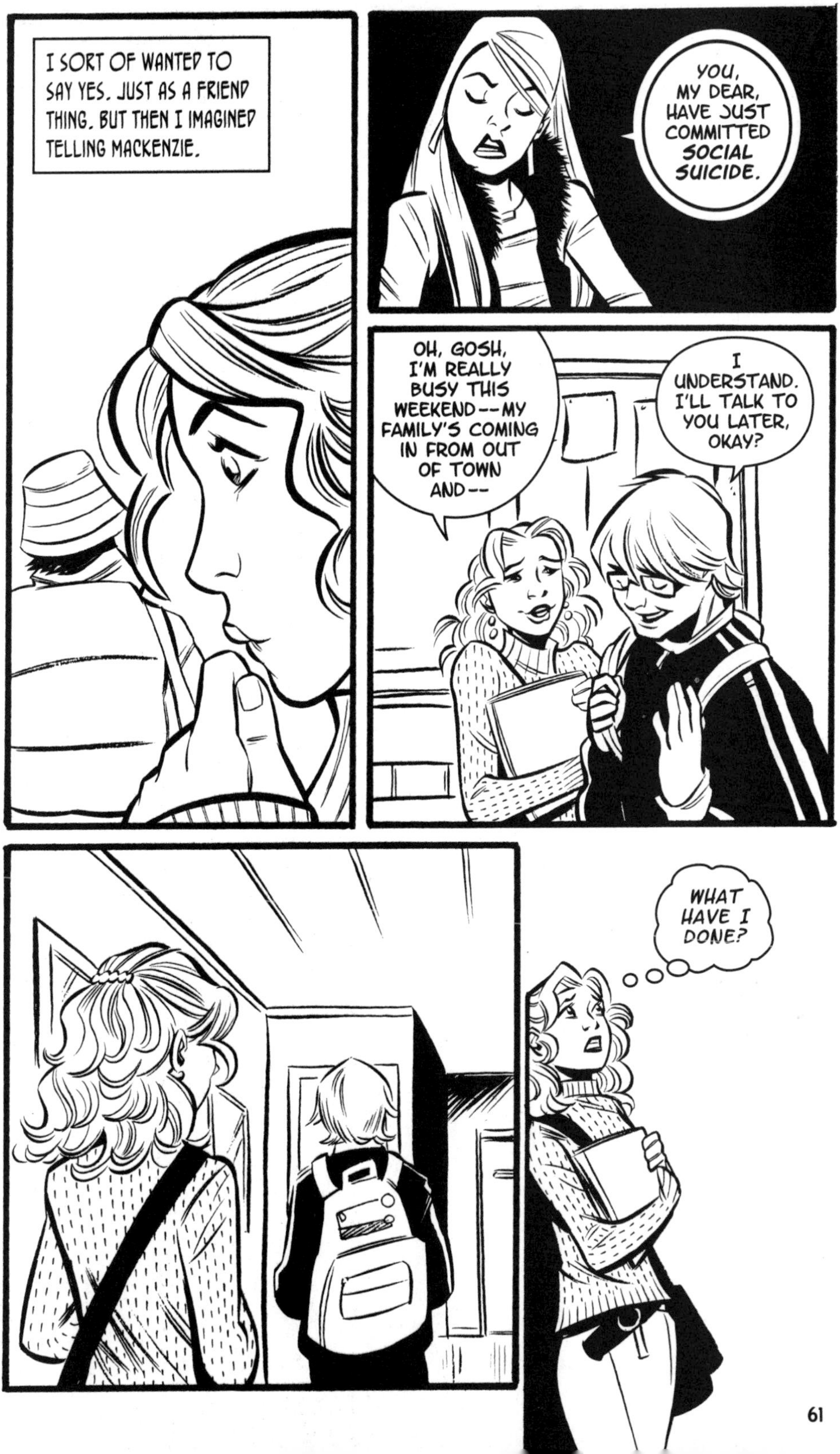
I SORT OF WANTED TO SAY YES. JUST AS A FRIEND THING. BUT THEN I IMAGINED TELLING MACKENZIE.
YOU, MY DEAR, HAVE JUST COMMITTED SOCIAL SUICIDE.
OH, GOSH, I'M REALLY BUSY THIS WEEKEND--MY FAMILY'S COMING IN FROM OUT OF TOWN AND--
I UNDERSTAND. I'LL TALK TO YOU LATER, OKAY?
WHAT HAVE I DONE?

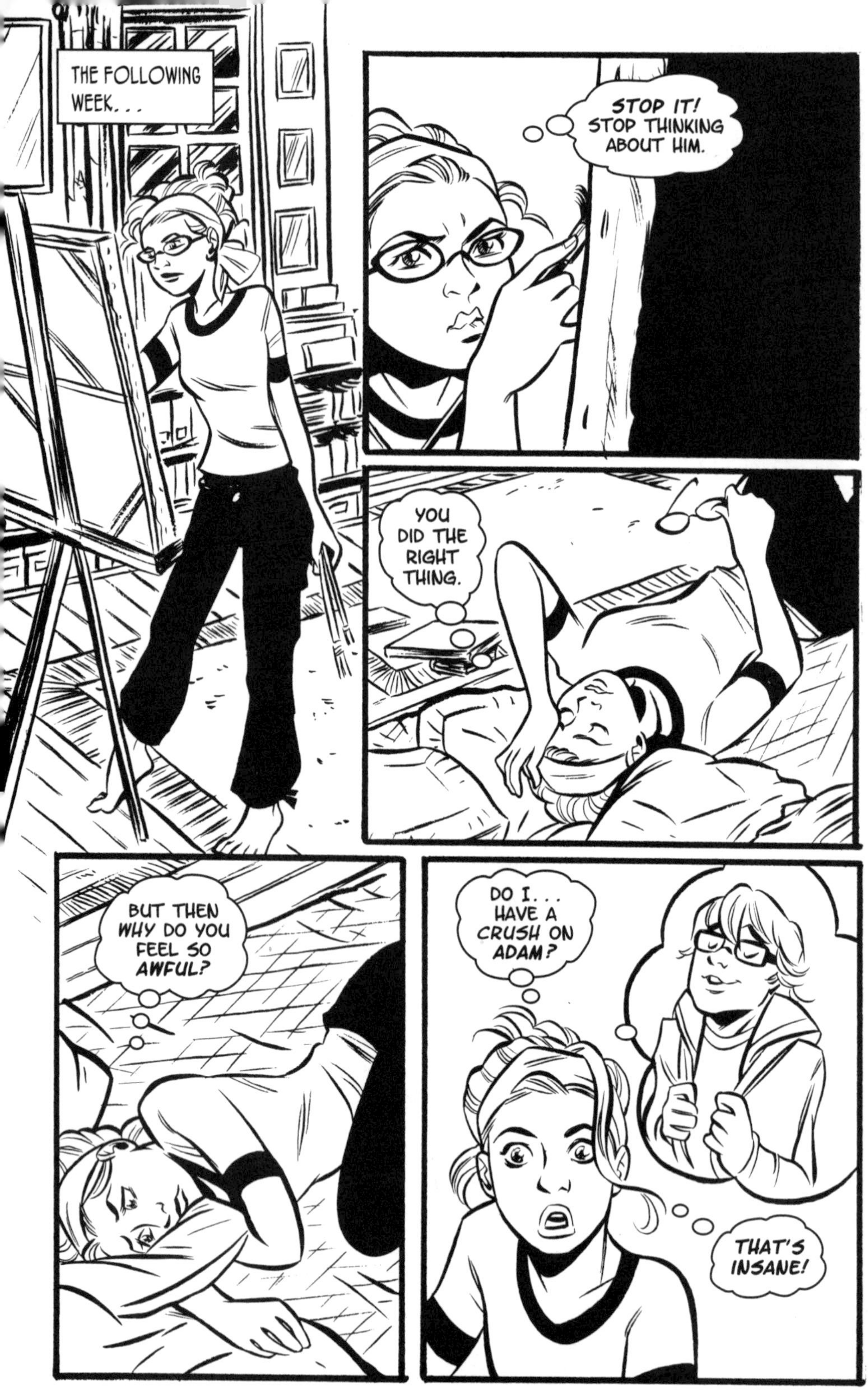
THE FOLLOWING WEEK. . .
STOP IT! STOP THINKING ABOUT HIM.
YOU DID THE RIGHT THING.
BUT THEN WHY DO YOU FEEL SO AWFUL?
DO I. . . HAVE A CRUSH ON ADAM?
THAT'S INSANE!

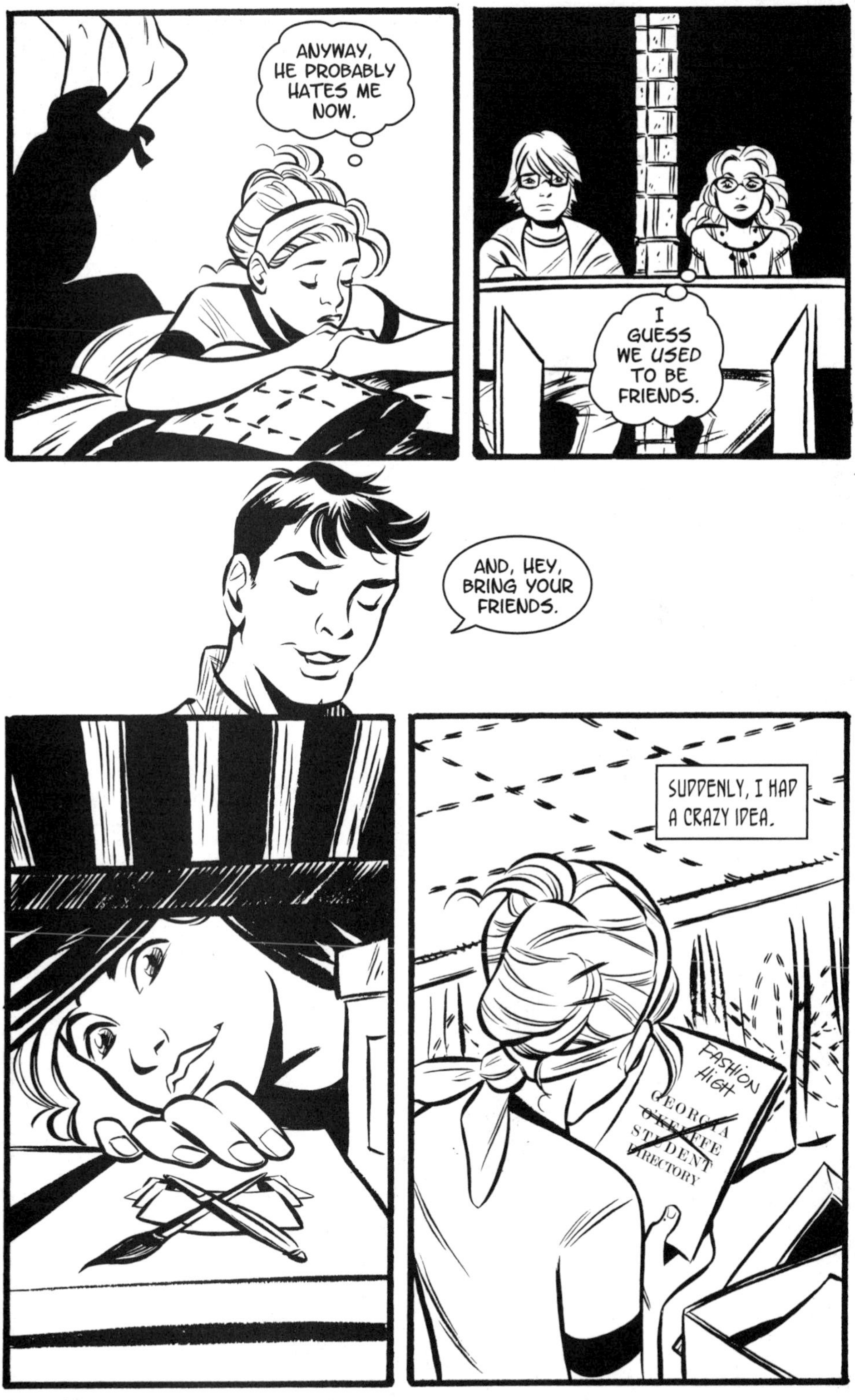
ANYWAY, HE PROBABLY HATES ME NOW.
I GUESS WE USED TO BE FRIENDS.
AND, HEY, BRING YOUR FRIENDS.
SUDDENLY, I HAD A CRAZY IDEA.
FASHION HIGH
GEORGIA O'KEEFFE STUDENT DIRECTORY

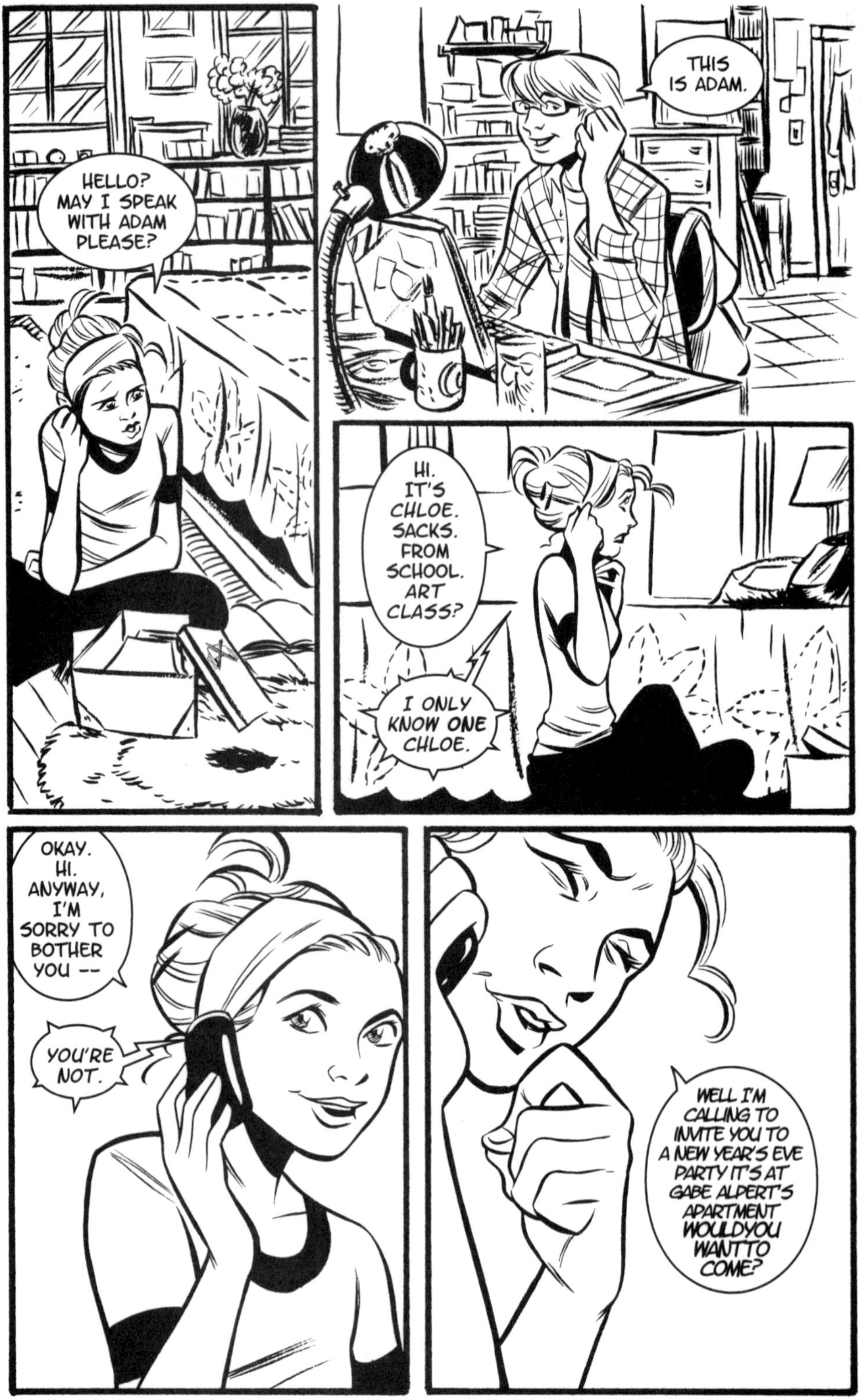
HELLO? MAY I SPEAK WITH ADAM PLEASE?
THIS IS ADAM.
HI. IT'S CHLOE. SACKS. FROM SCHOOL. ART CLASS?
I ONLY KNOW ONE CHLOE.
OKAY. HI. ANYWAY, I'M SORRY TO BOTHER YOU --
YOU'RE NOT.
WELL I'M CALLING TO INVITE YOU TO A NEW YEAR'S EVE PARTY IT'S AT GABE ALPERT'S APARTMENT WOULDYOU WANTTO COME?

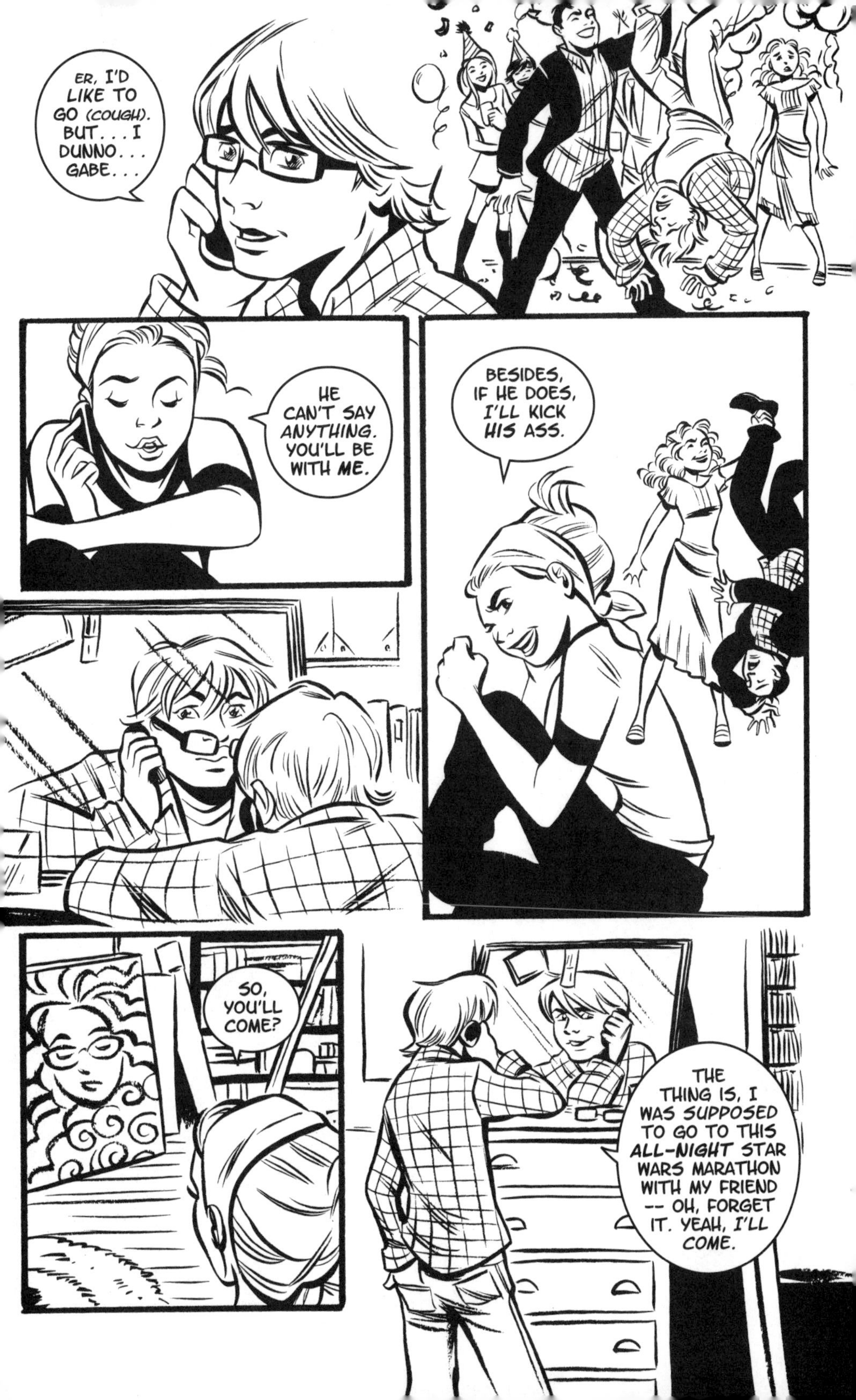
ER, I'D LIKE TO GO (COUGH). BUT . . . I DUNNO . . . GABE . . .
HE CAN'T SAY ANYTHING. YOU'LL BE WITH ME.
BESIDES, IF HE DOES, I'LL KICK HIS ASS.
SO, YOU'LL COME?
THE THING IS, I WAS SUPPOSED TO GO TO THIS ALL-NIGHT STAR WARS MARATHON WITH MY FRIEND -- OH, FORGET IT. YEAH, I'LL COME.

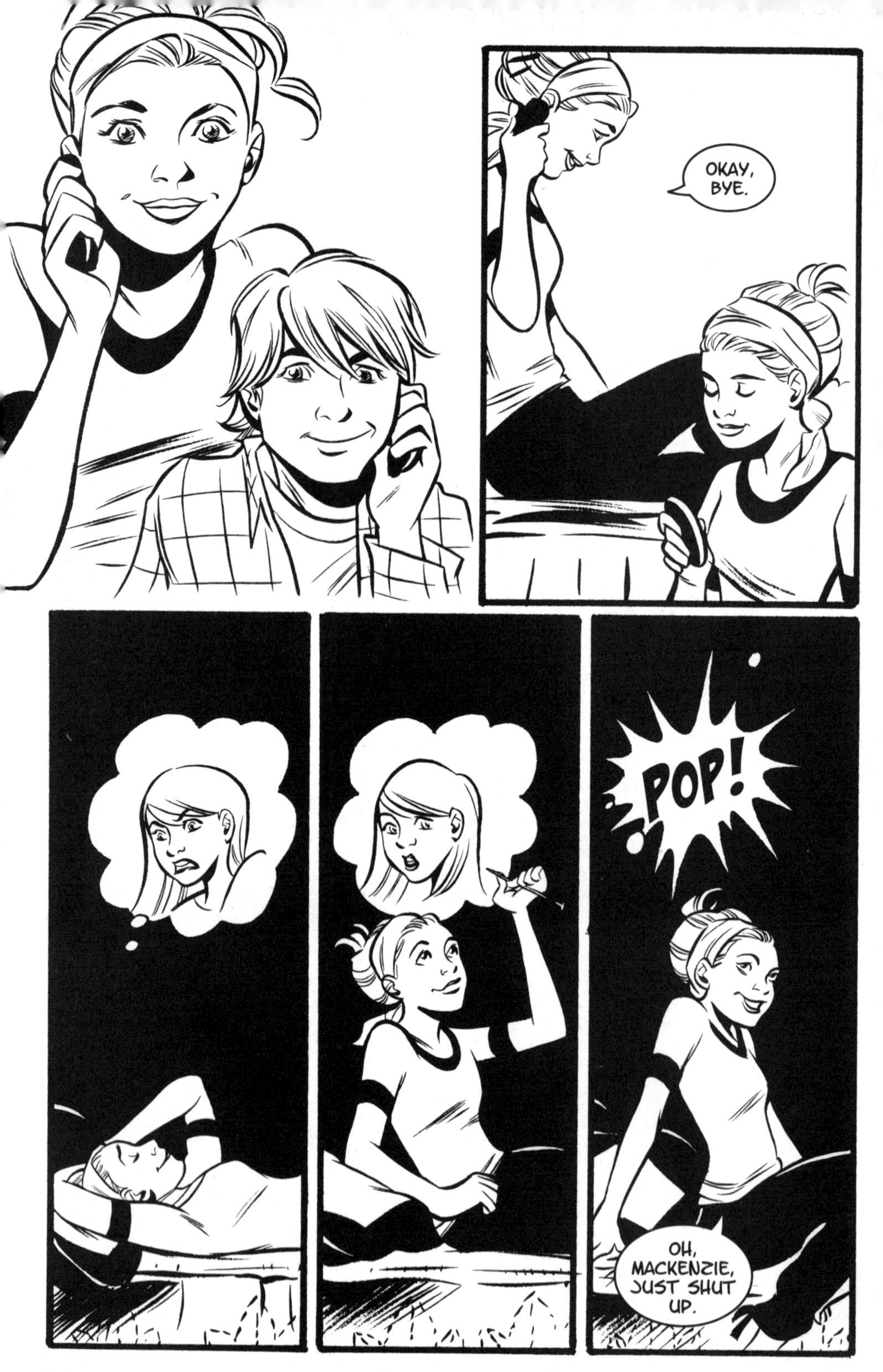
OKAY, BYE.
POP!
OH, MACKENZIE, JUST SHUT UP.

Chapter 6: Should Old Acquaintance Be Forgot?

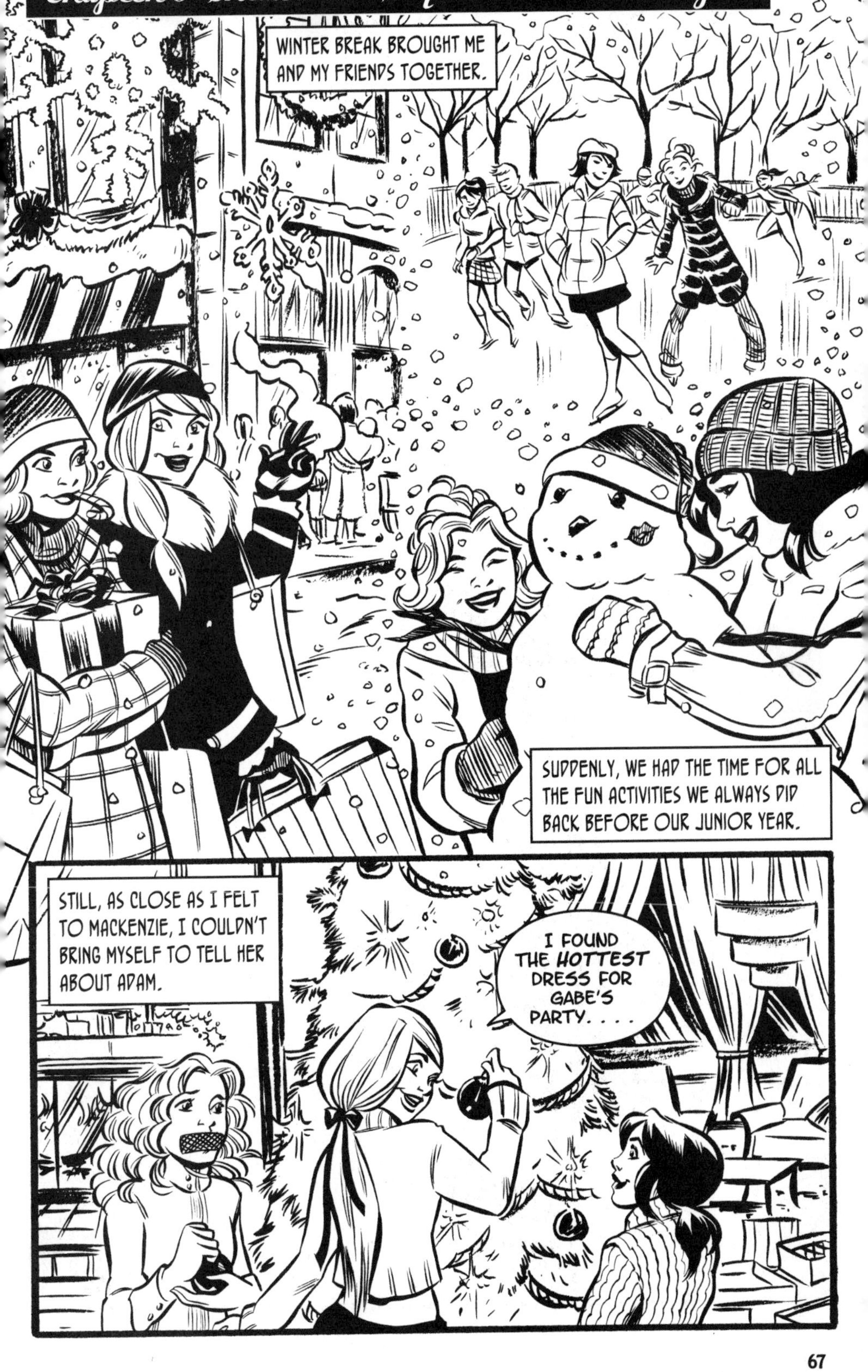
WINTER BREAK BROUGHT ME AND MY FRIENDS TOGETHER.
SUDDENLY, WE HAD THE TIME FOR ALL THE FUN ACTIVITIES WE ALWAYS DID BACK BEFORE OUR JUNIOR YEAR.
STILL, AS CLOSE AS I FELT TO MACKENZIE, I COULDN'T BRING MYSELF TO TELL HER ABOUT ADAM.
I FOUND THE *HOTTEST* DRESS FOR GABE'S PARTY. . . .

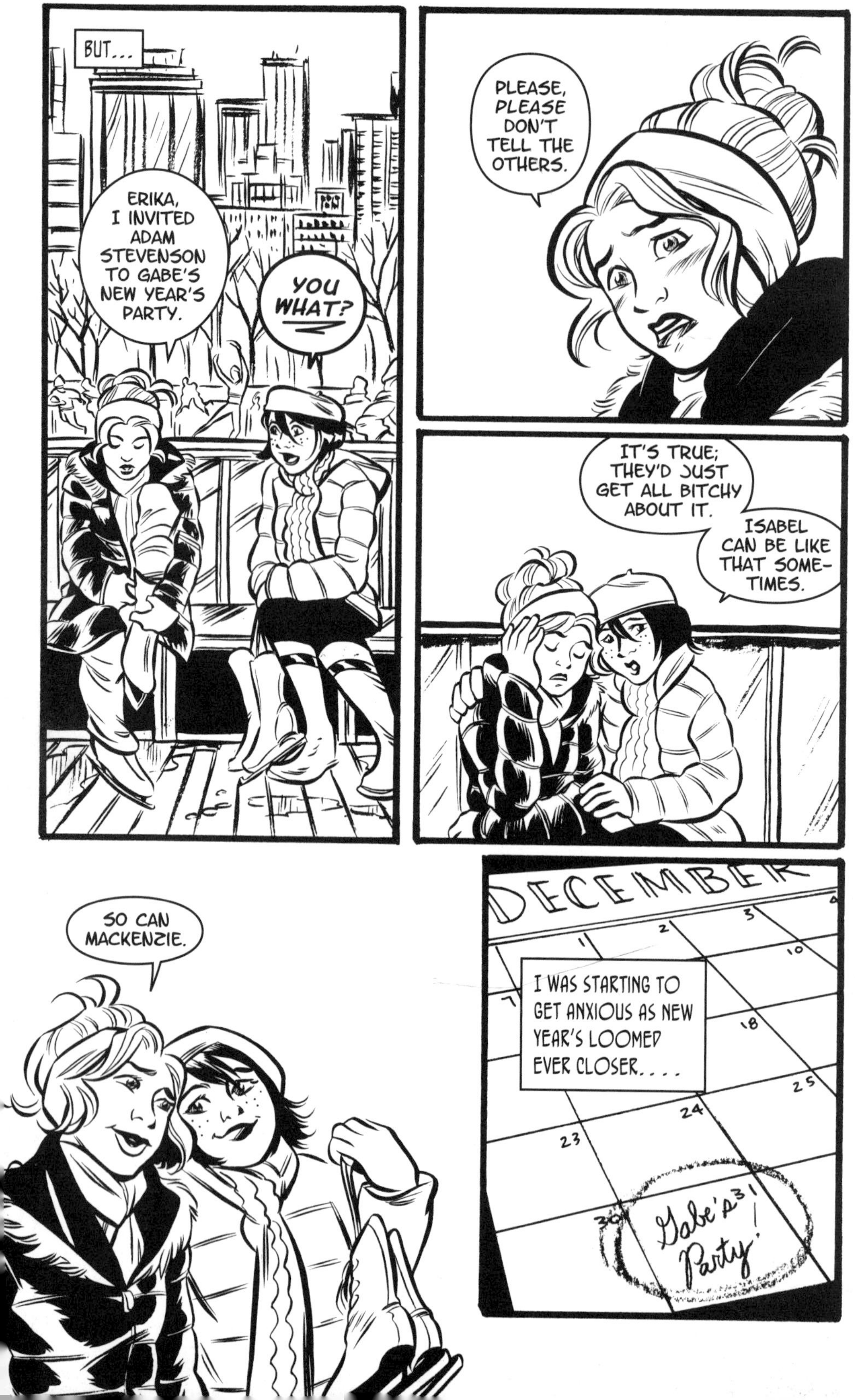
BUT...
ERIKA, I INVITED ADAM STEVENSON TO GABE'S NEW YEAR'S PARTY.
YOU WHAT?
PLEASE, PLEASE DON'T TELL THE OTHERS.
IT'S TRUE; THEY'D JUST GET ALL BITCHY ABOUT IT.
ISABEL CAN BE LIKE THAT SOME-TIMES.
SO CAN MACKENZIE.
DECEMBER
I WAS STARTING TO GET ANXIOUS AS NEW YEAR'S LOOMED EVER CLOSER....
Gabe's Party!

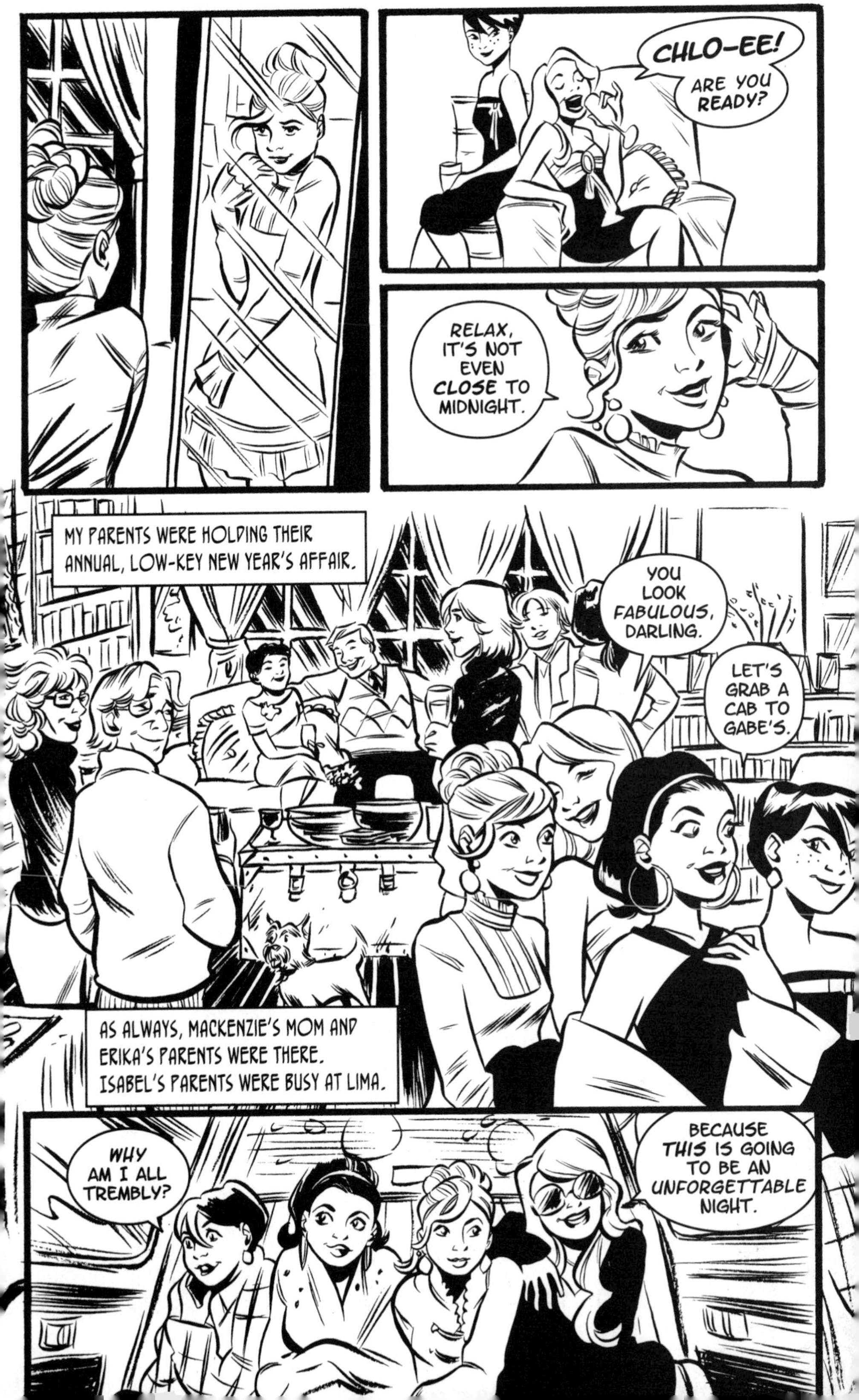
CHLO-EE!
ARE YOU READY?
RELAX, IT'S NOT EVEN CLOSE TO MIDNIGHT.
MY PARENTS WERE HOLDING THEIR ANNUAL, LOW-KEY NEW YEAR'S AFFAIR.
YOU LOOK FABULOUS, DARLING.
LET'S GRAB A CAB TO GABE'S.
AS ALWAYS, MACKENZIE'S MOM AND ERIKA'S PARENTS WERE THERE. ISABEL'S PARENTS WERE BUSY AT LIMA.
WHY AM I ALL TREMBLY?
BECAUSE THIS IS GOING TO BE AN UNFORGETTABLE NIGHT.

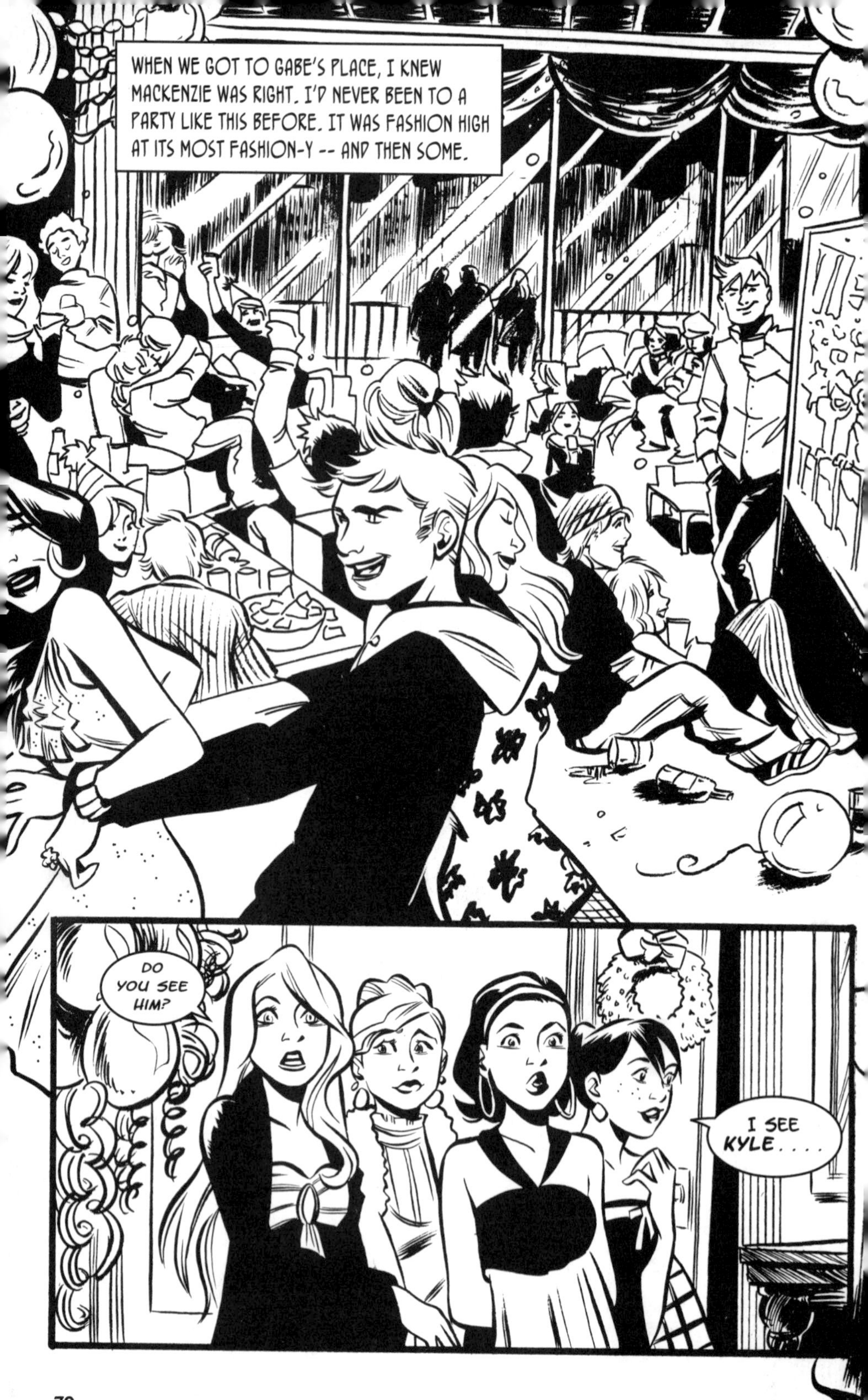
WHEN WE GOT TO GABE'S PLACE, I KNEW MACKENZIE WAS RIGHT. I'D NEVER BEEN TO A PARTY LIKE THIS BEFORE. IT WAS FASHION HIGH AT ITS MOST FASHION-Y -- AND THEN SOME.
DO YOU SEE HIM?
I SEE KYLE....

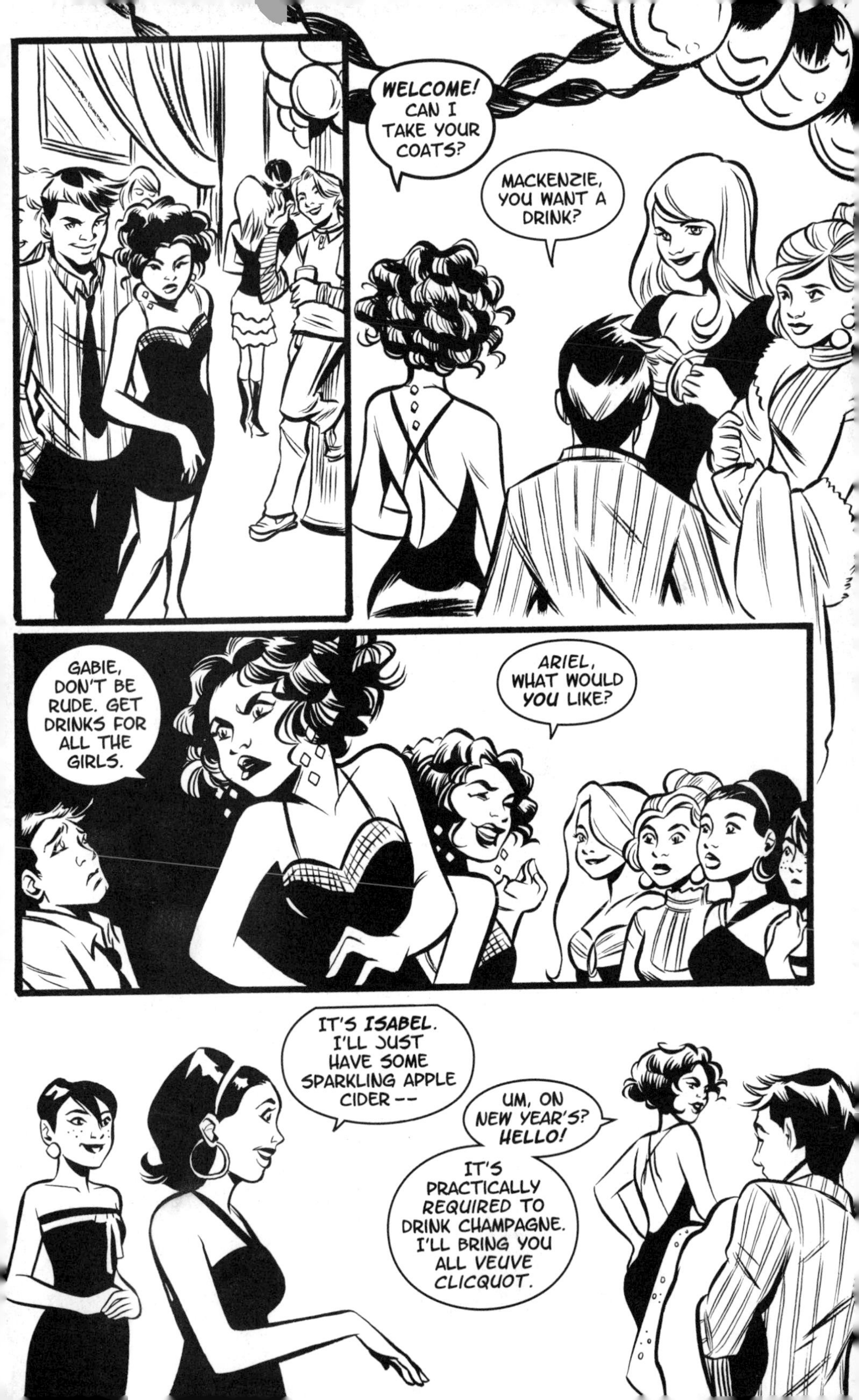
WELCOME! CAN I TAKE YOUR COATS?
MACKENZIE, YOU WANT A DRINK?
GABIE, DON'T BE RUDE. GET DRINKS FOR ALL THE GIRLS.
ARIEL, WHAT WOULD YOU LIKE?
IT'S ISABEL. I'LL JUST HAVE SOME SPARKLING APPLE CIDER --
UM, ON NEW YEAR'S? HELLO!
IT'S PRACTICALLY REQUIRED TO DRINK CHAMPAGNE. I'LL BRING YOU ALL VEUVE CLICQUOT.

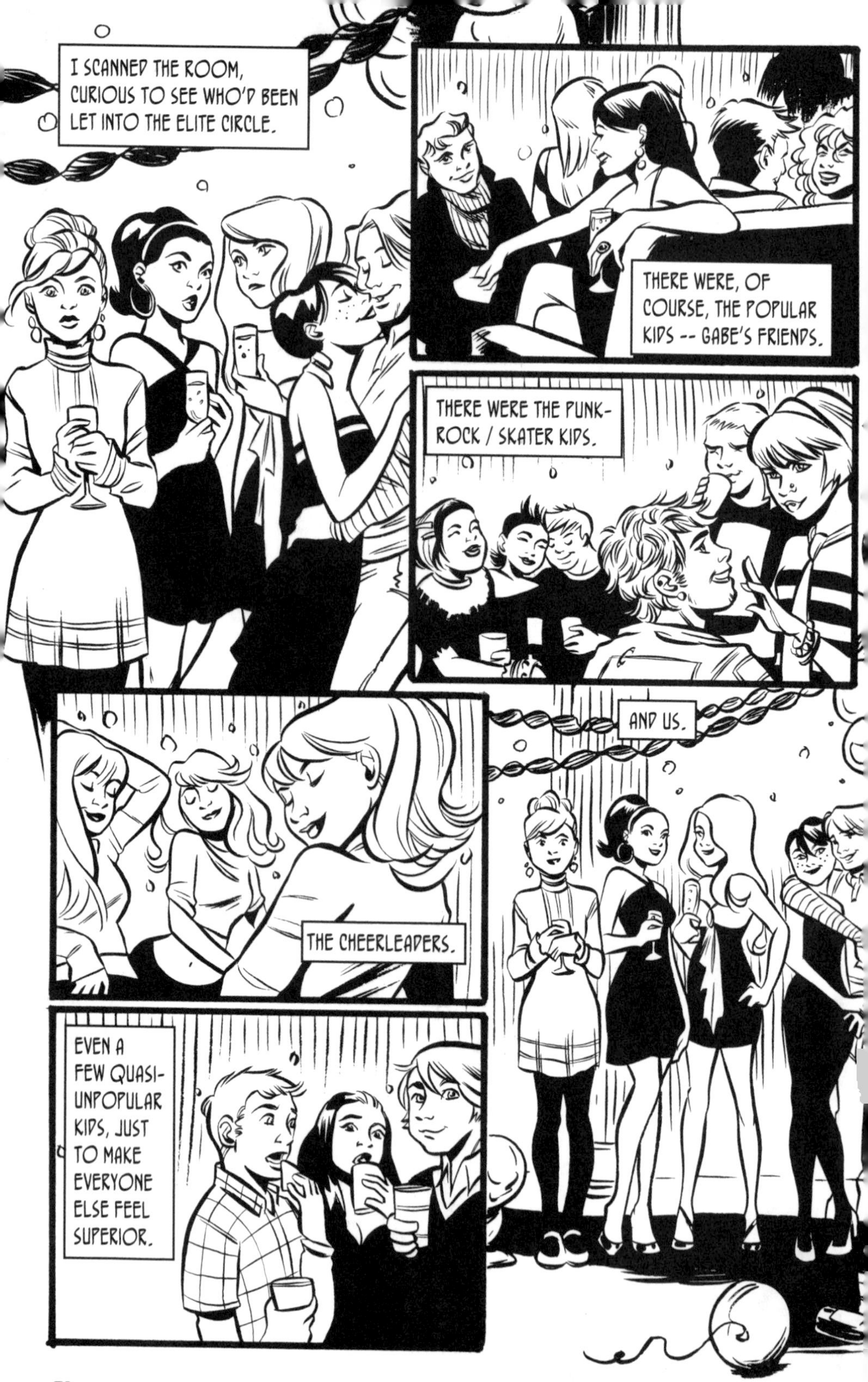
I SCANNED THE ROOM, CURIOUS TO SEE WHO'D BEEN LET INTO THE ELITE CIRCLE.
THERE WERE, OF COURSE, THE POPULAR KIDS -- GABE'S FRIENDS.
THERE WERE THE PUNK-ROCK / SKATER KIDS.
THE CHEERLEADERS.
EVEN A FEW QUASI-UNPOPULAR KIDS, JUST TO MAKE EVERYONE ELSE FEEL SUPERIOR.
AND US.

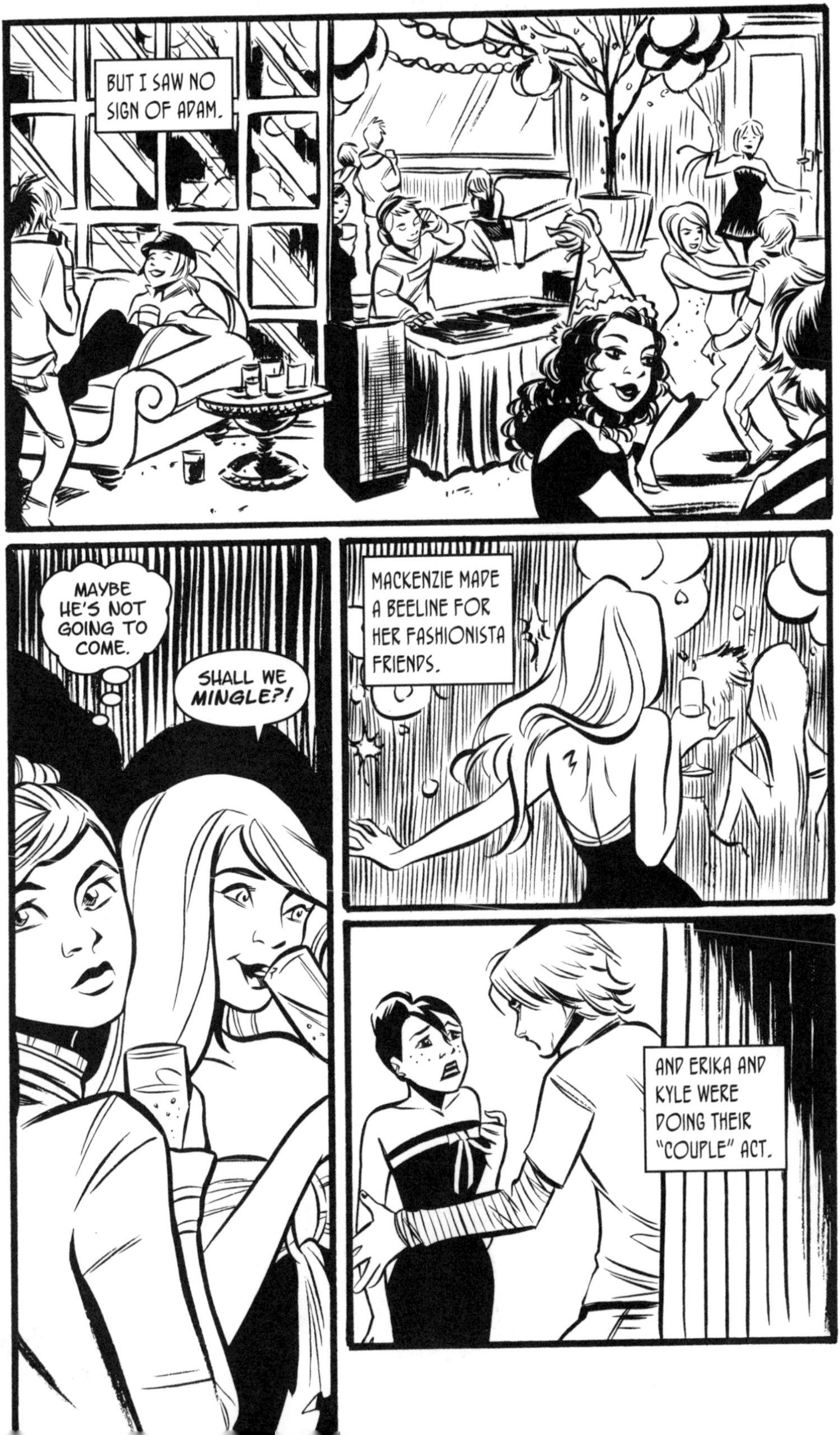
BUT I SAW NO SIGN OF ADAM.
MAYBE HE'S NOT GOING TO COME.
SHALL WE MINGLE?!
MACKENZIE MADE A BEELINE FOR HER FASHIONISTA FRIENDS.
AND ERIKA AND KYLE WERE DOING THEIR "COUPLE" ACT.

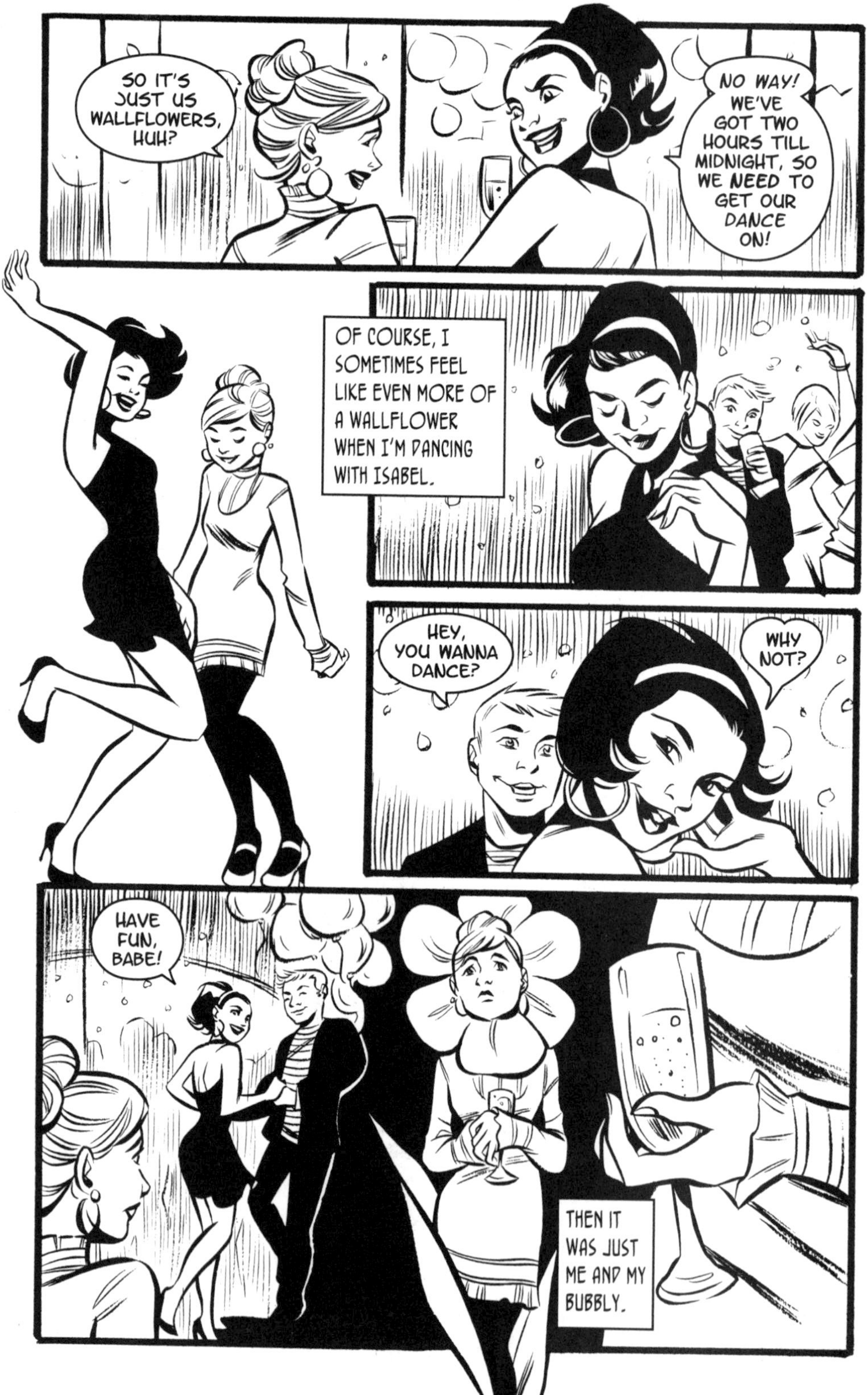
SO IT'S JUST US WALLFLOWERS, HUH?
NO WAY! WE'VE GOT TWO HOURS TILL MIDNIGHT, SO WE NEED TO GET OUR DANCE ON!
OF COURSE, I SOMETIMES FEEL LIKE EVEN MORE OF A WALLFLOWER WHEN I'M DANCING WITH ISABEL.
HEY, YOU WANNA DANCE?
WHY NOT?
HAVE FUN, BABE!
THEN IT WAS JUST ME AND MY BUBBLY.

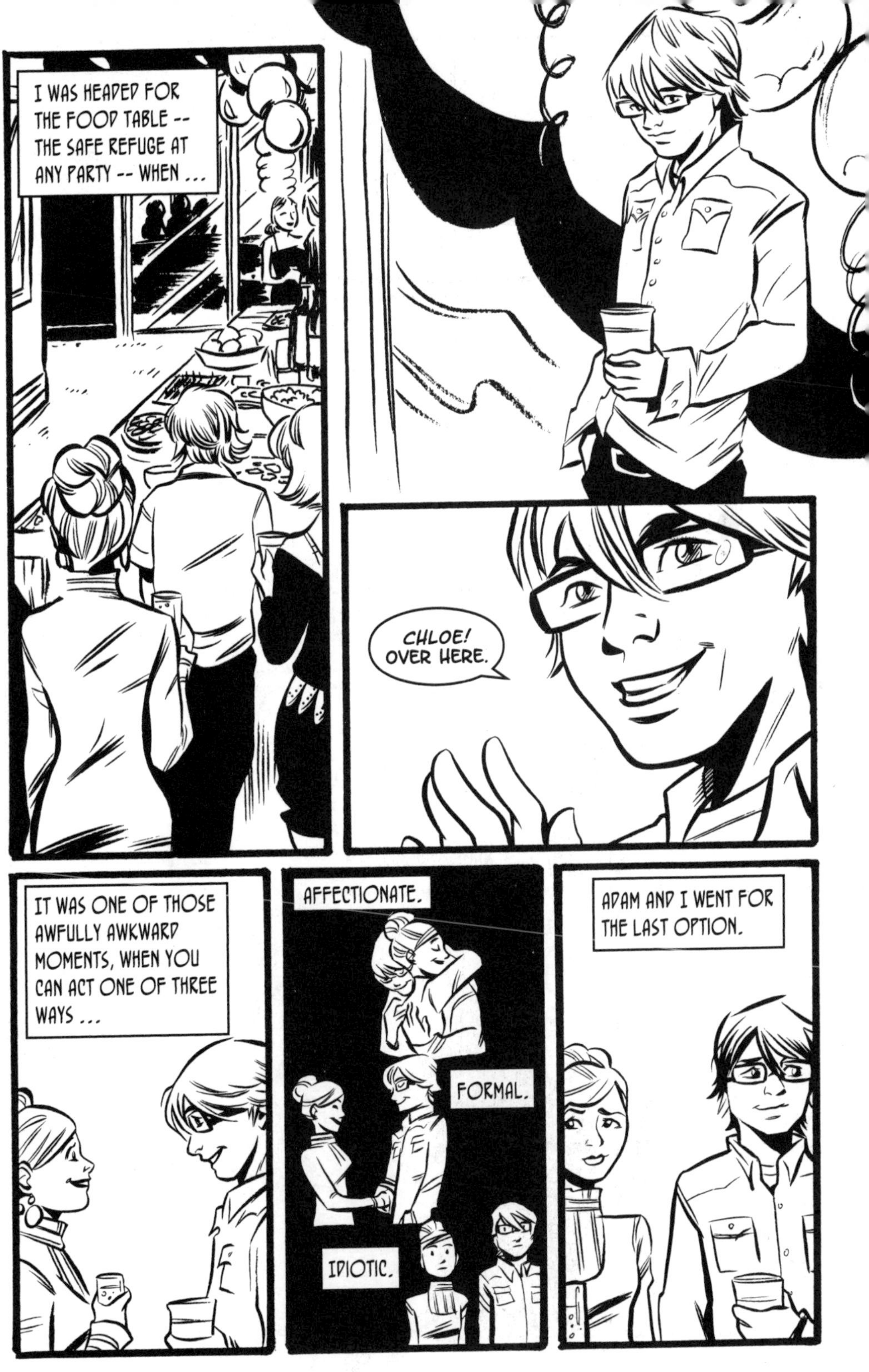
I WAS HEADED FOR THE FOOD TABLE -- THE SAFE REFUGE AT ANY PARTY -- WHEN ...
CHLOE! OVER HERE.
IT WAS ONE OF THOSE AWFULLY AWKWARD MOMENTS, WHEN YOU CAN ACT ONE OF THREE WAYS ...
AFFECTIONATE.
FORMAL.
IDIOTIC.
ADAM AND I WENT FOR THE LAST OPTION.

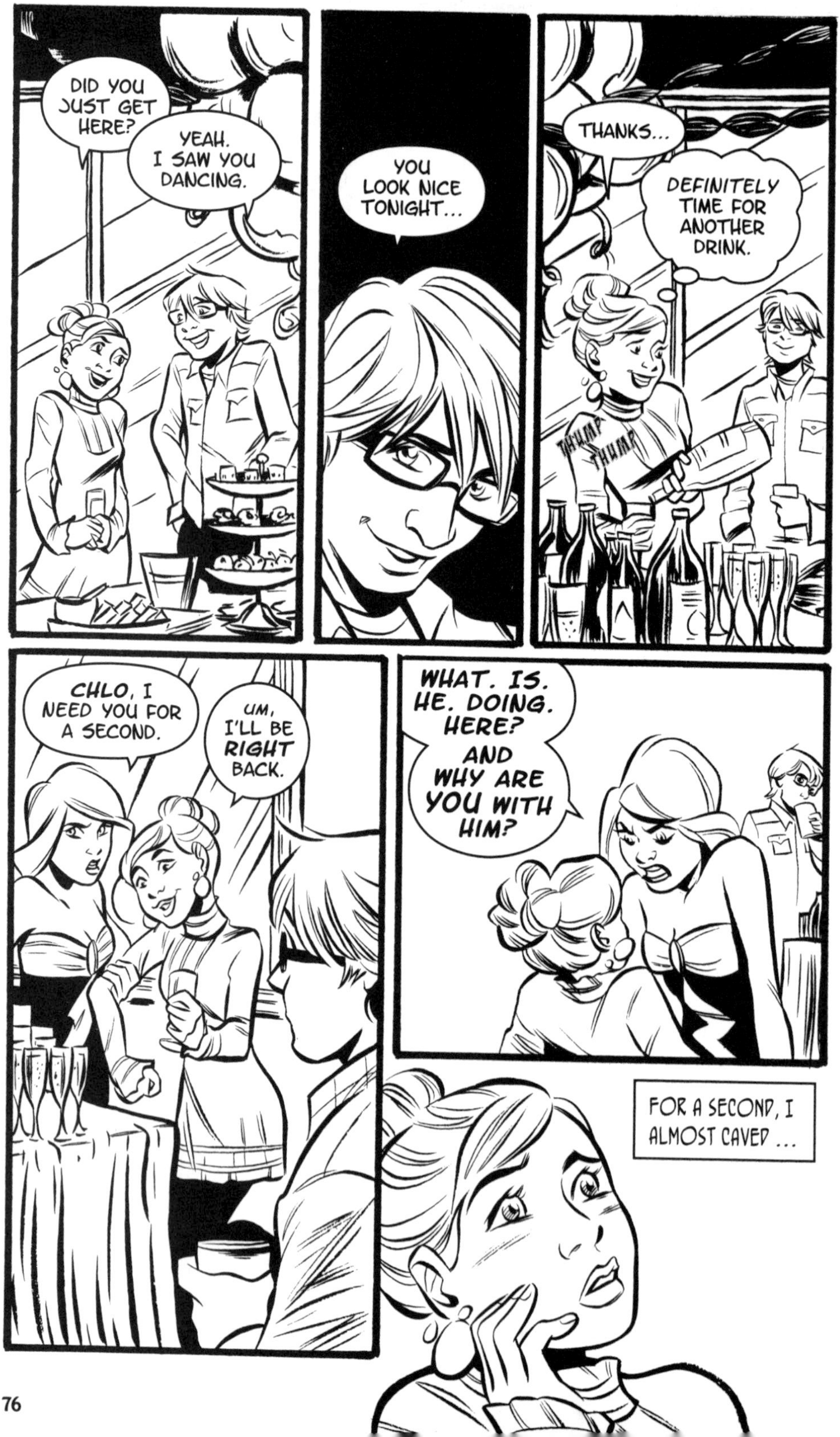
DID YOU JUST GET HERE?
YEAH. I SAW YOU DANCING.
YOU LOOK NICE TONIGHT...
THANKS...
DEFINITELY TIME FOR ANOTHER DRINK.
THUMP THUMP
CHLO, I NEED YOU FOR A SECOND.
UM, I'LL BE RIGHT BACK.
WHAT. IS. HE. DOING. HERE? AND WHY ARE YOU WITH HIM?
FOR A SECOND, I ALMOST CAVED ...

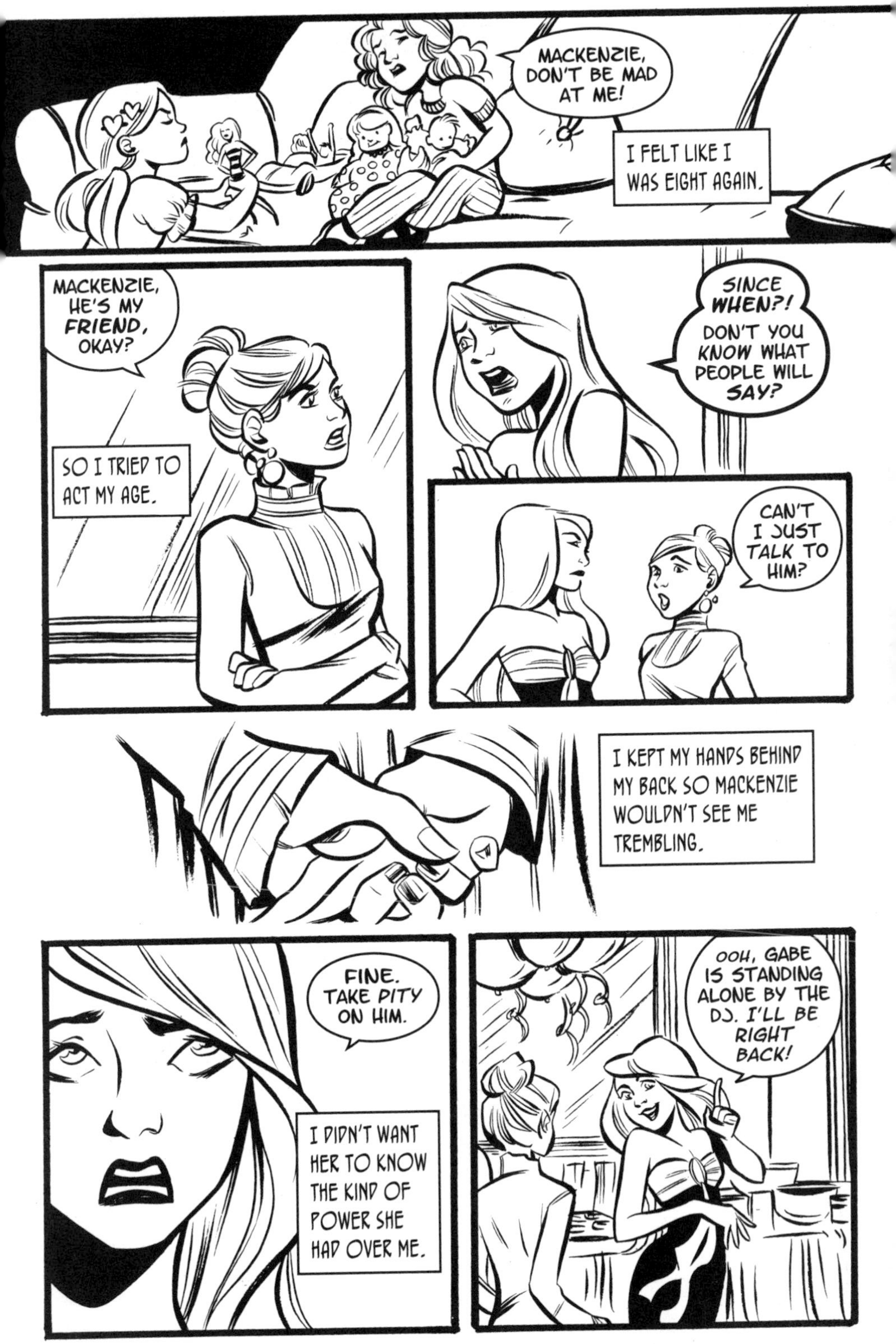
MACKENZIE, DON'T BE MAD AT ME!
I FELT LIKE I WAS EIGHT AGAIN.
MACKENZIE, HE'S MY FRIEND, OKAY?
SO I TRIED TO ACT MY AGE.
SINCE WHEN?! DON'T YOU KNOW WHAT PEOPLE WILL SAY?
CAN'T I JUST TALK TO HIM?
I KEPT MY HANDS BEHIND MY BACK SO MACKENZIE WOULDN'T SEE ME TREMBLING.
FINE. TAKE PITY ON HIM.
I DIDN'T WANT HER TO KNOW THE KIND OF POWER SHE HAD OVER ME.
OOH, GABE IS STANDING ALONE BY THE DJ. I'LL BE RIGHT BACK!

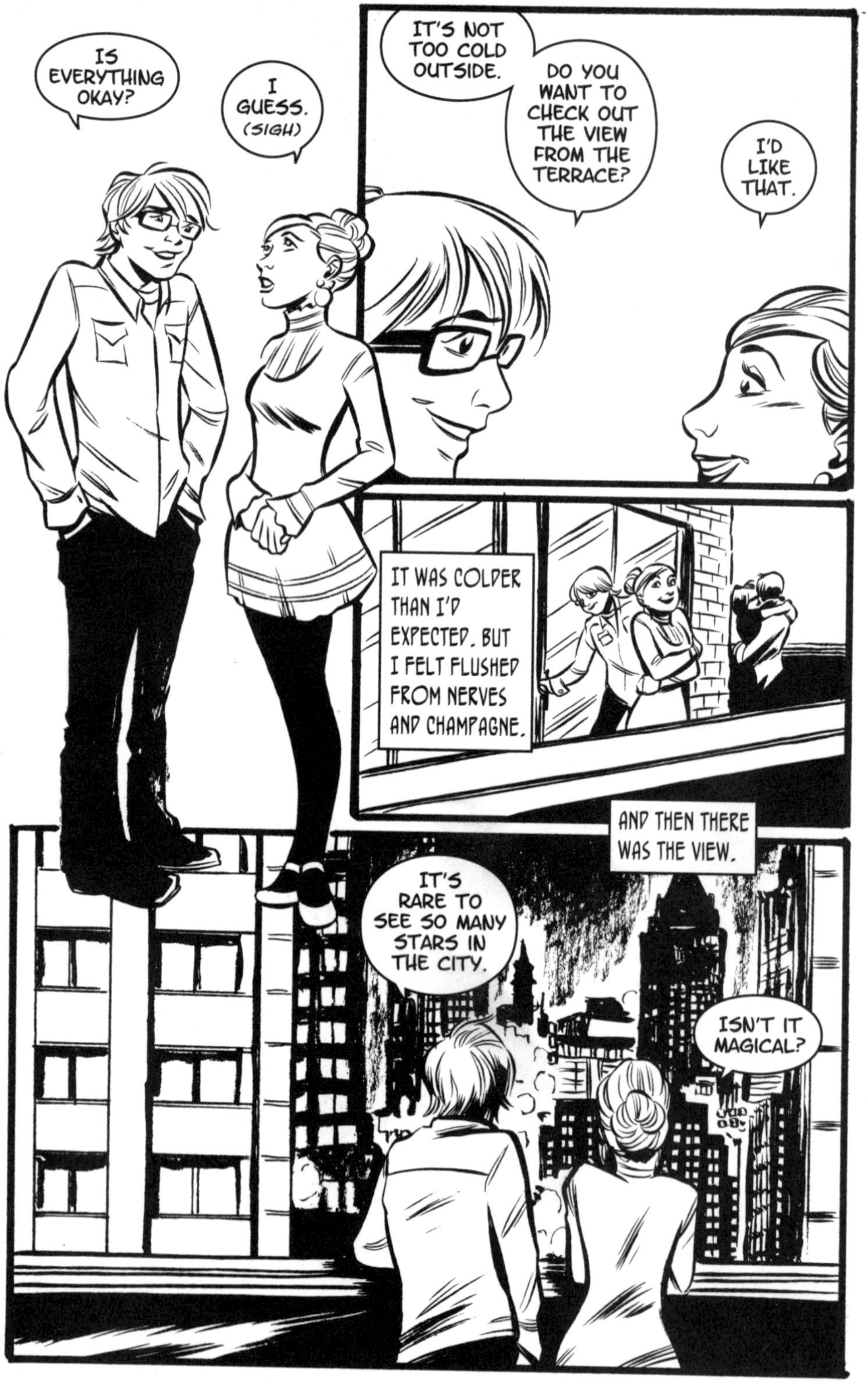
IS EVERYTHING OKAY?
I GUESS. (SIGH)
IT'S NOT TOO COLD OUTSIDE.
DO YOU WANT TO CHECK OUT THE VIEW FROM THE TERRACE?
I'D LIKE THAT.
IT WAS COLDER THAN I'D EXPECTED, BUT I FELT FLUSHED FROM NERVES AND CHAMPAGNE.
AND THEN THERE WAS THE VIEW.
IT'S RARE TO SEE SO MANY STARS IN THE CITY.
ISN'T IT MAGICAL?

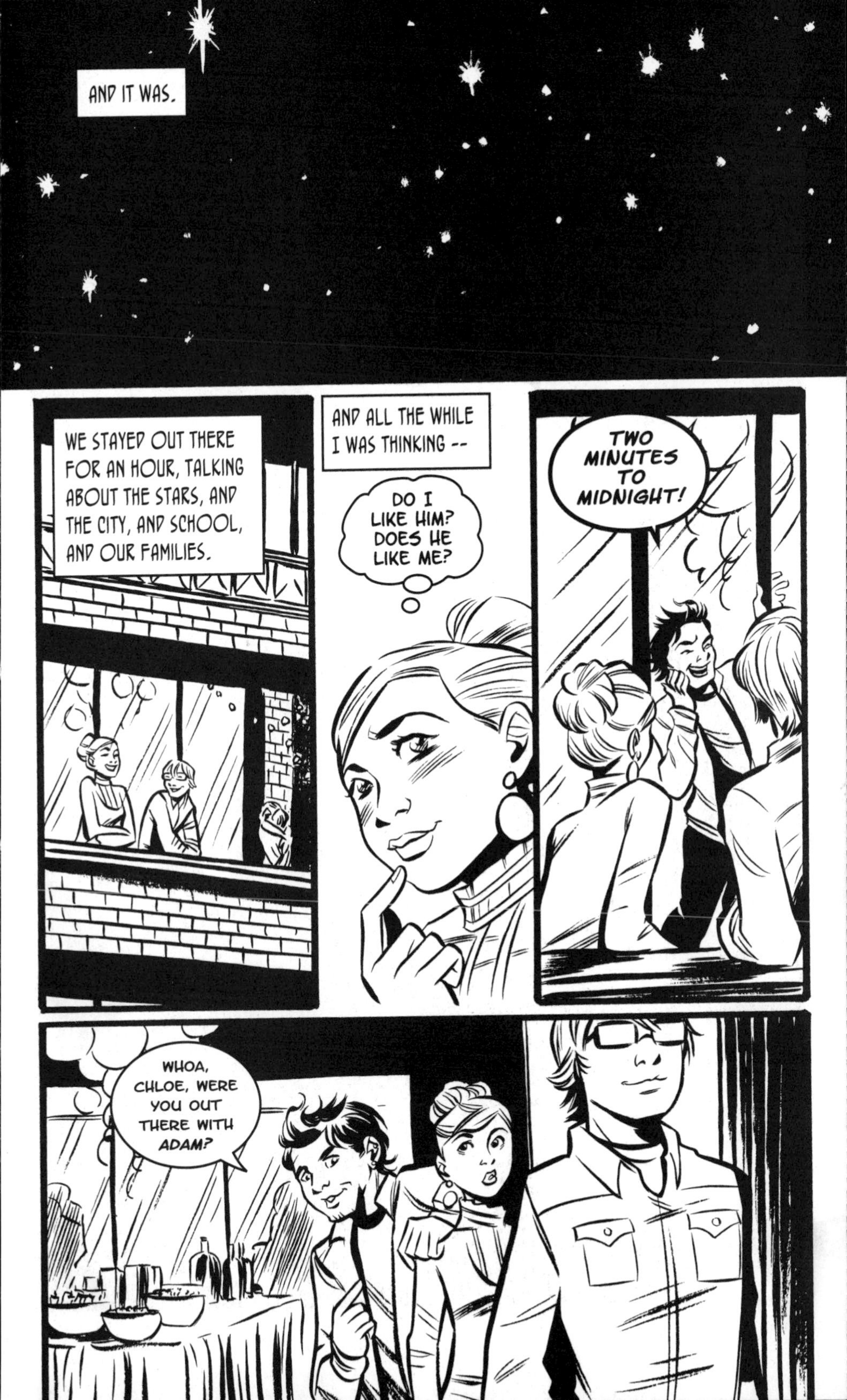
AND IT WAS.
WE STAYED OUT THERE FOR AN HOUR, TALKING ABOUT THE STARS, AND THE CITY, AND SCHOOL, AND OUR FAMILIES.
AND ALL THE WHILE I WAS THINKING --
DO I LIKE HIM? DOES HE LIKE ME?
TWO MINUTES TO MIDNIGHT!
WHOA, CHLOE, WERE YOU OUT THERE WITH ADAM?

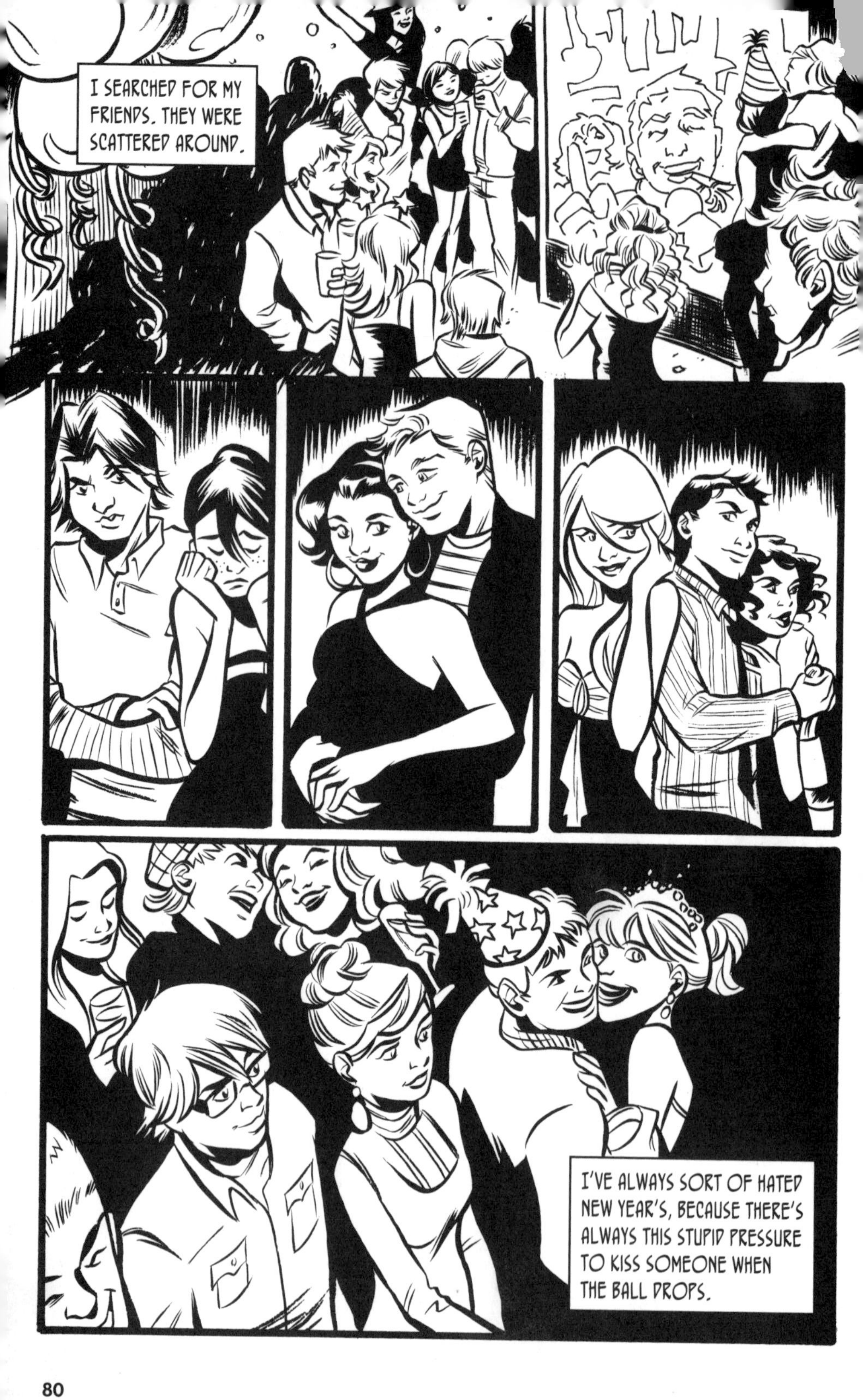
I SEARCHED FOR MY FRIENDS. THEY WERE SCATTERED AROUND.
I'VE ALWAYS SORT OF HATED NEW YEAR'S, BECAUSE THERE'S ALWAYS THIS STUPID PRESSURE TO KISS SOMEONE WHEN THE BALL DROPS.

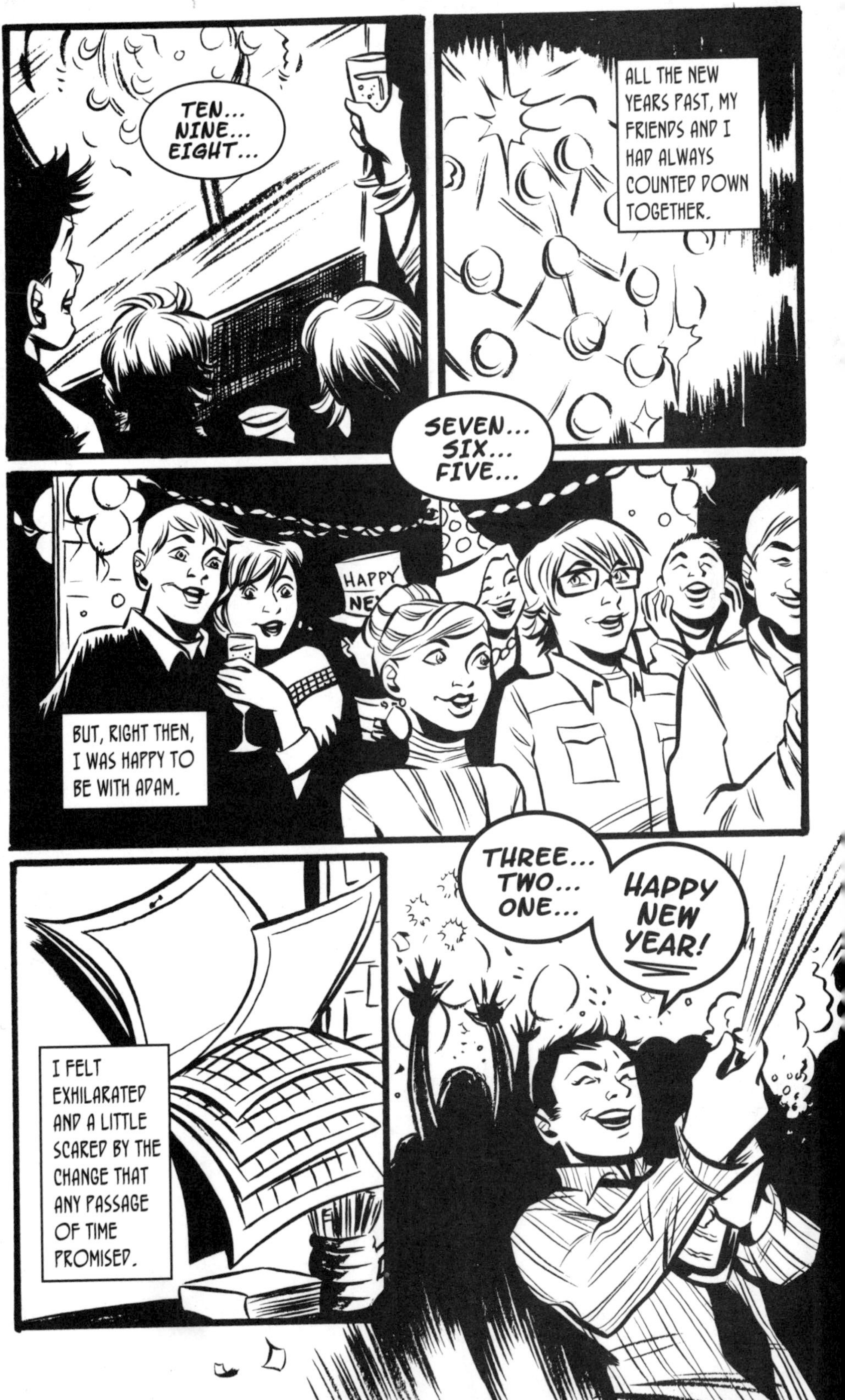

TEN... NINE... EIGHT...
ALL THE NEW YEARS PAST, MY FRIENDS AND I HAD ALWAYS COUNTED DOWN TOGETHER.
SEVEN... SIX... FIVE...
HAPPY NE
BUT, RIGHT THEN, I WAS HAPPY TO BE WITH ADAM.
I FELT EXHILARATED AND A LITTLE SCARED BY THE CHANGE THAT ANY PASSAGE OF TIME PROMISED.
THREE... TWO... ONE...
HAPPY NEW YEAR!

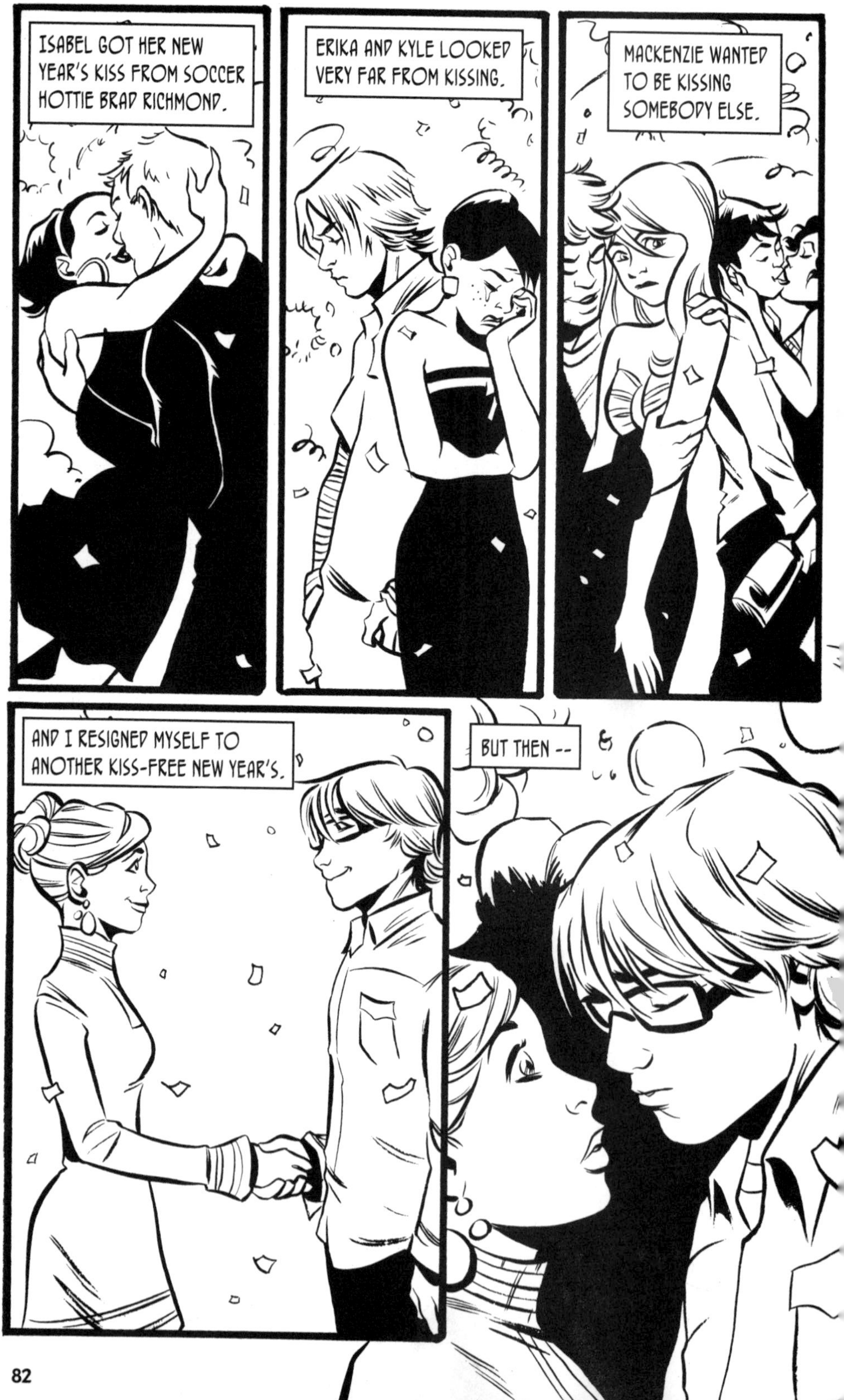
ISABEL GOT HER NEW YEAR'S KISS FROM SOCCER HOTTIE BRAD RICHMOND.
ERIKA AND KYLE LOOKED VERY FAR FROM KISSING.
MACKENZIE WANTED TO BE KISSING SOMEBODY ELSE.
AND I RESIGNED MYSELF TO ANOTHER KISS-FREE NEW YEAR'S.
BUT THEN --

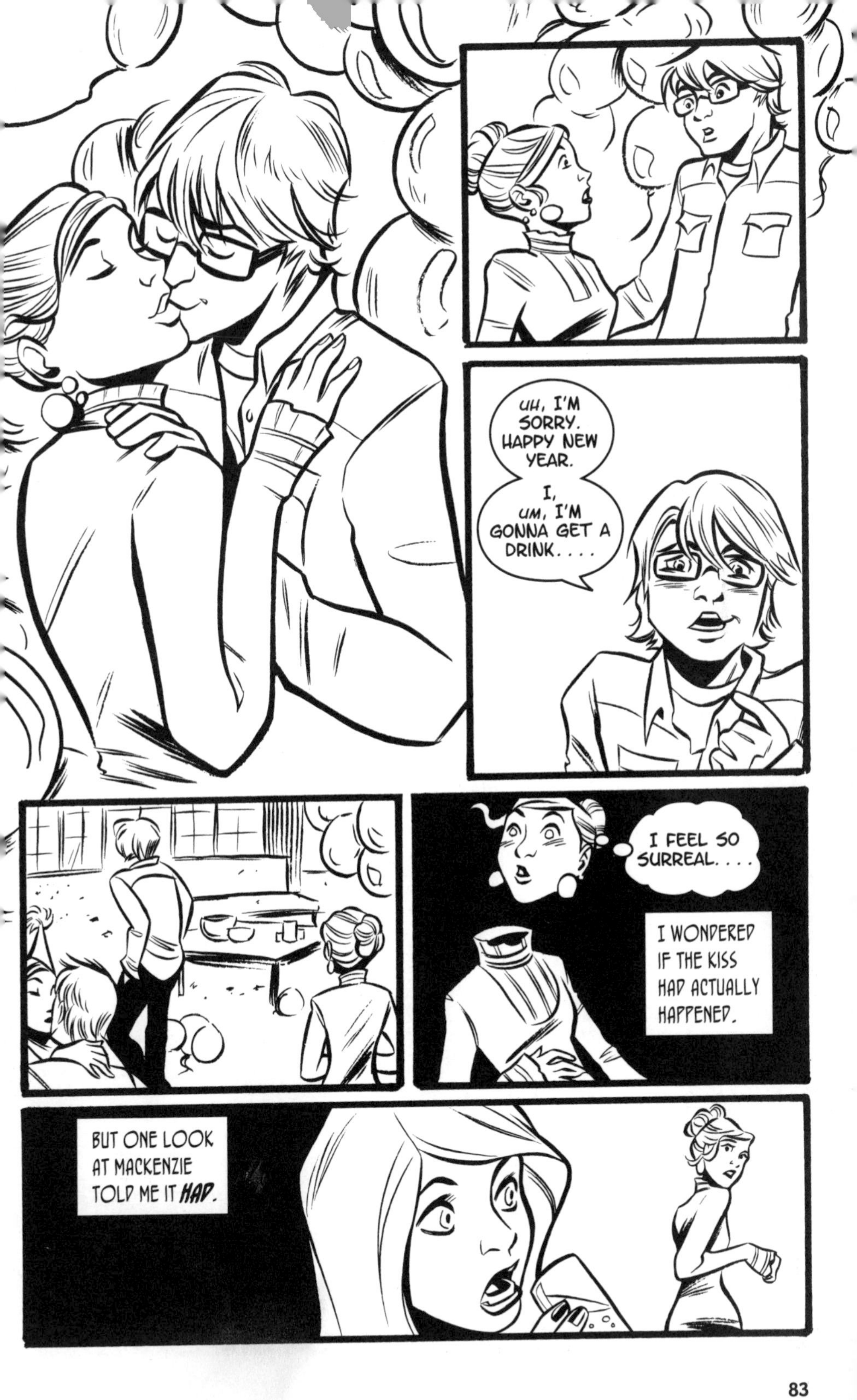
UH, I'M SORRY. HAPPY NEW YEAR.
I, UM, I'M GONNA GET A DRINK. . . .
I FEEL SO SURREAL. . . .
I WONDERED IF THE KISS HAD ACTUALLY HAPPENED.
BUT ONE LOOK AT MACKENZIE TOLD ME IT HAD.

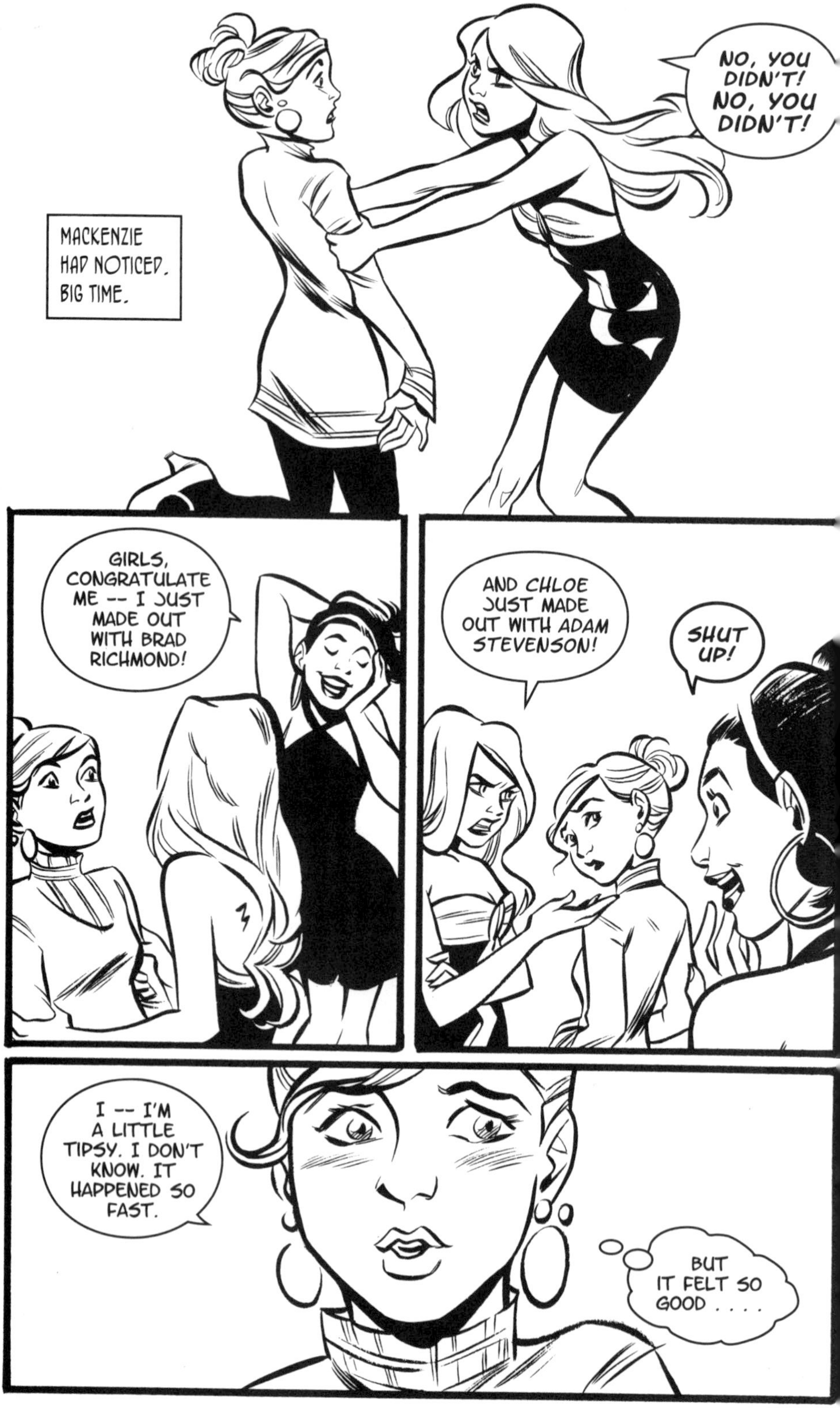
NO, YOU DIDN'T! NO, YOU DIDN'T!
MACKENZIE HAD NOTICED. BIG TIME.
GIRLS, CONGRATULATE ME -- I JUST MADE OUT WITH BRAD RICHMOND!
AND CHLOE JUST MADE OUT WITH ADAM STEVENSON!
SHUT UP!
I -- I'M A LITTLE TIPSY. I DON'T KNOW. IT HAPPENED SO FAST.
BUT IT FELT SO GOOD . . . .

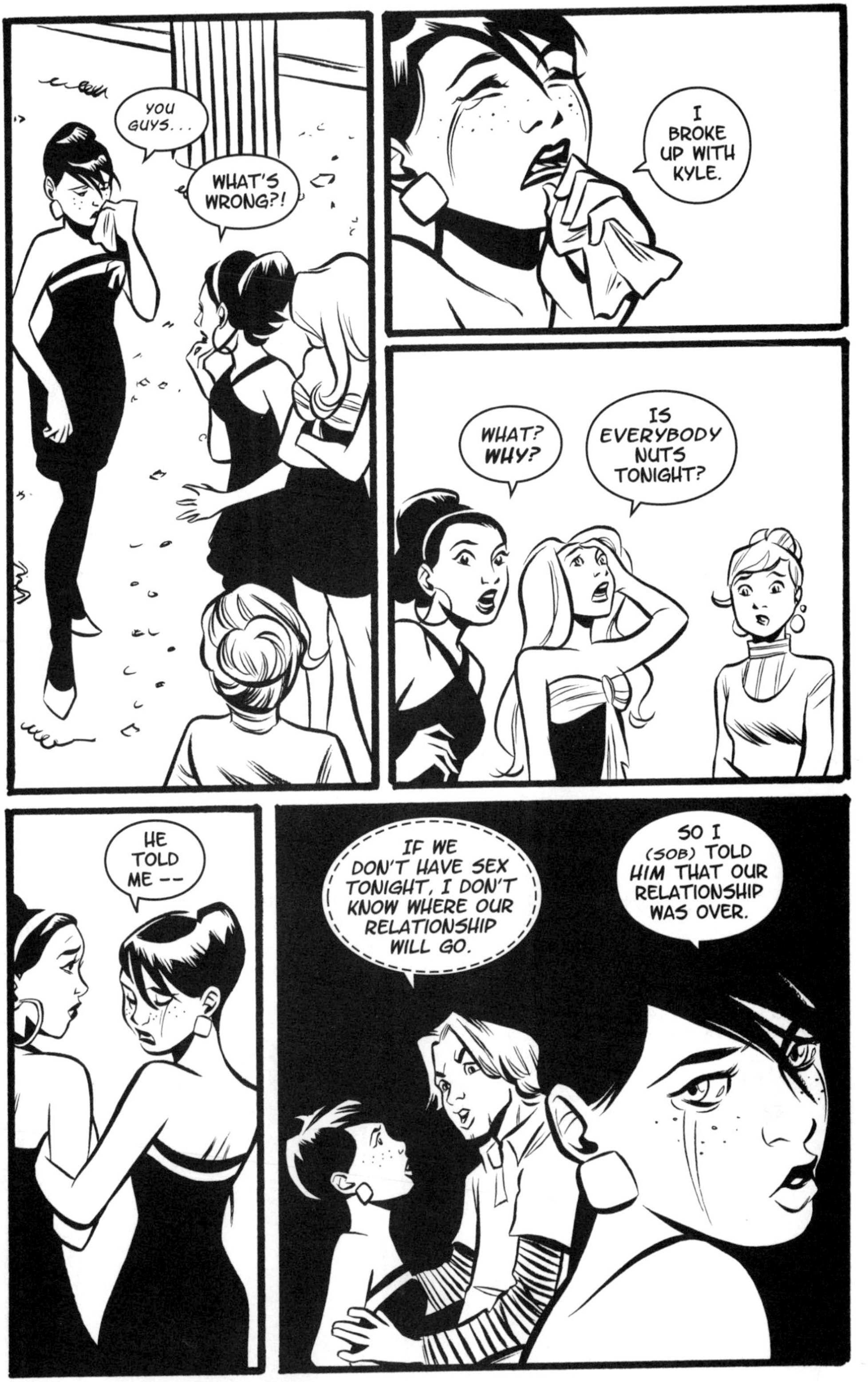
YOU GUYS...
WHAT'S WRONG?!
I BROKE UP WITH KYLE.
WHAT? WHY?
IS EVERYBODY NUTS TONIGHT?
HE TOLD ME --
IF WE DON'T HAVE SEX TONIGHT, I DON'T KNOW WHERE OUR RELATIONSHIP WILL GO.
SO I (SOB) TOLD HIM THAT OUR RELATIONSHIP WAS OVER.

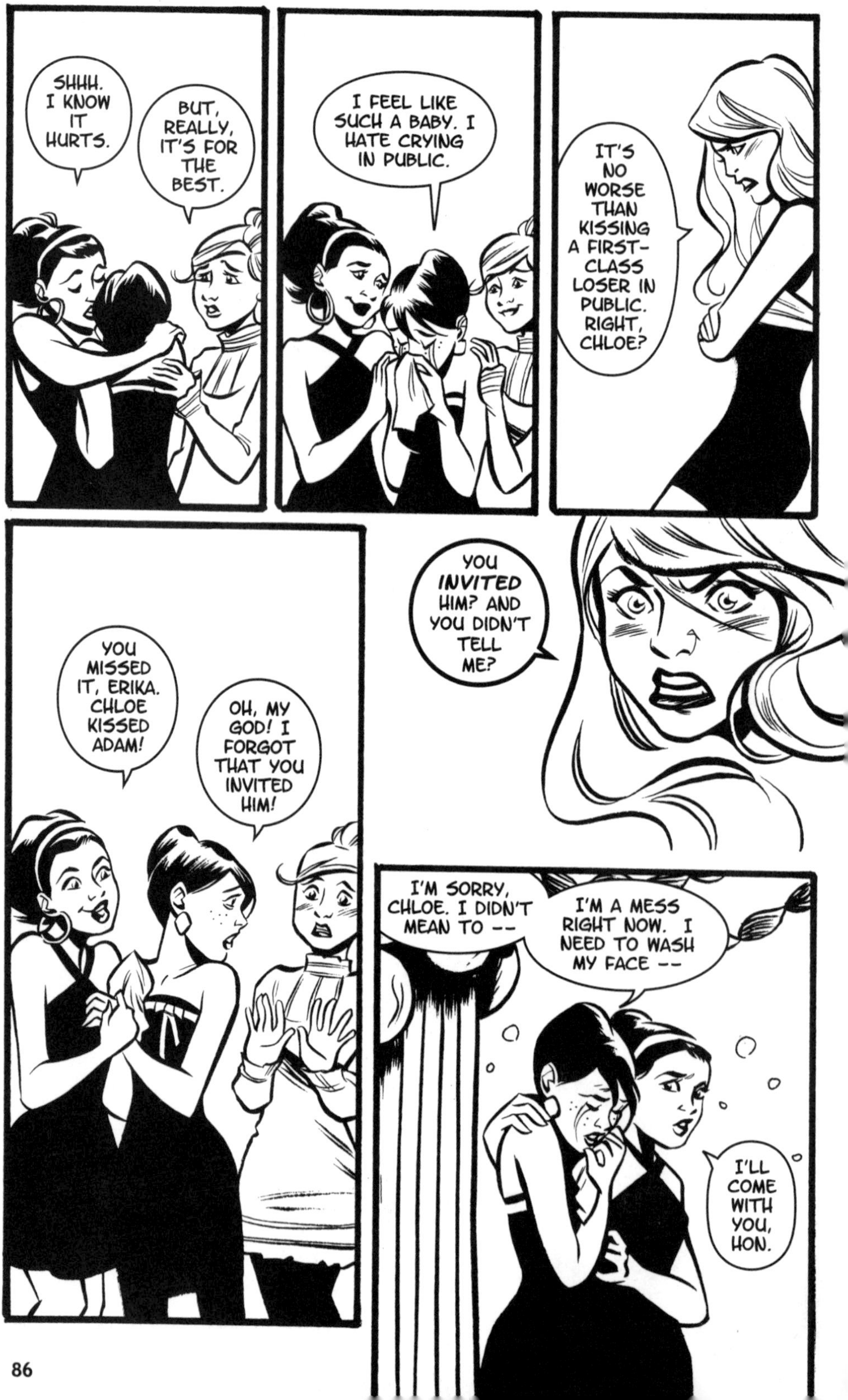

SHHH. I KNOW IT HURTS.
BUT, REALLY, IT'S FOR THE BEST.
I FEEL LIKE SUCH A BABY. I HATE CRYING IN PUBLIC.
IT'S NO WORSE THAN KISSING A FIRST-CLASS LOSER IN PUBLIC. RIGHT, CHLOE?
YOU MISSED IT, ERIKA. CHLOE KISSED ADAM!
OH, MY GOD! I FORGOT THAT YOU INVITED HIM!
YOU *INVITED* HIM? AND YOU DIDN'T TELL ME?
I'M SORRY, CHLOE. I DIDN'T MEAN TO --
I'M A MESS RIGHT NOW. I NEED TO WASH MY FACE --
I'LL COME WITH YOU, HON.

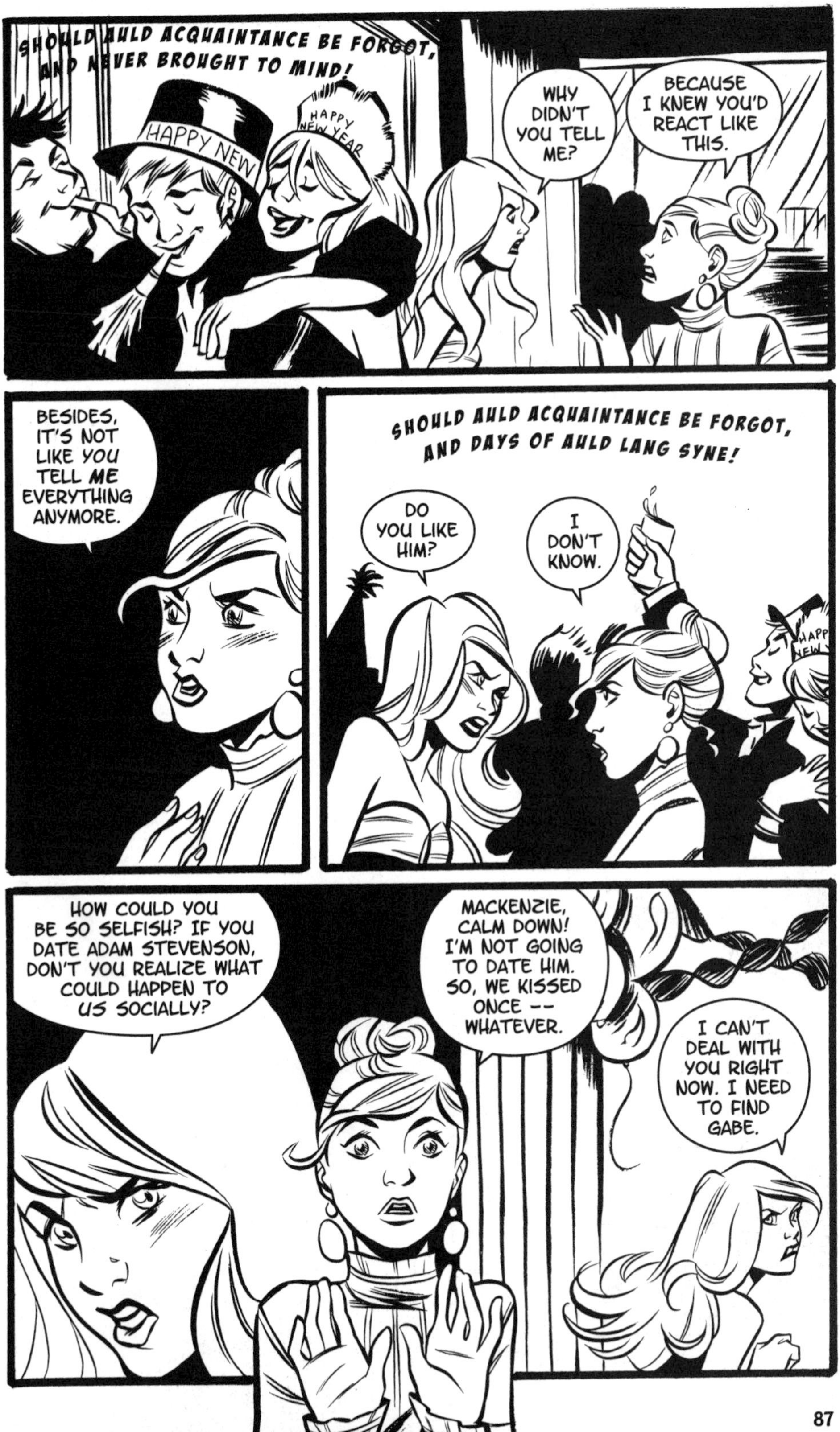
SHOULD AULD ACQUAINTANCE BE FORGOT, AND NEVER BROUGHT TO MIND!
HAPPY NEW
HAPPY NEW YEAR
WHY DIDN'T YOU TELL ME?
BECAUSE I KNEW YOU'D REACT LIKE THIS.
BESIDES, IT'S NOT LIKE YOU TELL ME EVERYTHING ANYMORE.
SHOULD AULD ACQUAINTANCE BE FORGOT, AND DAYS OF AULD LANG SYNE!
DO YOU LIKE HIM?
I DON'T KNOW.
HOW COULD YOU BE SO SELFISH? IF YOU DATE ADAM STEVENSON, DON'T YOU REALIZE WHAT COULD HAPPEN TO US SOCIALLY?
MACKENZIE, CALM DOWN! I'M NOT GOING TO DATE HIM. SO, WE KISSED ONCE -- WHATEVER.
I CAN'T DEAL WITH YOU RIGHT NOW. I NEED TO FIND GABE.

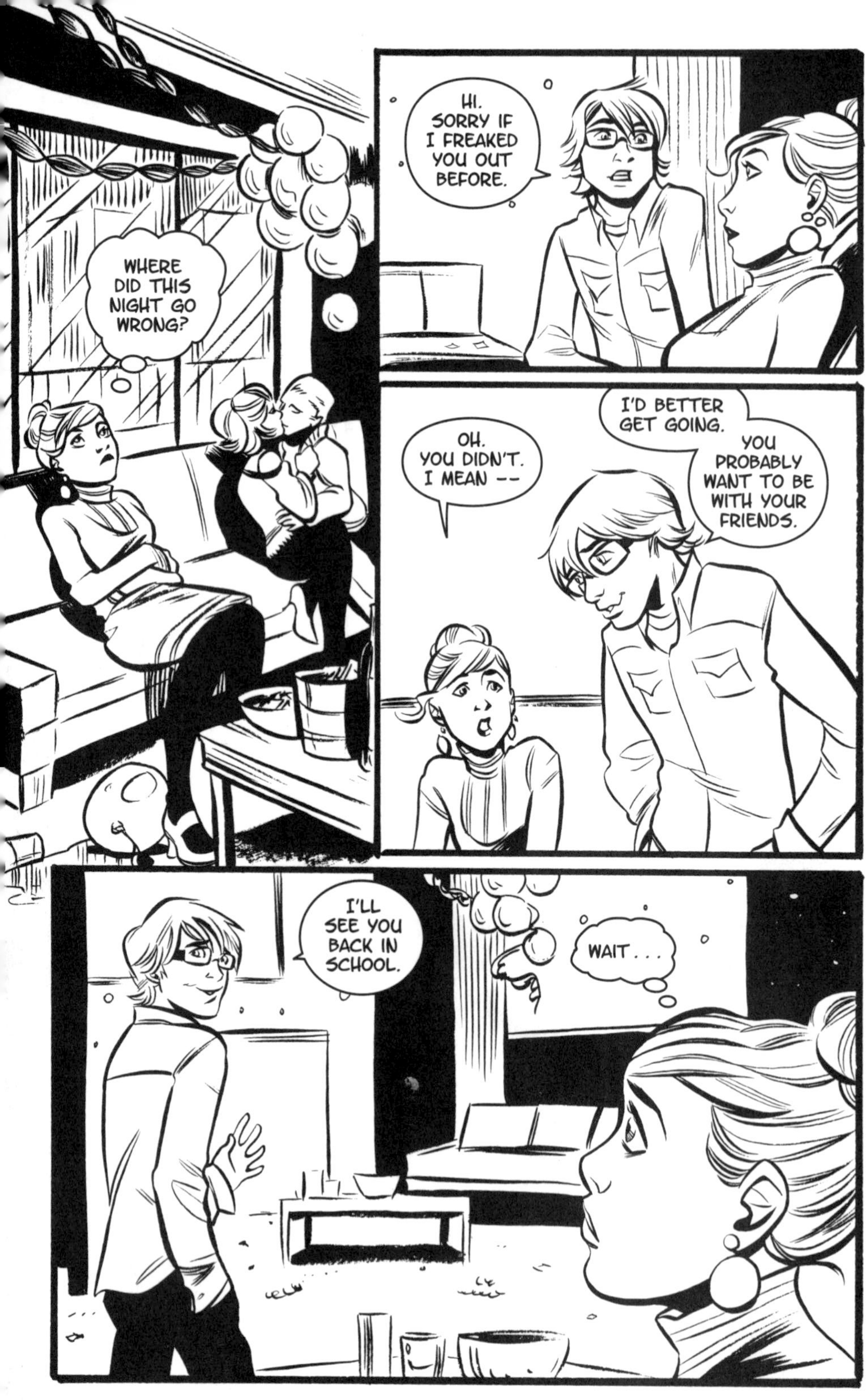
WHERE DID THIS NIGHT GO WRONG?
HI. SORRY IF I FREAKED YOU OUT BEFORE.
OH. YOU DIDN'T. I MEAN --
I'D BETTER GET GOING.
YOU PROBABLY WANT TO BE WITH YOUR FRIENDS.
I'LL SEE YOU BACK IN SCHOOL.
WAIT . . .

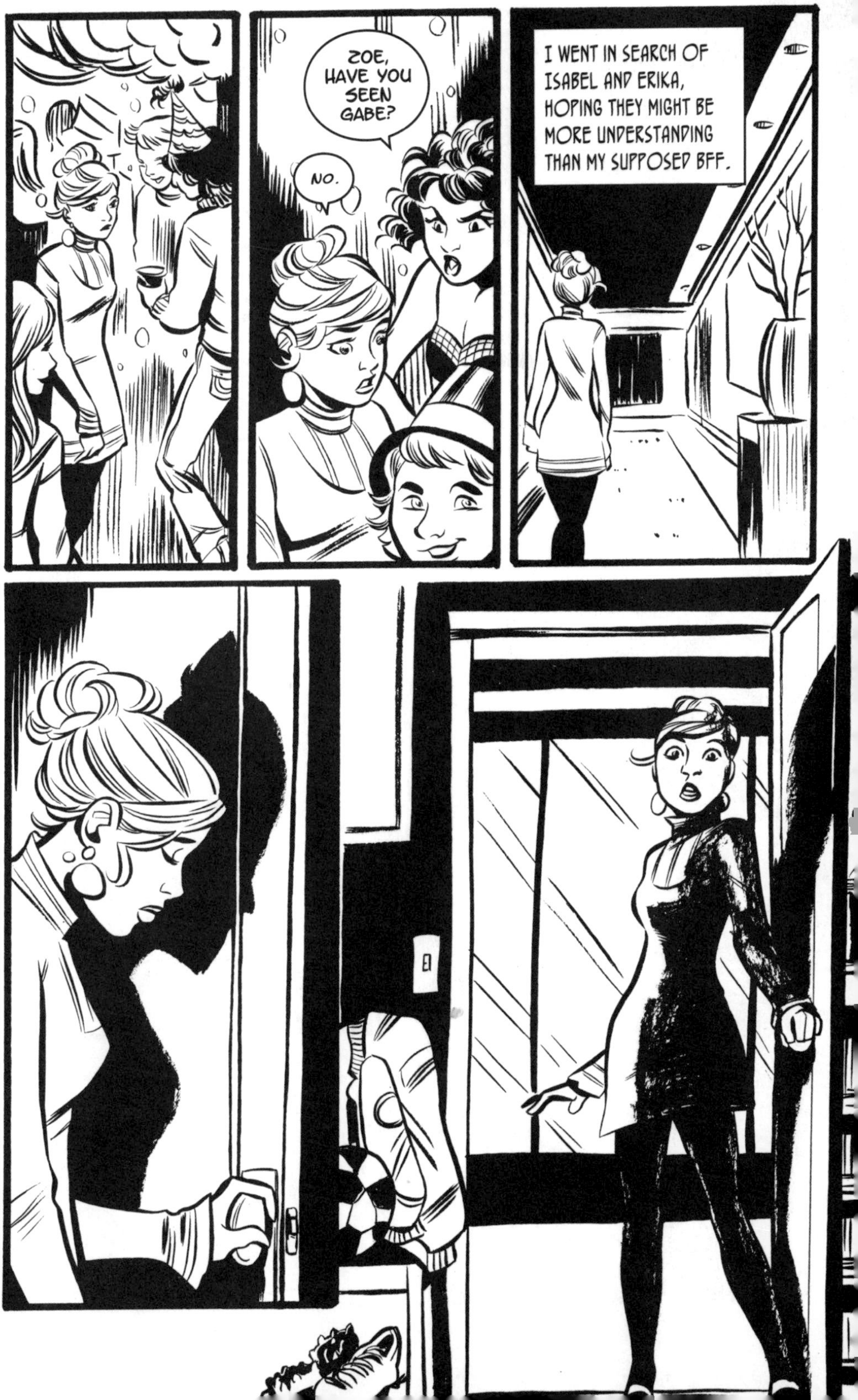
ZOE, HAVE YOU SEEN GABE?
NO.
I WENT IN SEARCH OF ISABEL AND ERIKA, HOPING THEY MIGHT BE MORE UNDERSTANDING THAN MY SUPPOSED BFF.

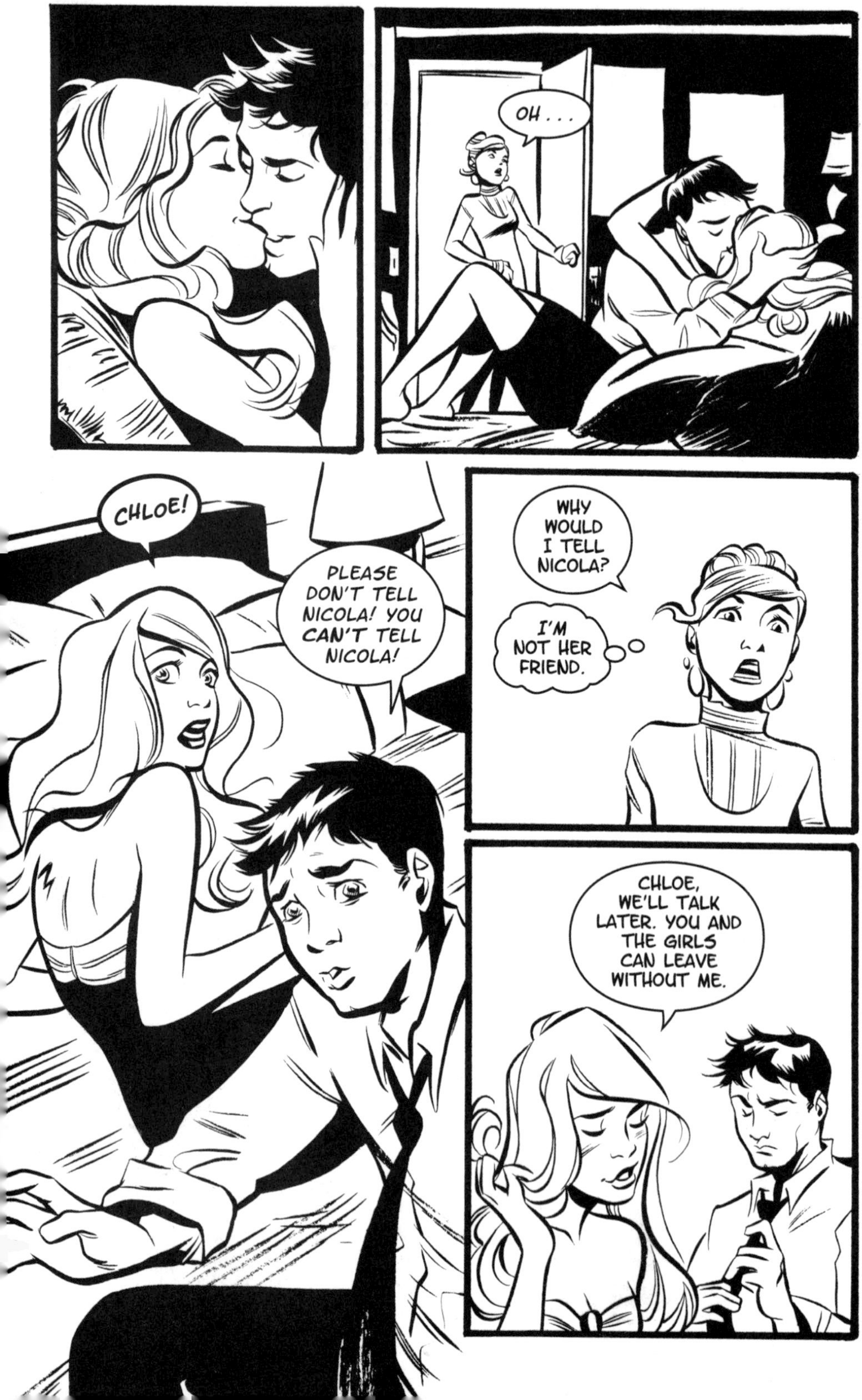
OH . . .
CHLOE!
PLEASE DON'T TELL NICOLA! YOU CAN'T TELL NICOLA!
WHY WOULD I TELL NICOLA?
I'M NOT HER FRIEND.
CHLOE, WE'LL TALK LATER. YOU AND THE GIRLS CAN LEAVE WITHOUT ME.

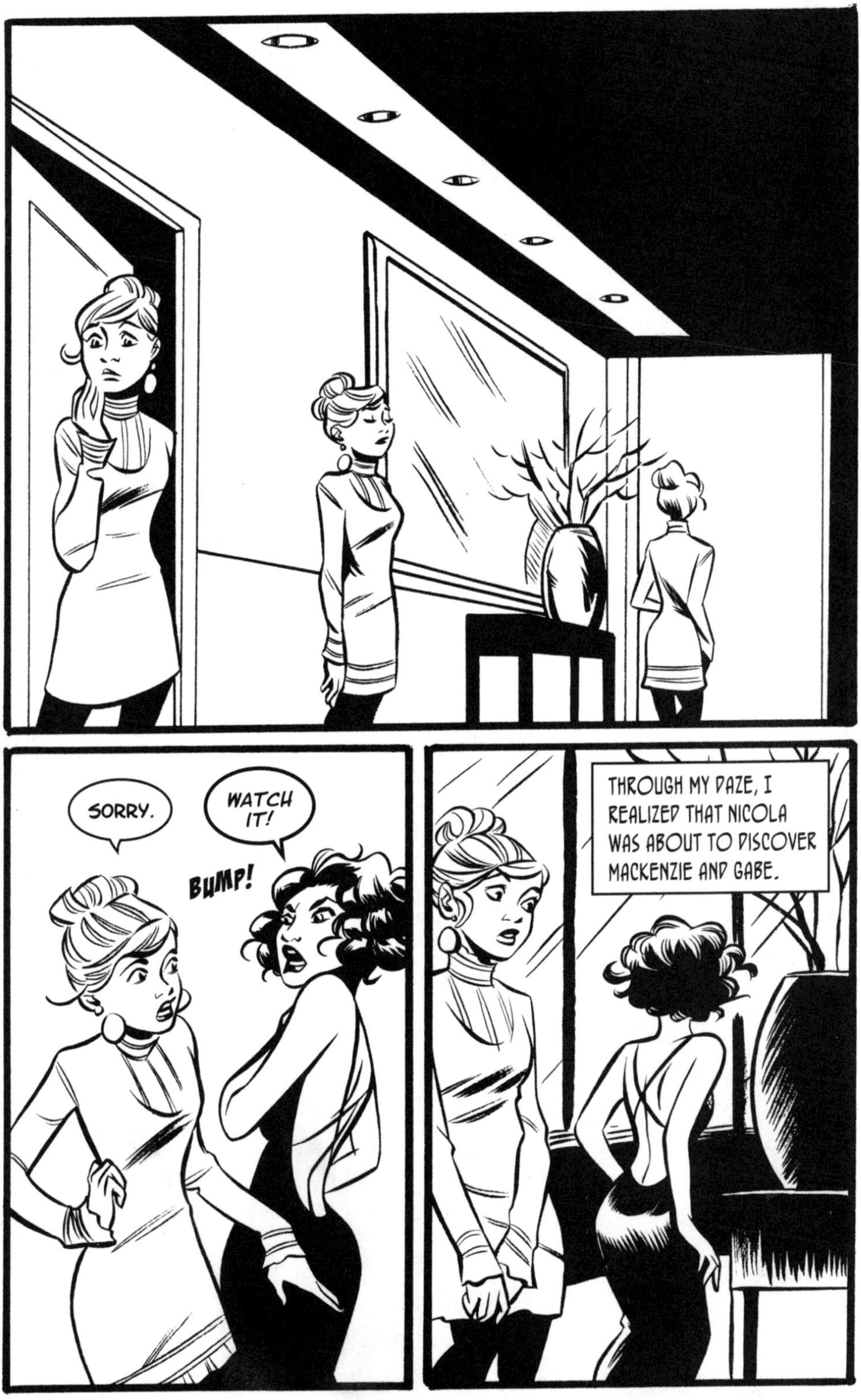
SORRY.
WATCH IT!
BUMP!
THROUGH MY DAZE, I REALIZED THAT NICOLA WAS ABOUT TO DISCOVER MACKENZIE AND GABE.

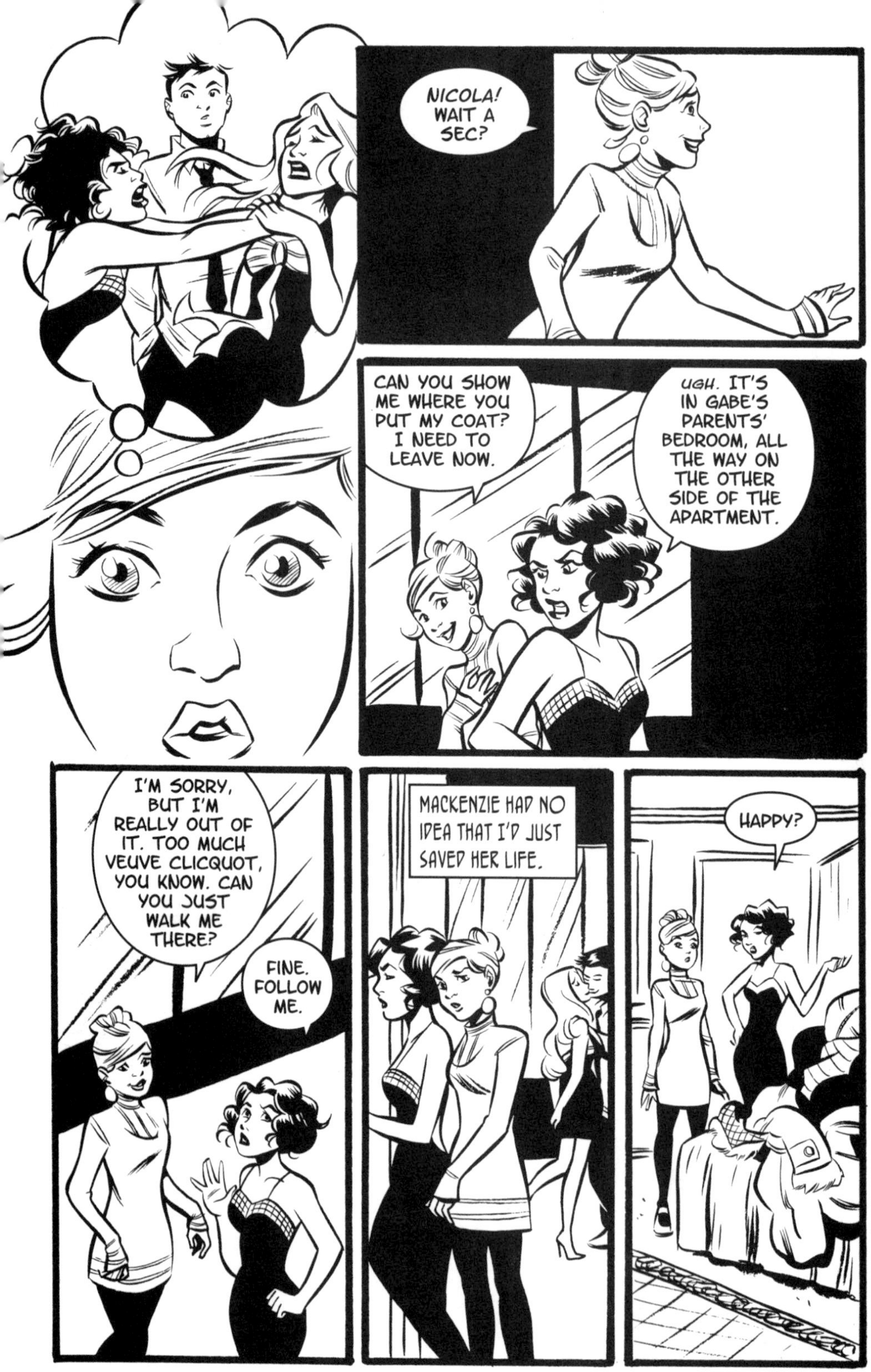
NICOLA! WAIT A SEC?
CAN YOU SHOW ME WHERE YOU PUT MY COAT? I NEED TO LEAVE NOW.
UGH. IT'S IN GABE'S PARENTS' BEDROOM, ALL THE WAY ON THE OTHER SIDE OF THE APARTMENT.
I'M SORRY, BUT I'M REALLY OUT OF IT. TOO MUCH VEUVE CLICQUOT, YOU KNOW. CAN YOU JUST WALK ME THERE?
FINE. FOLLOW ME.
MACKENZIE HAD NO IDEA THAT I'D JUST SAVED HER LIFE.
HAPPY?

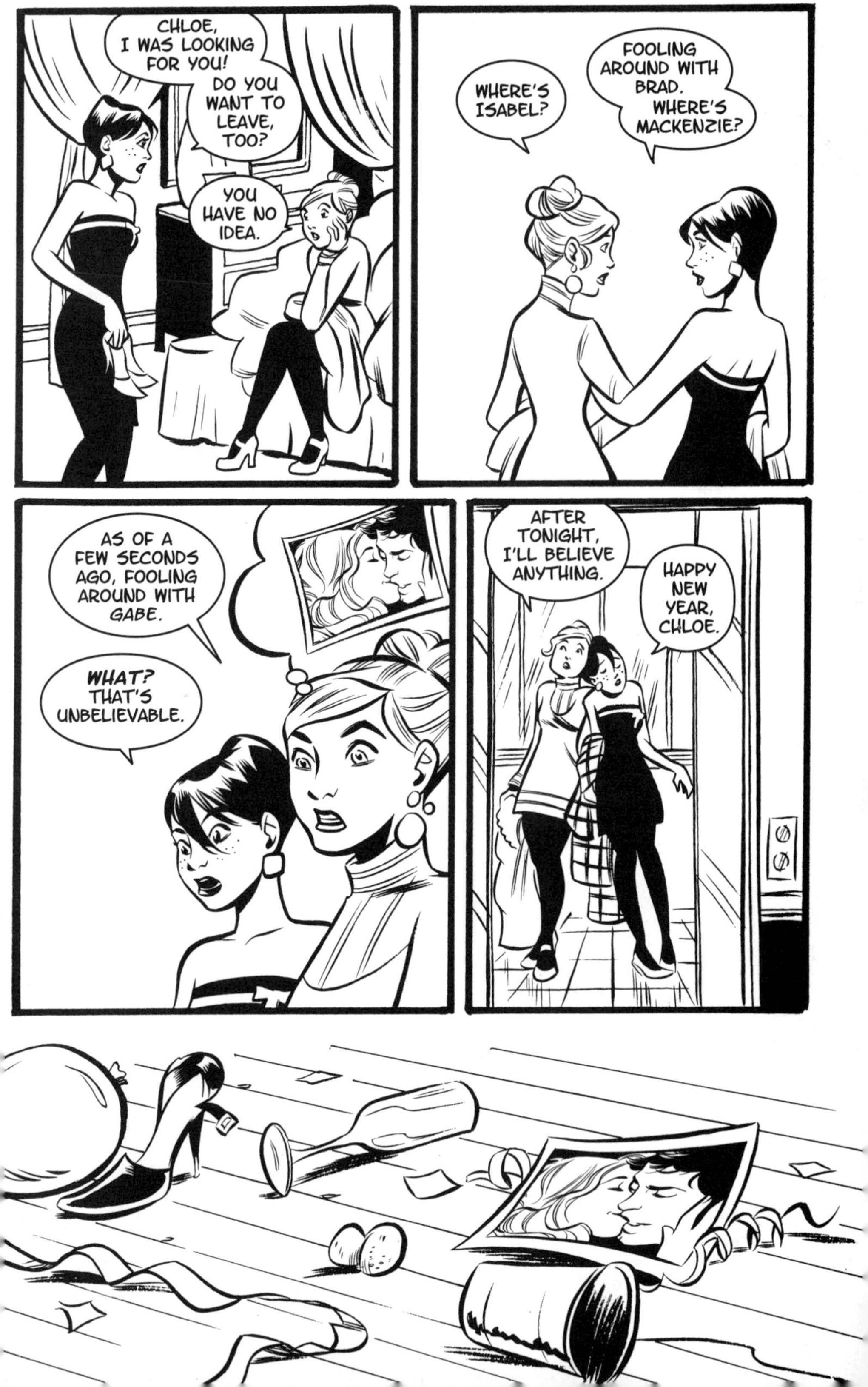
CHLOE, I WAS LOOKING FOR YOU!
DO YOU WANT TO LEAVE, TOO?
YOU HAVE NO IDEA.
WHERE'S ISABEL?
FOOLING AROUND WITH BRAD.
WHERE'S MACKENZIE?
AS OF A FEW SECONDS AGO, FOOLING AROUND WITH GABE.
WHAT? THAT'S UNBELIEVABLE.
AFTER TONIGHT, I'LL BELIEVE ANYTHING.
HAPPY NEW YEAR, CHLOE.

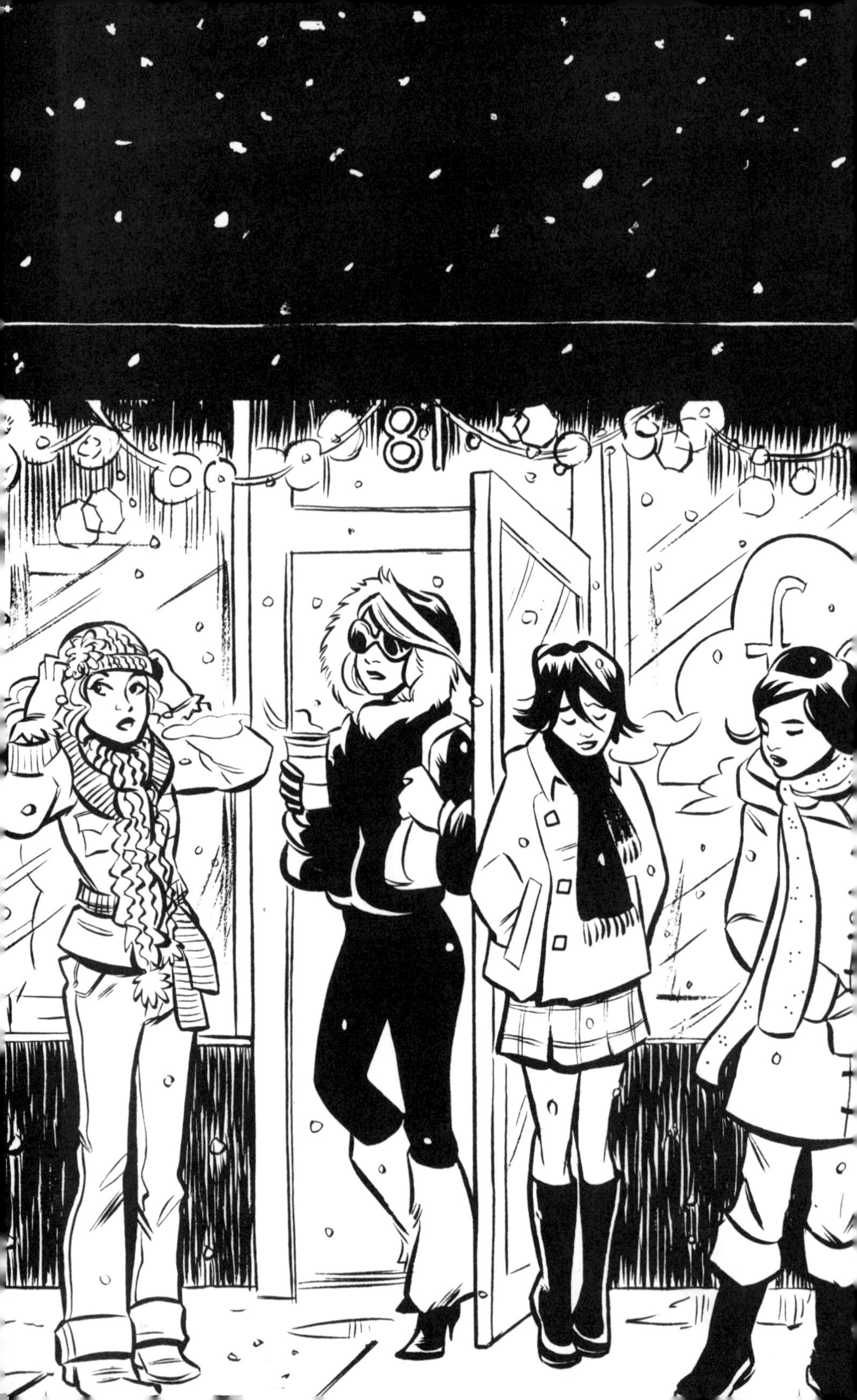
8

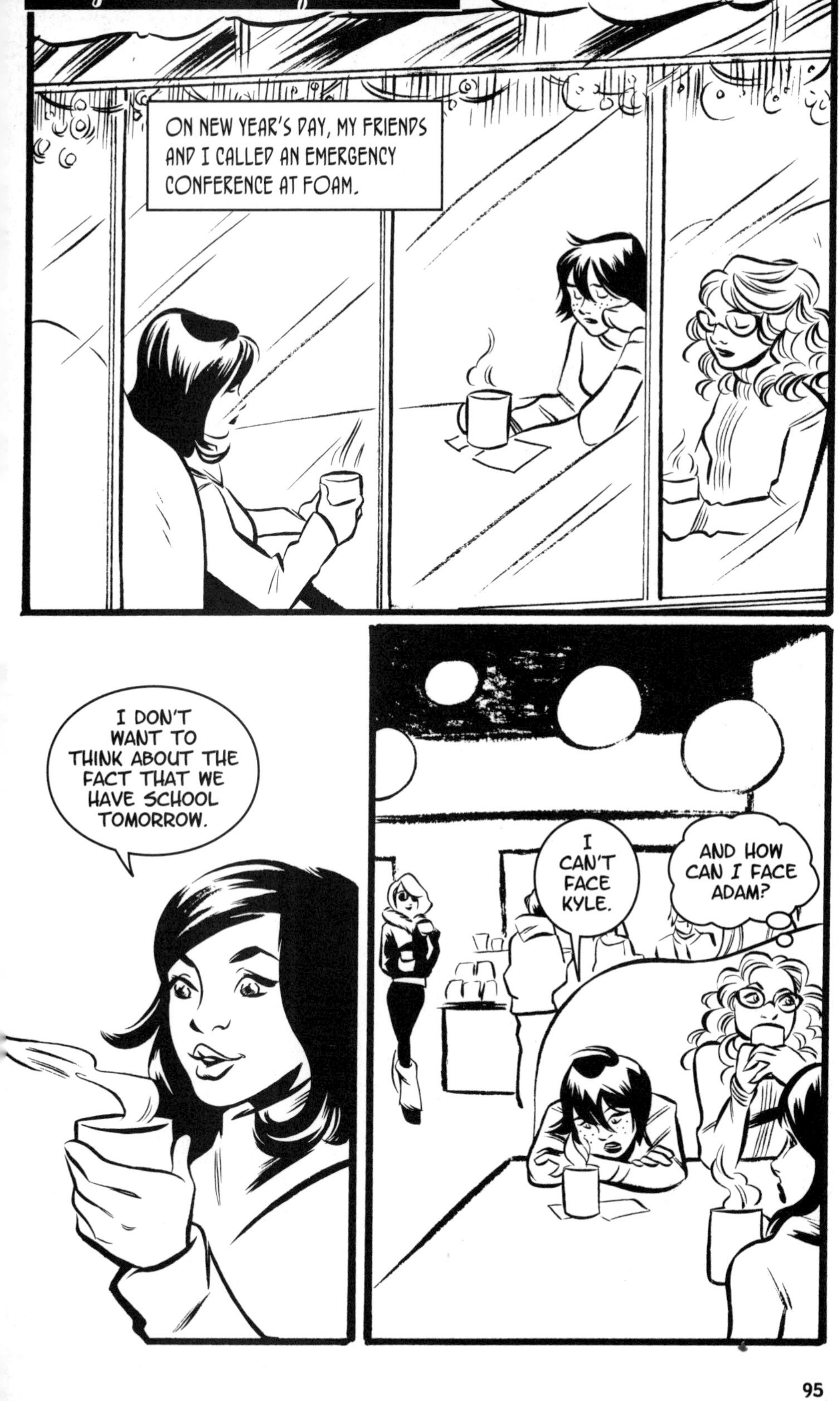
ON NEW YEAR'S DAY, MY FRIENDS AND I CALLED AN EMERGENCY CONFERENCE AT FOAM.
I DON'T WANT TO THINK ABOUT THE FACT THAT WE HAVE SCHOOL TOMORROW.
I CAN'T FACE KYLE.
AND HOW CAN I FACE ADAM?

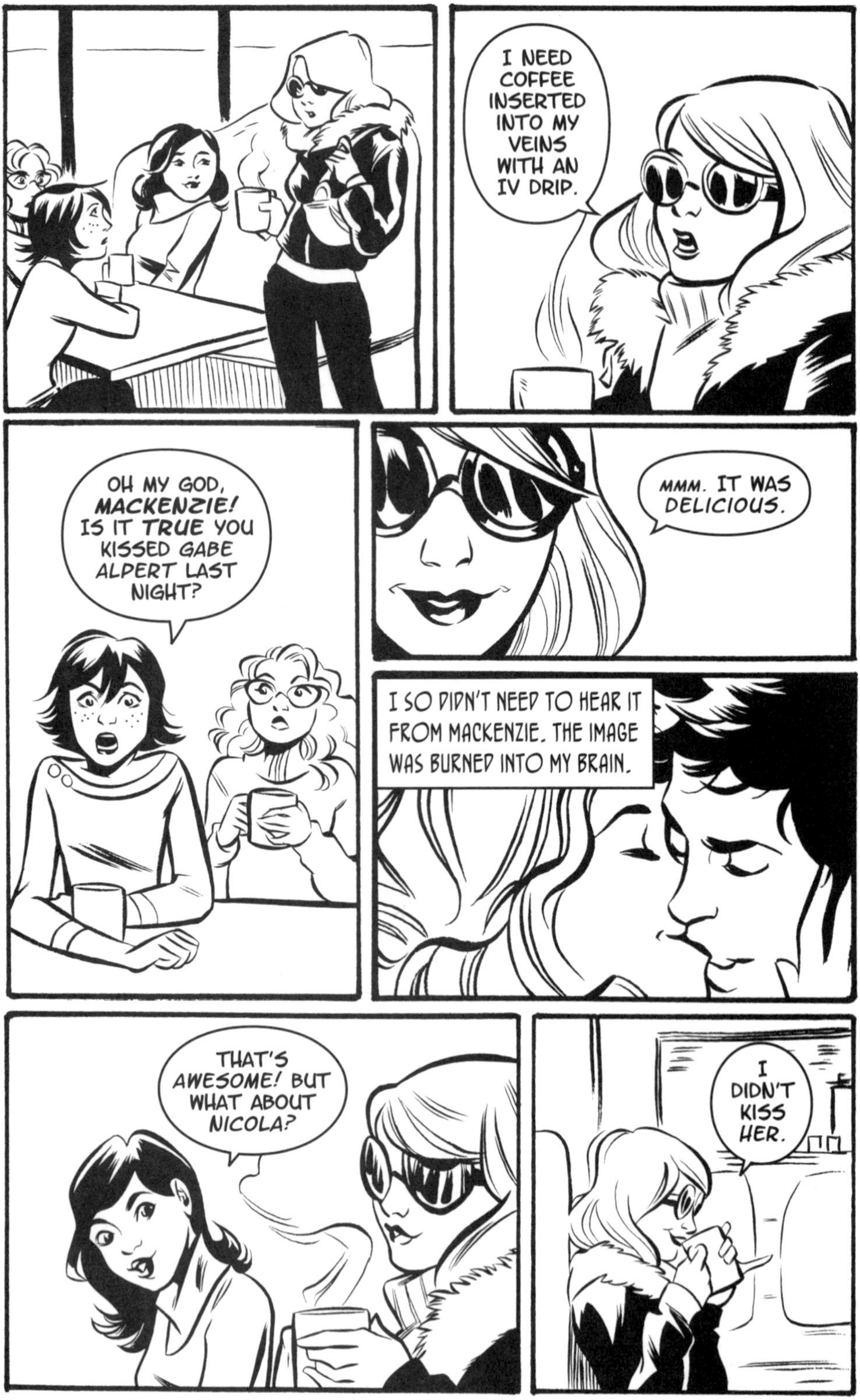
I NEED COFFEE INSERTED INTO MY VEINS WITH AN IV DRIP.
OH MY GOD, MACKENZIE! IS IT TRUE YOU KISSED GABE ALPERT LAST NIGHT?
MMM. IT WAS DELICIOUS.
I SO DIDN'T NEED TO HEAR IT FROM MACKENZIE. THE IMAGE WAS BURNED INTO MY BRAIN.
THAT'S AWESOME! BUT WHAT ABOUT NICOLA?
I DIDN'T KISS HER.

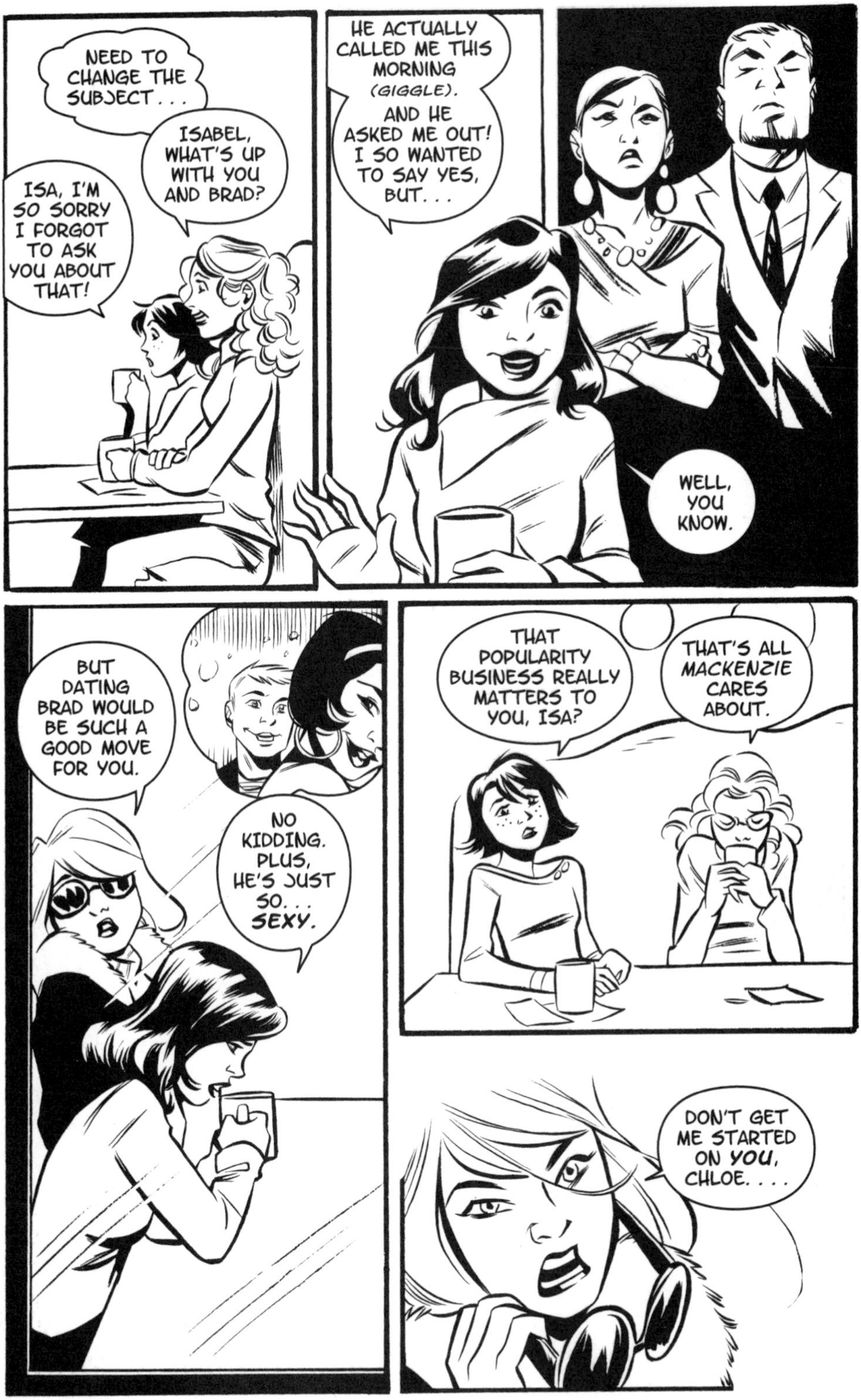
NEED TO CHANGE THE SUBJECT . . .
ISABEL, WHAT'S UP WITH YOU AND BRAD?
ISA, I'M SO SORRY I FORGOT TO ASK YOU ABOUT THAT!
HE ACTUALLY CALLED ME THIS MORNING (GIGGLE).
AND HE ASKED ME OUT! I SO WANTED TO SAY YES, BUT. . .
WELL, YOU KNOW.
BUT DATING BRAD WOULD BE SUCH A GOOD MOVE FOR YOU.
NO KIDDING. PLUS, HE'S JUST SO. . . SEXY.
THAT POPULARITY BUSINESS REALLY MATTERS TO YOU, ISA?
THAT'S ALL MACKENZIE CARES ABOUT.
DON'T GET ME STARTED ON YOU, CHLOE. . . .

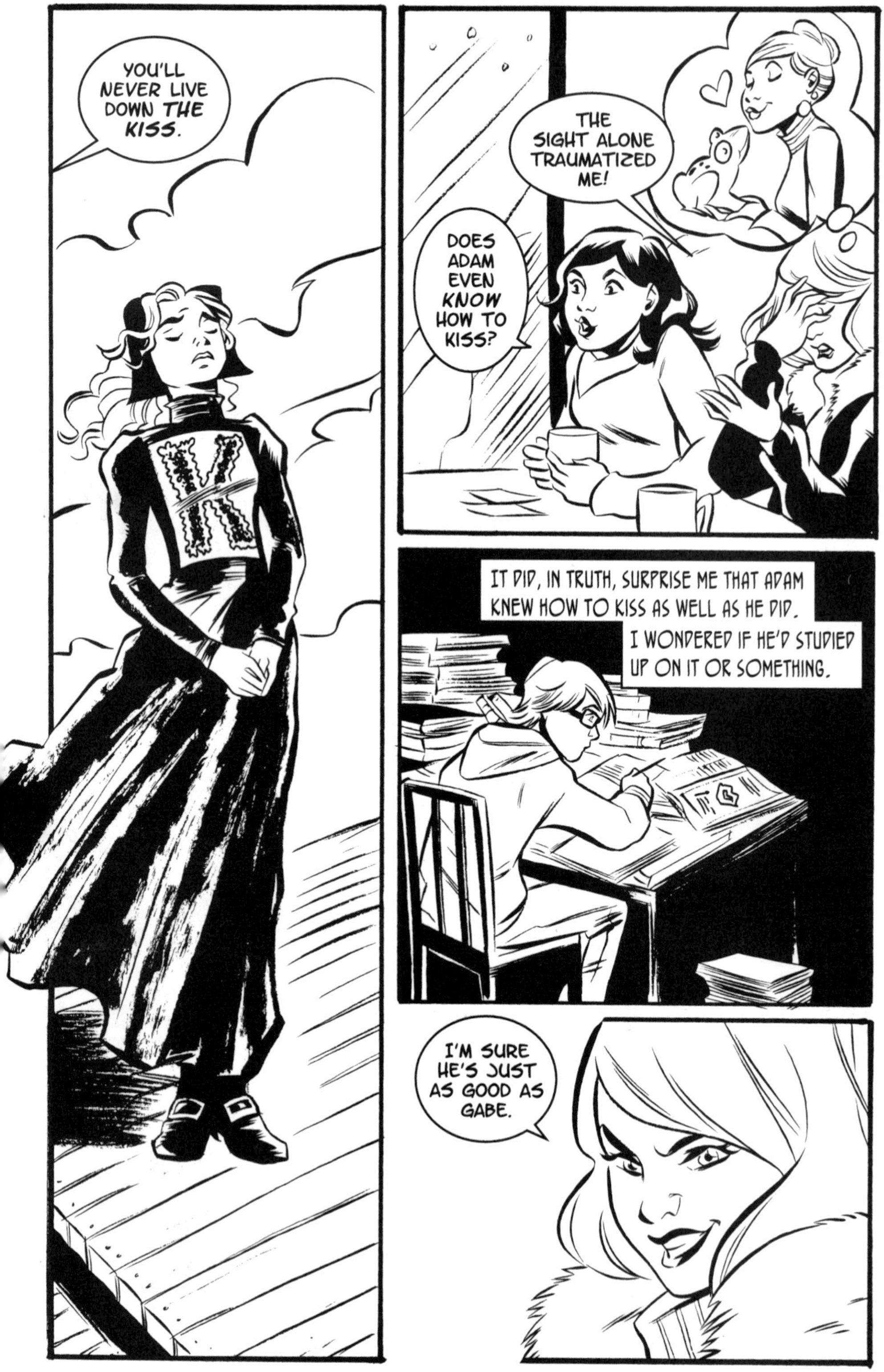
YOU'LL NEVER LIVE DOWN THE KISS.
THE SIGHT ALONE TRAUMATIZED ME!
DOES ADAM EVEN KNOW HOW TO KISS?
IT DID, IN TRUTH, SURPRISE ME THAT ADAM KNEW HOW TO KISS AS WELL AS HE DID.
I WONDERED IF HE'D STUDIED UP ON IT OR SOMETHING.
I'M SURE HE'S JUST AS GOOD AS GABE.

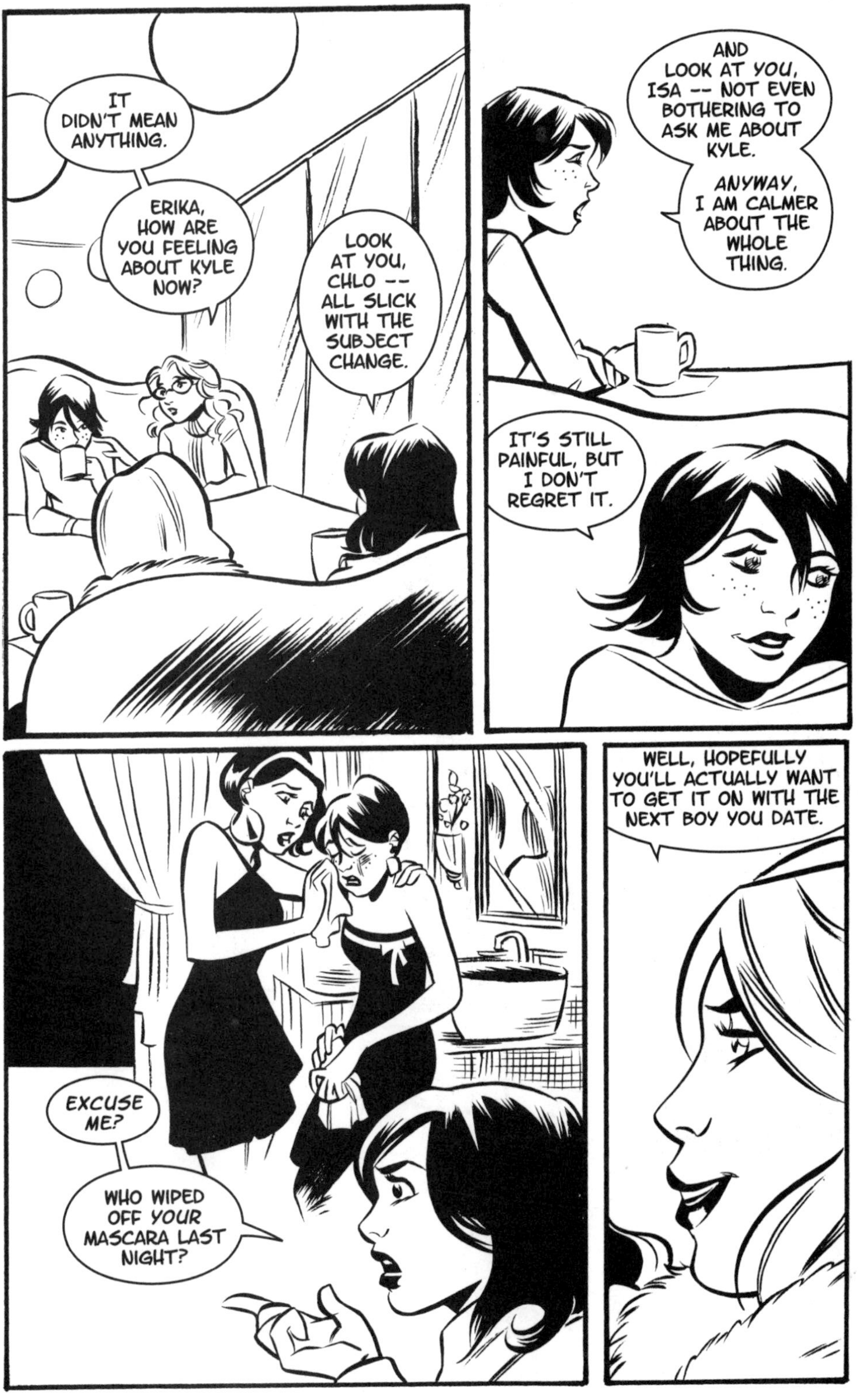
IT DIDN'T MEAN ANYTHING.
ERIKA, HOW ARE YOU FEELING ABOUT KYLE NOW?
LOOK AT YOU, CHLO -- ALL SLICK WITH THE SUBJECT CHANGE.
AND LOOK AT YOU, ISA -- NOT EVEN BOTHERING TO ASK ME ABOUT KYLE.
ANYWAY, I AM CALMER ABOUT THE WHOLE THING.
IT'S STILL PAINFUL, BUT I DON'T REGRET IT.
EXCUSE ME?
WHO WIPED OFF YOUR MASCARA LAST NIGHT?
WELL, HOPEFULLY YOU'LL ACTUALLY WANT TO GET IT ON WITH THE NEXT BOY YOU DATE.

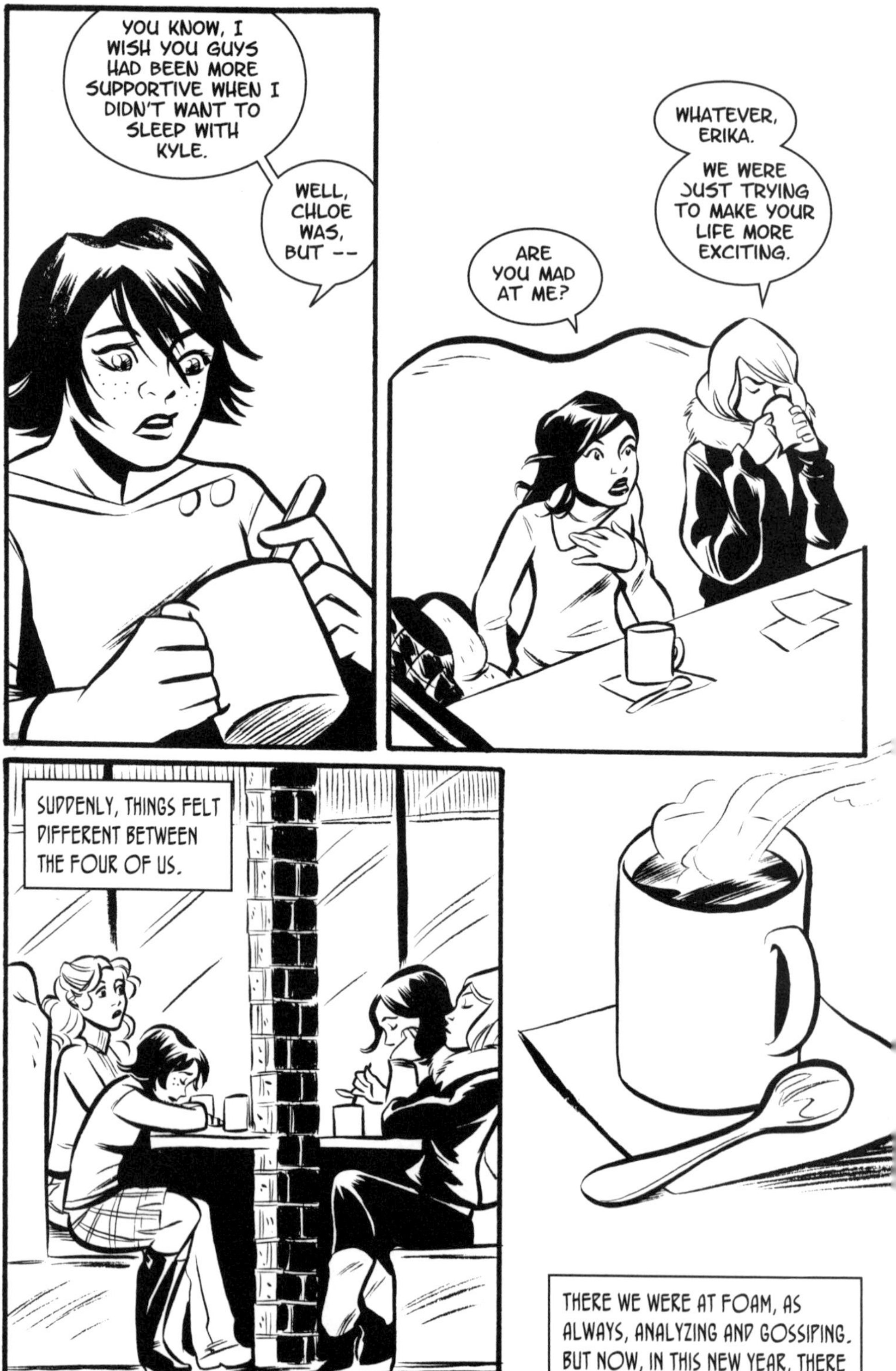
YOU KNOW, I WISH YOU GUYS HAD BEEN MORE SUPPORTIVE WHEN I DIDN'T WANT TO SLEEP WITH KYLE.
WELL, CHLOE WAS, BUT --
ARE YOU MAD AT ME?
WHATEVER, ERIKA.
WE WERE JUST TRYING TO MAKE YOUR LIFE MORE EXCITING.
SUDDENLY, THINGS FELT DIFFERENT BETWEEN THE FOUR OF US.
THERE WE WERE AT FOAM, AS ALWAYS, ANALYZING AND GOSSIPING. BUT NOW, IN THIS NEW YEAR, THERE WAS A TANGIBLE TENSION.

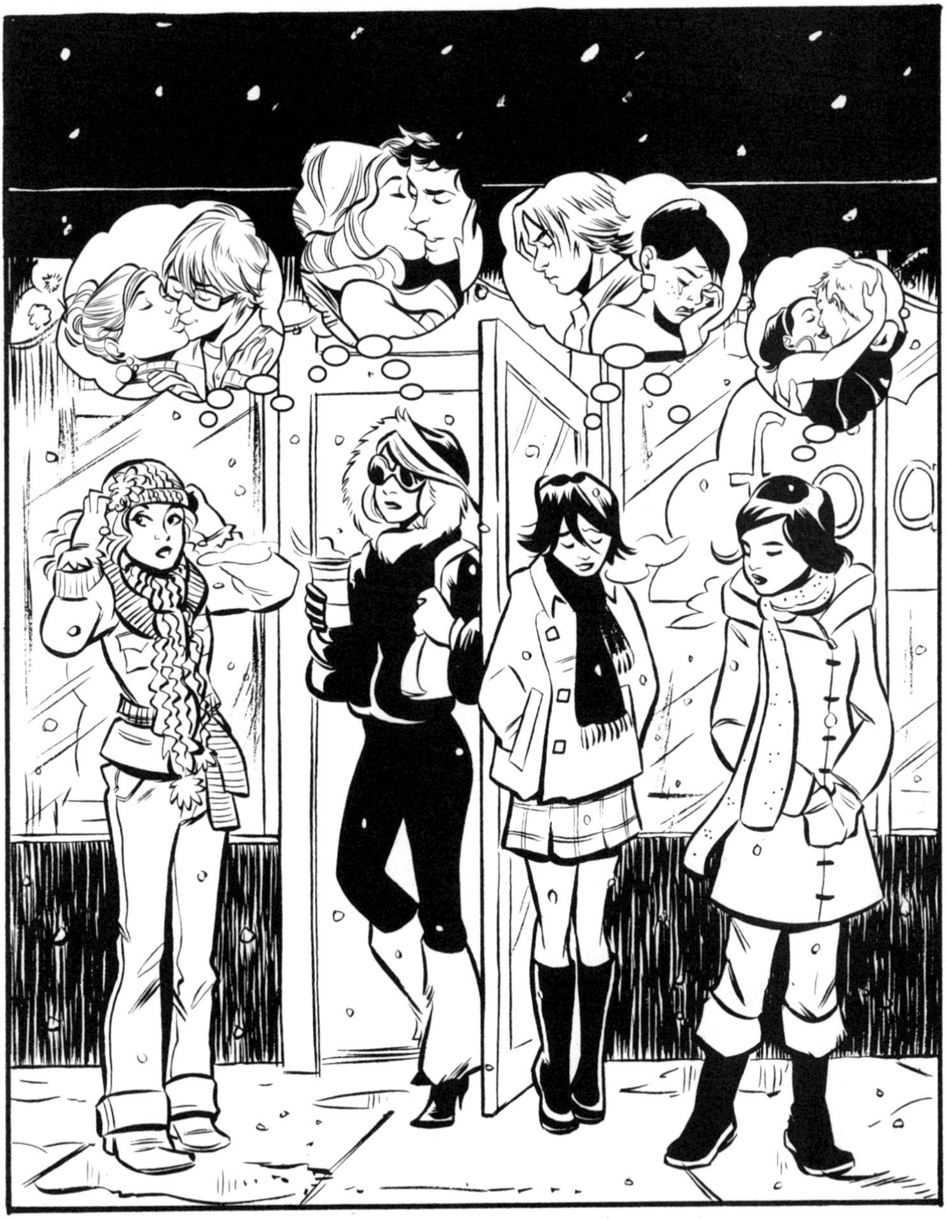

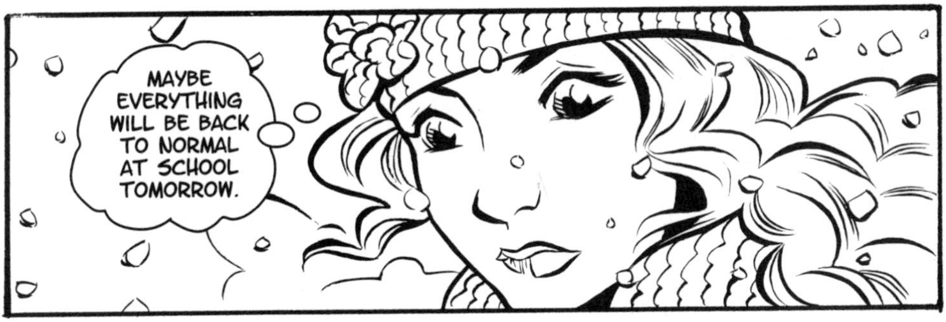
MAYBE EVERYTHING WILL BE BACK TO NORMAL AT SCHOOL TOMORROW.

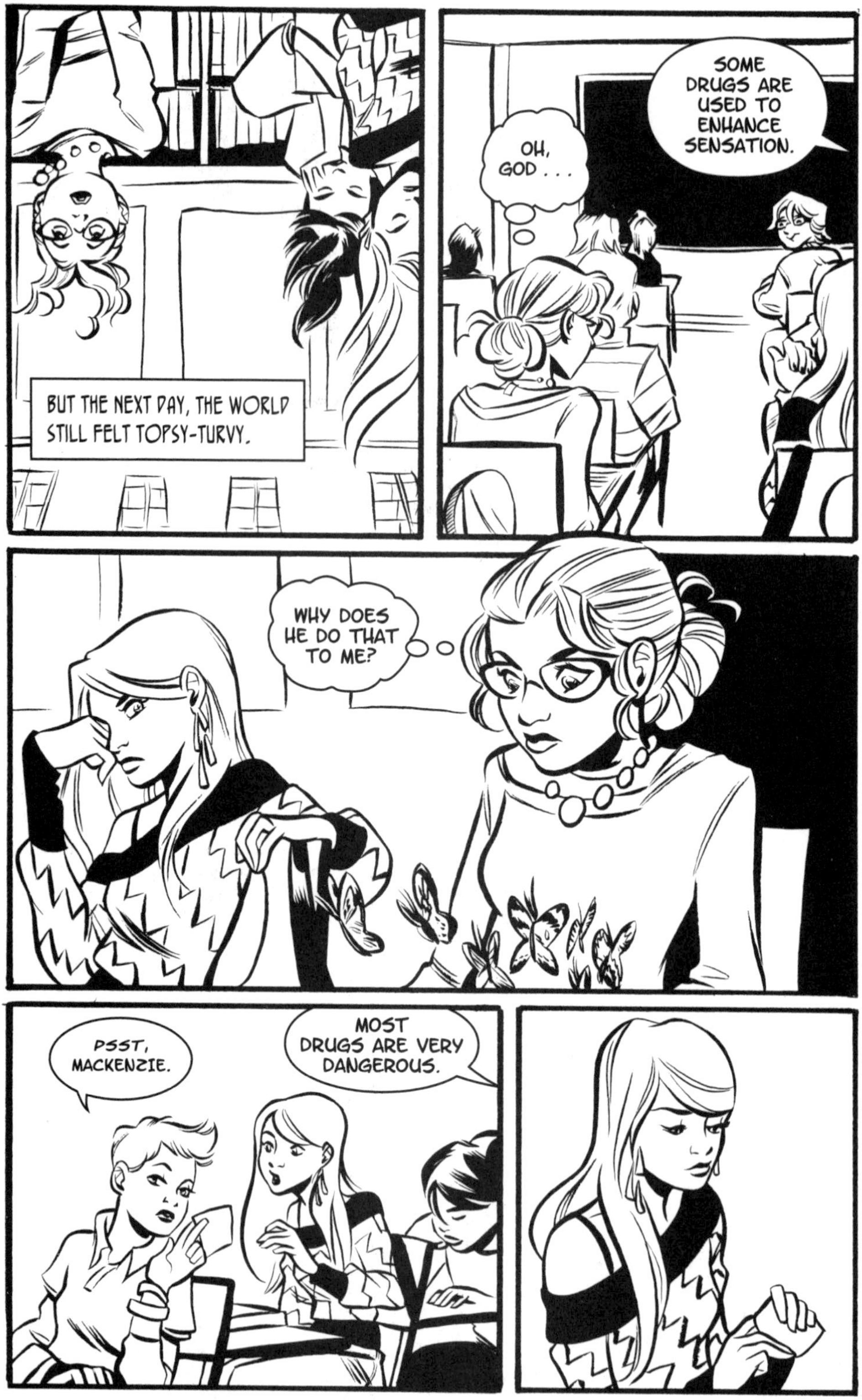
BUT THE NEXT DAY, THE WORLD STILL FELT TOPSY-TURVY.
OH, GOD . . .
SOME DRUGS ARE USED TO ENHANCE SENSATION.
WHY DOES HE DO THAT TO ME?
PSST, MACKENZIE.
MOST DRUGS ARE VERY DANGEROUS.

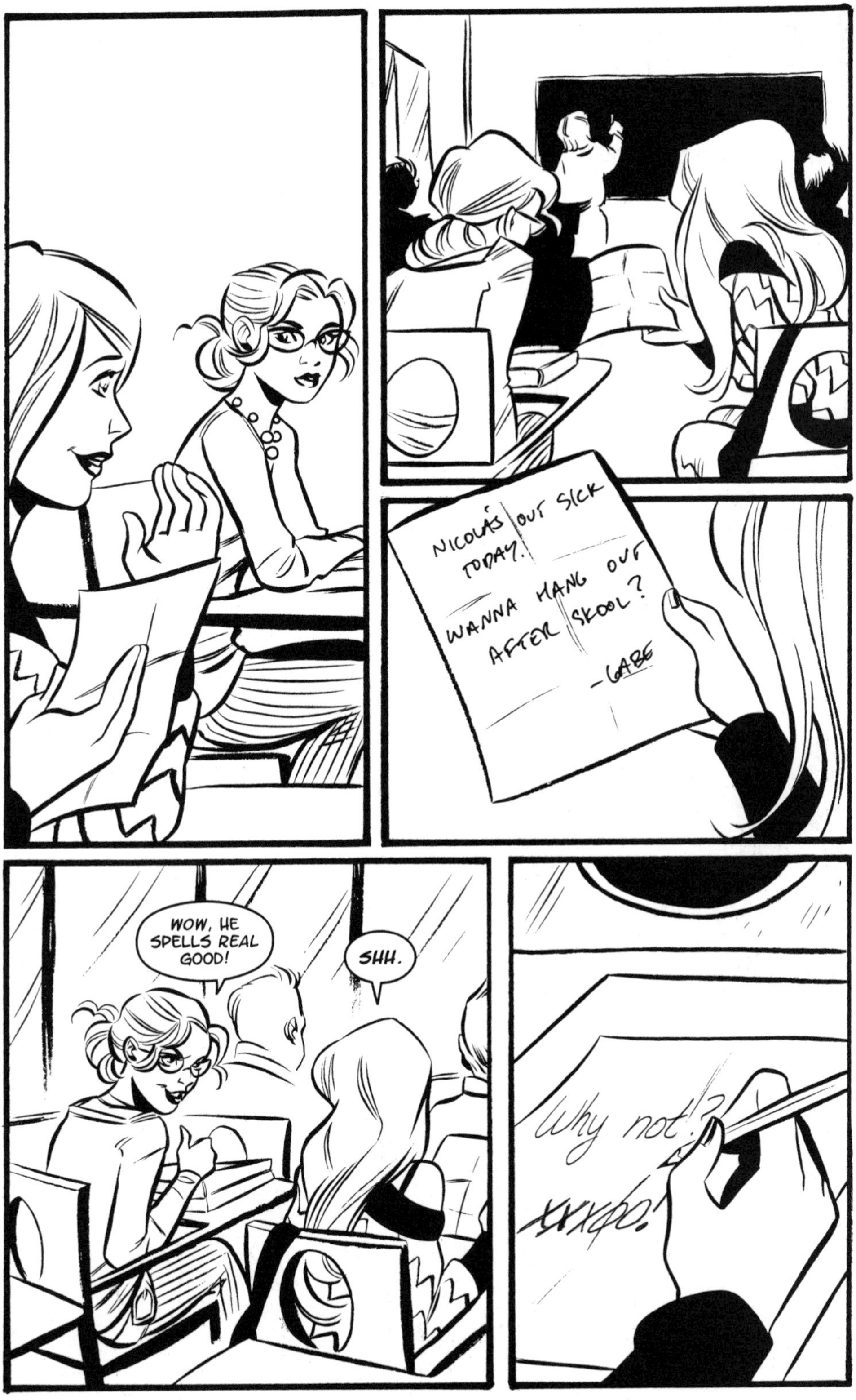
NICOLA'S OUT SICK TODAY.
WANNA HANG OUT AFTER SKOOL?
-GABE
WOW, HE SPELLS REAL GOOD!
SHH.
Why not!?
XXXOO!

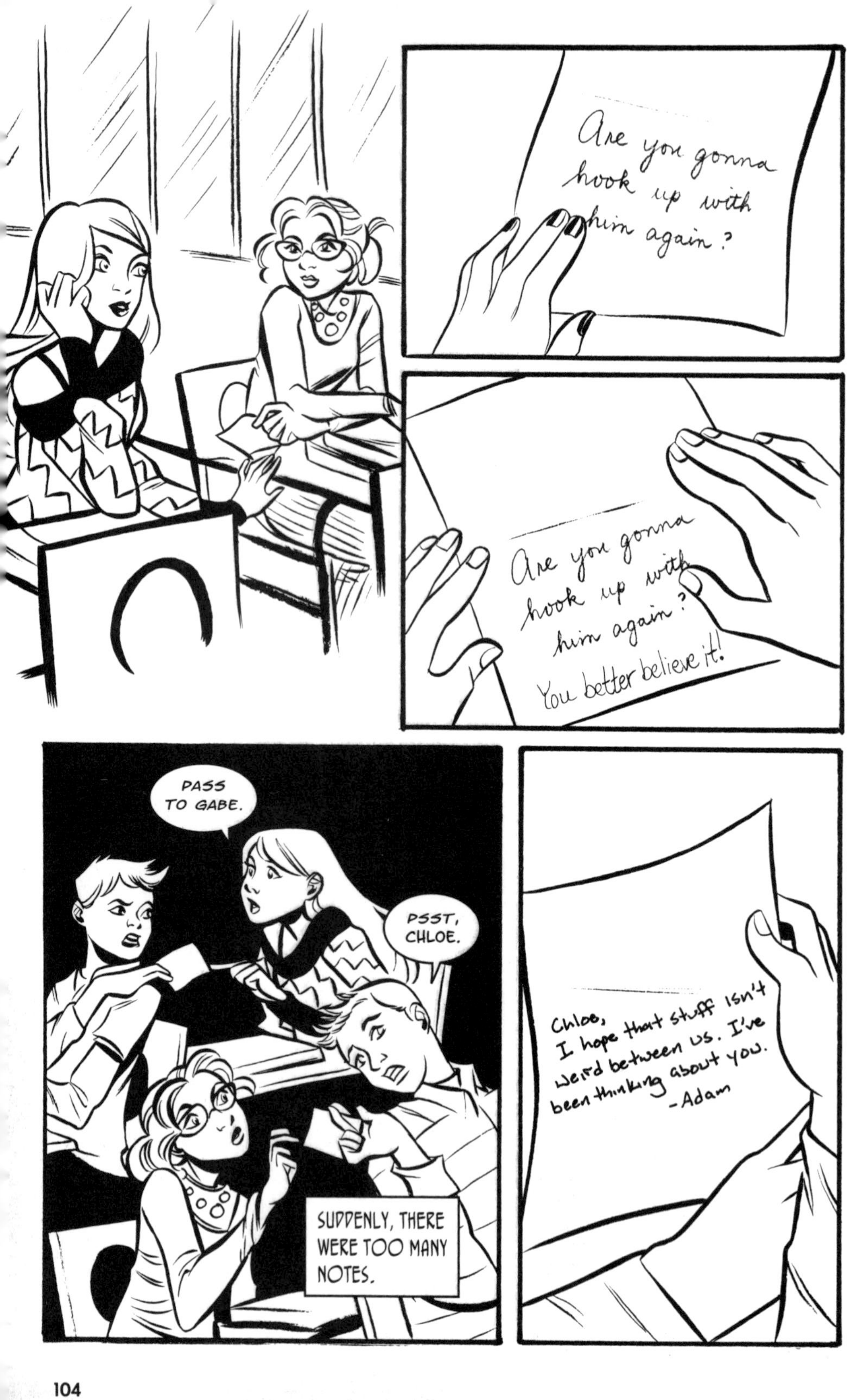

Are you gonna hook up with him again?
Are you gonna hook up with him again?
You better believe it!
PASS TO GABE.
PSST, CHLOE.
SUDDENLY, THERE WERE TOO MANY NOTES.
Chloe,
I hope that stuff isn't weird between us. I've been thinking about you.
-Adam

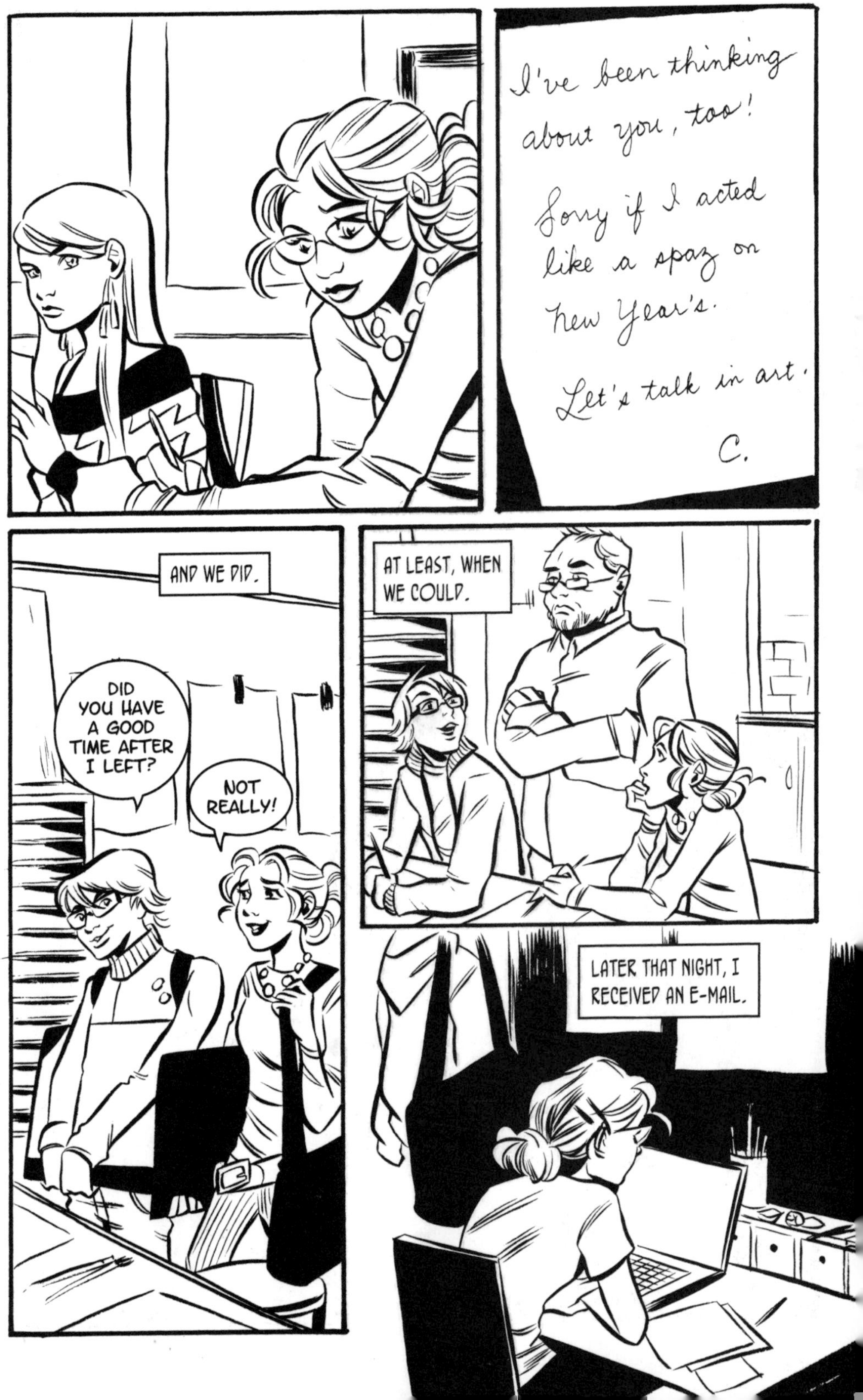
I've been thinking about you, too!
Sorry if I acted like a spaz on New Year's.
Let's talk in art.
C.
AND WE DID.
DID YOU HAVE A GOOD TIME AFTER I LEFT?
NOT REALLY!
AT LEAST, WHEN WE COULD.
LATER THAT NIGHT, I RECEIVED AN E-MAIL.

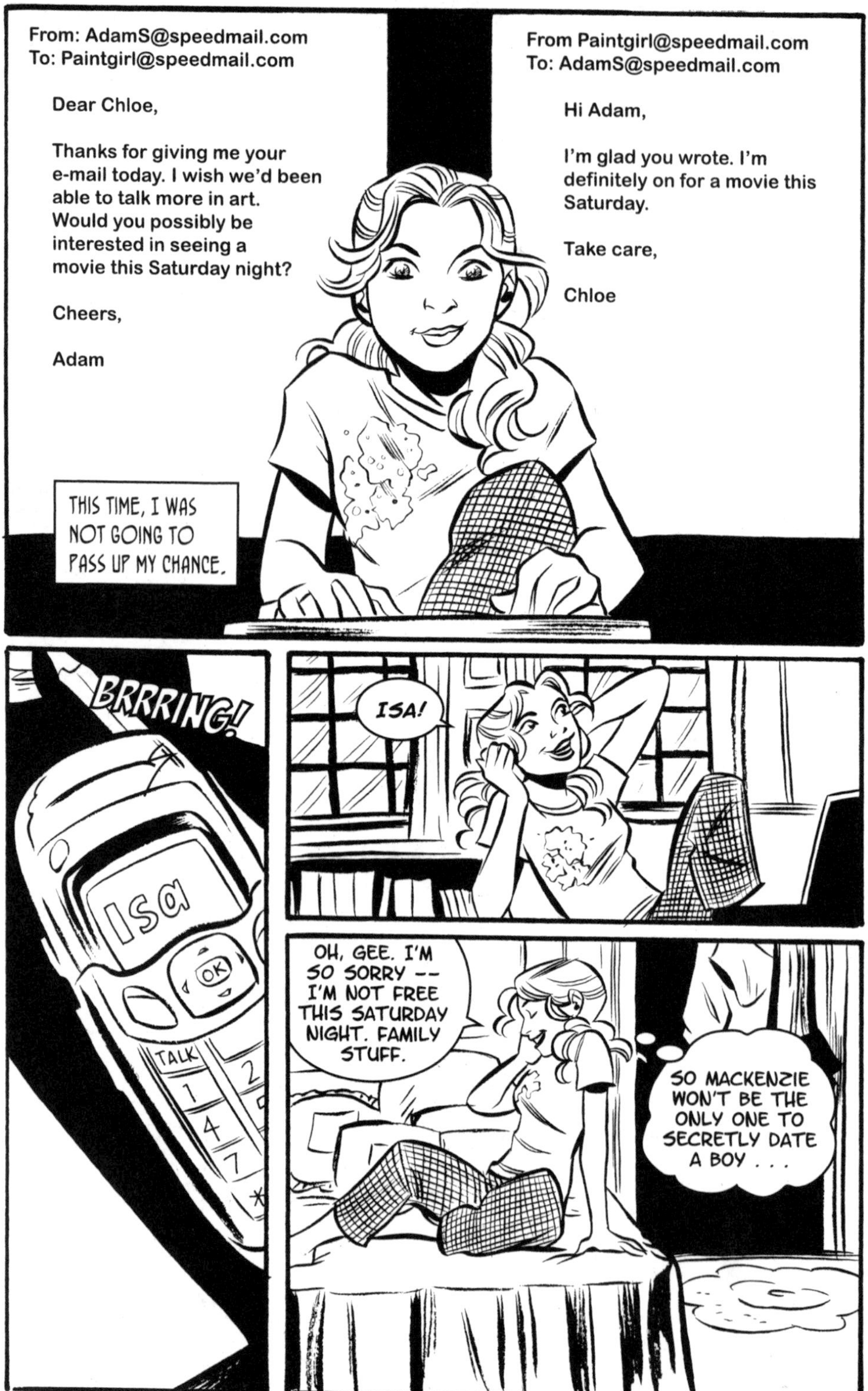
From: AdamS@speedmail.com
To: Paintgirl@speedmail.com
Dear Chloe,
Thanks for giving me your e-mail today. I wish we'd been able to talk more in art. Would you possibly be interested in seeing a movie this Saturday night?
Cheers,
Adam
From Paintgirl@speedmail.com
To: AdamS@speedmail.com
Hi Adam,
I'm glad you wrote. I'm definitely on for a movie this Saturday.
Take care,
Chloe
THIS TIME, I WAS NOT GOING TO PASS UP MY CHANCE.
BRRRING!
Isa
OK
TALK
ISA!
OH, GEE. I'M SO SORRY -- I'M NOT FREE THIS SATURDAY NIGHT. FAMILY STUFF.
SO MACKENZIE WON'T BE THE ONLY ONE TO SECRETLY DATE A BOY . . .

Chapter 8: Breaking Up

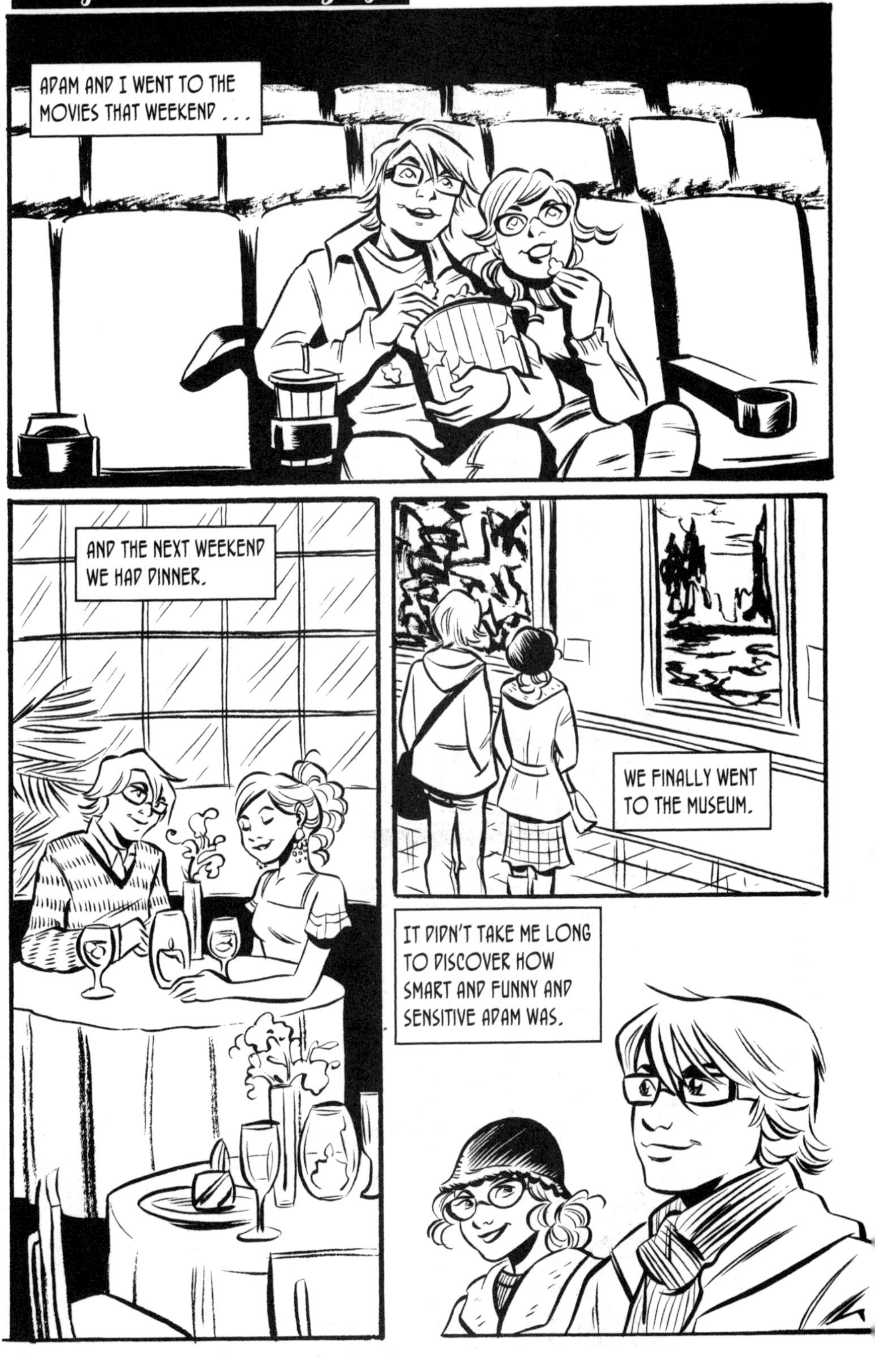
ADAM AND I WENT TO THE MOVIES THAT WEEKEND . . .
AND THE NEXT WEEKEND WE HAD DINNER.
WE FINALLY WENT TO THE MUSEUM.
IT DIDN'T TAKE ME LONG TO DISCOVER HOW SMART AND FUNNY AND SENSITIVE ADAM WAS.

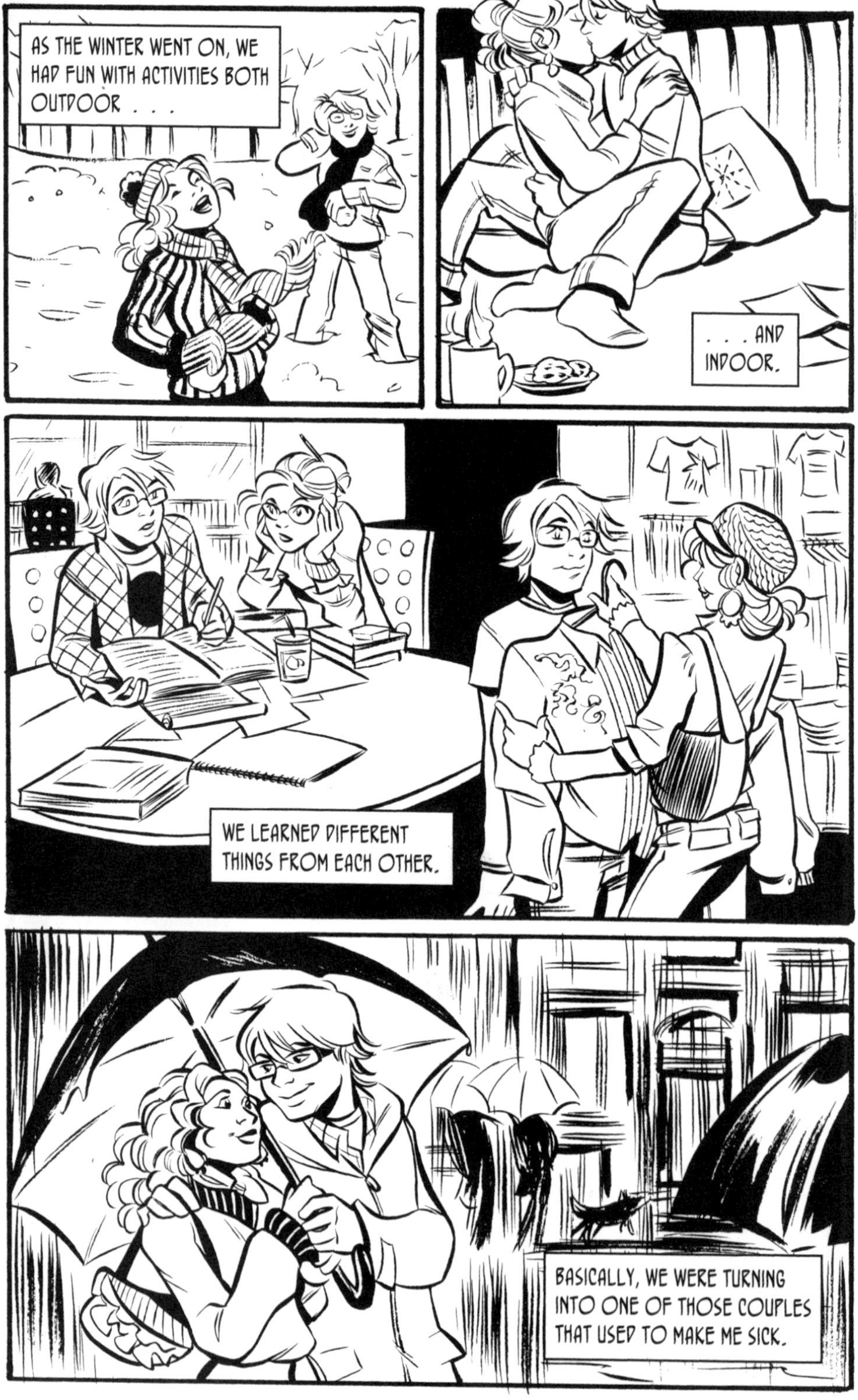
AS THE WINTER WENT ON, WE HAD FUN WITH ACTIVITIES BOTH OUTDOOR . . .
. . . AND INDOOR.
WE LEARNED DIFFERENT THINGS FROM EACH OTHER.
BASICALLY, WE WERE TURNING INTO ONE OF THOSE COUPLES THAT USED TO MAKE ME SICK.

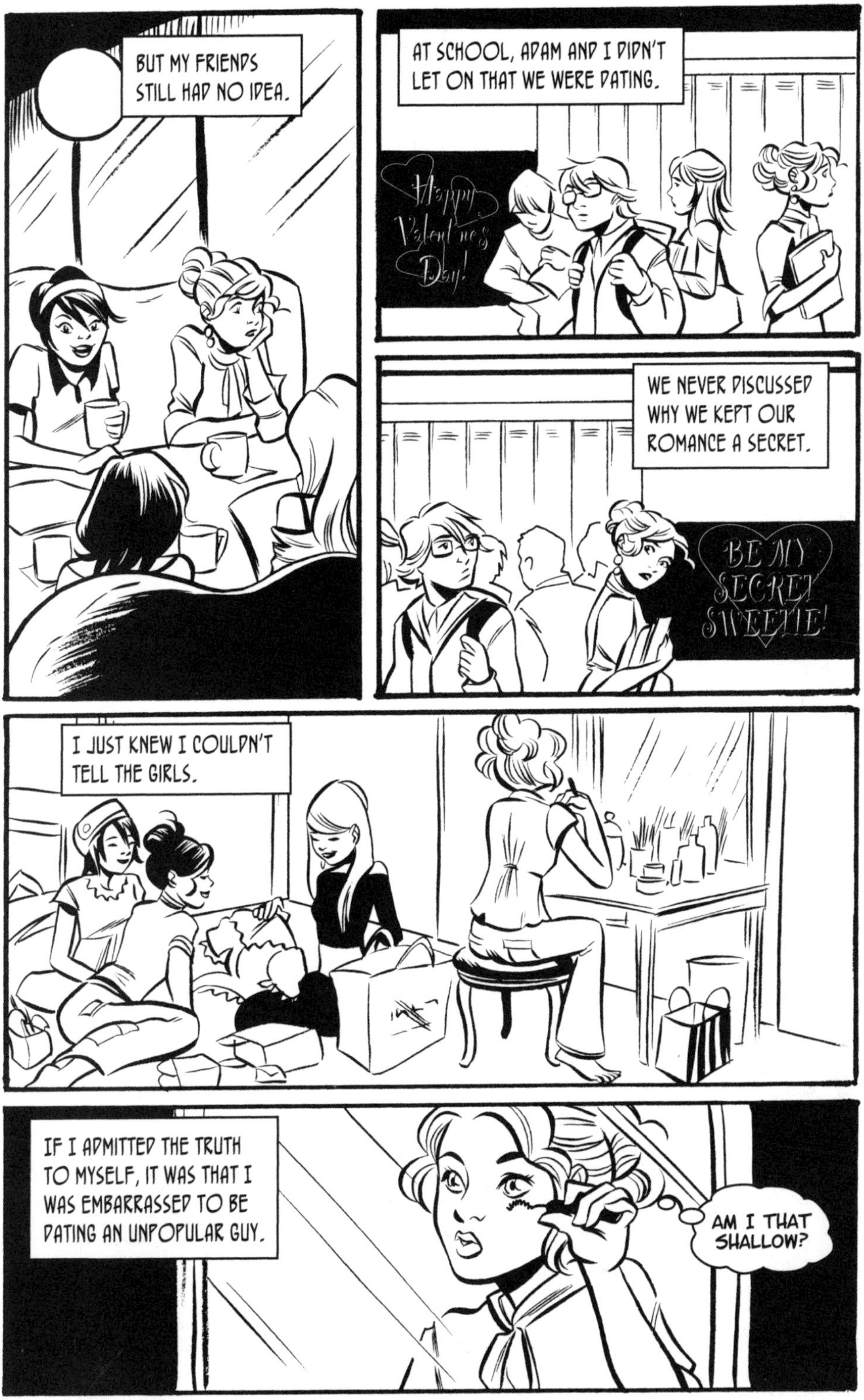
BUT MY FRIENDS STILL HAD NO IDEA.
AT SCHOOL, ADAM AND I DIDN'T LET ON THAT WE WERE DATING.
Happy Valentine's Day!
WE NEVER DISCUSSED WHY WE KEPT OUR ROMANCE A SECRET.
BE MY SECRET SWEETIE!
I JUST KNEW I COULDN'T TELL THE GIRLS.
IF I ADMITTED THE TRUTH TO MYSELF, IT WAS THAT I WAS EMBARRASSED TO BE DATING AN UNPOPULAR GUY.
AM I THAT SHALLOW?

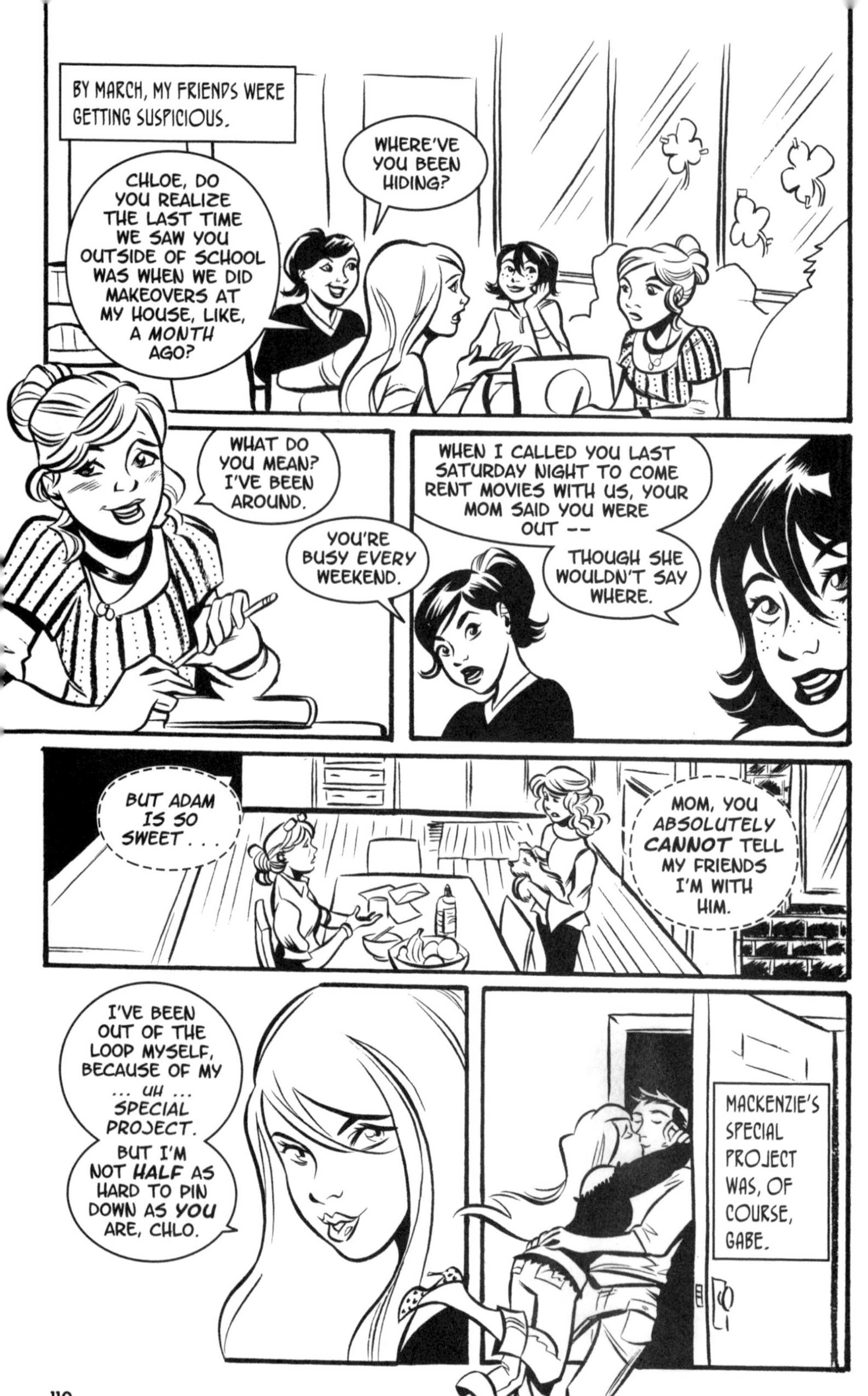
BY MARCH, MY FRIENDS WERE GETTING SUSPICIOUS.
CHLOE, DO YOU REALIZE THE LAST TIME WE SAW YOU OUTSIDE OF SCHOOL WAS WHEN WE DID MAKEOVERS AT MY HOUSE, LIKE, A *MONTH* AGO?
WHERE'VE YOU BEEN HIDING?
WHAT DO YOU MEAN? I'VE BEEN AROUND.
YOU'RE BUSY *EVERY* WEEKEND.
WHEN I CALLED YOU LAST SATURDAY NIGHT TO COME RENT MOVIES WITH US, YOUR MOM SAID YOU WERE OUT --
THOUGH SHE WOULDN'T SAY WHERE.
BUT ADAM IS SO SWEET . . .
MOM, YOU *ABSOLUTELY* **CANNOT** TELL MY FRIENDS I'M WITH HIM.
I'VE BEEN OUT OF THE LOOP MYSELF, BECAUSE OF MY ... UH ... *SPECIAL PROJECT*.
BUT I'M NOT **HALF** AS HARD TO PIN DOWN AS **YOU** ARE, CHLO.
MACKENZIE'S SPECIAL PROJECT WAS, OF COURSE, GABE.

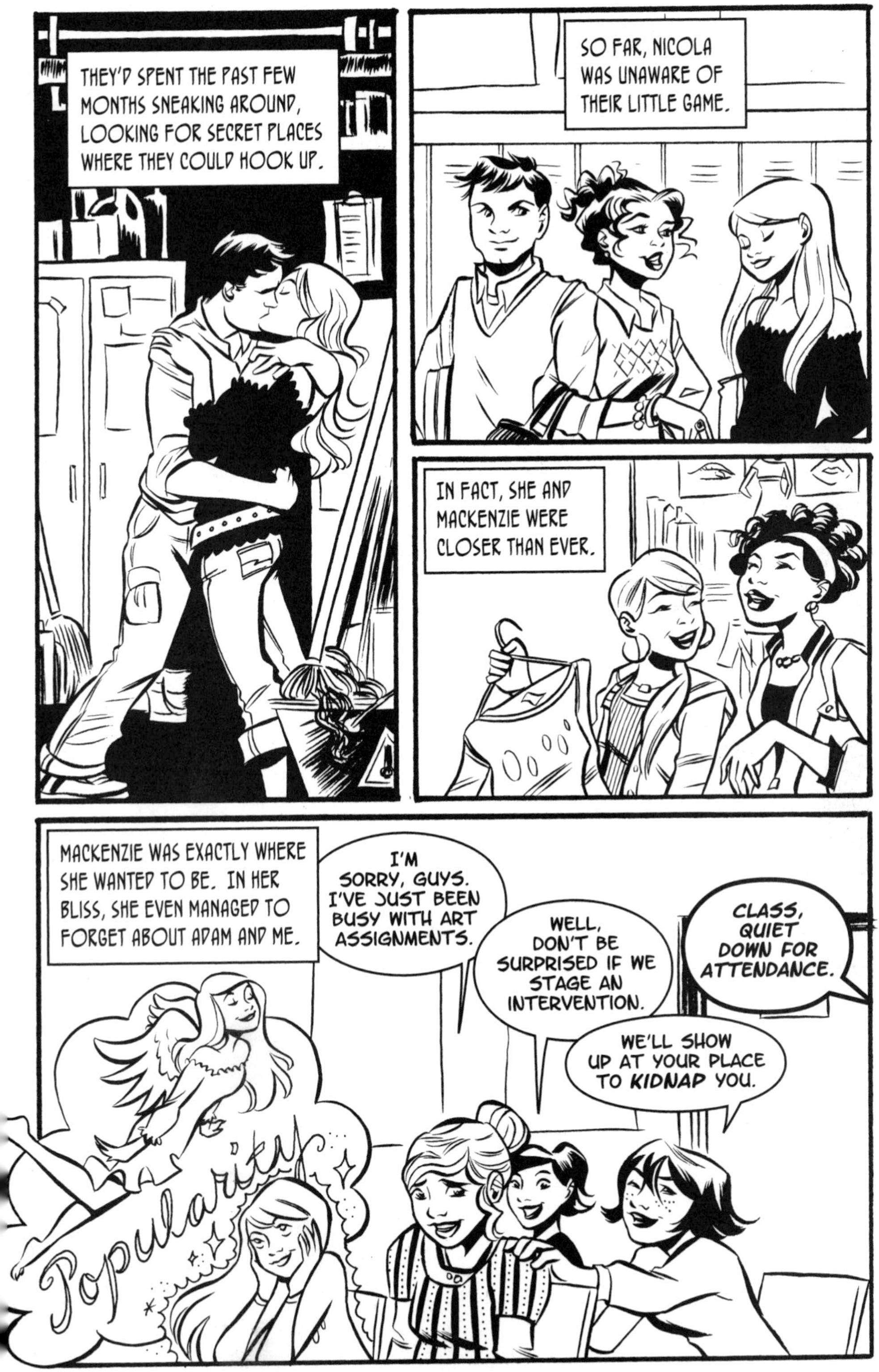
THEY'D SPENT THE PAST FEW MONTHS SNEAKING AROUND, LOOKING FOR SECRET PLACES WHERE THEY COULD HOOK UP.
SO FAR, NICOLA WAS UNAWARE OF THEIR LITTLE GAME.
IN FACT, SHE AND MACKENZIE WERE CLOSER THAN EVER.
MACKENZIE WAS EXACTLY WHERE SHE WANTED TO BE. IN HER BLISS, SHE EVEN MANAGED TO FORGET ABOUT ADAM AND ME.
I'M SORRY, GUYS. I'VE JUST BEEN BUSY WITH ART ASSIGNMENTS.
WELL, DON'T BE SURPRISED IF WE STAGE AN INTERVENTION.
CLASS, QUIET DOWN FOR ATTENDANCE.
WE'LL SHOW UP AT YOUR PLACE TO KIDNAP YOU.
Popularity

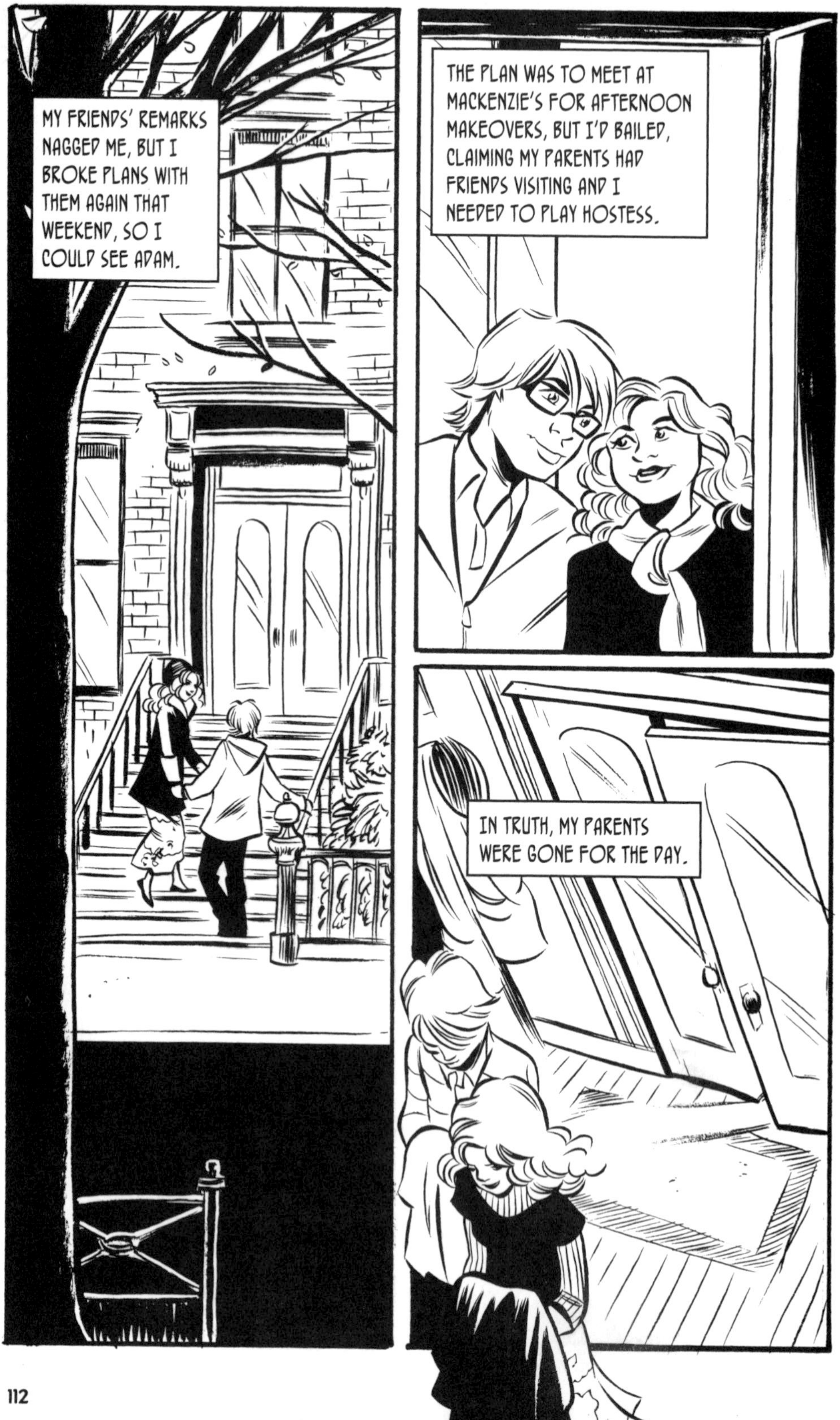
MY FRIENDS' REMARKS NAGGED ME, BUT I BROKE PLANS WITH THEM AGAIN THAT WEEKEND, SO I COULD SEE ADAM.
THE PLAN WAS TO MEET AT MACKENZIE'S FOR AFTERNOON MAKEOVERS, BUT I'D BAILED, CLAIMING MY PARENTS HAD FRIENDS VISITING AND I NEEDED TO PLAY HOSTESS.
IN TRUTH, MY PARENTS WERE GONE FOR THE DAY.

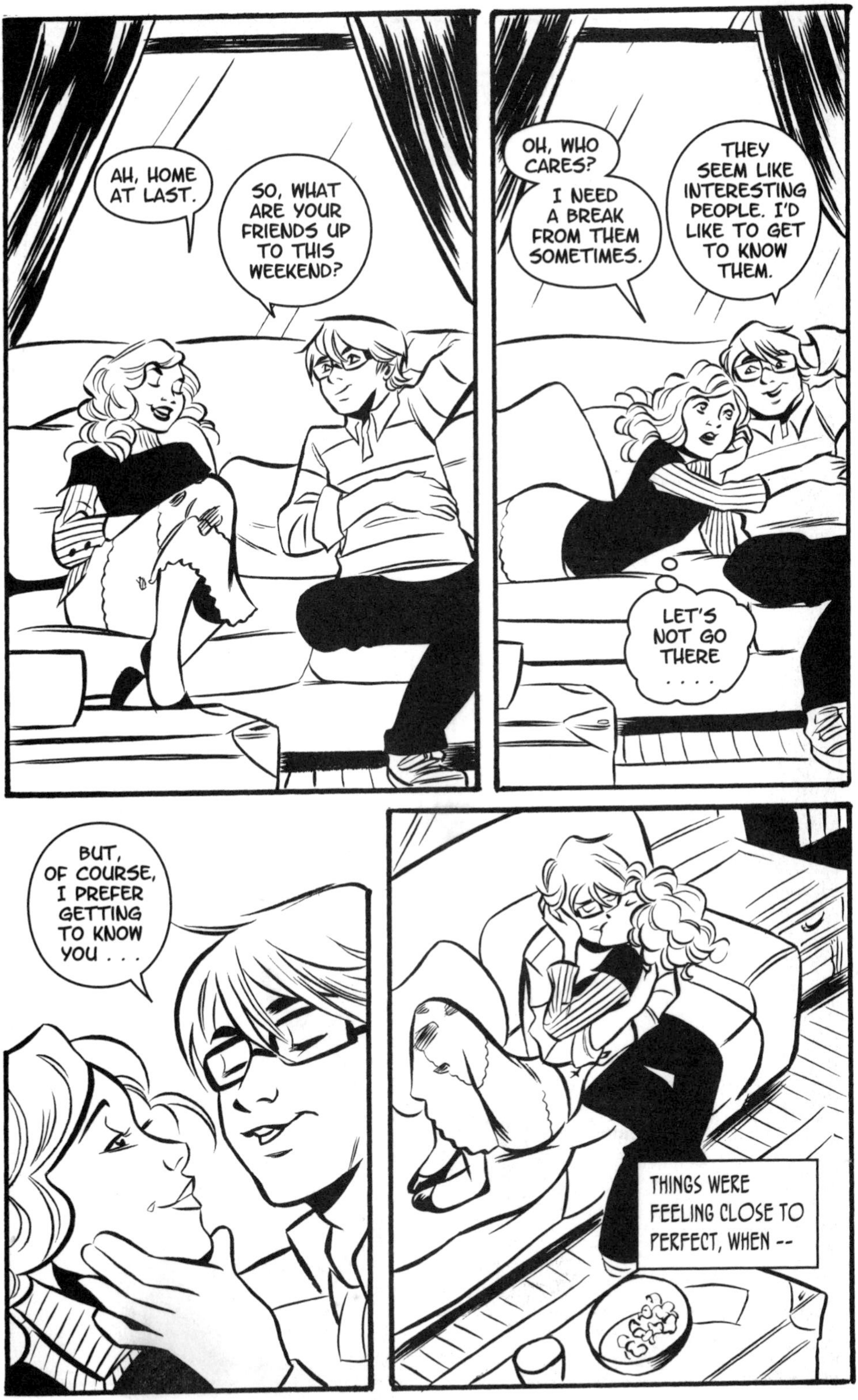
AH, HOME AT LAST.
SO, WHAT ARE YOUR FRIENDS UP TO THIS WEEKEND?
OH, WHO CARES?
I NEED A BREAK FROM THEM SOMETIMES.
THEY SEEM LIKE INTERESTING PEOPLE. I'D LIKE TO GET TO KNOW THEM.
LET'S NOT GO THERE . . . .
BUT, OF COURSE, I PREFER GETTING TO KNOW YOU . . .
THINGS WERE FEELING CLOSE TO PERFECT, WHEN --

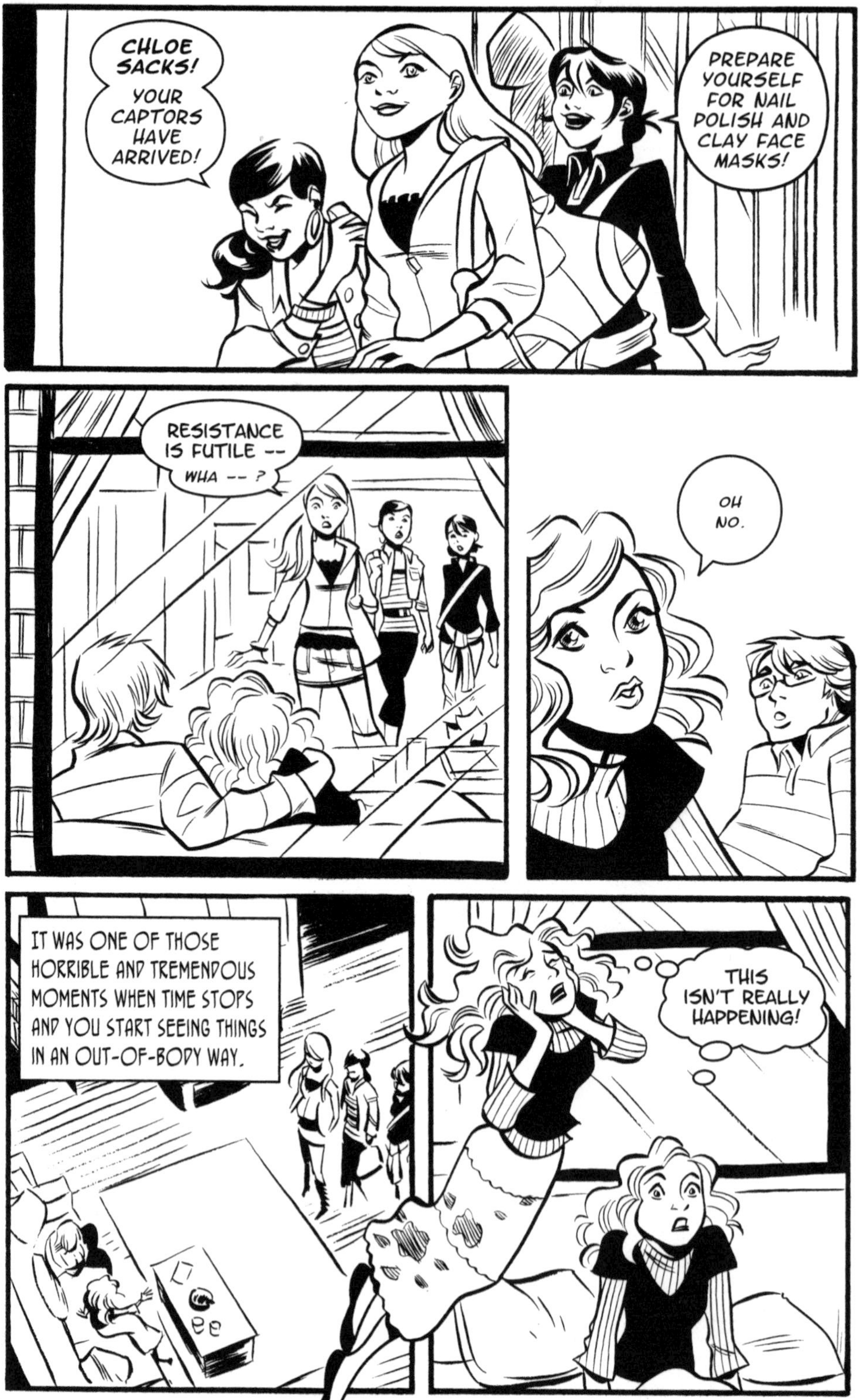
CHLOE SACKS! YOUR CAPTORS HAVE ARRIVED!
PREPARE YOURSELF FOR NAIL POLISH AND CLAY FACE MASKS!
RESISTANCE IS FUTILE -- WHA -- ?
OH NO.
IT WAS ONE OF THOSE HORRIBLE AND TREMENDOUS MOMENTS WHEN TIME STOPS AND YOU START SEEING THINGS IN AN OUT-OF-BODY WAY.
THIS ISN'T REALLY HAPPENING!

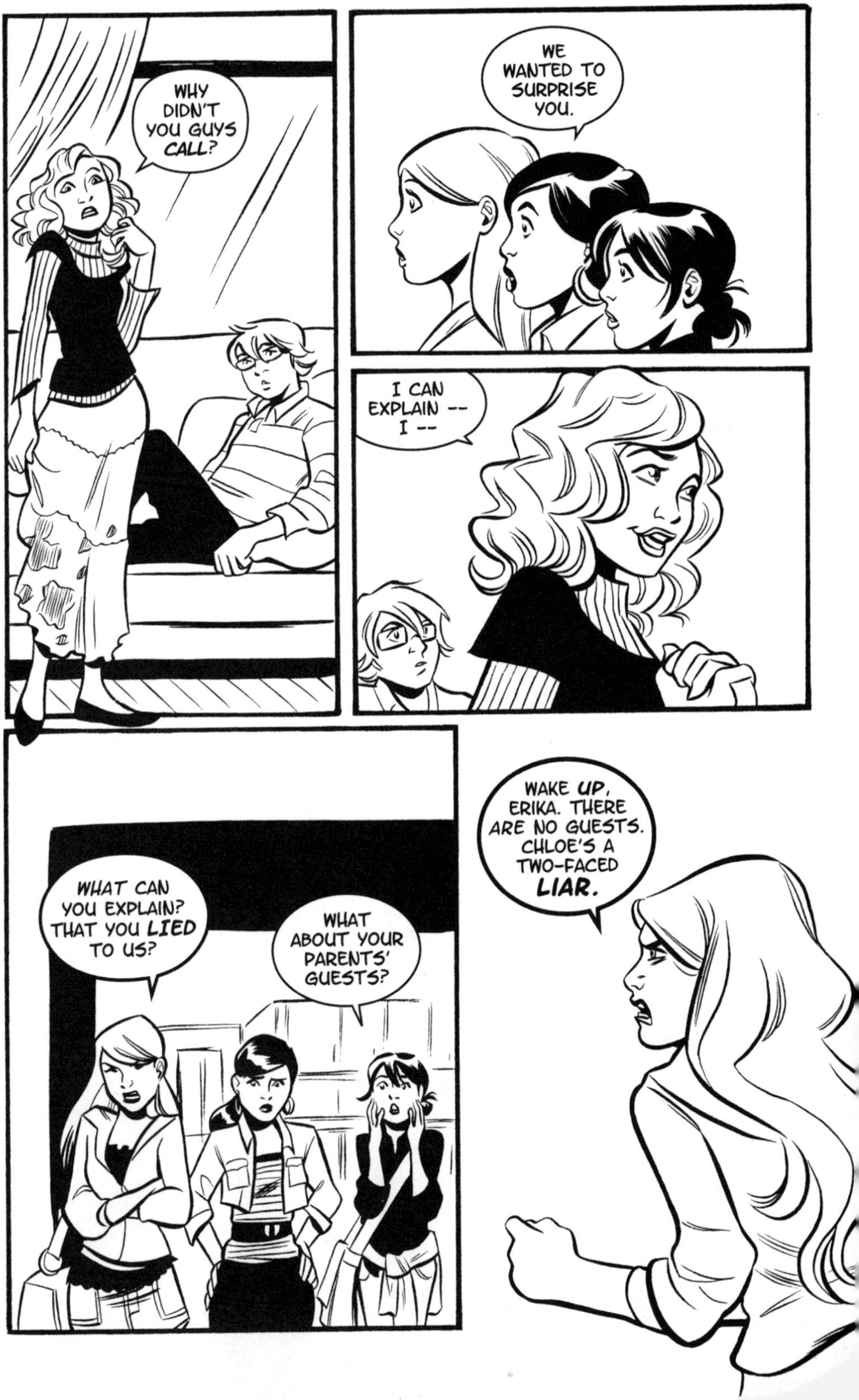
WHY DIDN'T YOU GUYS CALL?
WE WANTED TO SURPRISE YOU.
I CAN EXPLAIN -- I --
WHAT CAN YOU EXPLAIN? THAT YOU LIED TO US?
WHAT ABOUT YOUR PARENTS' GUESTS?
WAKE UP, ERIKA. THERE ARE NO GUESTS. CHLOE'S A TWO-FACED LIAR.

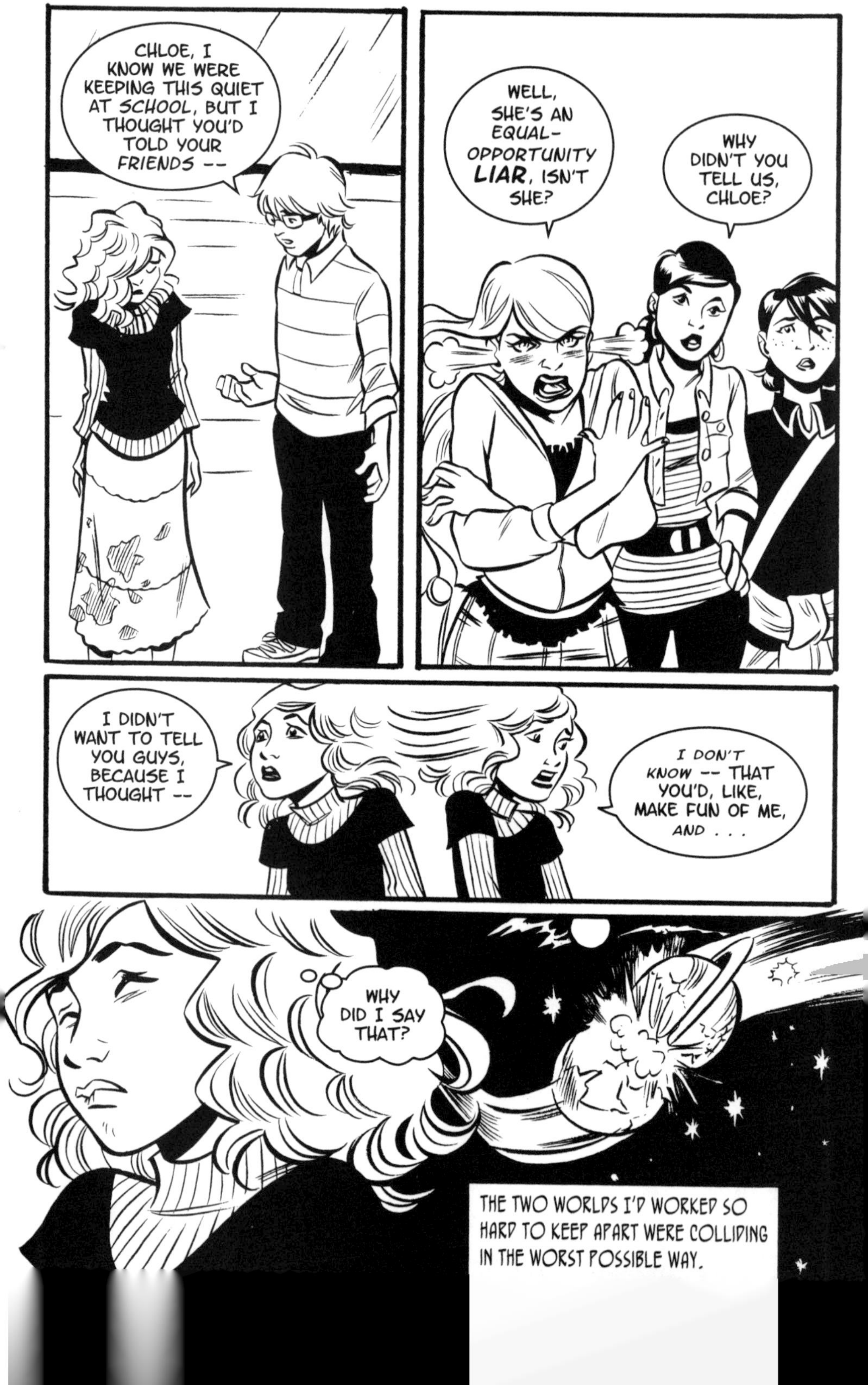

CHLOE, I KNOW WE WERE KEEPING THIS QUIET AT SCHOOL, BUT I THOUGHT YOU'D TOLD YOUR FRIENDS --
WELL, SHE'S AN EQUAL-OPPORTUNITY LIAR, ISN'T SHE?
WHY DIDN'T YOU TELL US, CHLOE?
I DIDN'T WANT TO TELL YOU GUYS, BECAUSE I THOUGHT --
I DON'T KNOW -- THAT YOU'D, LIKE, MAKE FUN OF ME, AND . . .
WHY DID I SAY THAT?
THE TWO WORLDS I'D WORKED SO HARD TO KEEP APART WERE COLLIDING IN THE WORST POSSIBLE WAY.

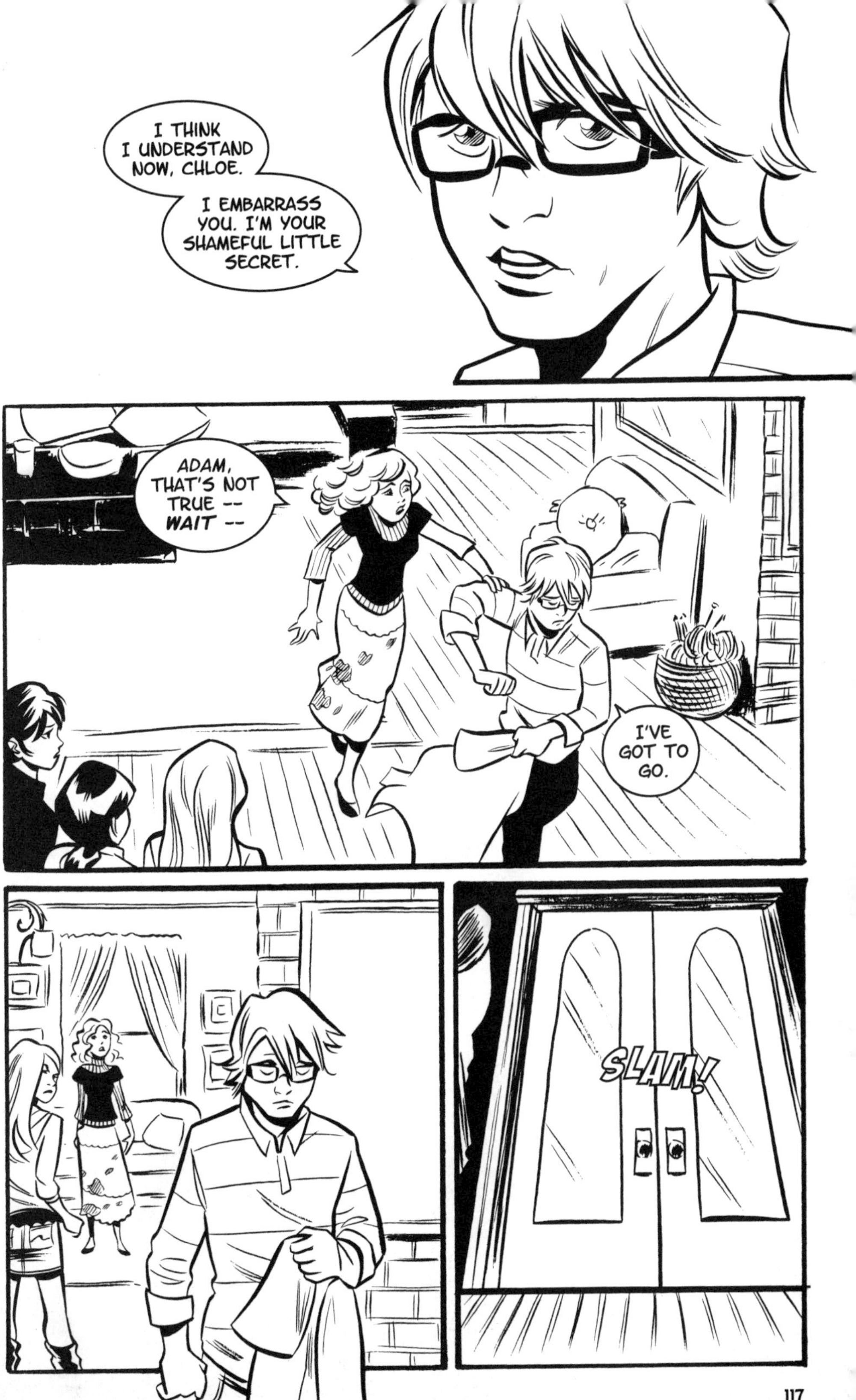
I THINK I UNDERSTAND NOW, CHLOE.
I EMBARRASS YOU. I'M YOUR SHAMEFUL LITTLE SECRET.
ADAM, THAT'S NOT TRUE -- WAIT --
I'VE GOT TO GO.
SLAM!

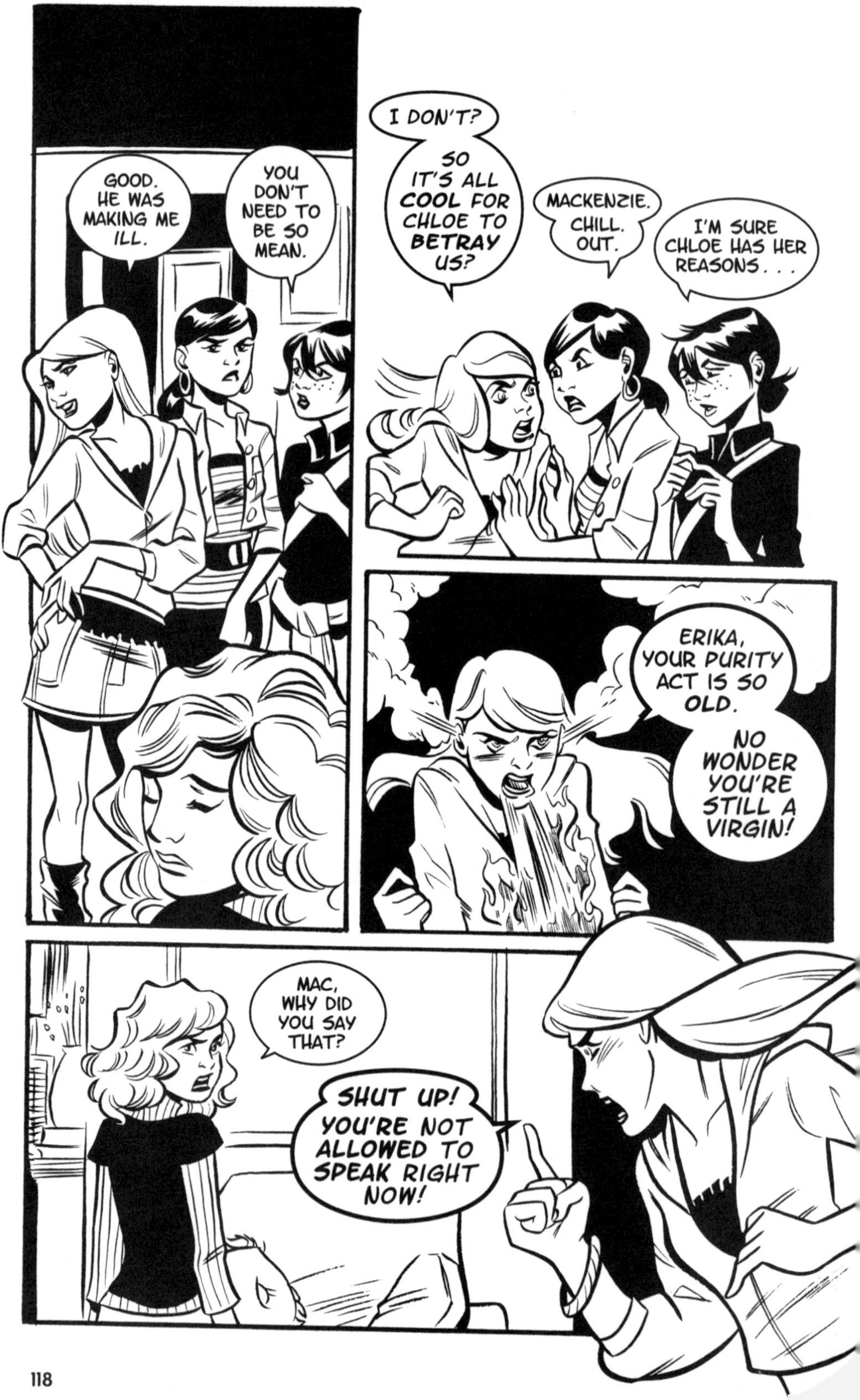
GOOD. HE WAS MAKING ME ILL.
YOU DON'T NEED TO BE SO MEAN.
I DON'T?
SO IT'S ALL COOL FOR CHLOE TO BETRAY US?
MACKENZIE. CHILL. OUT.
I'M SURE CHLOE HAS HER REASONS . . .
ERIKA, YOUR PURITY ACT IS SO OLD.
NO WONDER YOU'RE STILL A VIRGIN!
MAC, WHY DID YOU SAY THAT?
SHUT UP! YOU'RE NOT ALLOWED TO SPEAK RIGHT NOW!

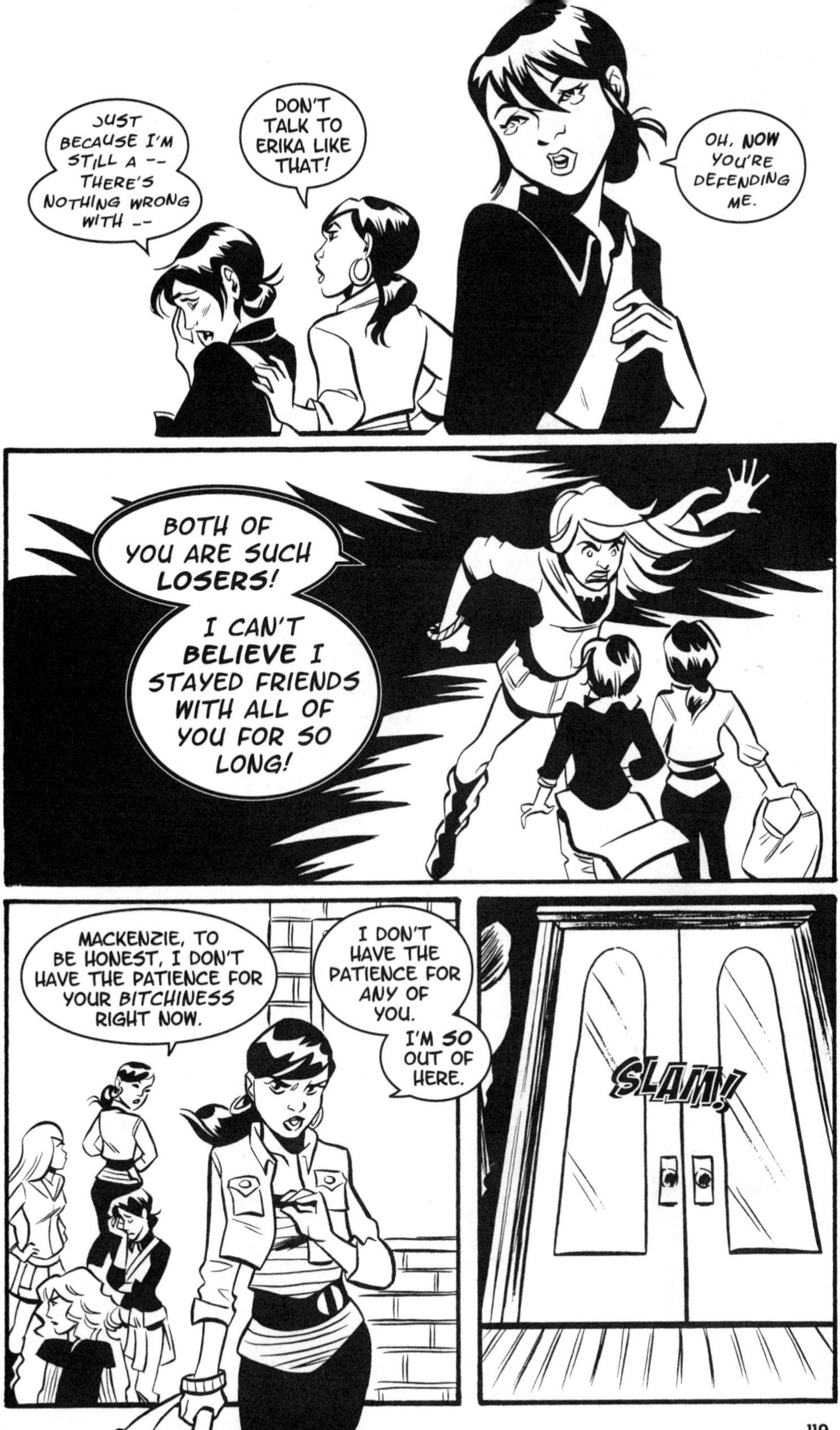
JUST BECAUSE I'M STILL A -- THERE'S NOTHING WRONG WITH --
DON'T TALK TO ERIKA LIKE THAT!
OH, NOW YOU'RE DEFENDING ME.
BOTH OF YOU ARE SUCH LOSERS!
I CAN'T BELIEVE I STAYED FRIENDS WITH ALL OF YOU FOR SO LONG!
MACKENZIE, TO BE HONEST, I DON'T HAVE THE PATIENCE FOR YOUR BITCHINESS RIGHT NOW.
I DON'T HAVE THE PATIENCE FOR ANY OF YOU.
I'M SO OUT OF HERE.
SLAM!

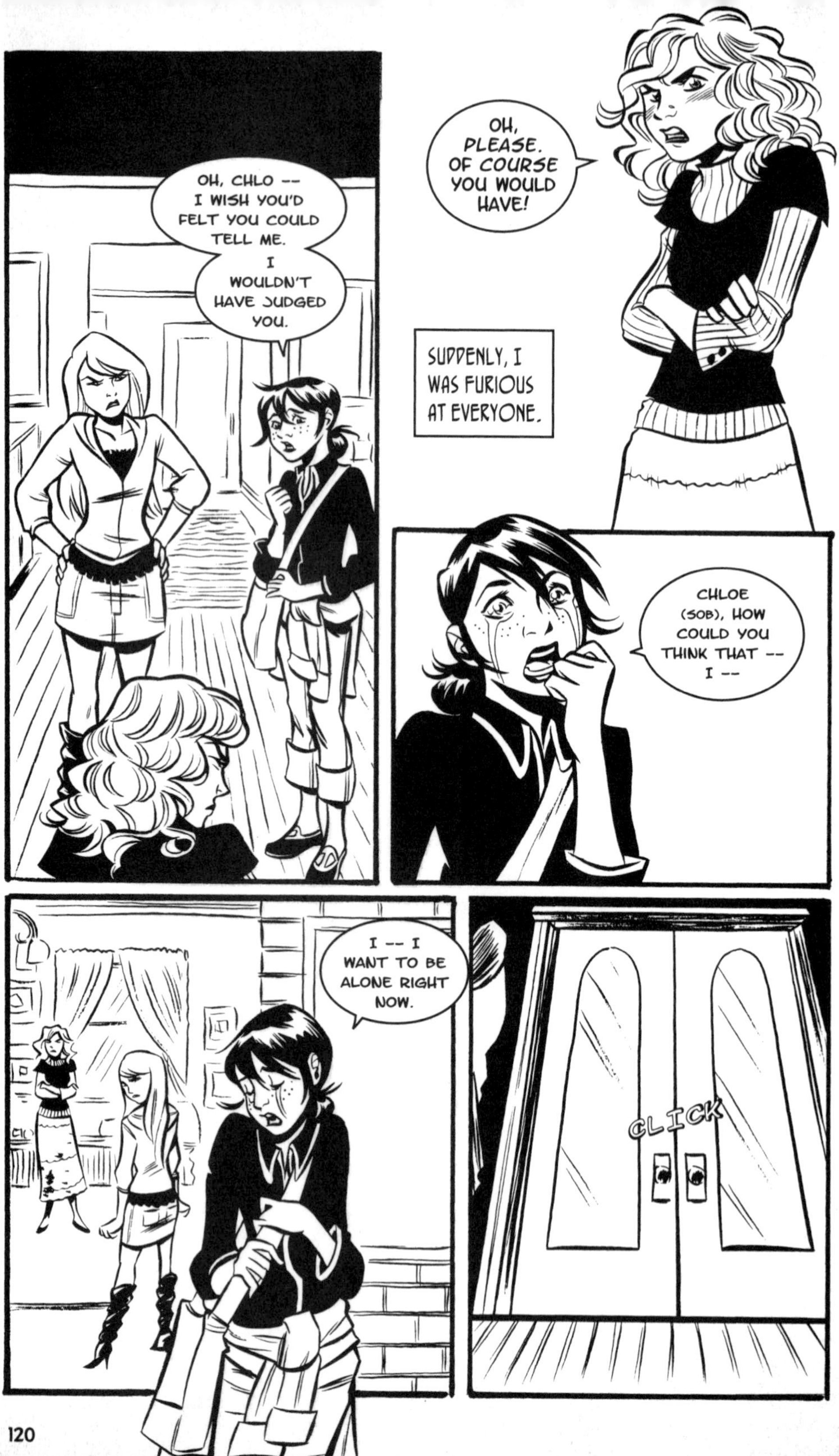
OH, CHLO -- I WISH YOU'D FELT YOU COULD TELL ME.
I WOULDN'T HAVE JUDGED YOU.
OH, PLEASE. OF COURSE YOU WOULD HAVE!
SUDDENLY, I WAS FURIOUS AT EVERYONE.
CHLOE (SOB), HOW COULD YOU THINK THAT -- I --
I -- I WANT TO BE ALONE RIGHT NOW.
CLICK

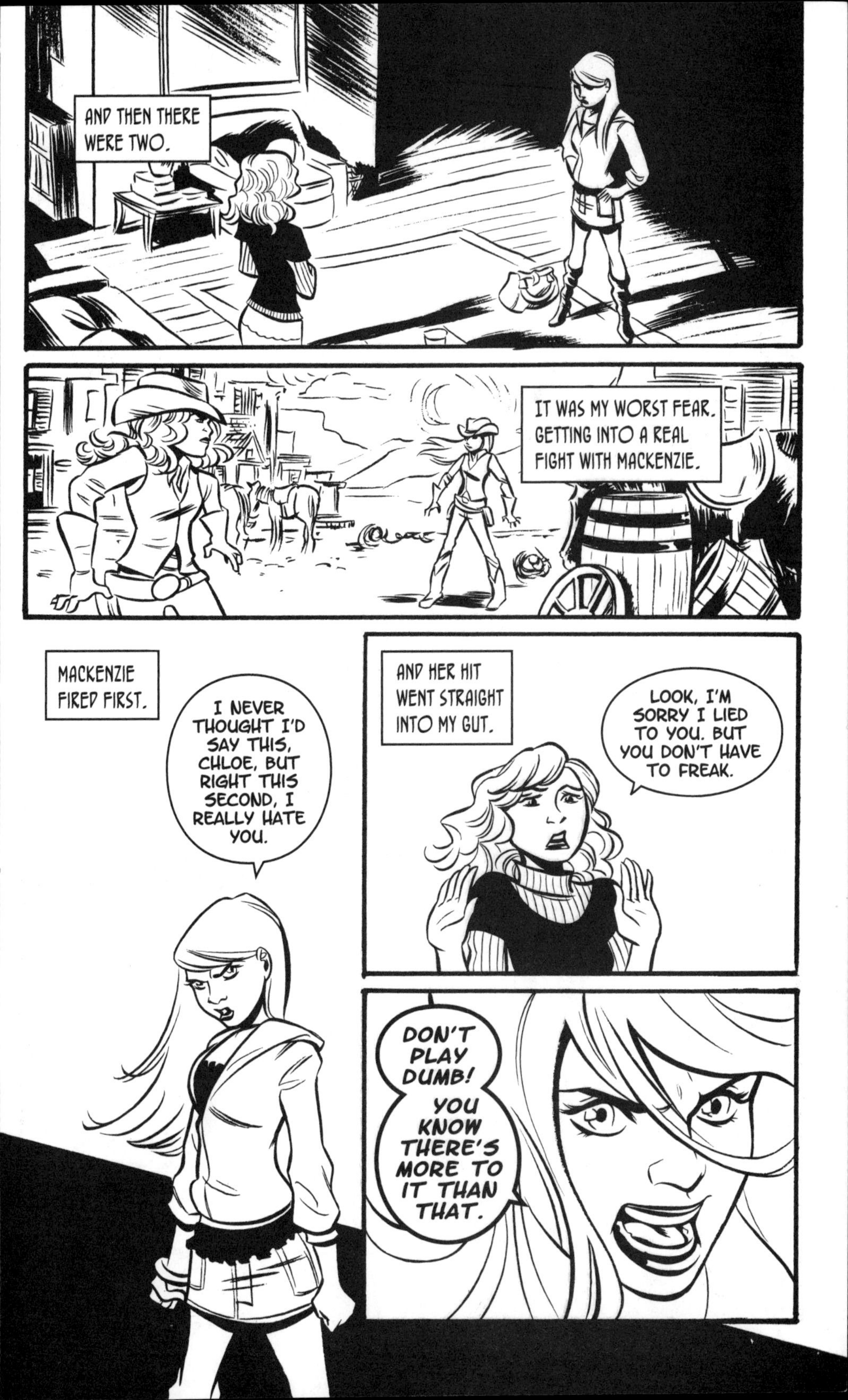
AND THEN THERE WERE TWO.
IT WAS MY WORST FEAR. GETTING INTO A REAL FIGHT WITH MACKENZIE.
MACKENZIE FIRED FIRST.
I NEVER THOUGHT I'D SAY THIS, CHLOE, BUT RIGHT THIS SECOND, I REALLY HATE YOU.
AND HER HIT WENT STRAIGHT INTO MY GUT.
LOOK, I'M SORRY I LIED TO YOU. BUT YOU DON'T HAVE TO FREAK.
DON'T PLAY DUMB!
YOU KNOW THERE'S MORE TO IT THAN THAT.

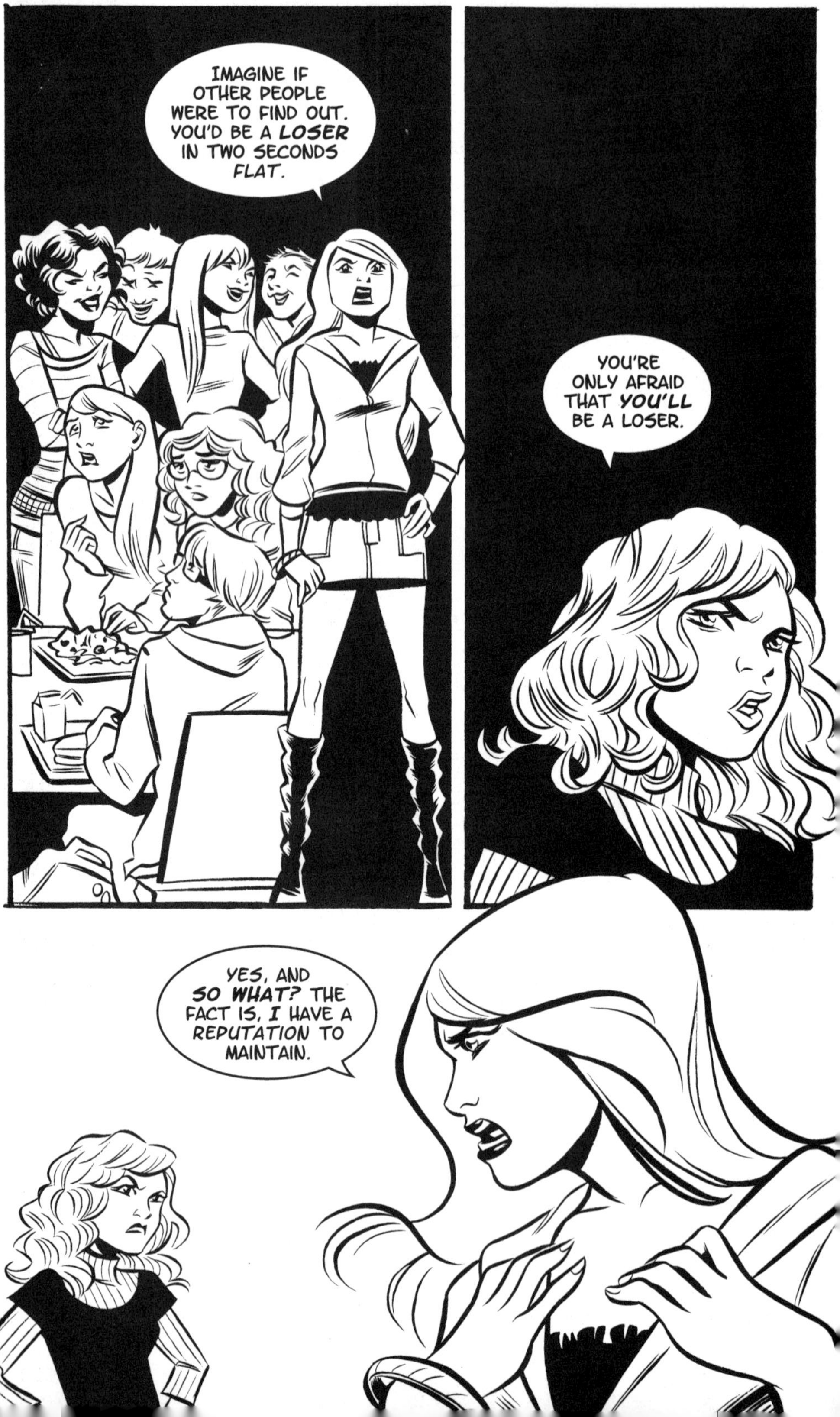
IMAGINE IF OTHER PEOPLE WERE TO FIND OUT. YOU'D BE A **LOSER** IN TWO SECONDS FLAT.
YOU'RE ONLY AFRAID THAT **YOU'LL** BE A LOSER.
YES, AND **SO WHAT?** THE FACT IS, **I** HAVE A REPUTATION TO MAINTAIN.

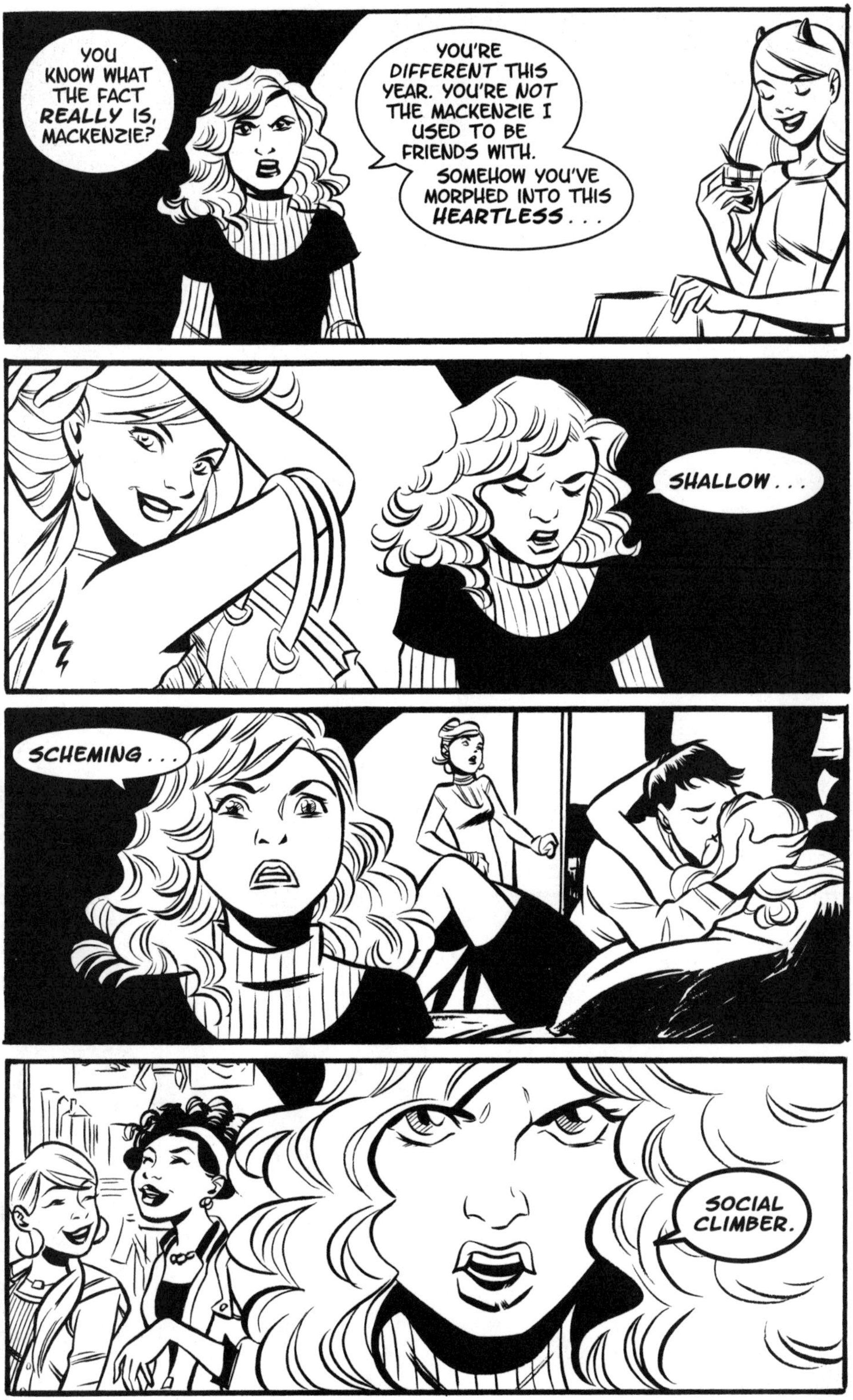
YOU KNOW WHAT THE FACT REALLY IS, MACKENZIE?
YOU'RE DIFFERENT THIS YEAR. YOU'RE NOT THE MACKENZIE I USED TO BE FRIENDS WITH.
SOMEHOW YOU'VE MORPHED INTO THIS HEARTLESS . . .
SHALLOW . . .
SCHEMING . . .
SOCIAL CLIMBER.

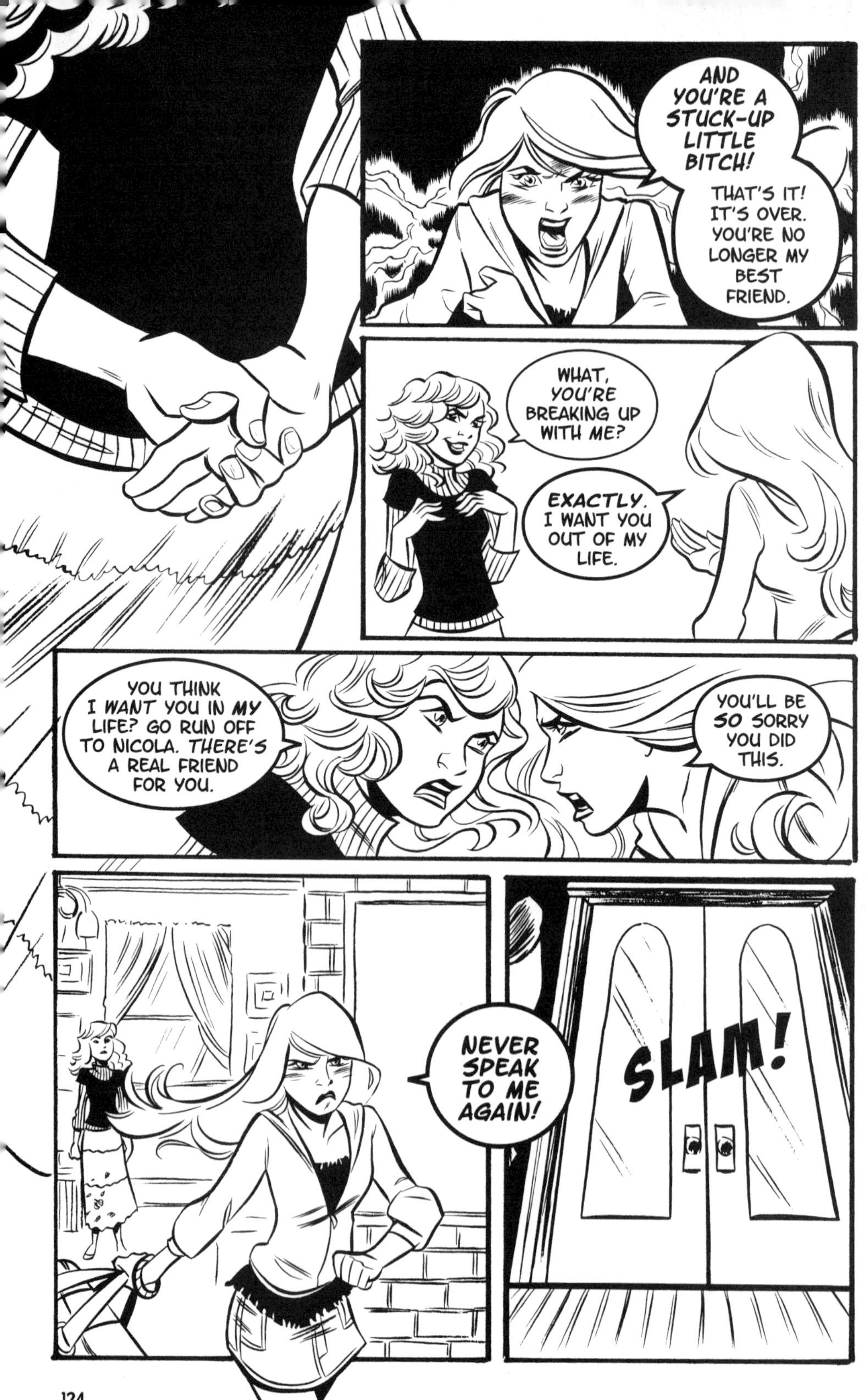
AND YOU'RE A STUCK-UP LITTLE BITCH!
THAT'S IT! IT'S OVER. YOU'RE NO LONGER MY BEST FRIEND.
WHAT, YOU'RE BREAKING UP WITH ME?
EXACTLY. I WANT YOU OUT OF MY LIFE.
YOU THINK I WANT YOU IN MY LIFE? GO RUN OFF TO NICOLA. THERE'S A REAL FRIEND FOR YOU.
YOU'LL BE SO SORRY YOU DID THIS.
NEVER SPEAK TO ME AGAIN!
SLAM!

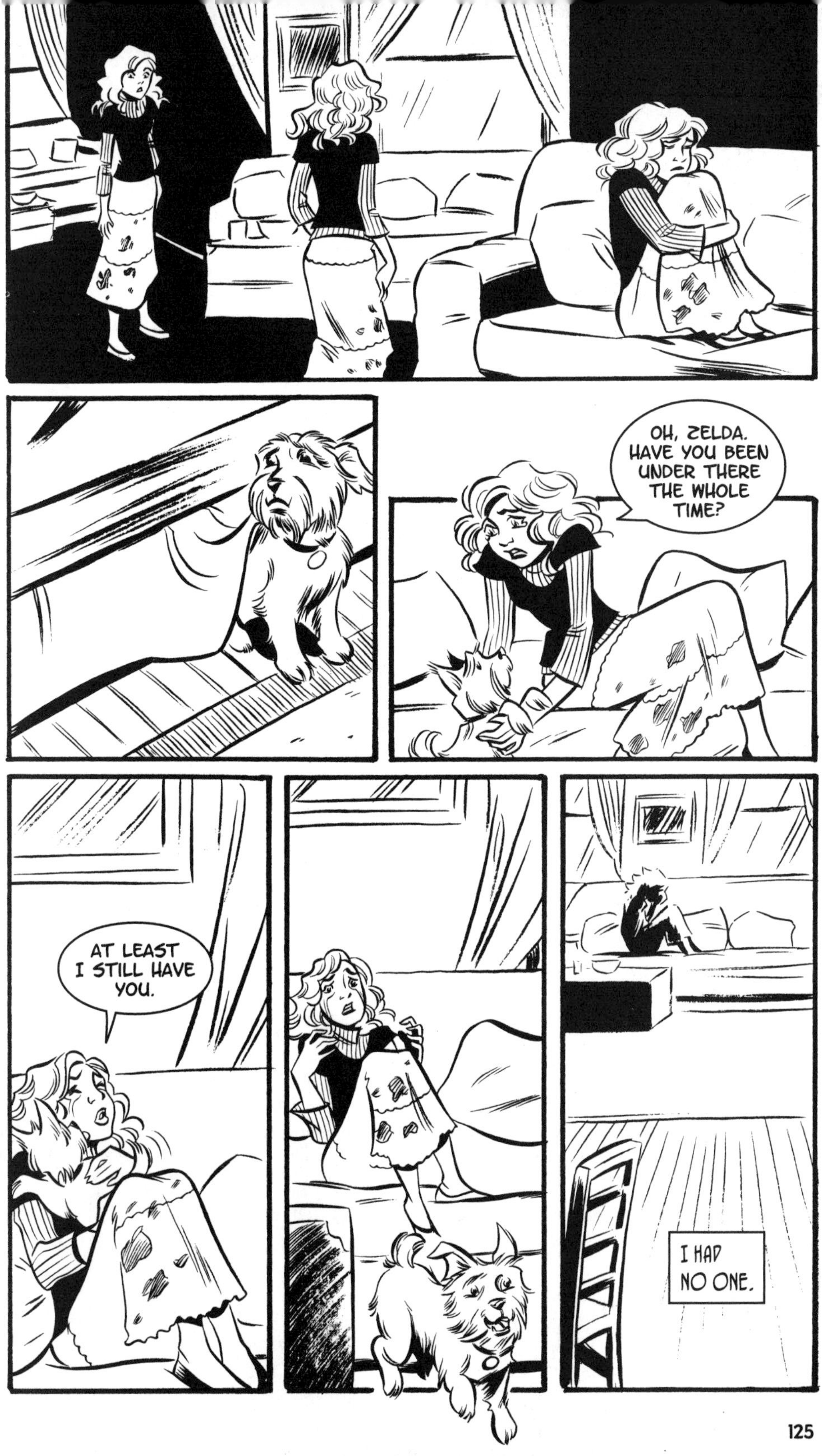
OH, ZELDA. HAVE YOU BEEN UNDER THERE THE WHOLE TIME?
AT LEAST I STILL HAVE YOU.
I HAD NO ONE.

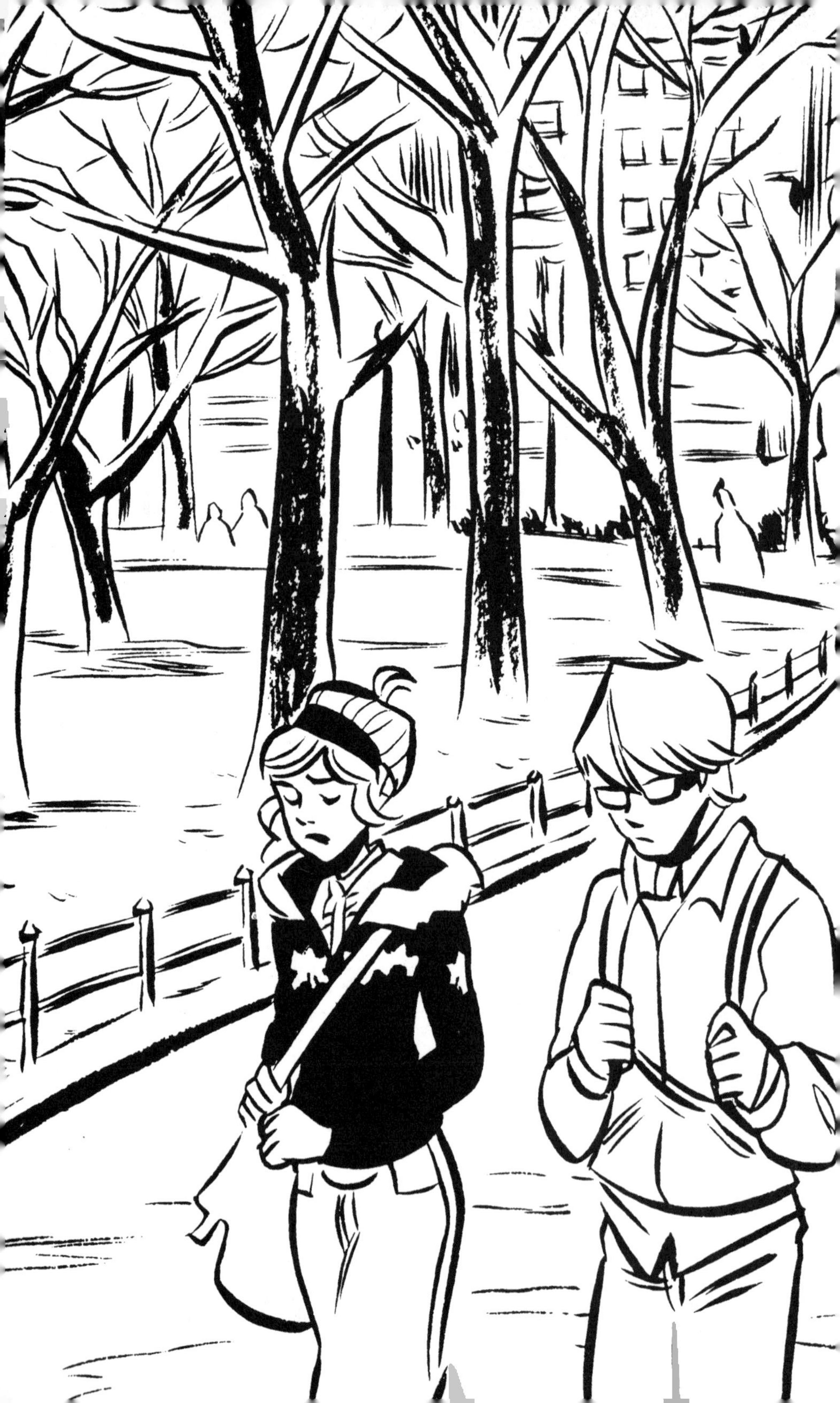

Chapter 9: The Way We Were

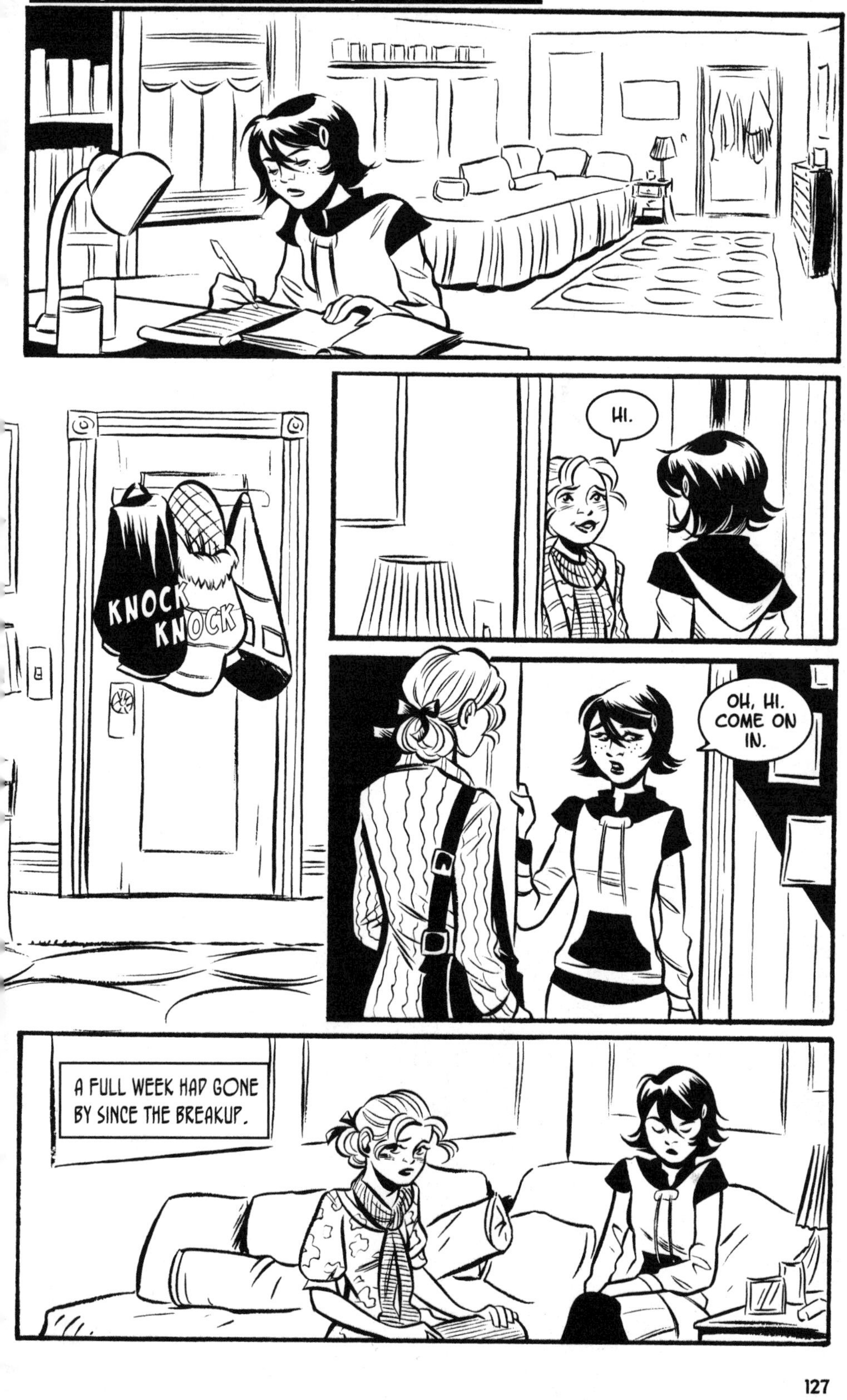
KNOCK KNOCK
HI.
OH, HI. COME ON IN.
A FULL WEEK HAD GONE BY SINCE THE BREAKUP.

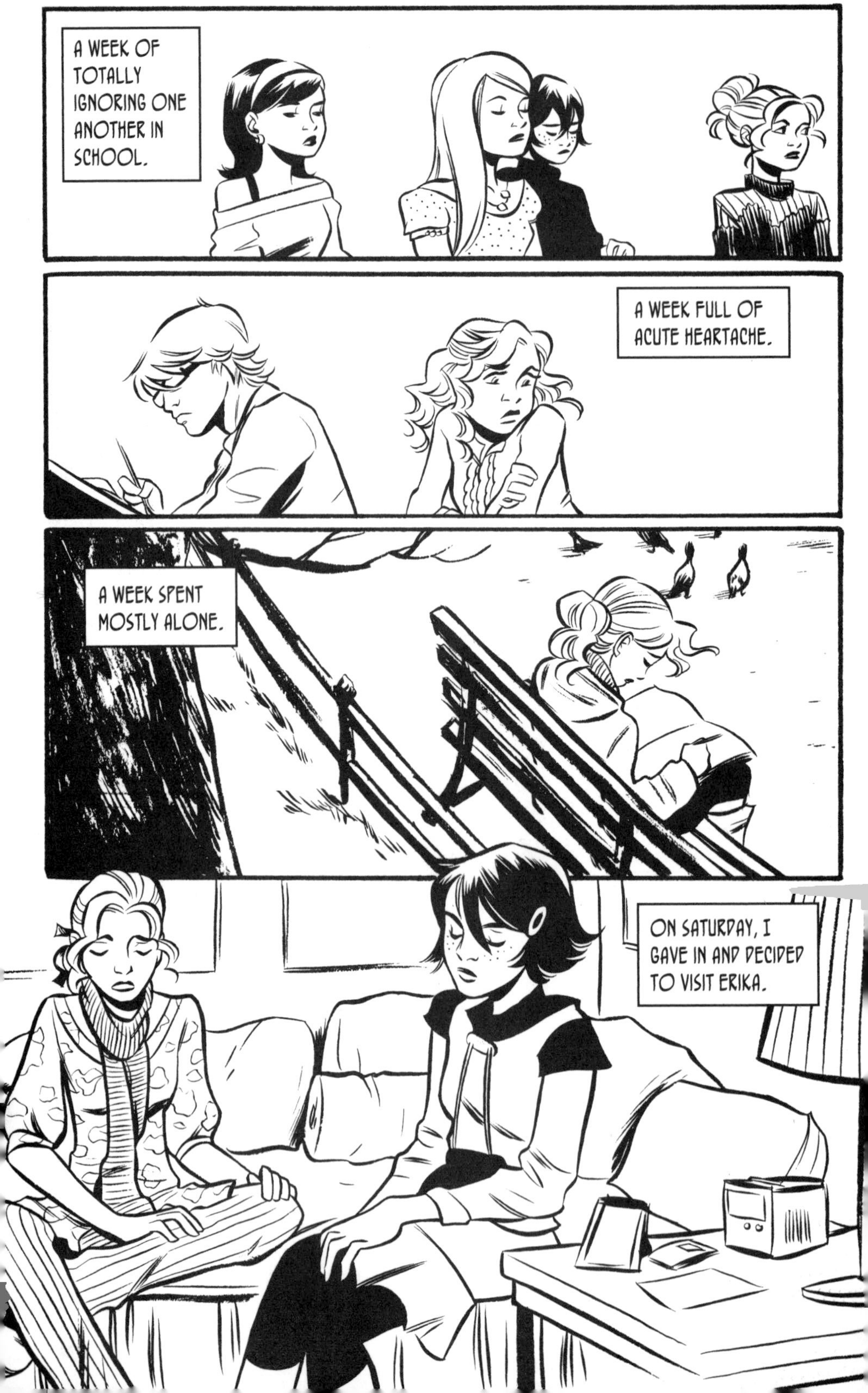
A WEEK OF TOTALLY IGNORING ONE ANOTHER IN SCHOOL.
A WEEK FULL OF ACUTE HEARTACHE.
A WEEK SPENT MOSTLY ALONE.
ON SATURDAY, I GAVE IN AND DECIDED TO VISIT ERIKA.

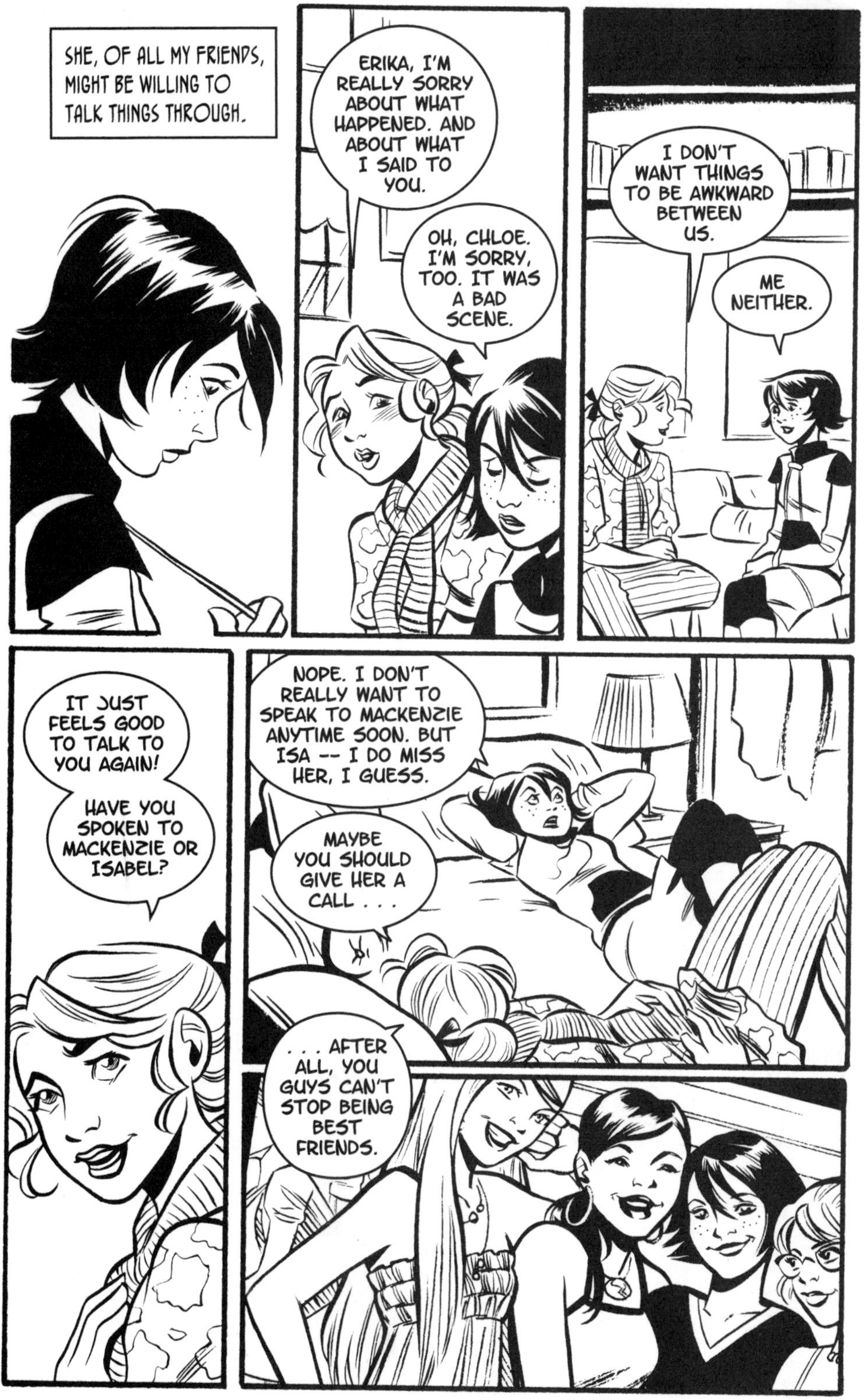
SHE, OF ALL MY FRIENDS, MIGHT BE WILLING TO TALK THINGS THROUGH.
ERIKA, I'M REALLY SORRY ABOUT WHAT HAPPENED. AND ABOUT WHAT I SAID TO YOU.
OH, CHLOE. I'M SORRY, TOO. IT WAS A BAD SCENE.
I DON'T WANT THINGS TO BE AWKWARD BETWEEN US.
ME NEITHER.
IT JUST FEELS GOOD TO TALK TO YOU AGAIN!
HAVE YOU SPOKEN TO MACKENZIE OR ISABEL?
NOPE. I DON'T REALLY WANT TO SPEAK TO MACKENZIE ANYTIME SOON. BUT ISA -- I DO MISS HER, I GUESS.
MAYBE YOU SHOULD GIVE HER A CALL . . .
. . . AFTER ALL, YOU GUYS CAN'T STOP BEING BEST FRIENDS.

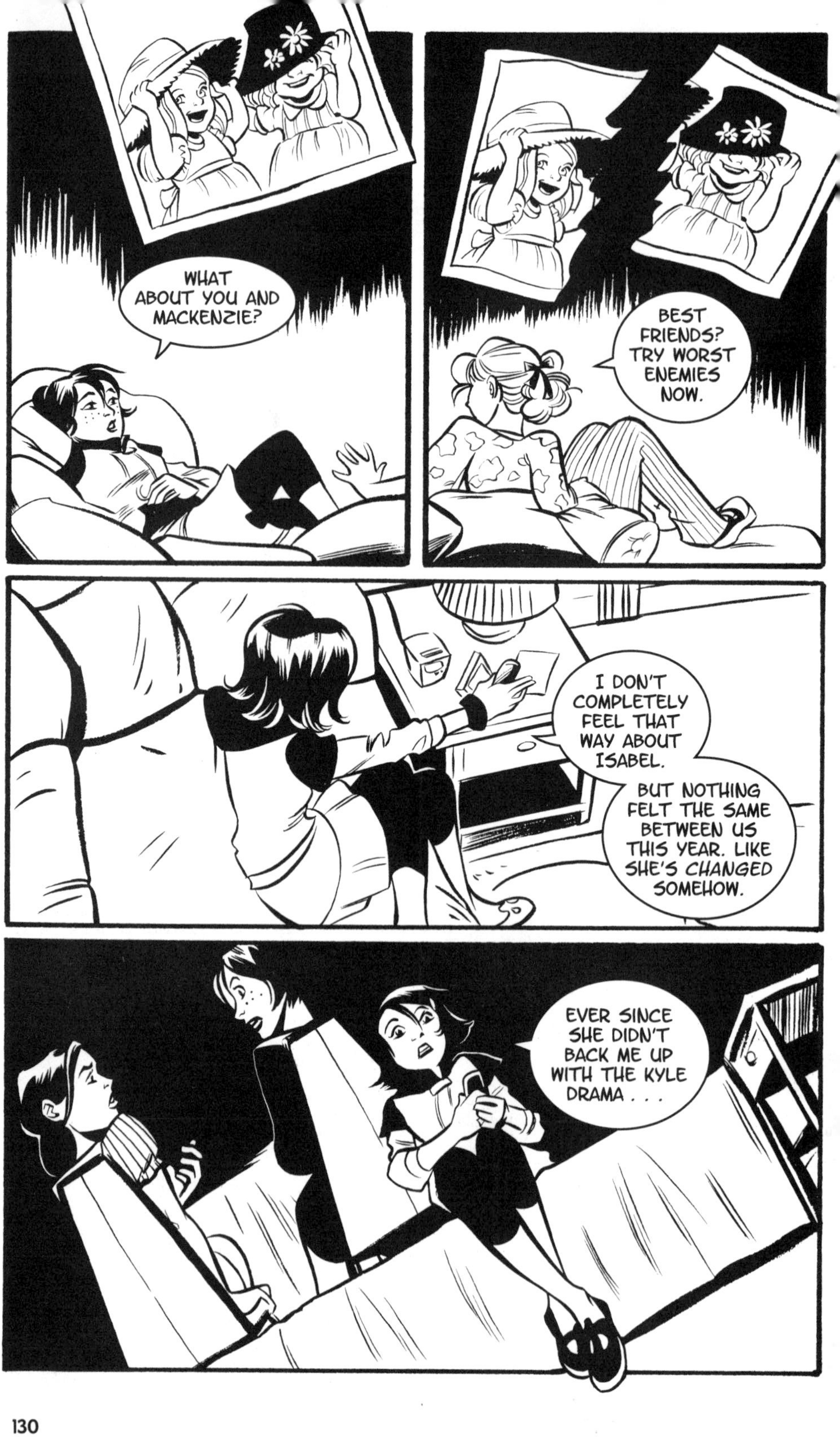
WHAT ABOUT YOU AND MACKENZIE?
BEST FRIENDS? TRY WORST ENEMIES NOW.
I DON'T COMPLETELY FEEL THAT WAY ABOUT ISABEL.
BUT NOTHING FELT THE SAME BETWEEN US THIS YEAR. LIKE SHE'S *CHANGED* SOMEHOW.
EVER SINCE SHE DIDN'T BACK ME UP WITH THE KYLE DRAMA . . .

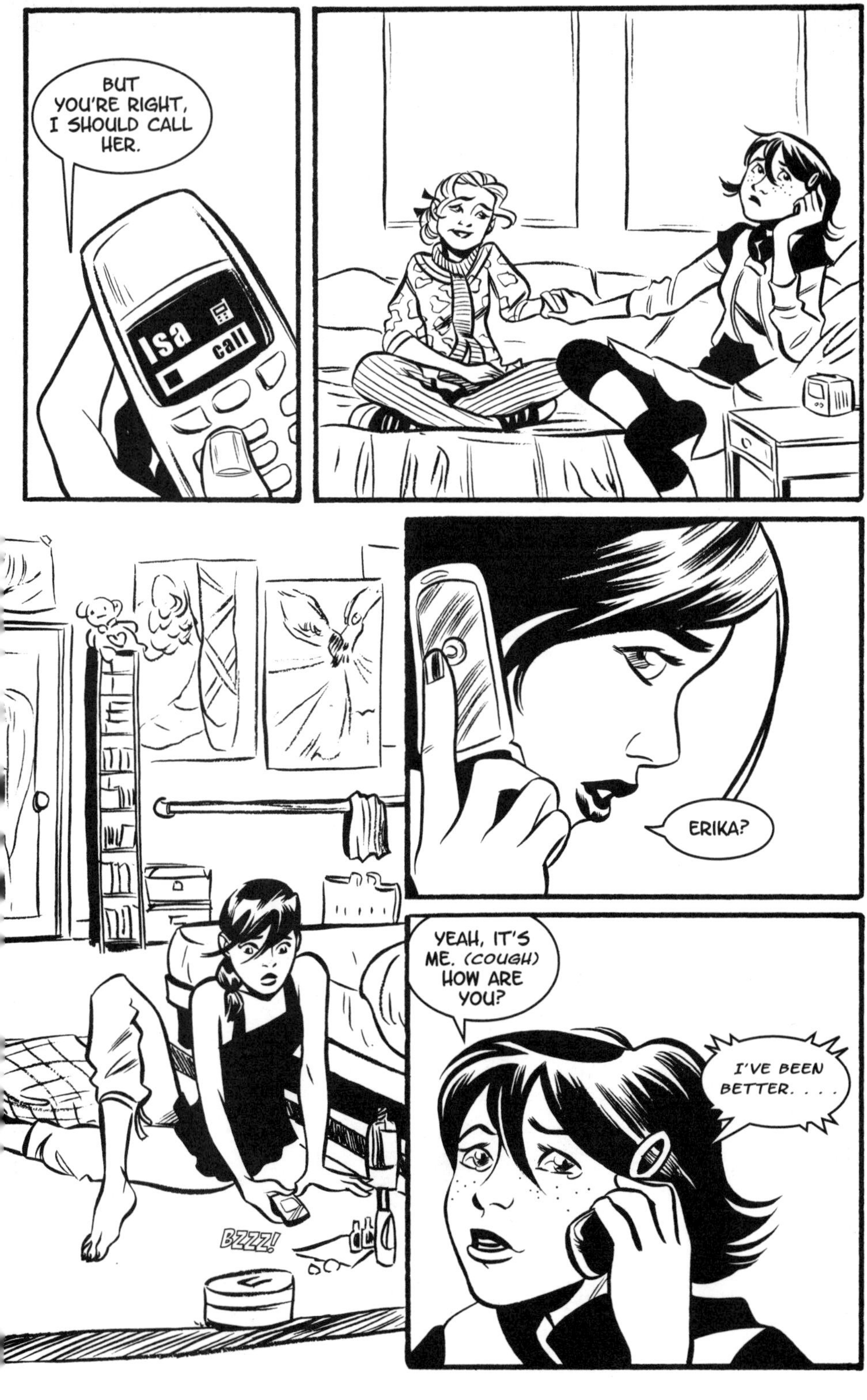
BUT YOU'RE RIGHT, I SHOULD CALL HER.
Isa
call
ERIKA?
BZZZ!
YEAH, IT'S ME. (COUGH) HOW ARE YOU?
I'VE BEEN BETTER. . . .

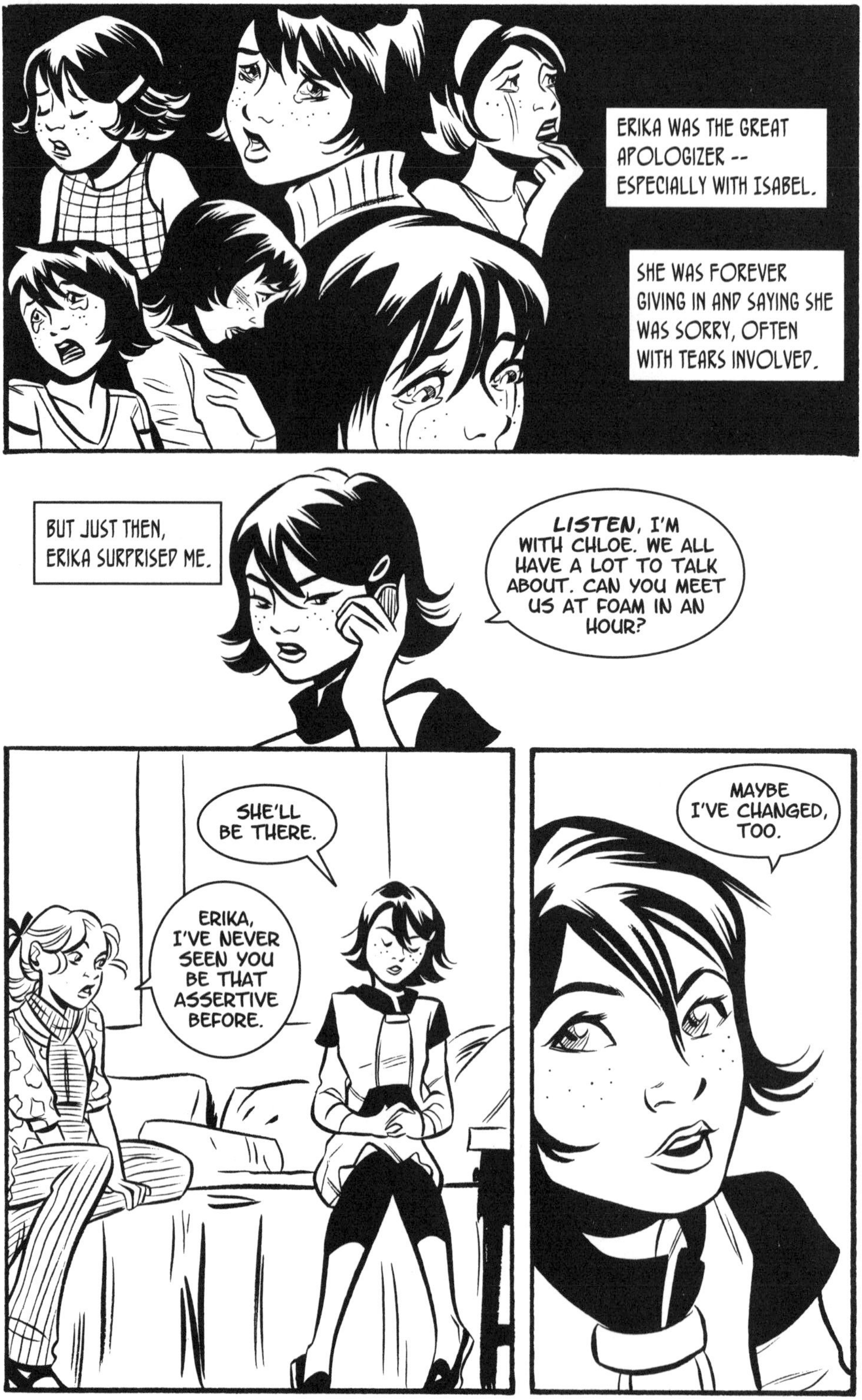
ERIKA WAS THE GREAT APOLOGIZER -- ESPECIALLY WITH ISABEL.
SHE WAS FOREVER GIVING IN AND SAYING SHE WAS SORRY, OFTEN WITH TEARS INVOLVED.
BUT JUST THEN, ERIKA SURPRISED ME.
LISTEN, I'M WITH CHLOE. WE ALL HAVE A LOT TO TALK ABOUT. CAN YOU MEET US AT FOAM IN AN HOUR?
SHE'LL BE THERE.
ERIKA, I'VE NEVER SEEN YOU BE THAT ASSERTIVE BEFORE.
MAYBE I'VE CHANGED, TOO.

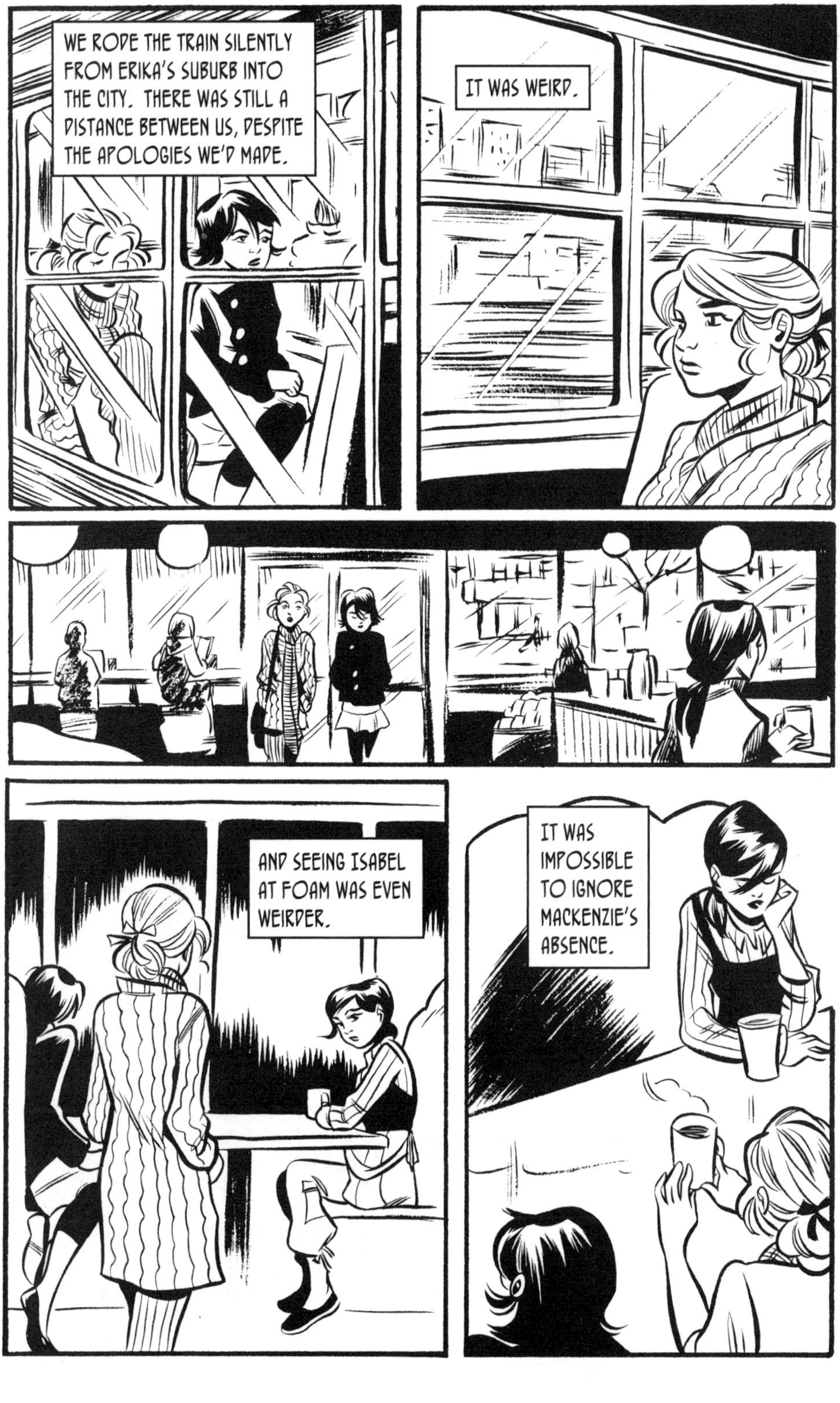
WE RODE THE TRAIN SILENTLY FROM ERIKA'S SUBURB INTO THE CITY. THERE WAS STILL A DISTANCE BETWEEN US, DESPITE THE APOLOGIES WE'D MADE.
IT WAS WEIRD.
AND SEEING ISABEL AT FOAM WAS EVEN WEIRDER.
IT WAS IMPOSSIBLE TO IGNORE MACKENZIE'S ABSENCE.

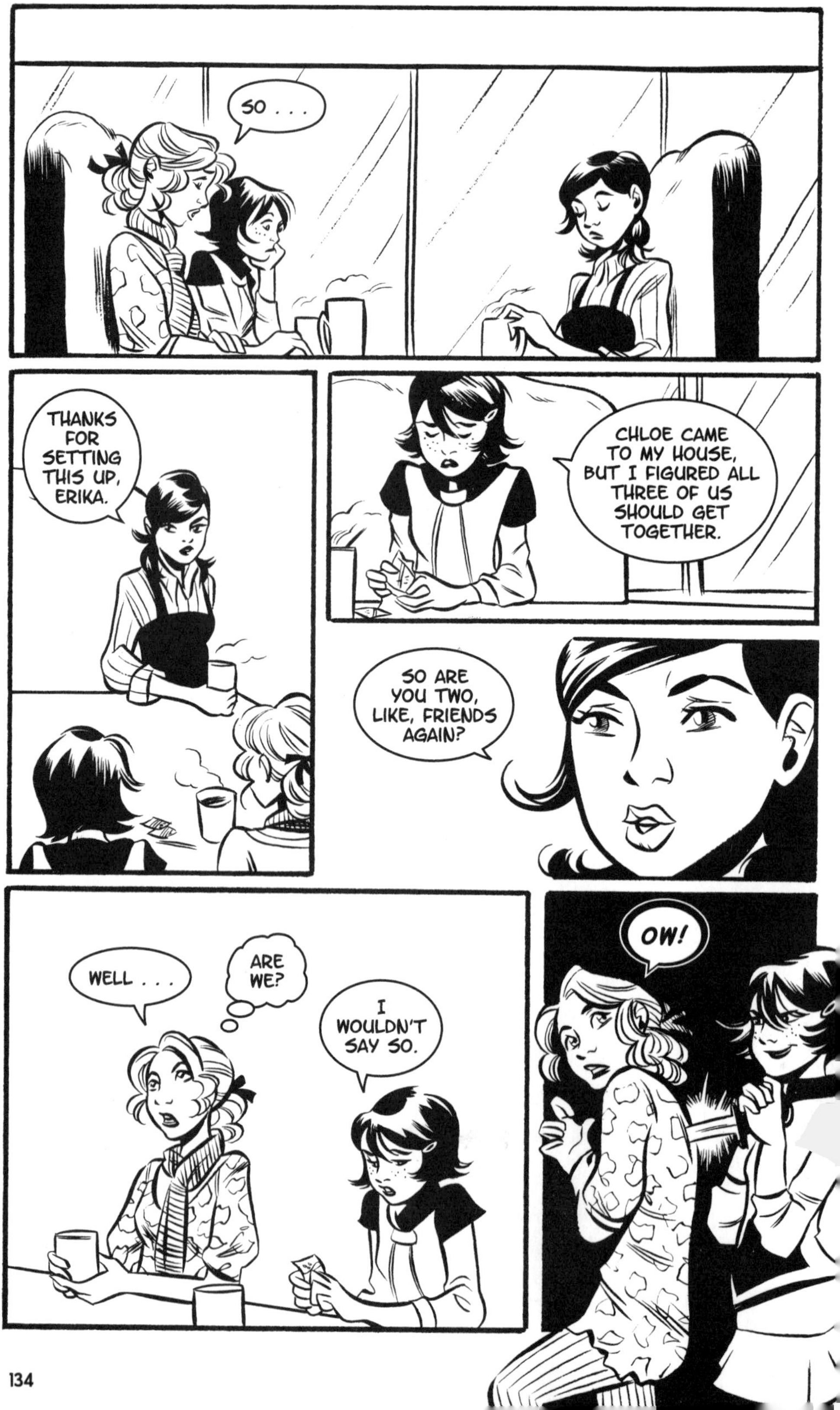
SO . . .
THANKS FOR SETTING THIS UP, ERIKA.
CHLOE CAME TO MY HOUSE, BUT I FIGURED ALL THREE OF US SHOULD GET TOGETHER.
SO ARE YOU TWO, LIKE, FRIENDS AGAIN?
WELL . . .
ARE WE?
I WOULDN'T SAY SO.
OW!

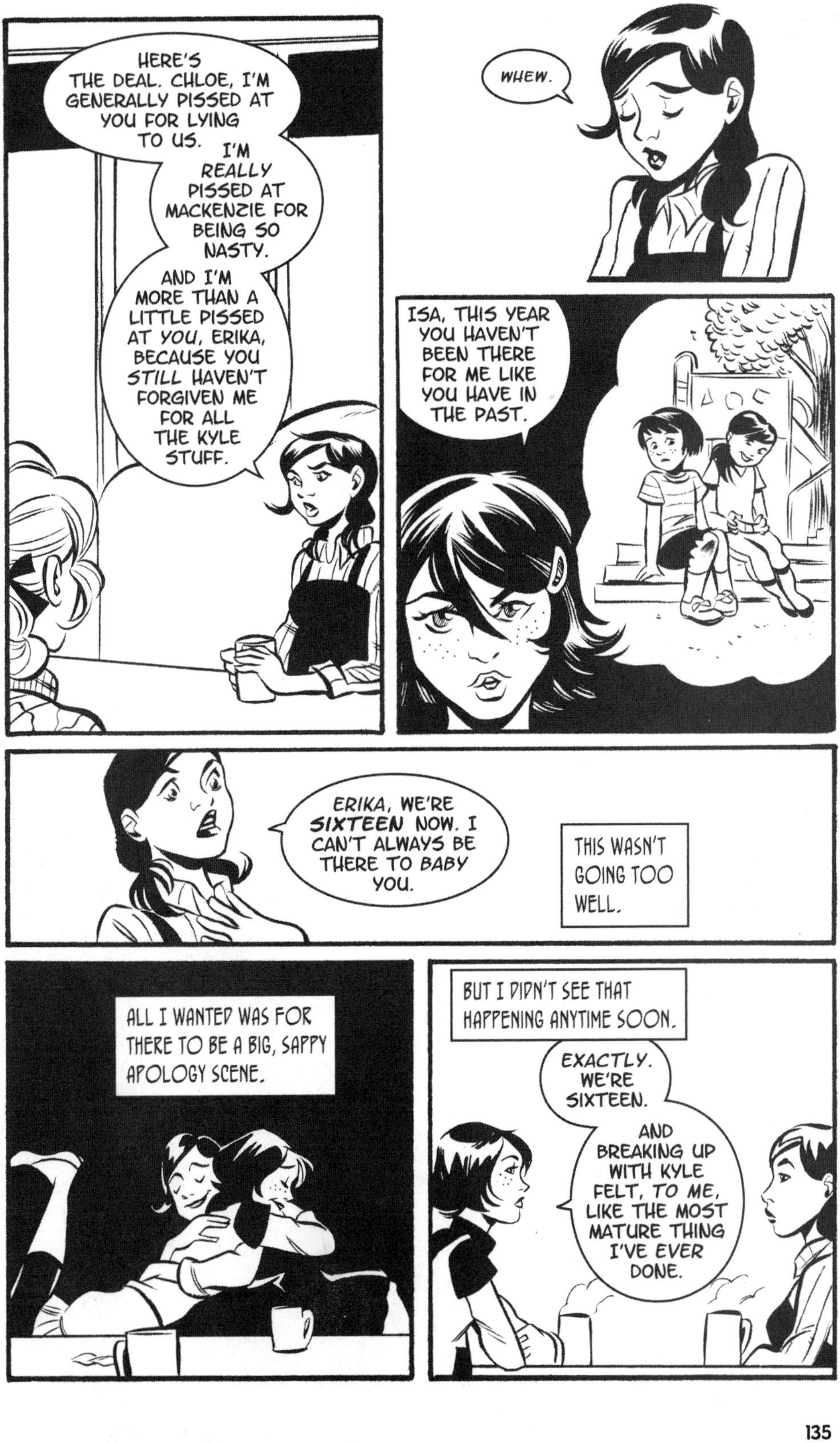
HERE'S THE DEAL. CHLOE, I'M GENERALLY PISSED AT YOU FOR LYING TO US.
I'M REALLY PISSED AT MACKENZIE FOR BEING SO NASTY.
AND I'M MORE THAN A LITTLE PISSED AT YOU, ERIKA, BECAUSE YOU STILL HAVEN'T FORGIVEN ME FOR ALL THE KYLE STUFF.
WHEW.
ISA, THIS YEAR YOU HAVEN'T BEEN THERE FOR ME LIKE YOU HAVE IN THE PAST.
ERIKA, WE'RE SIXTEEN NOW. I CAN'T ALWAYS BE THERE TO BABY YOU.
THIS WASN'T GOING TOO WELL.
ALL I WANTED WAS FOR THERE TO BE A BIG, SAPPY APOLOGY SCENE.
BUT I DIDN'T SEE THAT HAPPENING ANYTIME SOON.
EXACTLY. WE'RE SIXTEEN.
AND BREAKING UP WITH KYLE FELT, TO ME, LIKE THE MOST MATURE THING I'VE EVER DONE.

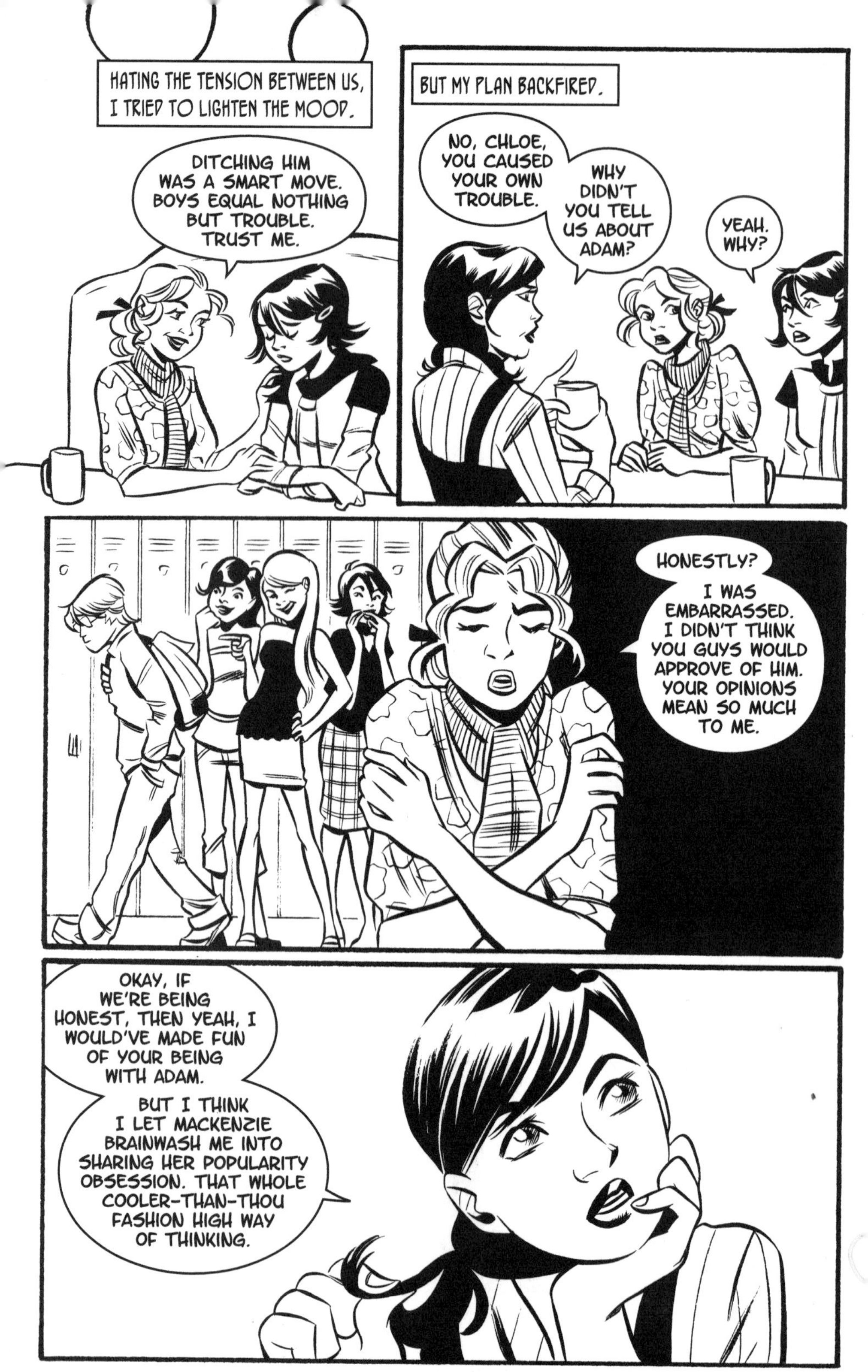
HATING THE TENSION BETWEEN US, I TRIED TO LIGHTEN THE MOOD.
DITCHING HIM WAS A SMART MOVE. BOYS EQUAL NOTHING BUT TROUBLE. TRUST ME.
BUT MY PLAN BACKFIRED.
NO, CHLOE, YOU CAUSED YOUR OWN TROUBLE.
WHY DIDN'T YOU TELL US ABOUT ADAM?
YEAH. WHY?
HONESTLY?
I WAS EMBARRASSED. I DIDN'T THINK YOU GUYS WOULD APPROVE OF HIM. YOUR OPINIONS MEAN SO MUCH TO ME.
OKAY, IF WE'RE BEING HONEST, THEN YEAH, I WOULD'VE MADE FUN OF YOUR BEING WITH ADAM.
BUT I THINK I LET MACKENZIE BRAINWASH ME INTO SHARING HER POPULARITY OBSESSION. THAT WHOLE COOLER-THAN-THOU FASHION HIGH WAY OF THINKING.

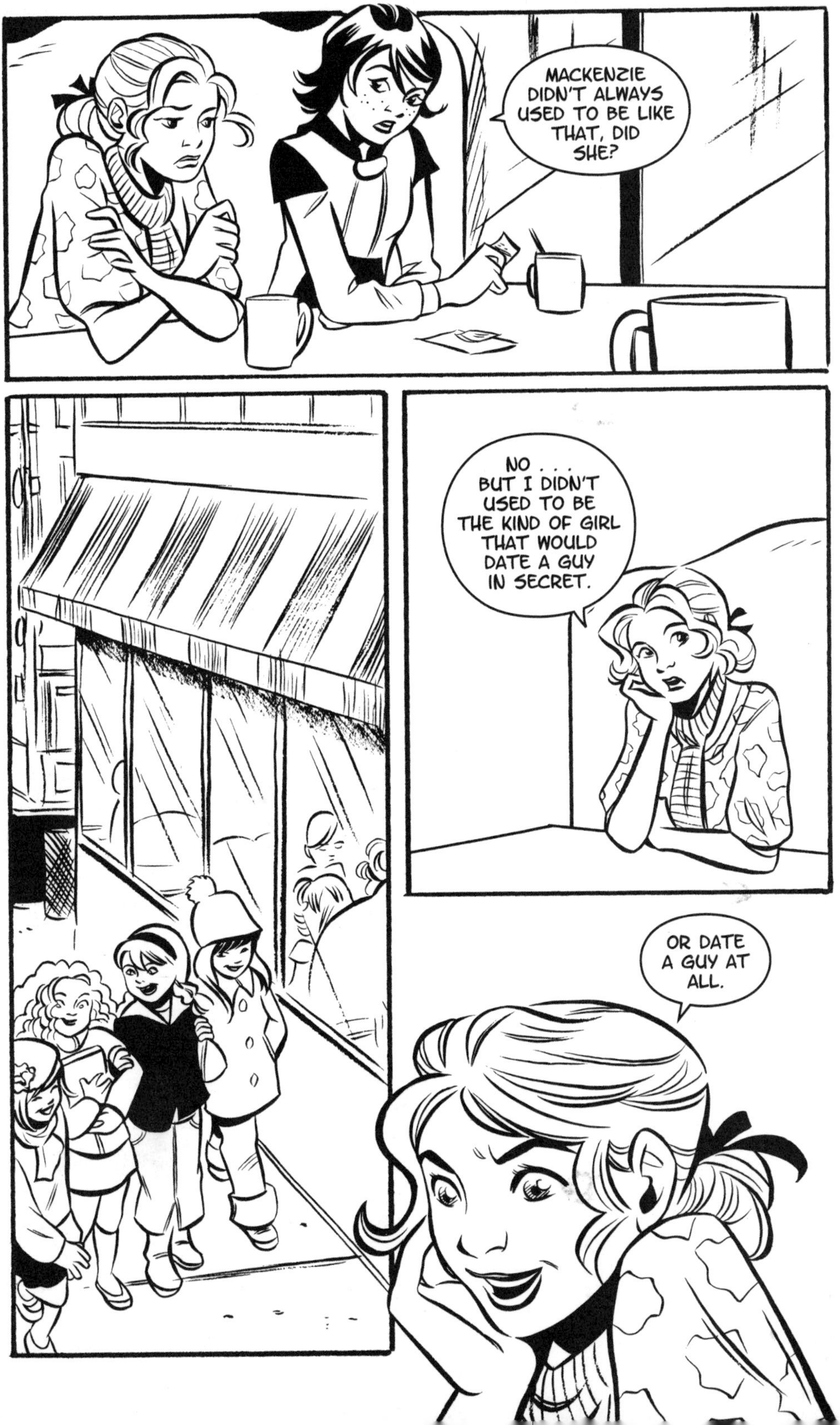
MACKENZIE DIDN'T ALWAYS USED TO BE LIKE THAT, DID SHE?
NO . . . BUT I DIDN'T USED TO BE THE KIND OF GIRL THAT WOULD DATE A GUY IN SECRET.
OR DATE A GUY AT ALL.

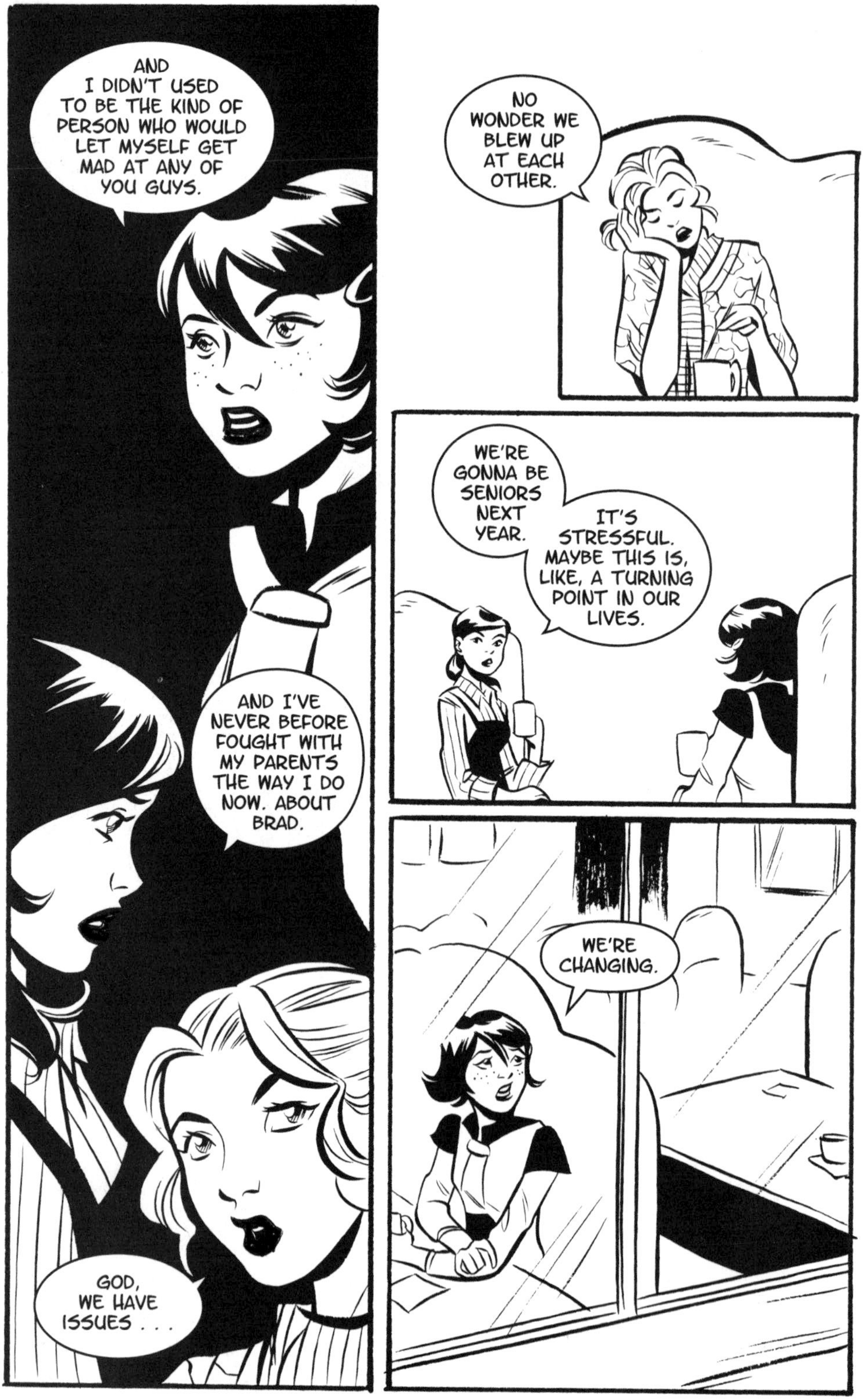
AND I DIDN'T USED TO BE THE KIND OF PERSON WHO WOULD LET MYSELF GET MAD AT ANY OF YOU GUYS.
AND I'VE NEVER BEFORE FOUGHT WITH MY PARENTS THE WAY I DO NOW. ABOUT BRAD.
GOD, WE HAVE ISSUES . . .
NO WONDER WE BLEW UP AT EACH OTHER.
WE'RE GONNA BE SENIORS NEXT YEAR.
IT'S STRESSFUL. MAYBE THIS IS, LIKE, A TURNING POINT IN OUR LIVES.
WE'RE CHANGING.

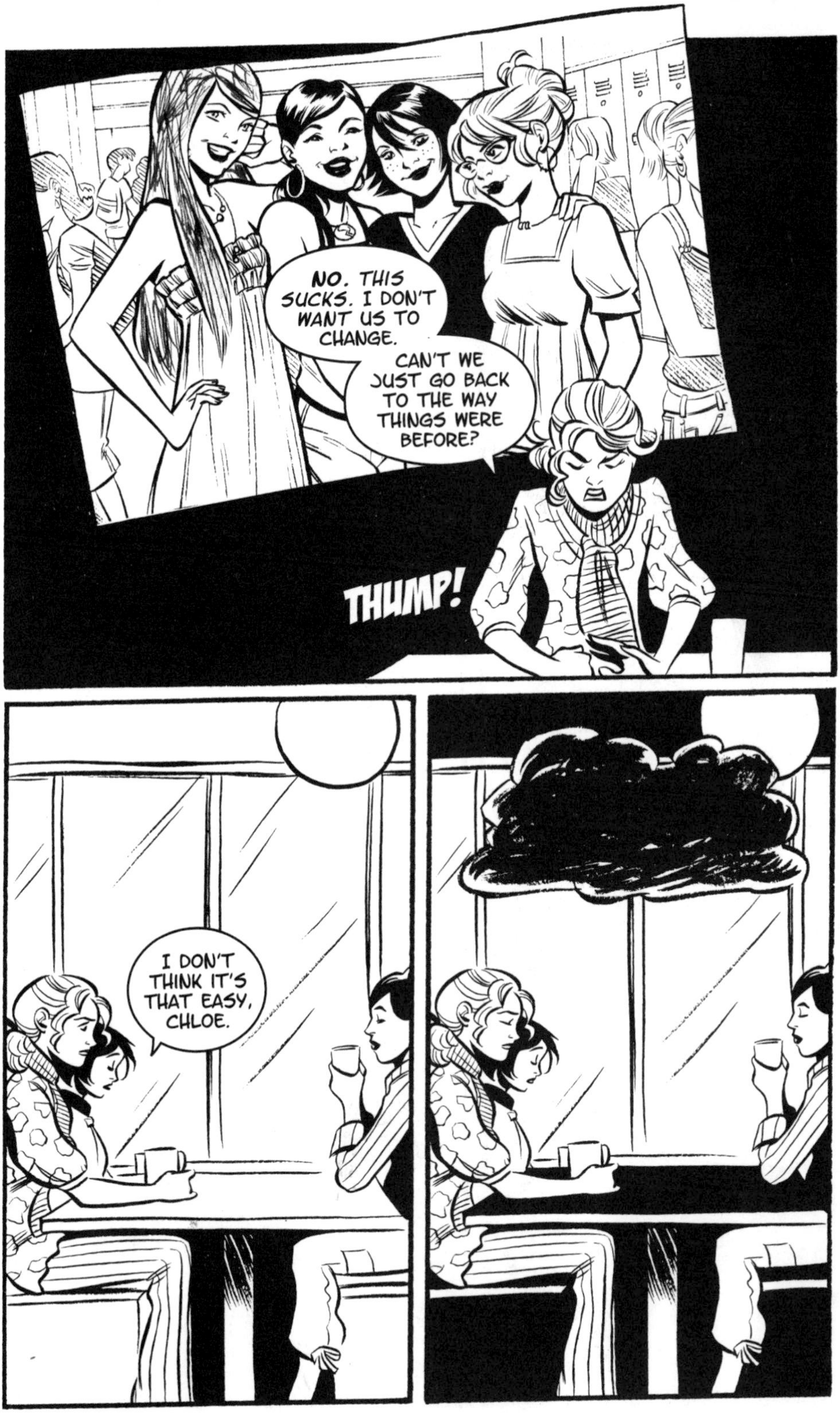
NO. THIS SUCKS. I DON'T WANT US TO CHANGE.
CAN'T WE JUST GO BACK TO THE WAY THINGS WERE BEFORE?
THUMP!
I DON'T THINK IT'S THAT EASY, CHLOE.

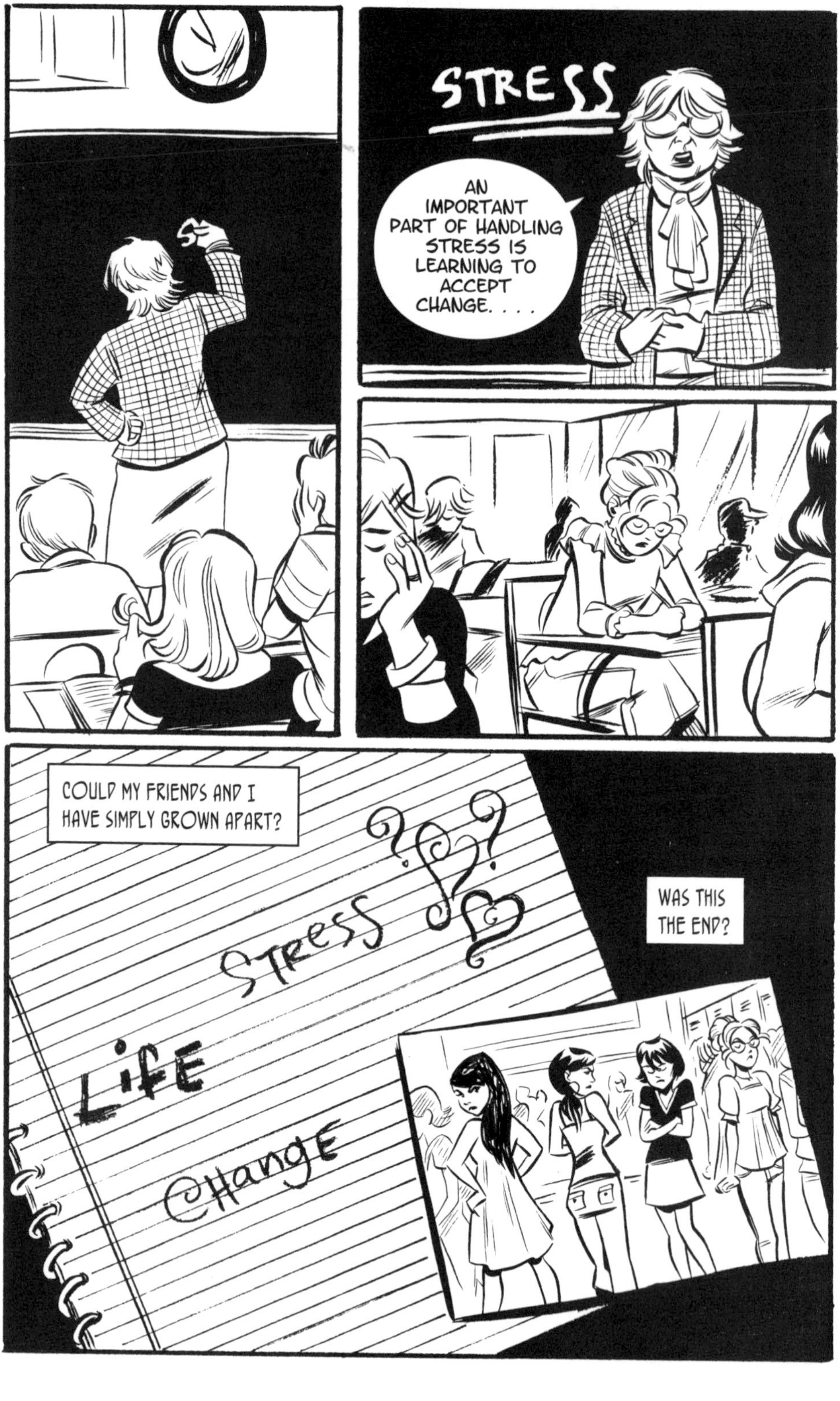
STRESS
AN IMPORTANT PART OF HANDLING STRESS IS LEARNING TO ACCEPT CHANGE. . . .
COULD MY FRIENDS AND I HAVE SIMPLY GROWN APART?
WAS THIS THE END?
STRESS
LIFE
CHANGE

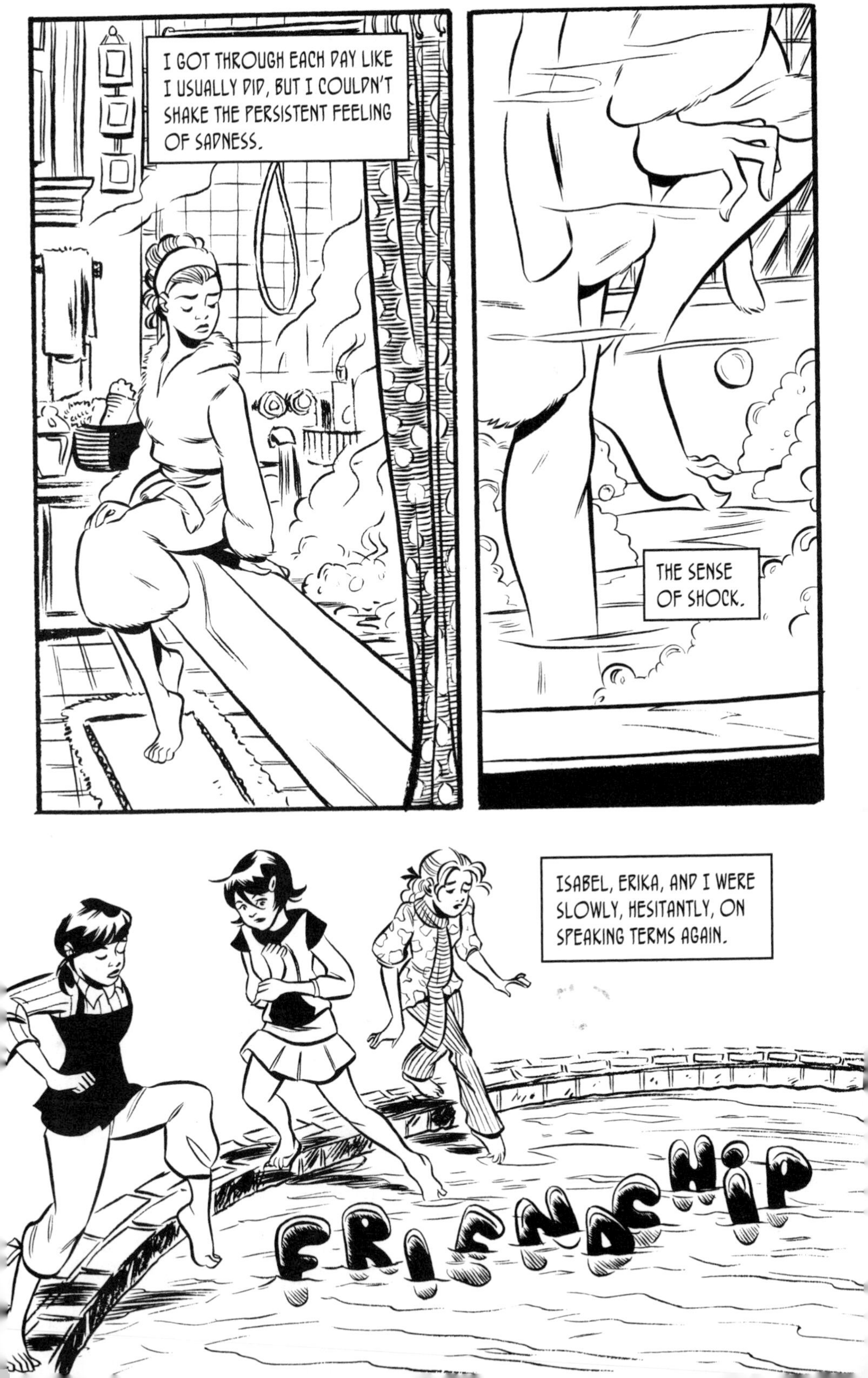
I GOT THROUGH EACH DAY LIKE I USUALLY DID, BUT I COULDN'T SHAKE THE PERSISTENT FEELING OF SADNESS.
THE SENSE OF SHOCK.
ISABEL, ERIKA, AND I WERE SLOWLY, HESITANTLY, ON SPEAKING TERMS AGAIN.
FRIENDSHIP

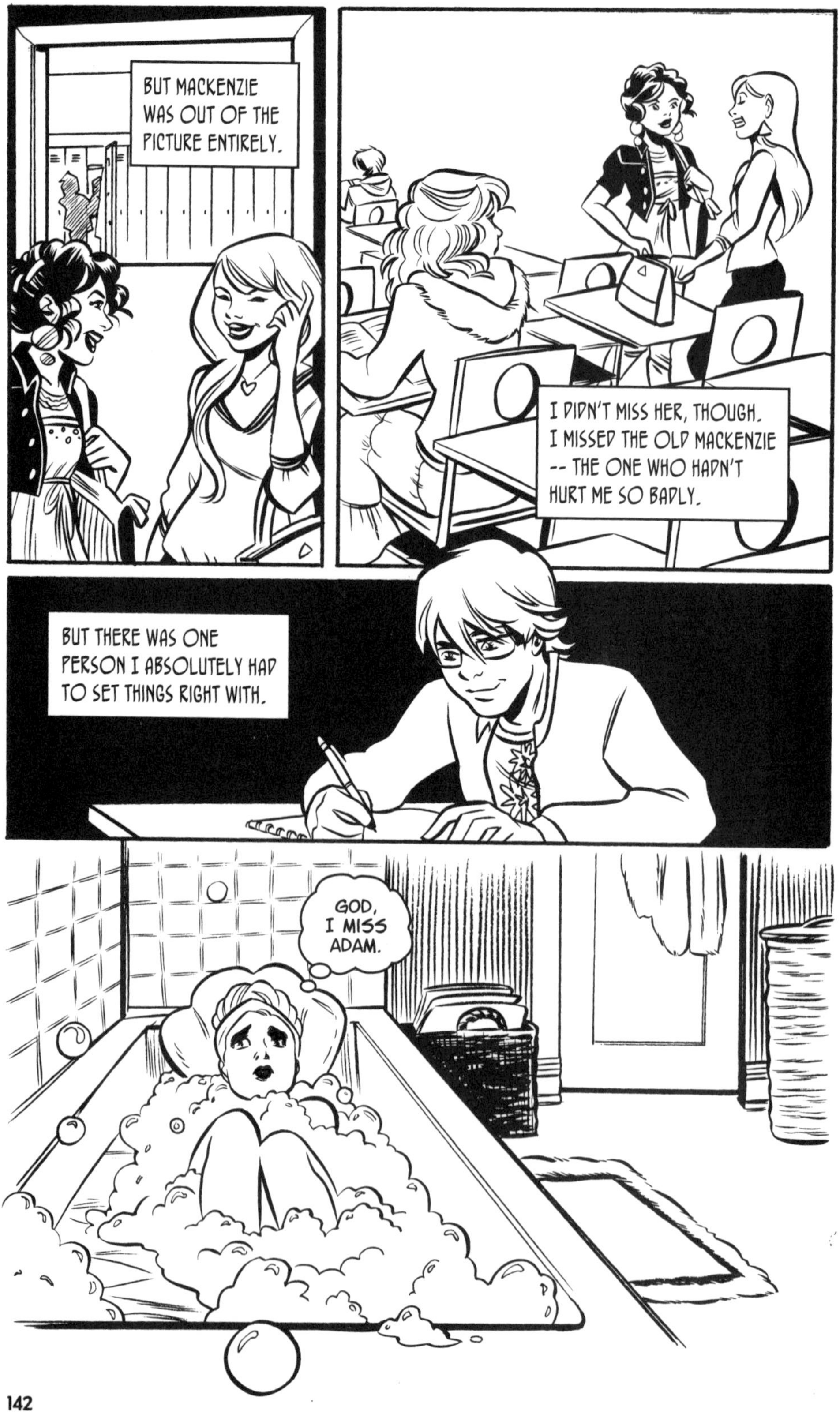
BUT MACKENZIE WAS OUT OF THE PICTURE ENTIRELY.
I DIDN'T MISS HER, THOUGH. I MISSED THE OLD MACKENZIE -- THE ONE WHO HADN'T HURT ME SO BADLY.
BUT THERE WAS ONE PERSON I ABSOLUTELY HAD TO SET THINGS RIGHT WITH.
GOD, I MISS ADAM.

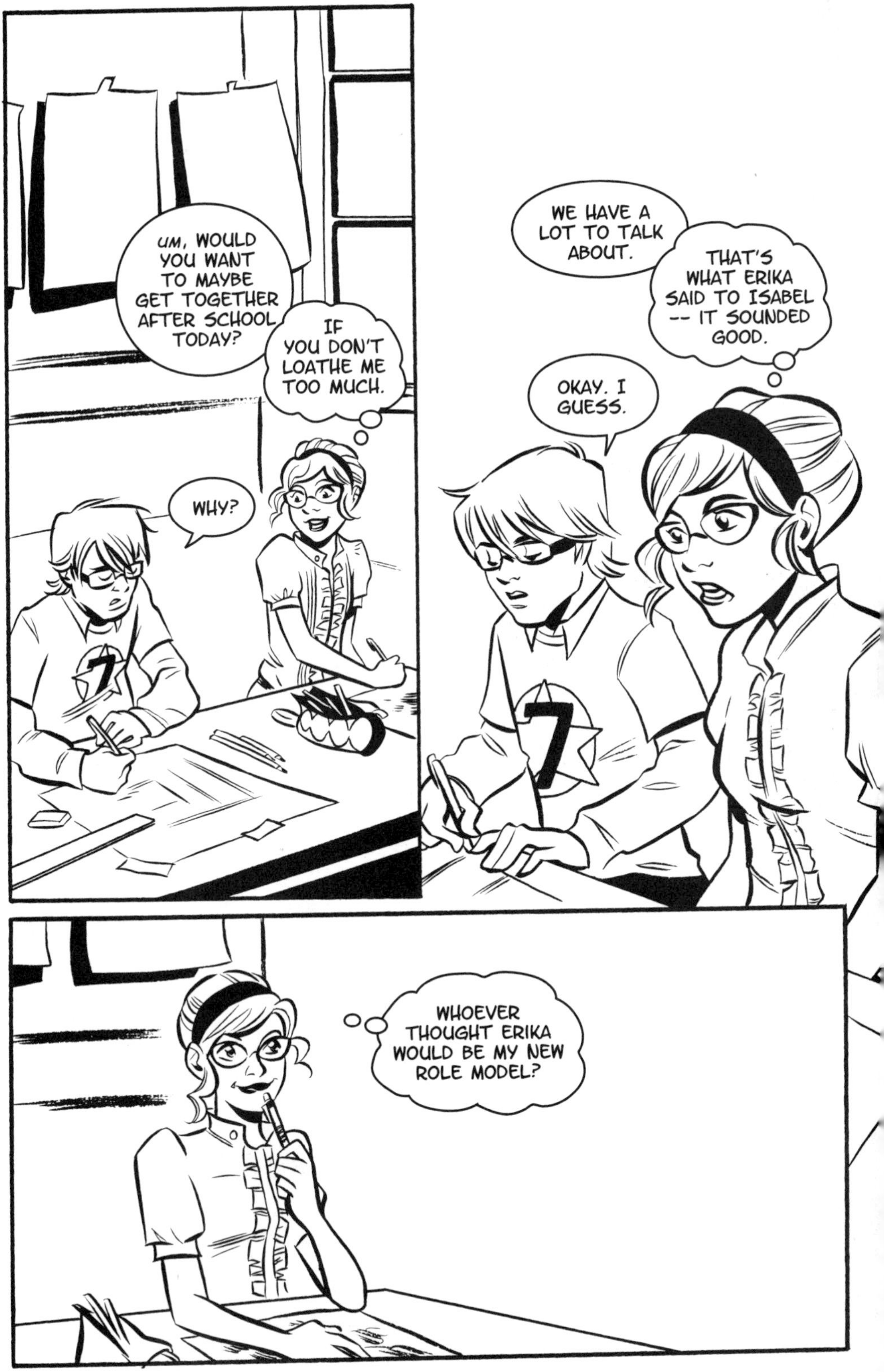
UM, WOULD YOU WANT TO MAYBE GET TOGETHER AFTER SCHOOL TODAY?
IF YOU DON'T LOATHE ME TOO MUCH.
WHY?
WE HAVE A LOT TO TALK ABOUT.
THAT'S WHAT ERIKA SAID TO ISABEL -- IT SOUNDED GOOD.
OKAY. I GUESS.
WHOEVER THOUGHT ERIKA WOULD BE MY NEW ROLE MODEL?

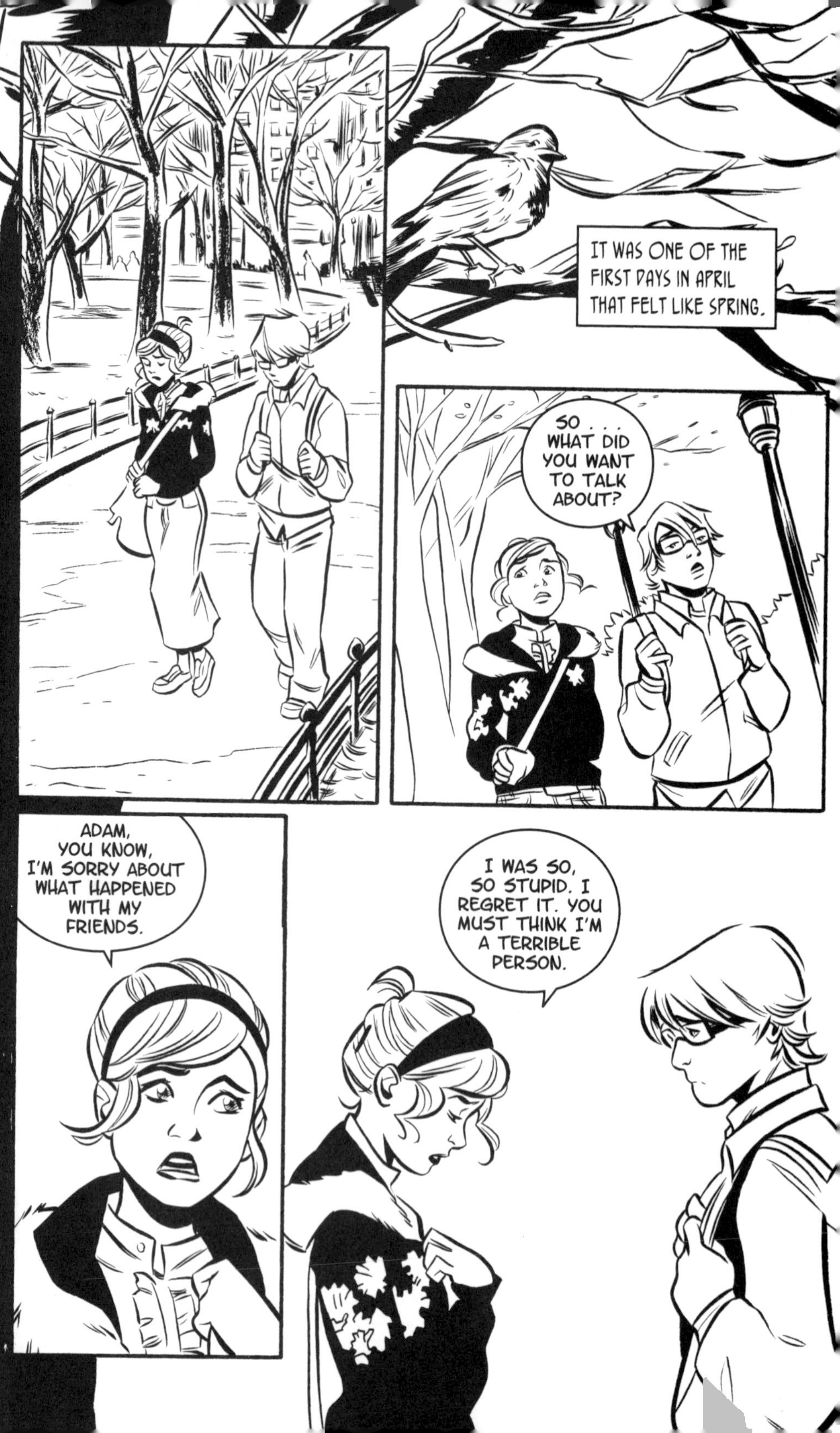
IT WAS ONE OF THE FIRST DAYS IN APRIL THAT FELT LIKE SPRING.
SO . . . WHAT DID YOU WANT TO TALK ABOUT?
ADAM, YOU KNOW, I'M SORRY ABOUT WHAT HAPPENED WITH MY FRIENDS.
I WAS SO, SO STUPID. I REGRET IT. YOU MUST THINK I'M A TERRIBLE PERSON.

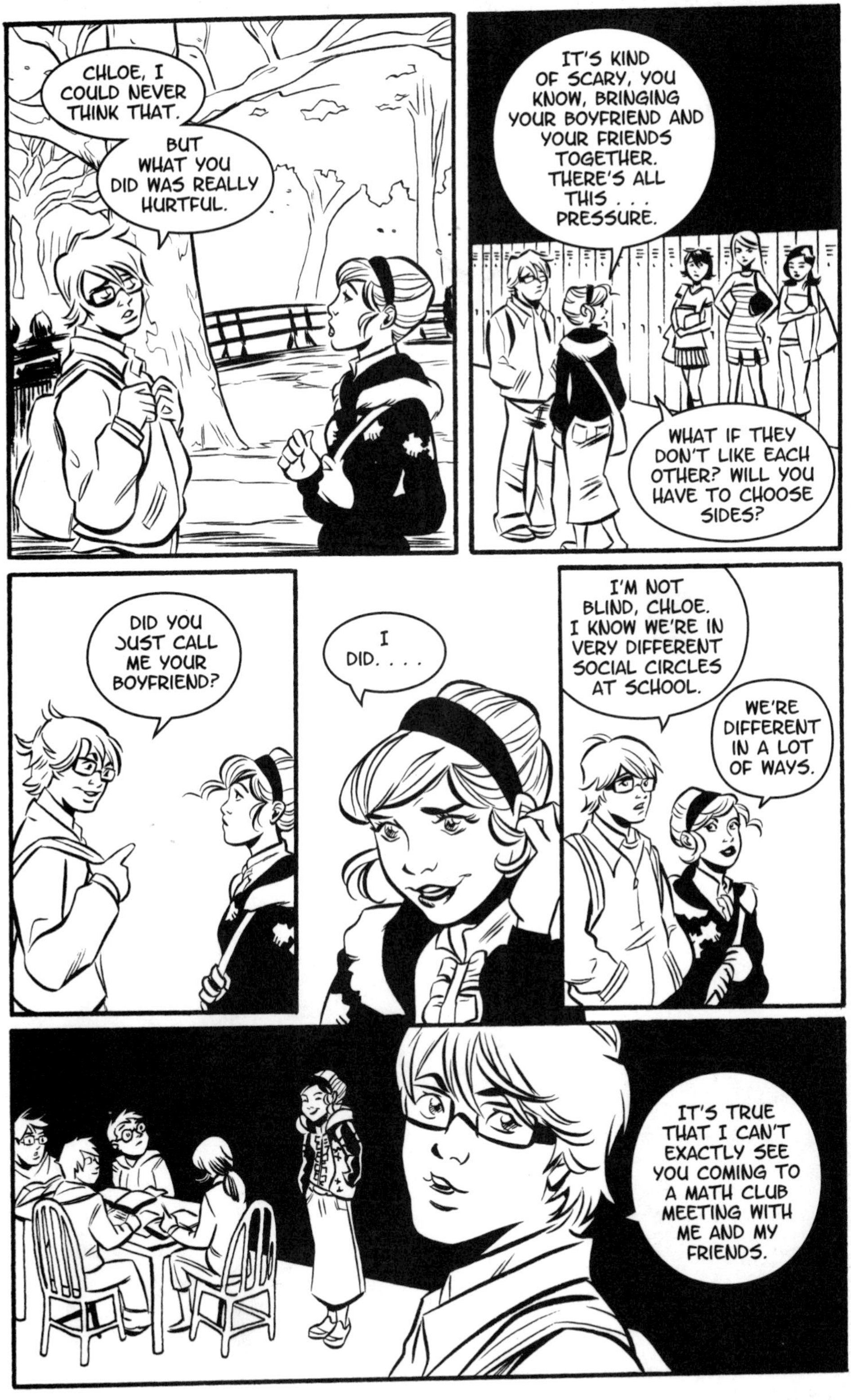
CHLOE, I COULD NEVER THINK THAT.
BUT WHAT YOU DID WAS REALLY HURTFUL.
IT'S KIND OF SCARY, YOU KNOW, BRINGING YOUR BOYFRIEND AND YOUR FRIENDS TOGETHER. THERE'S ALL THIS . . . PRESSURE.
WHAT IF THEY DON'T LIKE EACH OTHER? WILL YOU HAVE TO CHOOSE SIDES?
DID YOU JUST CALL ME YOUR BOYFRIEND?
I DID. . . .
I'M NOT BLIND, CHLOE. I KNOW WE'RE IN VERY DIFFERENT SOCIAL CIRCLES AT SCHOOL.
WE'RE DIFFERENT IN A LOT OF WAYS.
IT'S TRUE THAT I CAN'T EXACTLY SEE YOU COMING TO A MATH CLUB MEETING WITH ME AND MY FRIENDS.

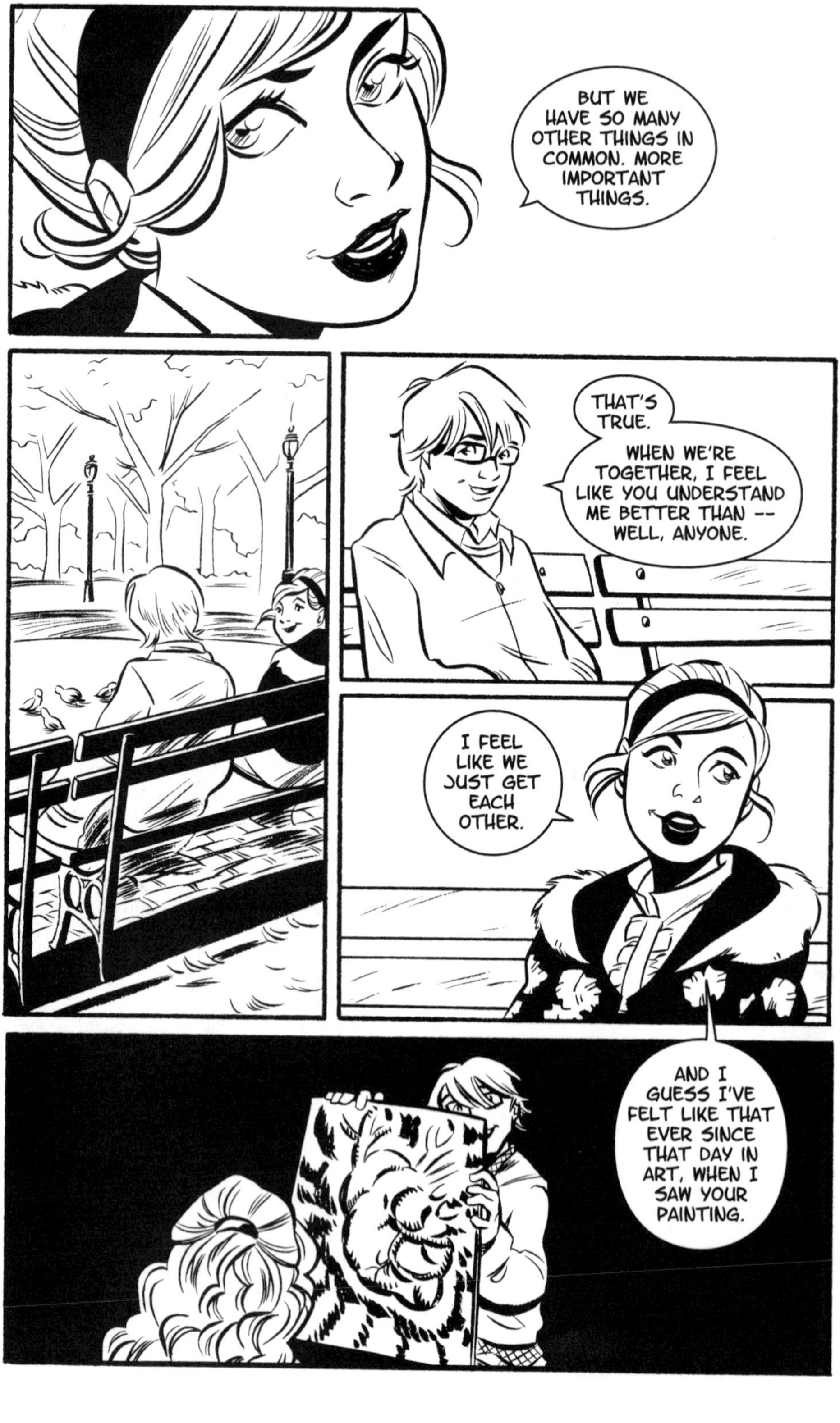
BUT WE HAVE SO MANY OTHER THINGS IN COMMON. MORE IMPORTANT THINGS.
THAT'S TRUE.
WHEN WE'RE TOGETHER, I FEEL LIKE YOU UNDERSTAND ME BETTER THAN -- WELL, ANYONE.
I FEEL LIKE WE JUST GET EACH OTHER.
AND I GUESS I'VE FELT LIKE THAT EVER SINCE THAT DAY IN ART, WHEN I SAW YOUR PAINTING.

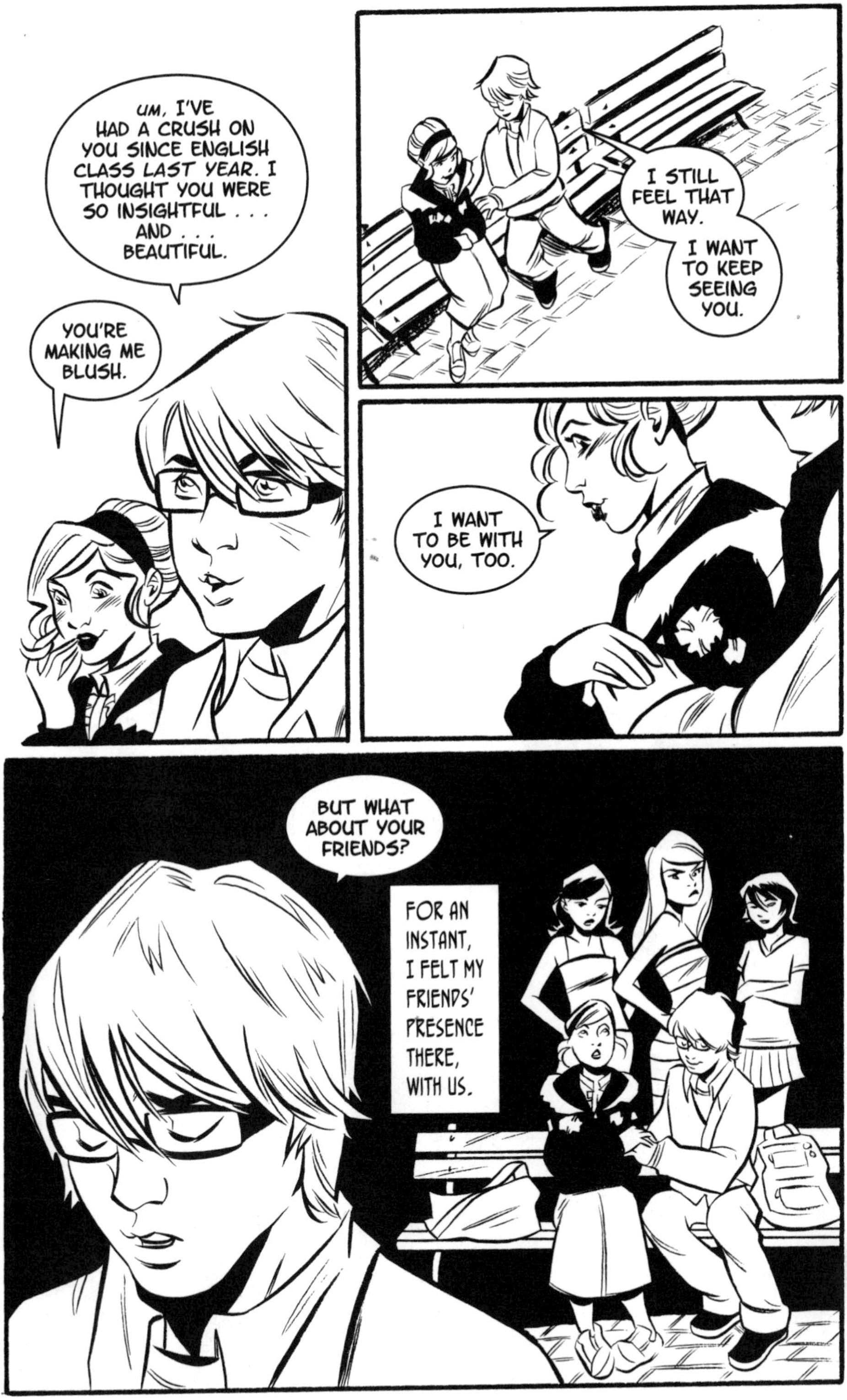

UM, I'VE HAD A CRUSH ON YOU SINCE ENGLISH CLASS LAST YEAR. I THOUGHT YOU WERE SO INSIGHTFUL . . . AND . . . BEAUTIFUL.
YOU'RE MAKING ME BLUSH.
I STILL FEEL THAT WAY.
I WANT TO KEEP SEEING YOU.
I WANT TO BE WITH YOU, TOO.
BUT WHAT ABOUT YOUR FRIENDS?
FOR AN INSTANT, I FELT MY FRIENDS' PRESENCE THERE, WITH US.

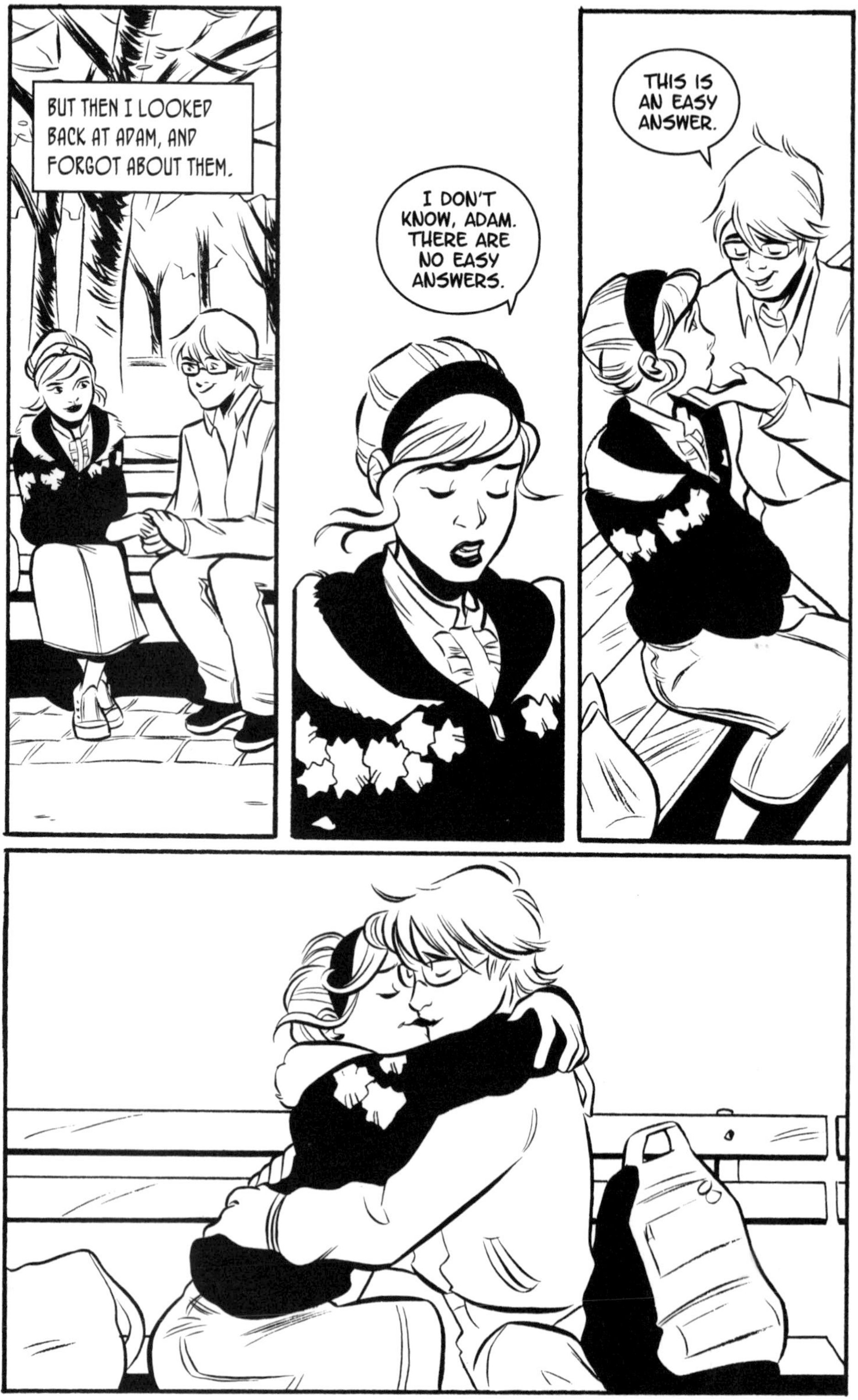
BUT THEN I LOOKED BACK AT ADAM, AND FORGOT ABOUT THEM.
I DON'T KNOW, ADAM. THERE ARE NO EASY ANSWERS.
THIS IS AN EASY ANSWER.

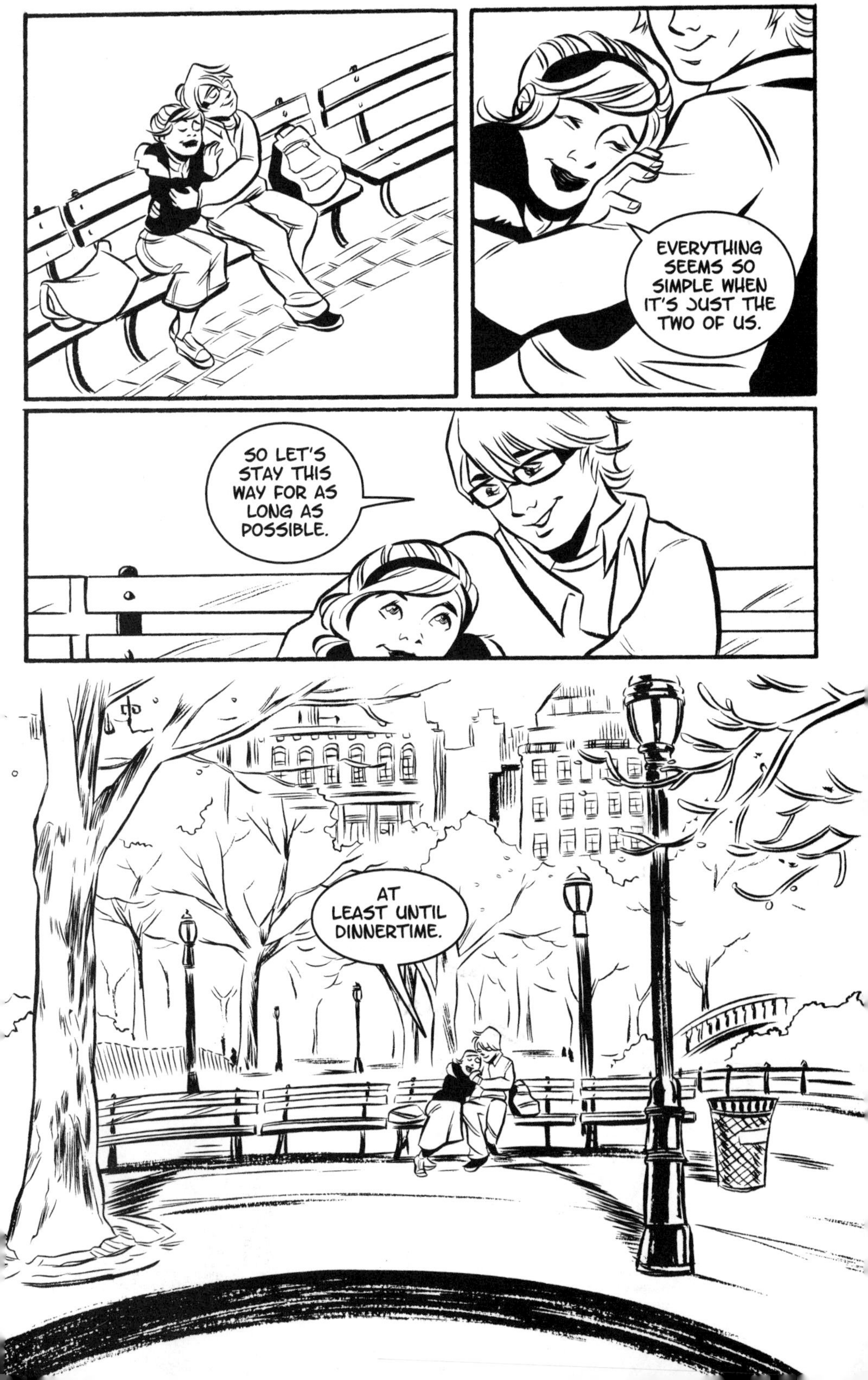
EVERYTHING SEEMS SO SIMPLE WHEN IT'S JUST THE TWO OF US.
SO LET'S STAY THIS WAY FOR AS LONG AS POSSIBLE.
AT LEAST UNTIL DINNERTIME.

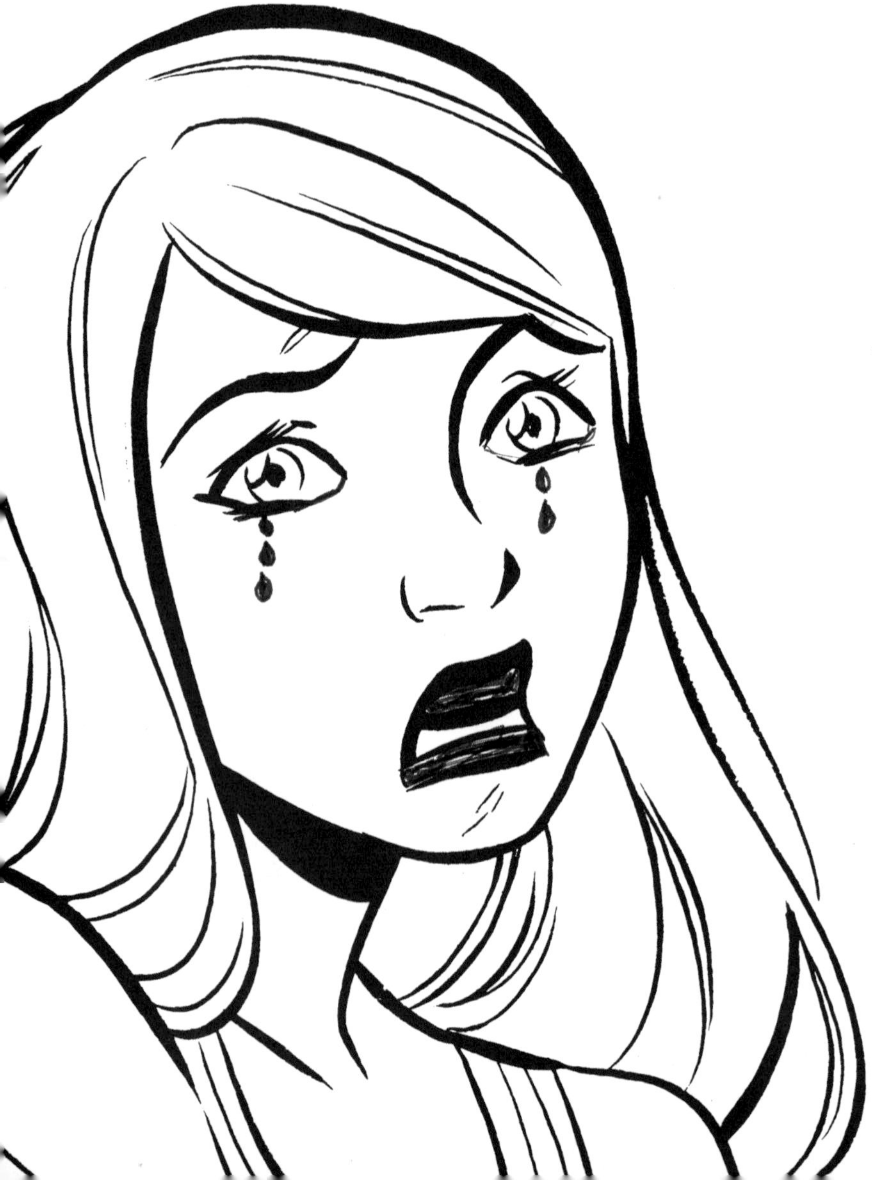

Chapter 10: Final Exam

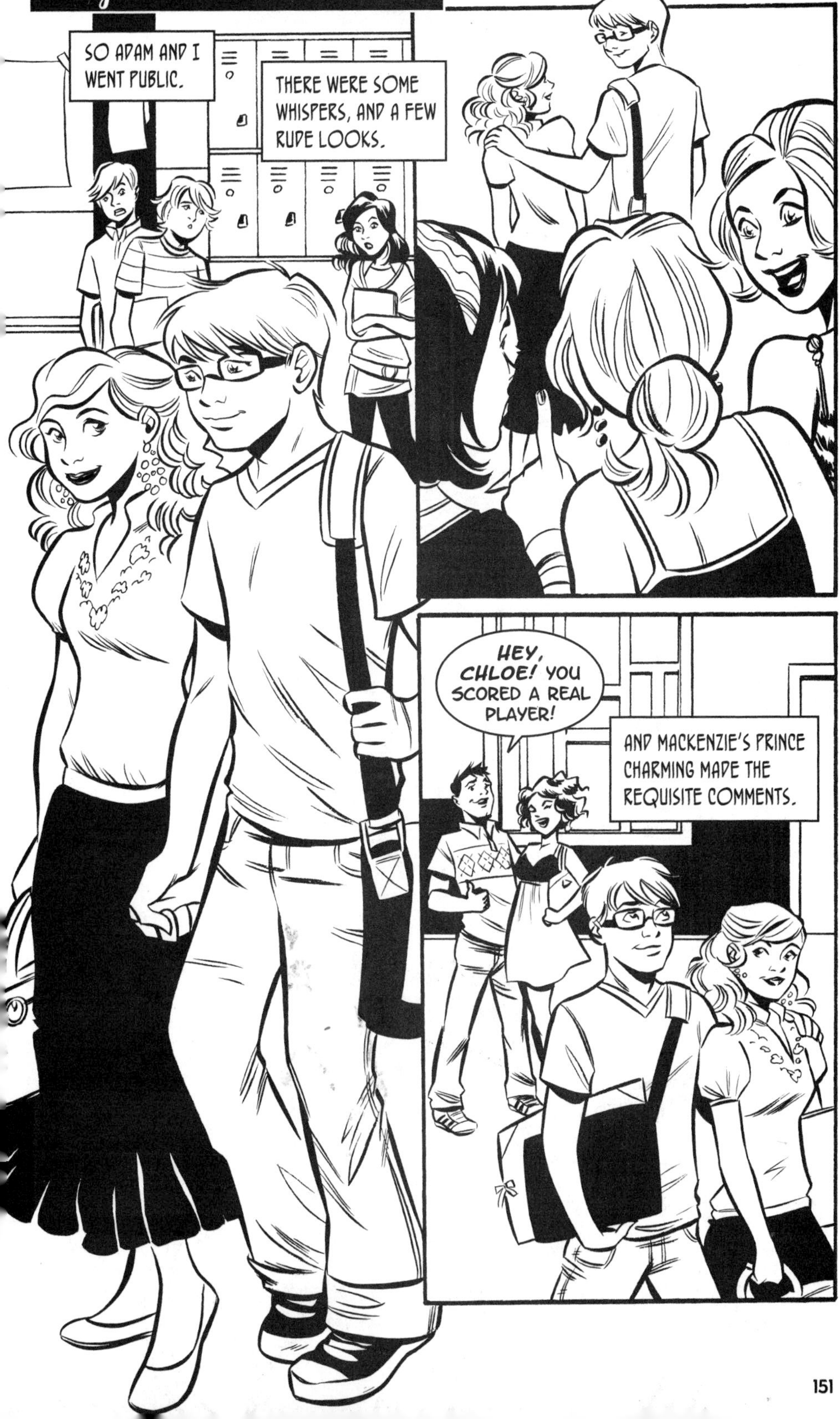
SO ADAM AND I WENT PUBLIC.
THERE WERE SOME WHISPERS, AND A FEW RUDE LOOKS.
HEY, CHLOE! YOU SCORED A REAL PLAYER!
AND MACKENZIE'S PRINCE CHARMING MADE THE REQUISITE COMMENTS.

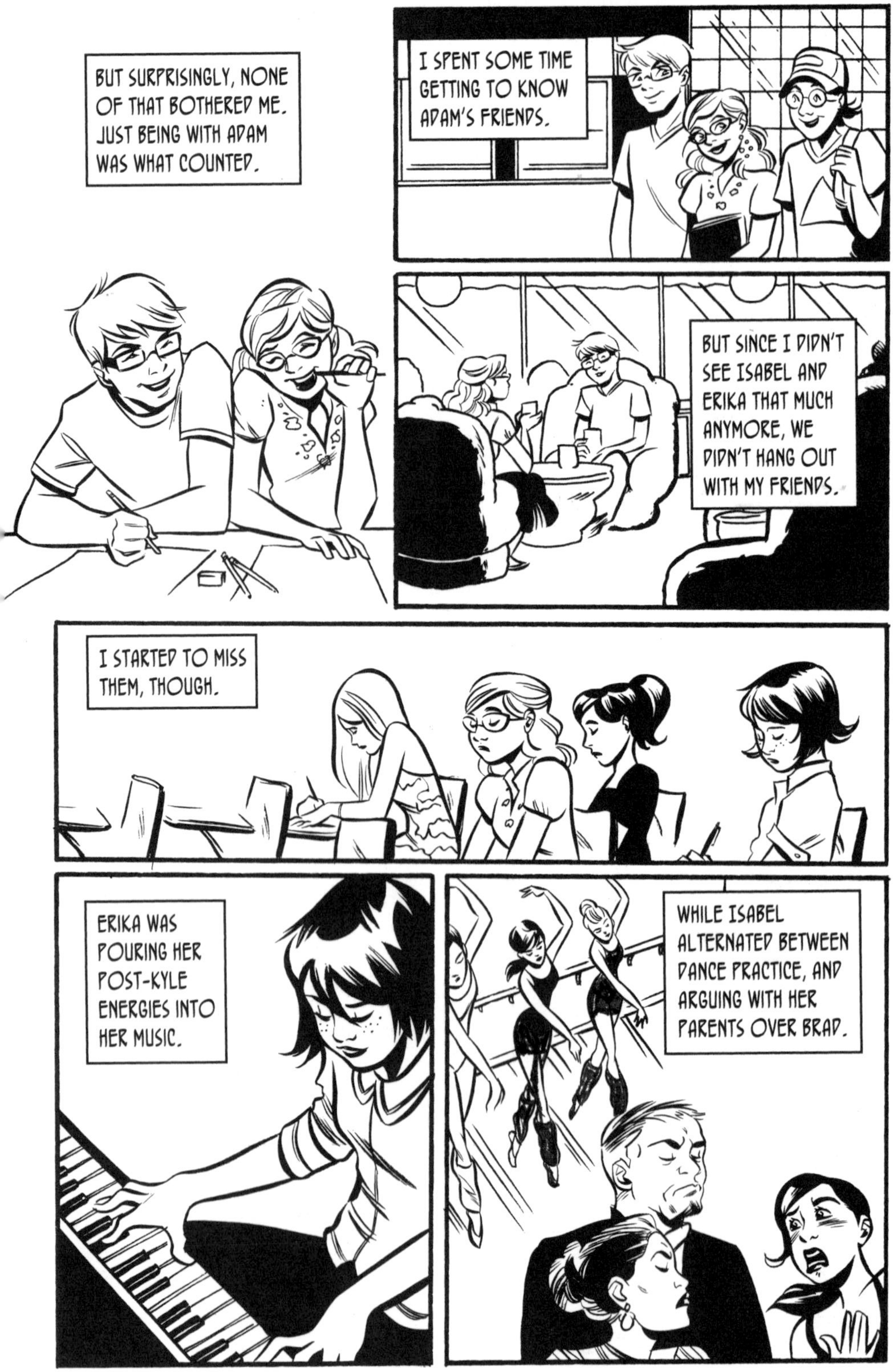
BUT SURPRISINGLY, NONE OF THAT BOTHERED ME. JUST BEING WITH ADAM WAS WHAT COUNTED.
I SPENT SOME TIME GETTING TO KNOW ADAM'S FRIENDS.
BUT SINCE I DIDN'T SEE ISABEL AND ERIKA THAT MUCH ANYMORE, WE DIDN'T HANG OUT WITH MY FRIENDS.
I STARTED TO MISS THEM, THOUGH.
ERIKA WAS POURING HER POST-KYLE ENERGIES INTO HER MUSIC.
WHILE ISABEL ALTERNATED BETWEEN DANCE PRACTICE, AND ARGUING WITH HER PARENTS OVER BRAD.

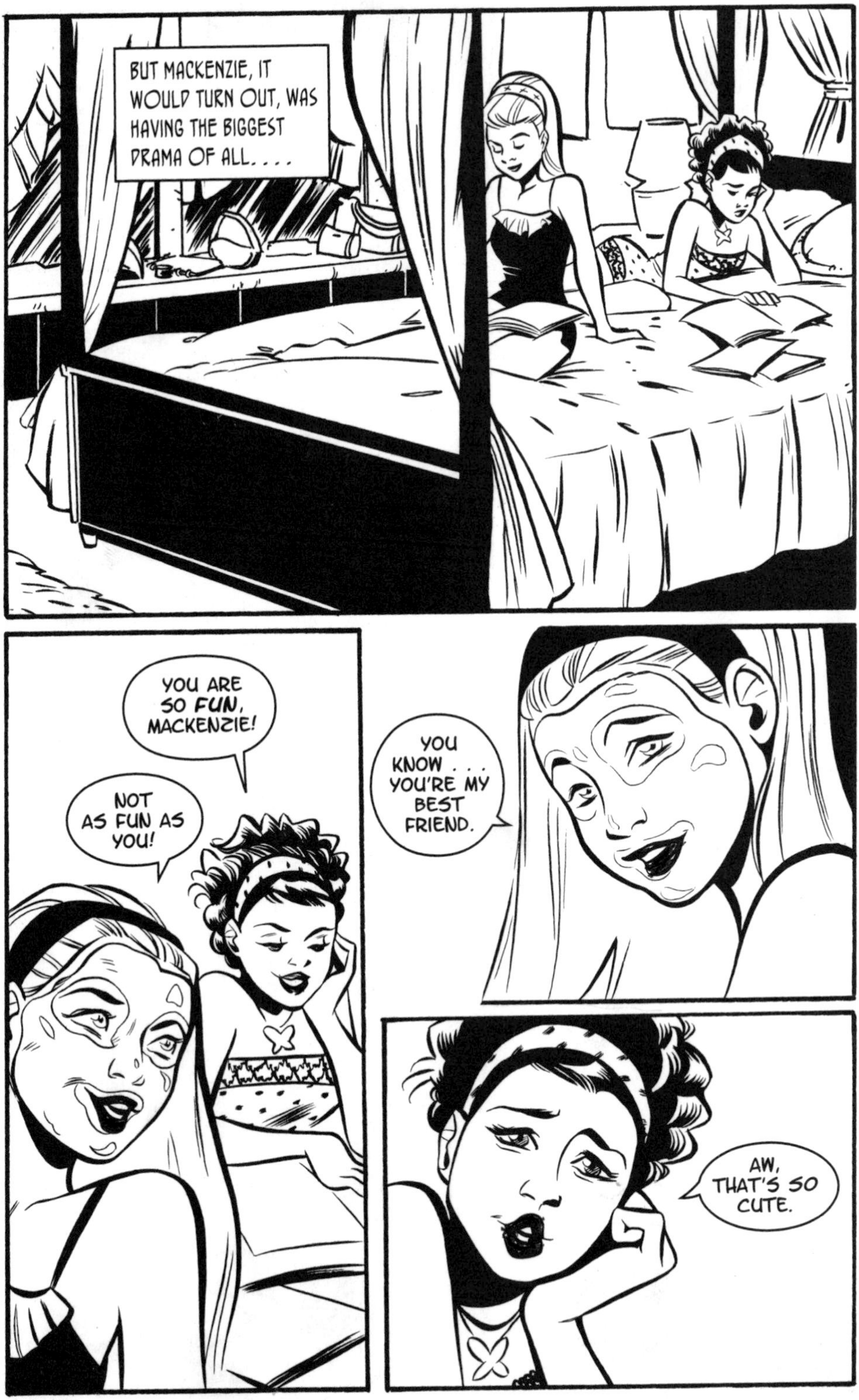
BUT MACKENZIE, IT WOULD TURN OUT, WAS HAVING THE BIGGEST DRAMA OF ALL. . . .
YOU ARE SO FUN, MACKENZIE!
NOT AS FUN AS YOU!
YOU KNOW . . . YOU'RE MY BEST FRIEND.
AW, THAT'S SO CUTE.

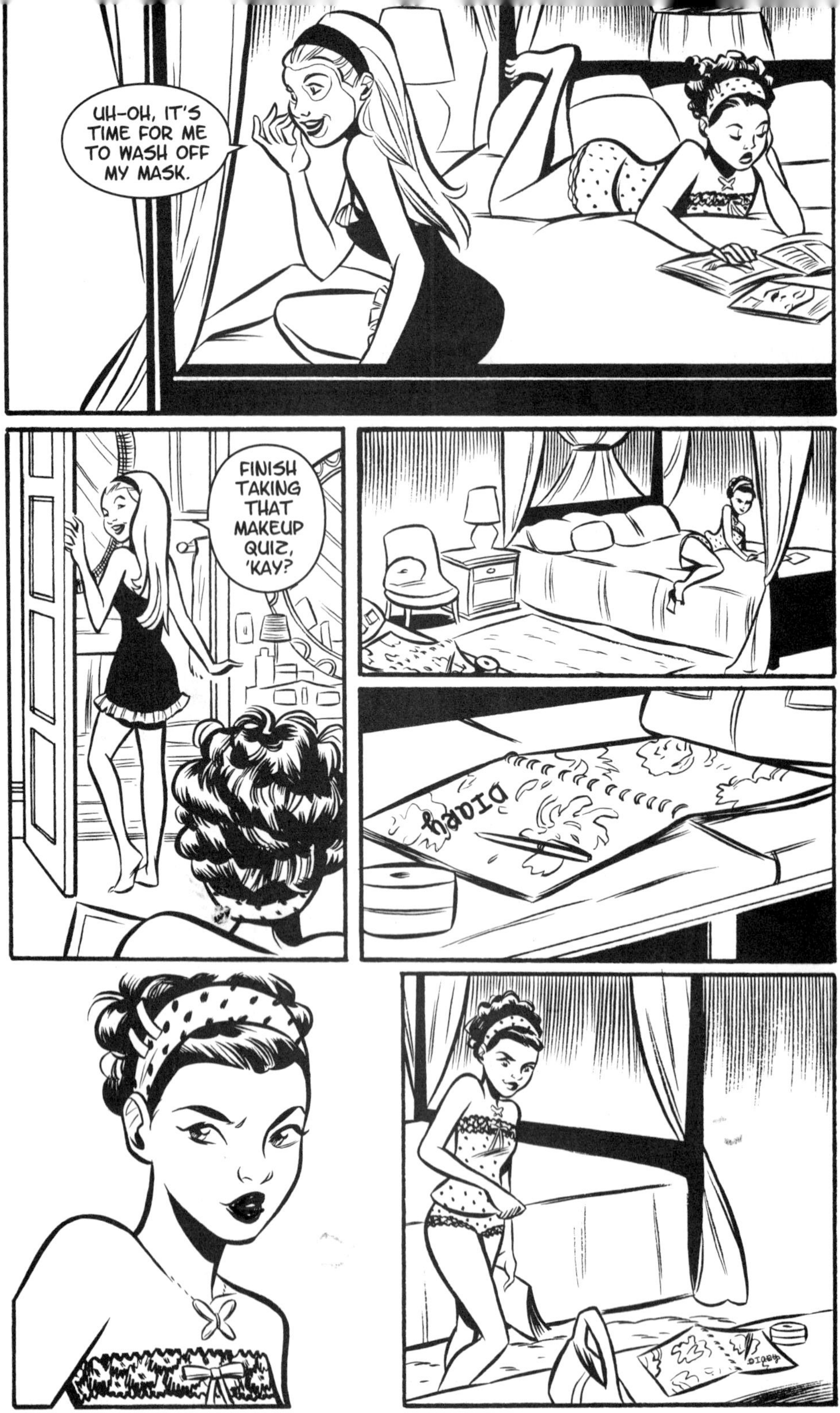
UH-OH, IT'S TIME FOR ME TO WASH OFF MY MASK.
FINISH TAKING THAT MAKEUP QUIZ, 'KAY?
Diary

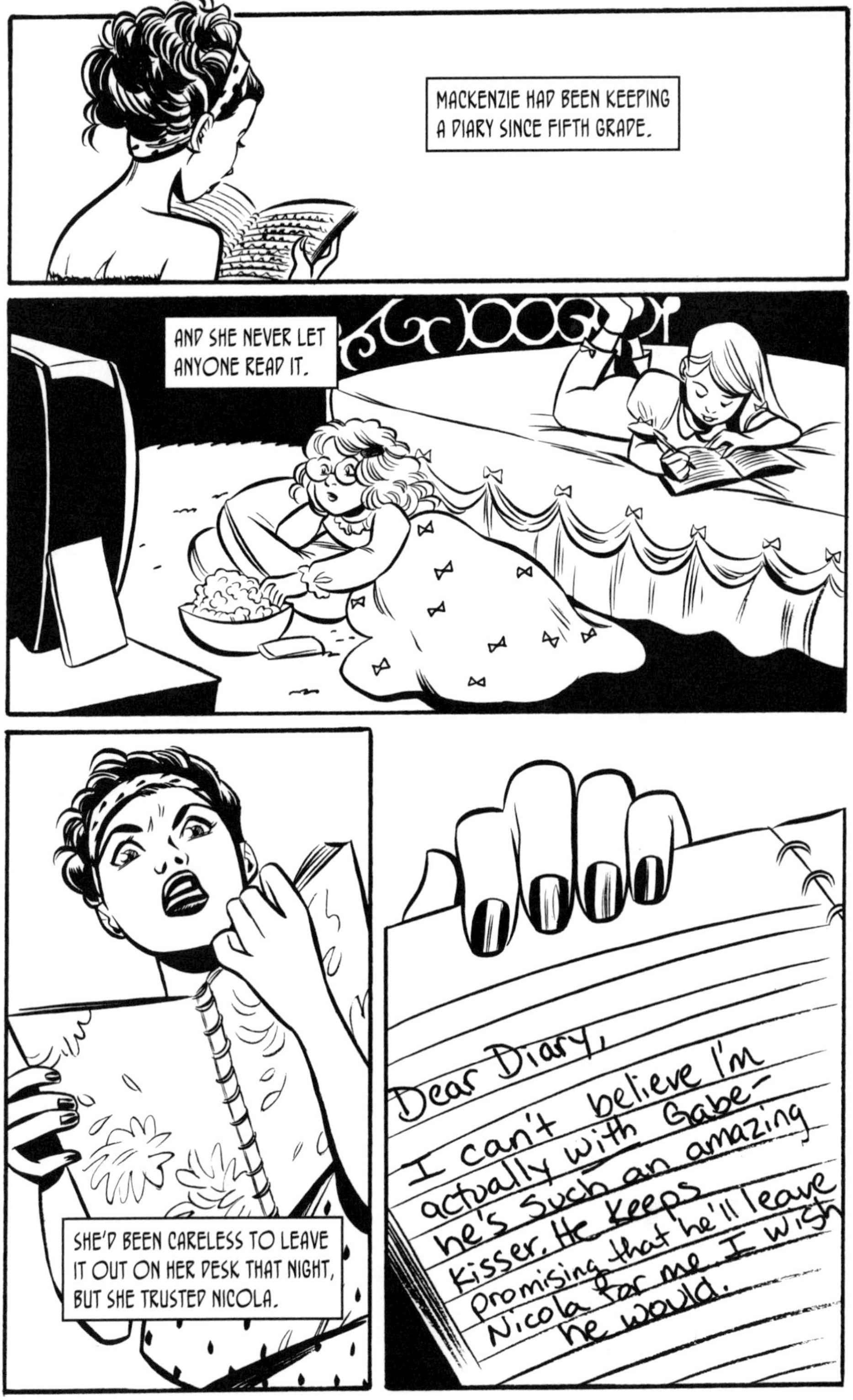
MACKENZIE HAD BEEN KEEPING A DIARY SINCE FIFTH GRADE.
AND SHE NEVER LET ANYONE READ IT.
SHE'D BEEN CARELESS TO LEAVE IT OUT ON HER DESK THAT NIGHT, BUT SHE TRUSTED NICOLA.
Dear Diary,
I can't believe I'm actually with Gabe-
he's such an amazing kisser. He keeps promising that he'll leave Nicola for me. I wish he would.

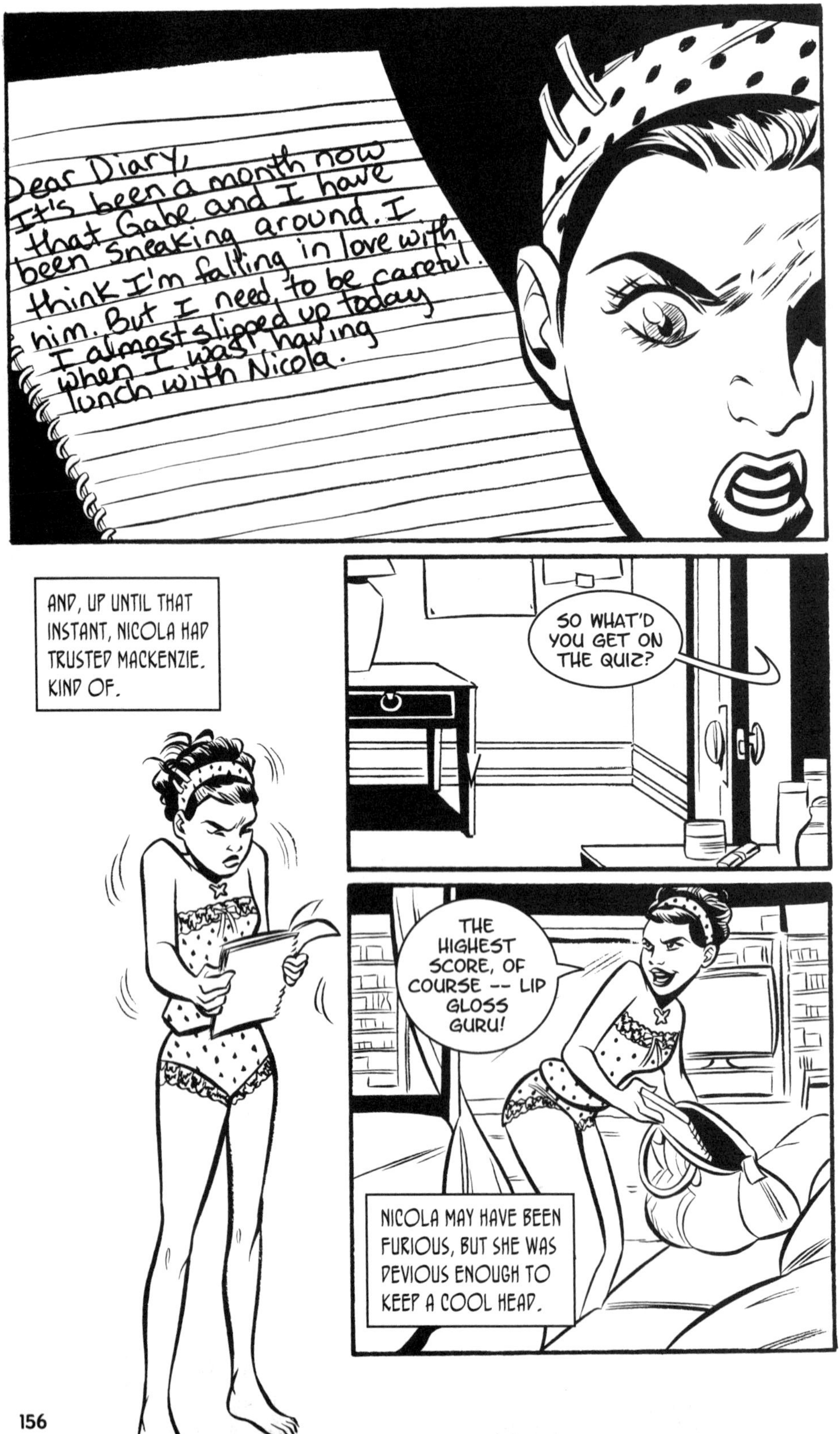
Dear Diary,
It's been a month now
that Gabe and I have
been sneaking around. I
think I'm falling in love with
him. But I need to be careful.
I almost slipped up today
when I was having
lunch with Nicola.
AND, UP UNTIL THAT INSTANT, NICOLA HAD TRUSTED MACKENZIE. KIND OF.
SO WHAT'D YOU GET ON THE QUIZ?
THE HIGHEST SCORE, OF COURSE -- LIP GLOSS GURU!
NICOLA MAY HAVE BEEN FURIOUS, BUT SHE WAS DEVIOUS ENOUGH TO KEEP A COOL HEAD.

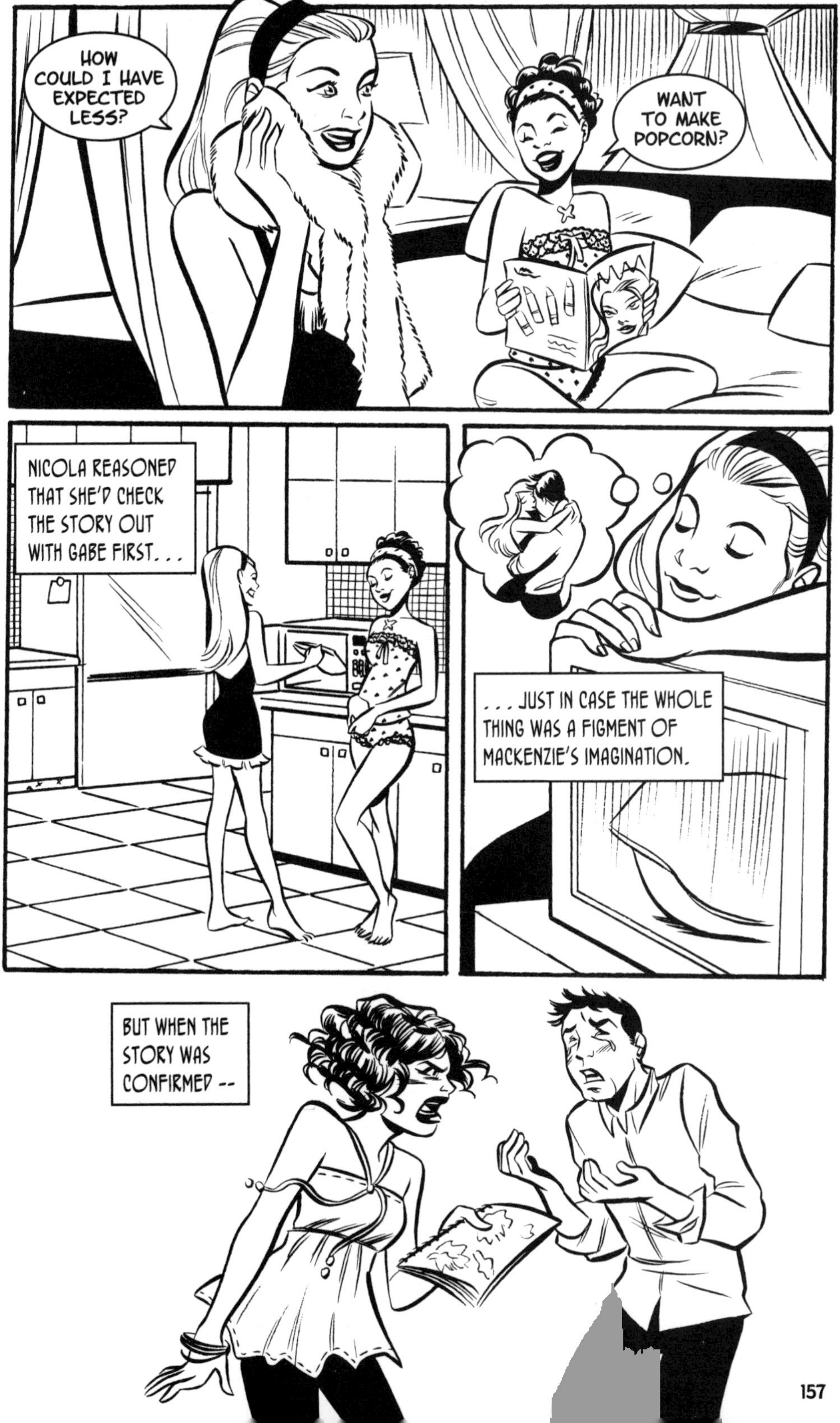
HOW COULD I HAVE EXPECTED LESS?
WANT TO MAKE POPCORN?
NICOLA REASONED THAT SHE'D CHECK THE STORY OUT WITH GABE FIRST. . .
. . . JUST IN CASE THE WHOLE THING WAS A FIGMENT OF MACKENZIE'S IMAGINATION.
BUT WHEN THE STORY WAS CONFIRMED --

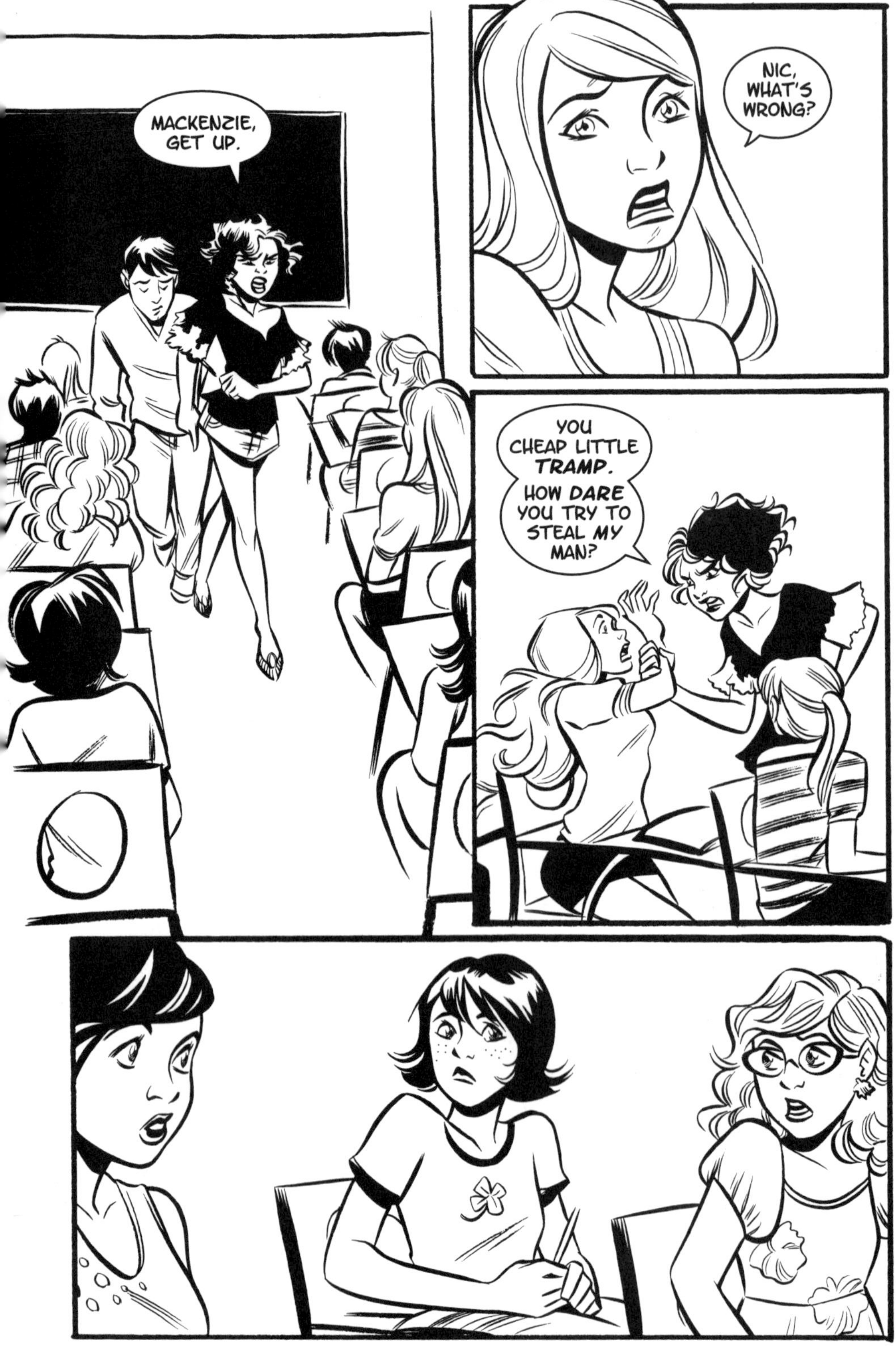
MACKENZIE, GET UP.
NIC, WHAT'S WRONG?
YOU CHEAP LITTLE ***TRAMP.*** HOW ***DARE*** YOU TRY TO STEAL ***MY*** MAN?

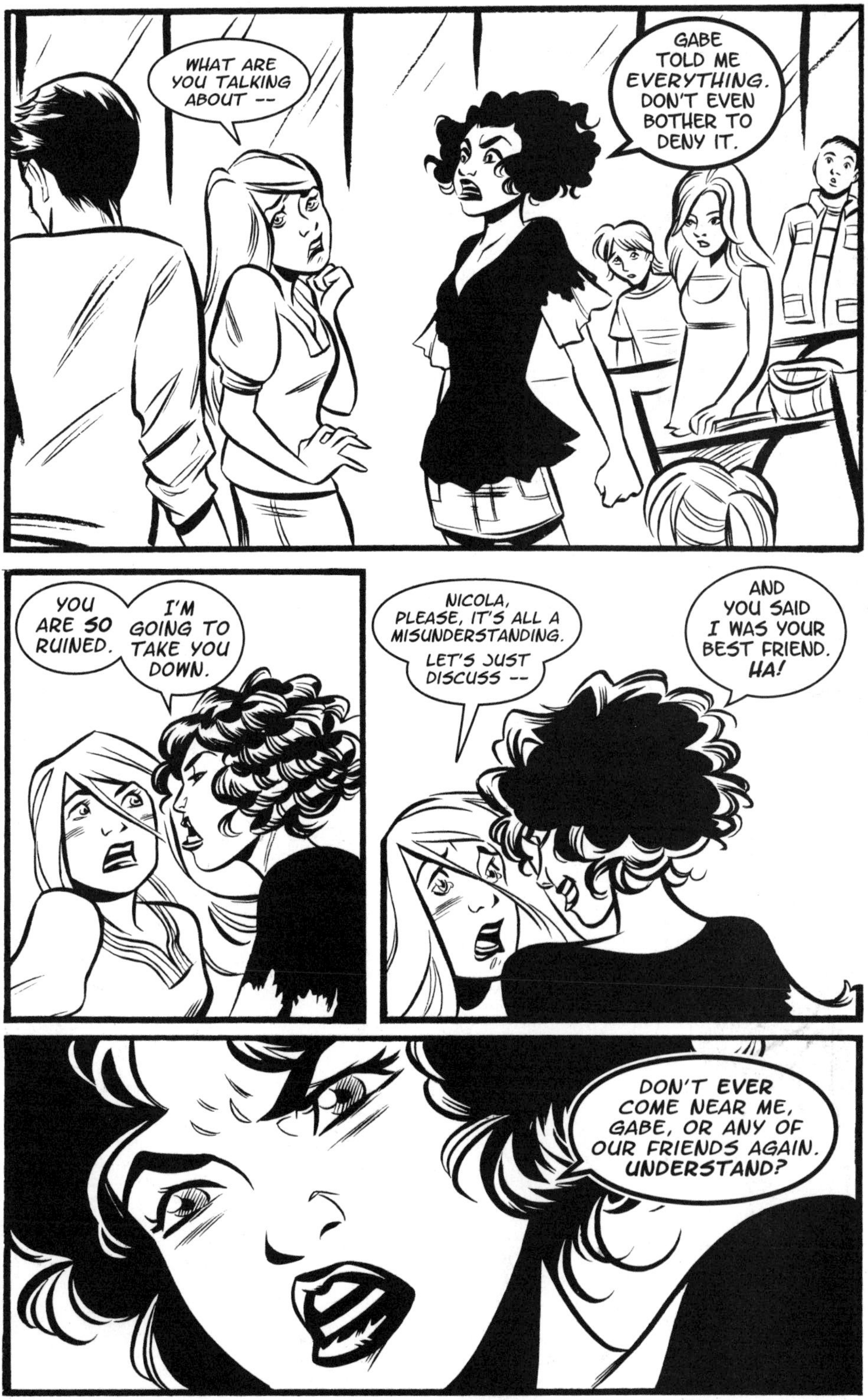
WHAT ARE YOU TALKING ABOUT --
GABE TOLD ME EVERYTHING. DON'T EVEN BOTHER TO DENY IT.
YOU ARE SO RUINED.
I'M GOING TO TAKE YOU DOWN.
NICOLA, PLEASE, IT'S ALL A MISUNDERSTANDING.
LET'S JUST DISCUSS --
AND YOU SAID I WAS YOUR BEST FRIEND. HA!
DON'T EVER COME NEAR ME, GABE, OR ANY OF OUR FRIENDS AGAIN. UNDERSTAND?

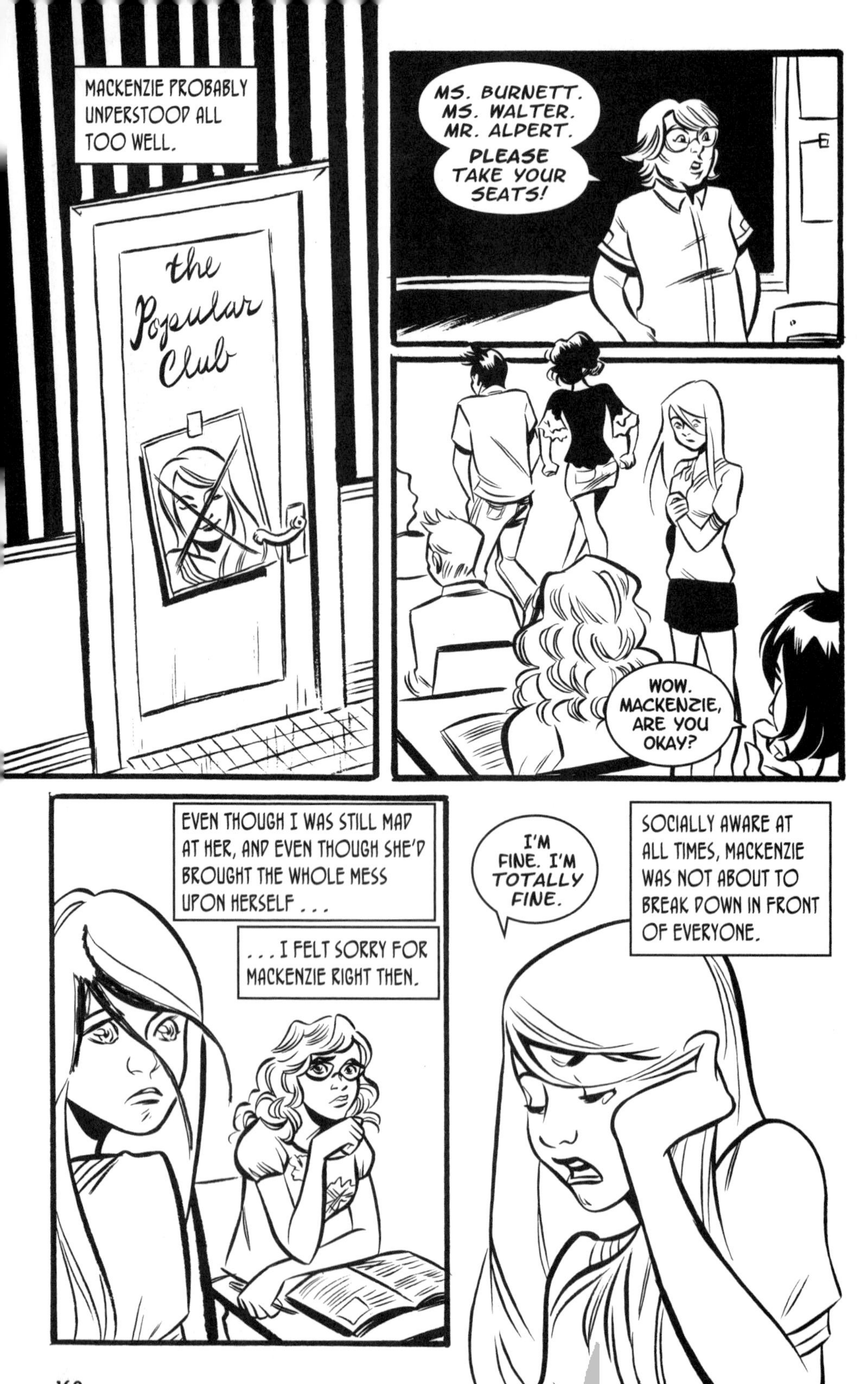

MACKENZIE PROBABLY UNDERSTOOD ALL TOO WELL.
the Popular Club
MS. BURNETT. MS. WALTER. MR. ALPERT.
PLEASE TAKE YOUR SEATS!
WOW. MACKENZIE, ARE YOU OKAY?
EVEN THOUGH I WAS STILL MAD AT HER, AND EVEN THOUGH SHE'D BROUGHT THE WHOLE MESS UPON HERSELF . . .
. . . I FELT SORRY FOR MACKENZIE RIGHT THEN.
I'M FINE. I'M *TOTALLY* FINE.
SOCIALLY AWARE AT ALL TIMES, MACKENZIE WAS NOT ABOUT TO BREAK DOWN IN FRONT OF EVERYONE.

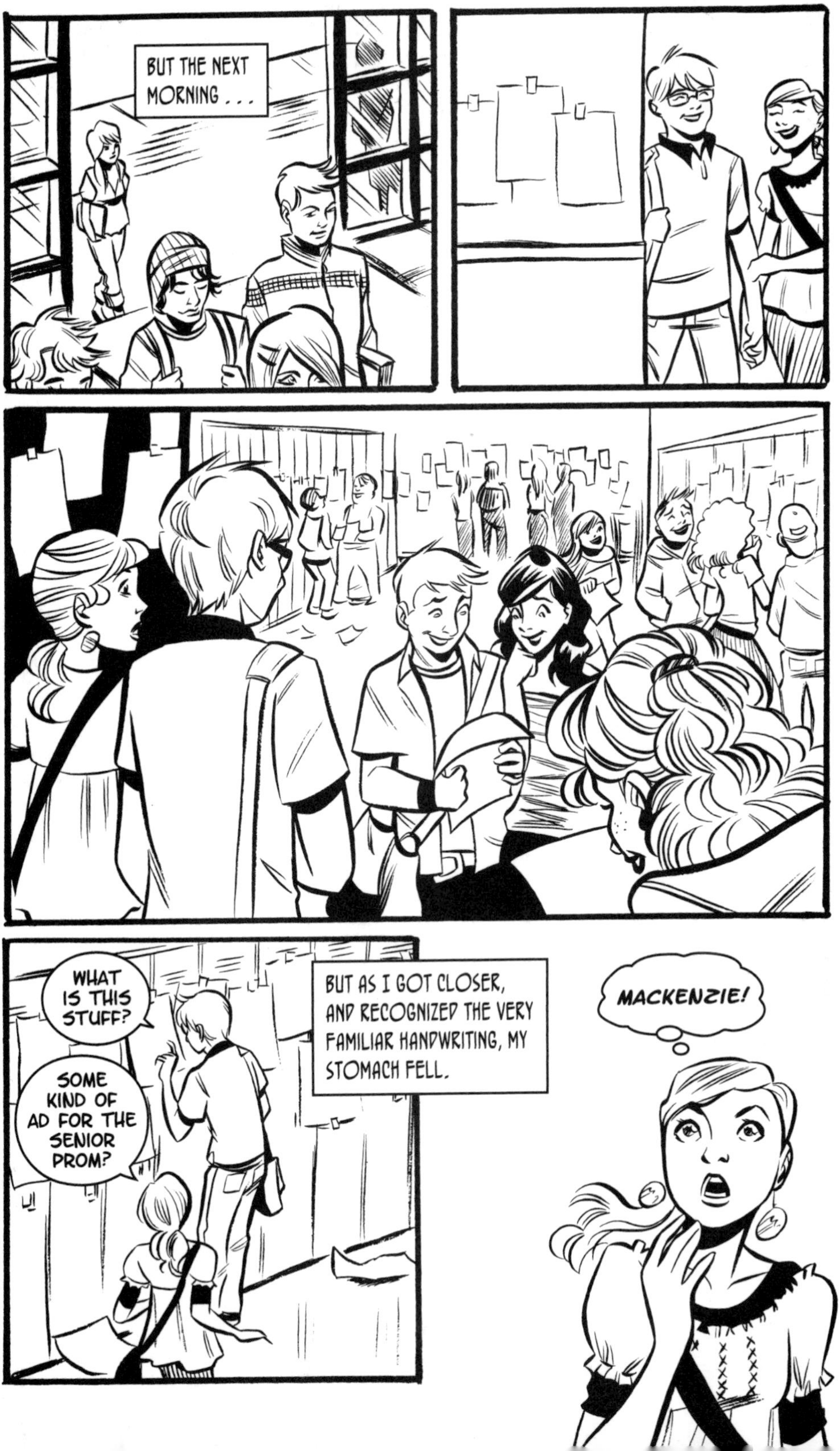
BUT THE NEXT MORNING . . .
WHAT IS THIS STUFF?
SOME KIND OF AD FOR THE SENIOR PROM?
BUT AS I GOT CLOSER, AND RECOGNIZED THE VERY FAMILIAR HANDWRITING, MY STOMACH FELL.
MACKENZIE!

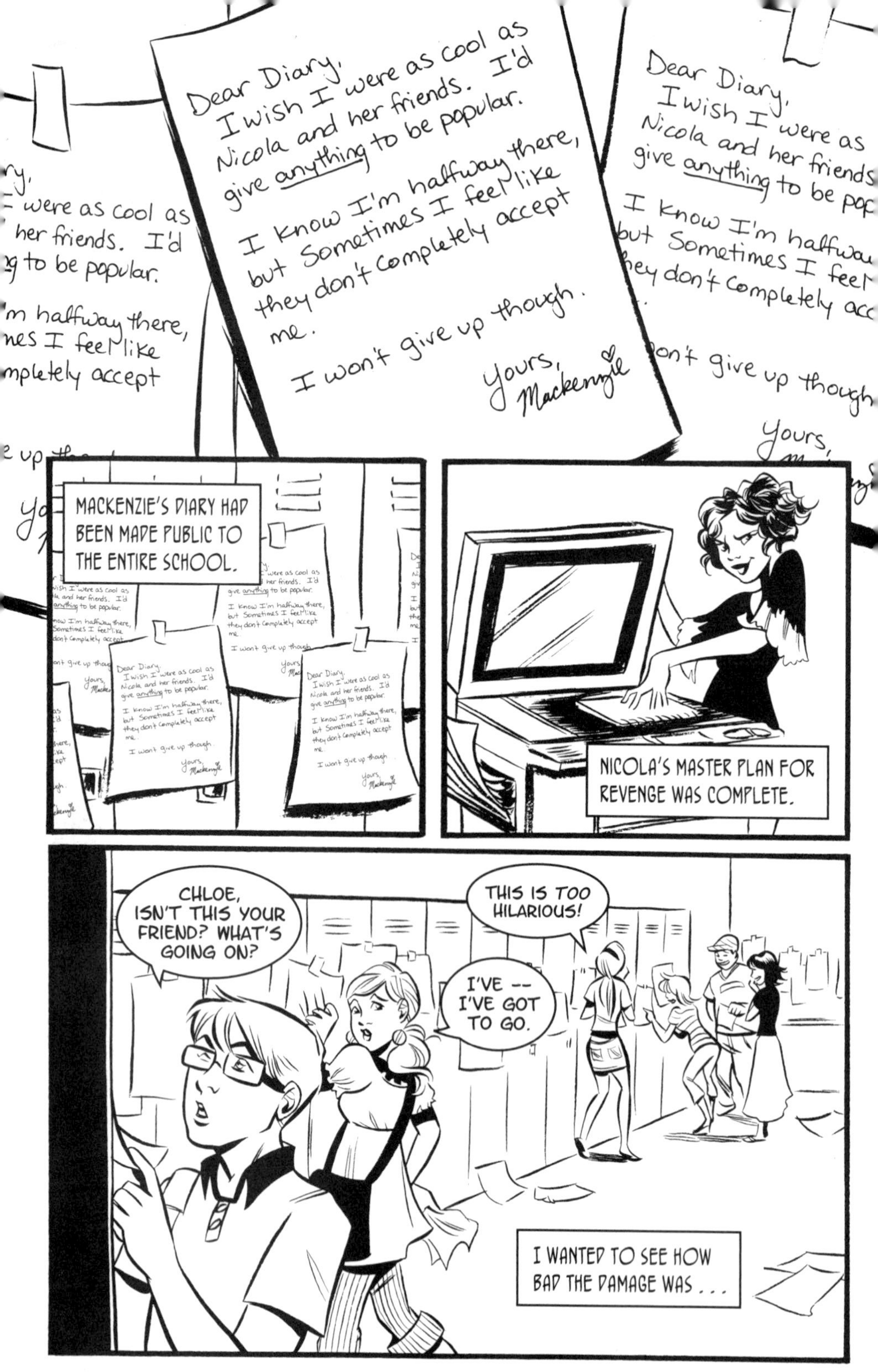
Dear Diary,
I wish I were as cool as Nicola and her friends. I'd give anything to be popular.
I know I'm halfway there, but Sometimes I feel like they don't completely accept me.
I won't give up though.
Yours, Mackenzie
MACKENZIE'S DIARY HAD BEEN MADE PUBLIC TO THE ENTIRE SCHOOL.
NICOLA'S MASTER PLAN FOR REVENGE WAS COMPLETE.
CHLOE, ISN'T THIS YOUR FRIEND? WHAT'S GOING ON?
THIS IS TOO HILARIOUS!
I'VE -- I'VE GOT TO GO.
I WANTED TO SEE HOW BAD THE DAMAGE WAS . . .

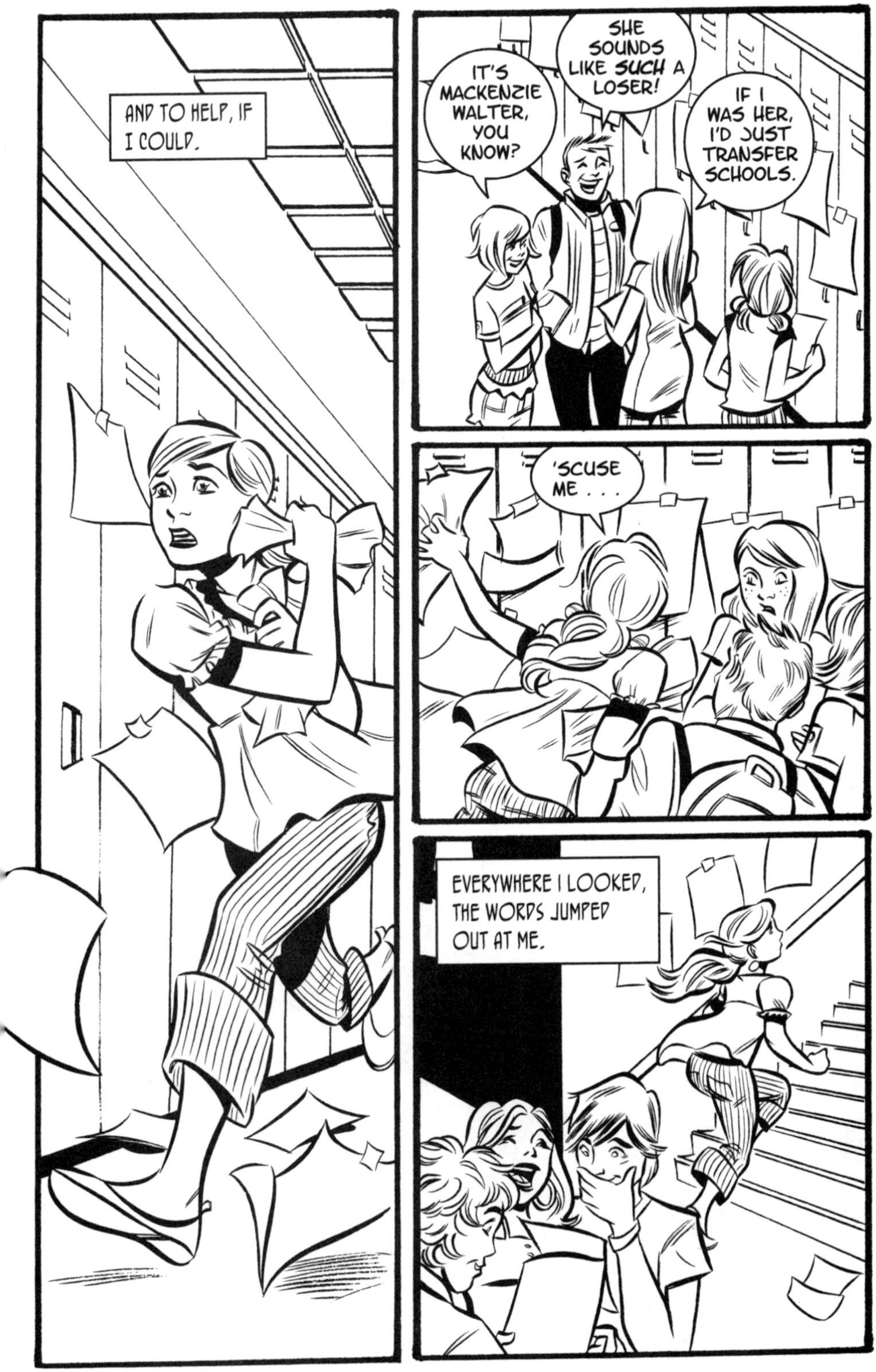
AND TO HELP, IF I COULD.
IT'S MACKENZIE WALTER, YOU KNOW?
SHE SOUNDS LIKE SUCH A LOSER!
IF I WAS HER, I'D JUST TRANSFER SCHOOLS.
'SCUSE ME . . .
EVERYWHERE I LOOKED, THE WORDS JUMPED OUT AT ME.

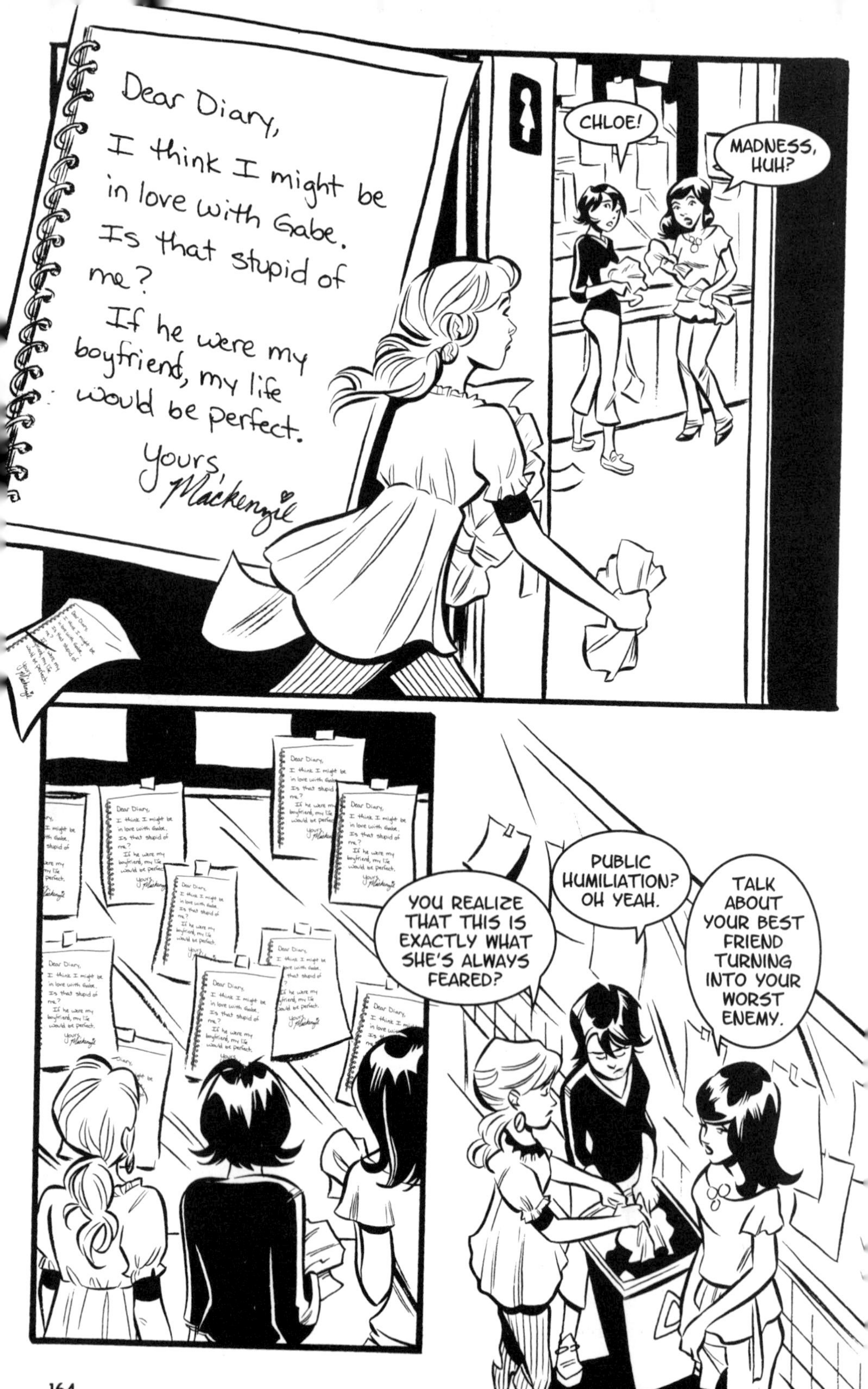
Dear Diary,
I think I might be in love with Gabe. Is that stupid of me?
If he were my boyfriend, my life would be perfect.
Yours, Mackenzie
CHLOE!
MADNESS, HUH?
YOU REALIZE THAT THIS IS EXACTLY WHAT SHE'S ALWAYS FEARED?
PUBLIC HUMILIATION? OH YEAH.
TALK ABOUT YOUR BEST FRIEND TURNING INTO YOUR WORST ENEMY.

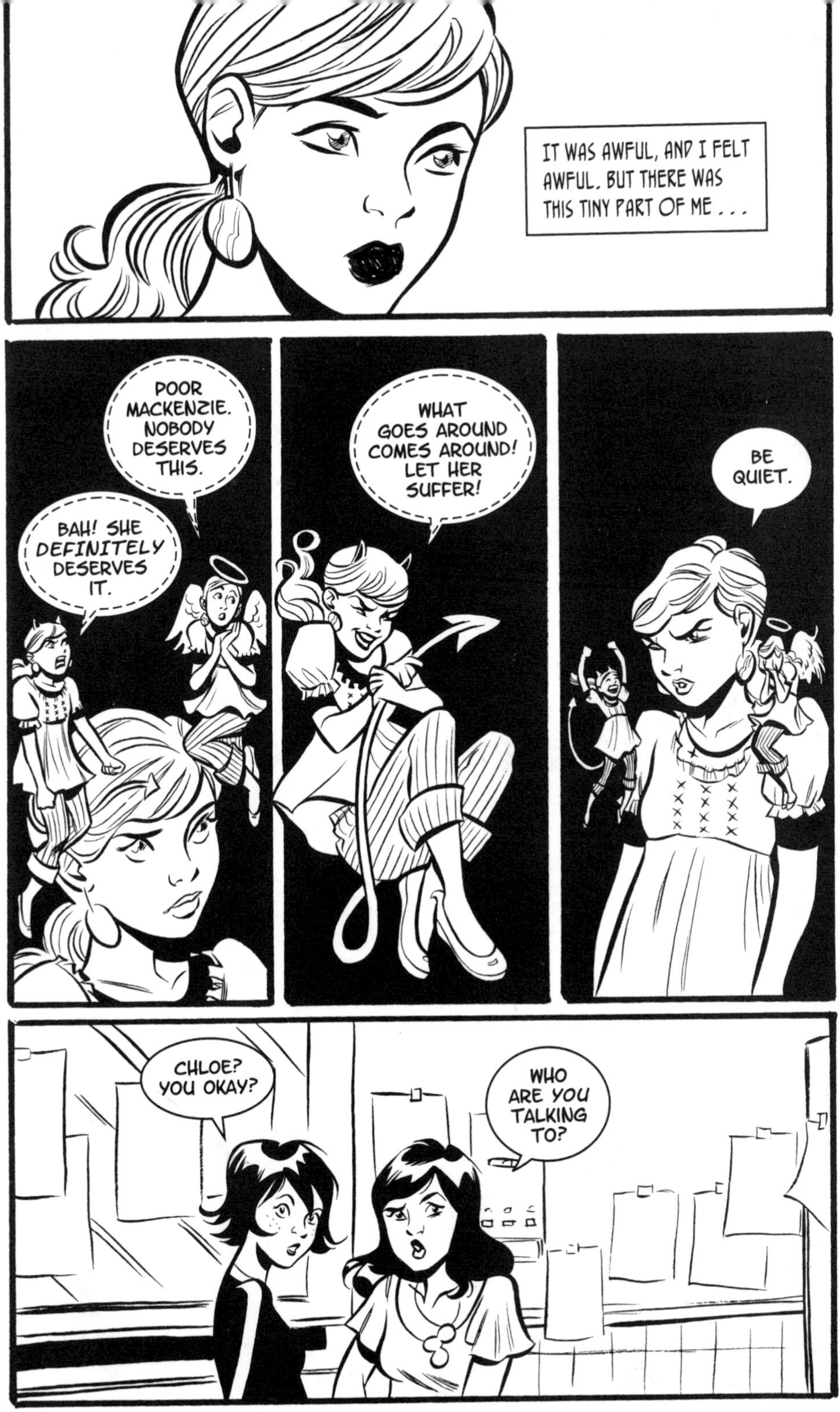
IT WAS AWFUL, AND I FELT AWFUL. BUT THERE WAS THIS TINY PART OF ME . . .
POOR MACKENZIE. NOBODY DESERVES THIS.
BAH! SHE DEFINITELY DESERVES IT.
WHAT GOES AROUND COMES AROUND! LET HER SUFFER!
BE QUIET.
CHLOE? YOU OKAY?
WHO ARE YOU TALKING TO?

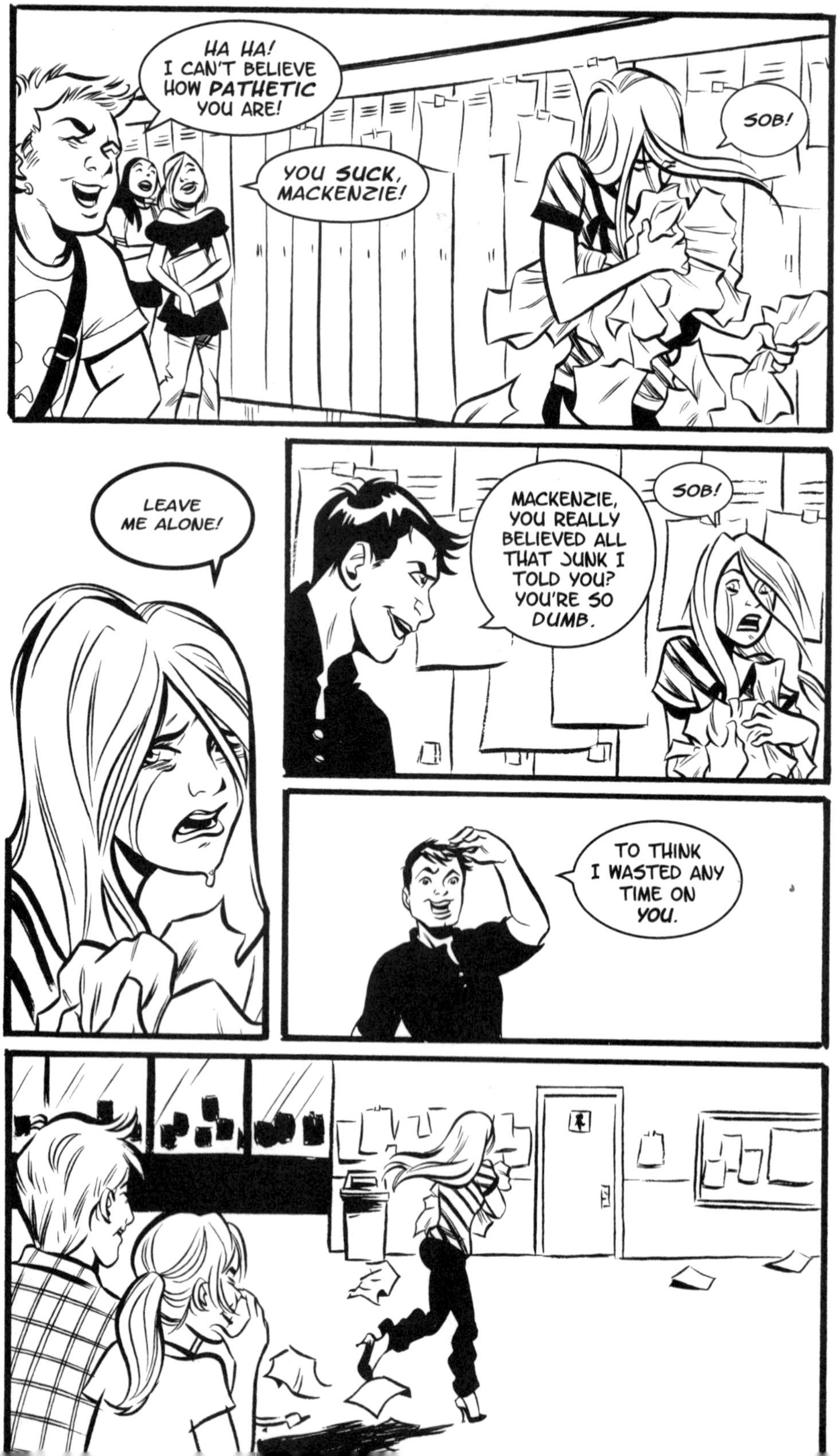
HA HA! I CAN'T BELIEVE HOW PATHETIC YOU ARE!
YOU SUCK, MACKENZIE!
SOB!
LEAVE ME ALONE!
MACKENZIE, YOU REALLY BELIEVED ALL THAT JUNK I TOLD YOU? YOU'RE SO DUMB.
SOB!
TO THINK I WASTED ANY TIME ON YOU.

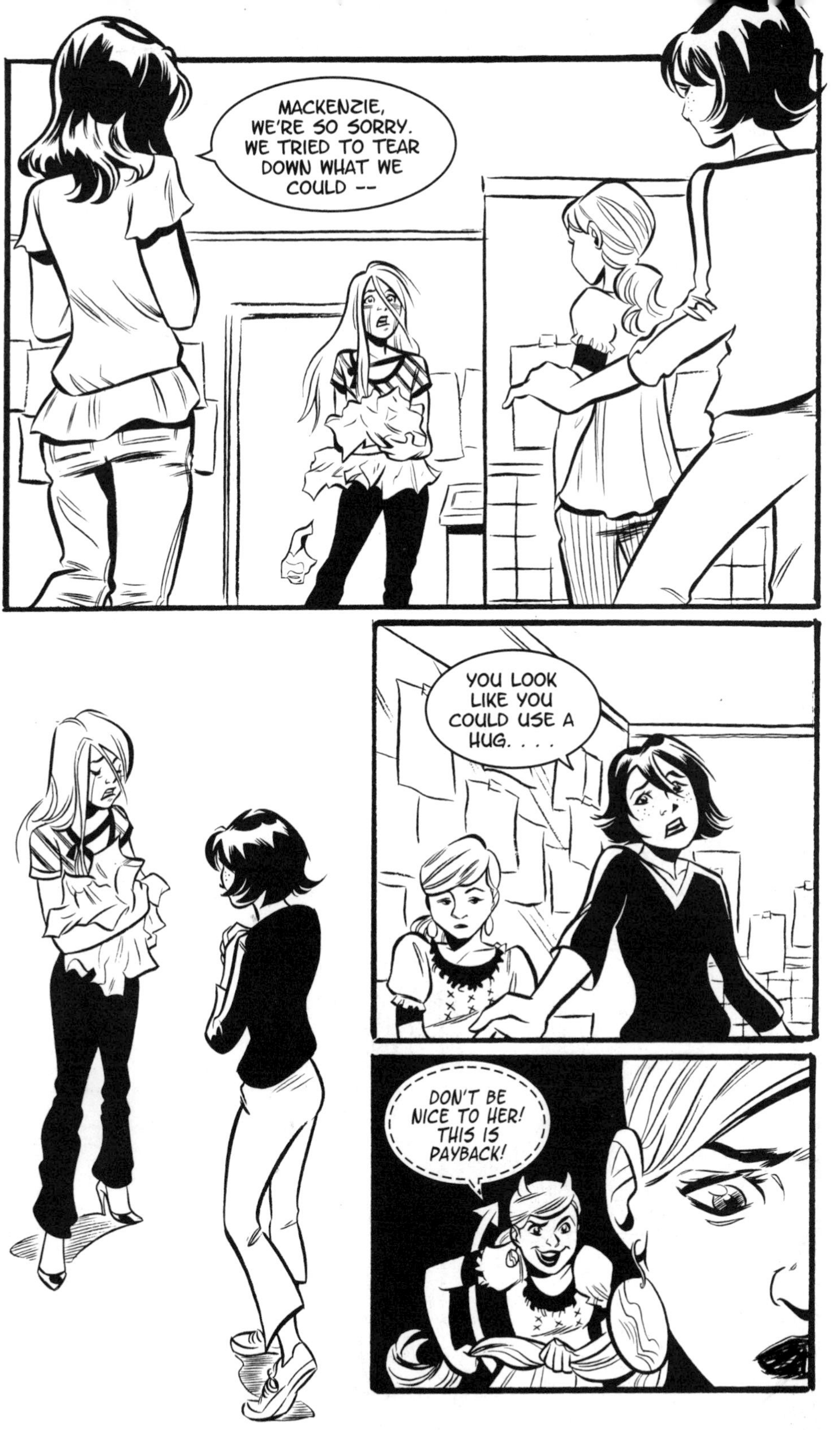
MACKENZIE, WE'RE SO SORRY. WE TRIED TO TEAR DOWN WHAT WE COULD --
YOU LOOK LIKE YOU COULD USE A HUG. . . .
DON'T BE NICE TO HER! THIS IS PAYBACK!

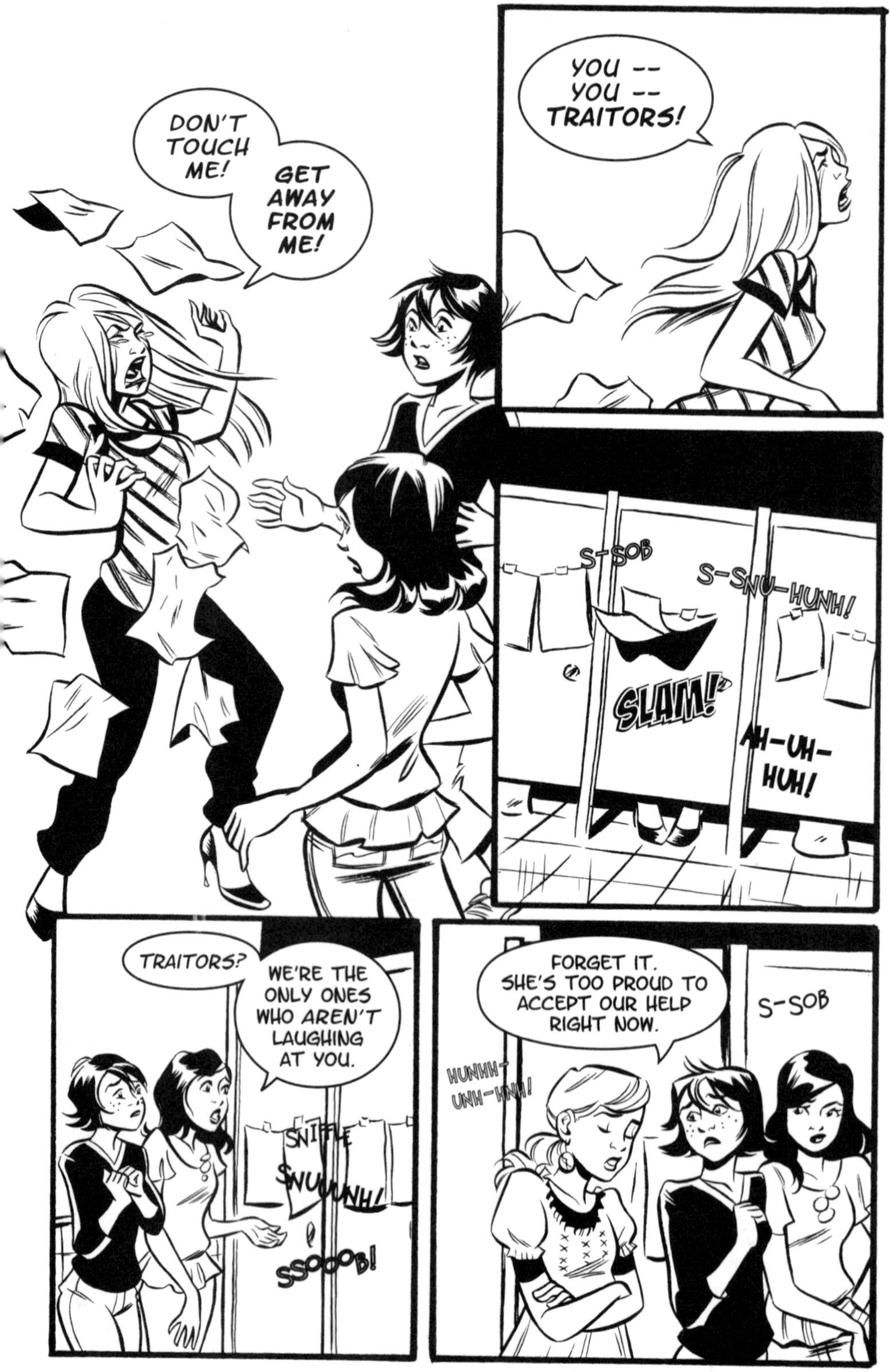
DON'T TOUCH ME!
GET AWAY FROM ME!
YOU -- YOU -- TRAITORS!
S-SOB
S-SNU-HUNH!
SLAM!
AH-UH-HUH!
TRAITORS?
WE'RE THE ONLY ONES WHO AREN'T LAUGHING AT YOU.
SNIFFLE
SNUUUNH!
SSOOOB!
FORGET IT. SHE'S TOO PROUD TO ACCEPT OUR HELP RIGHT NOW.
S-SOB
HUNHH-UNH-HNH!

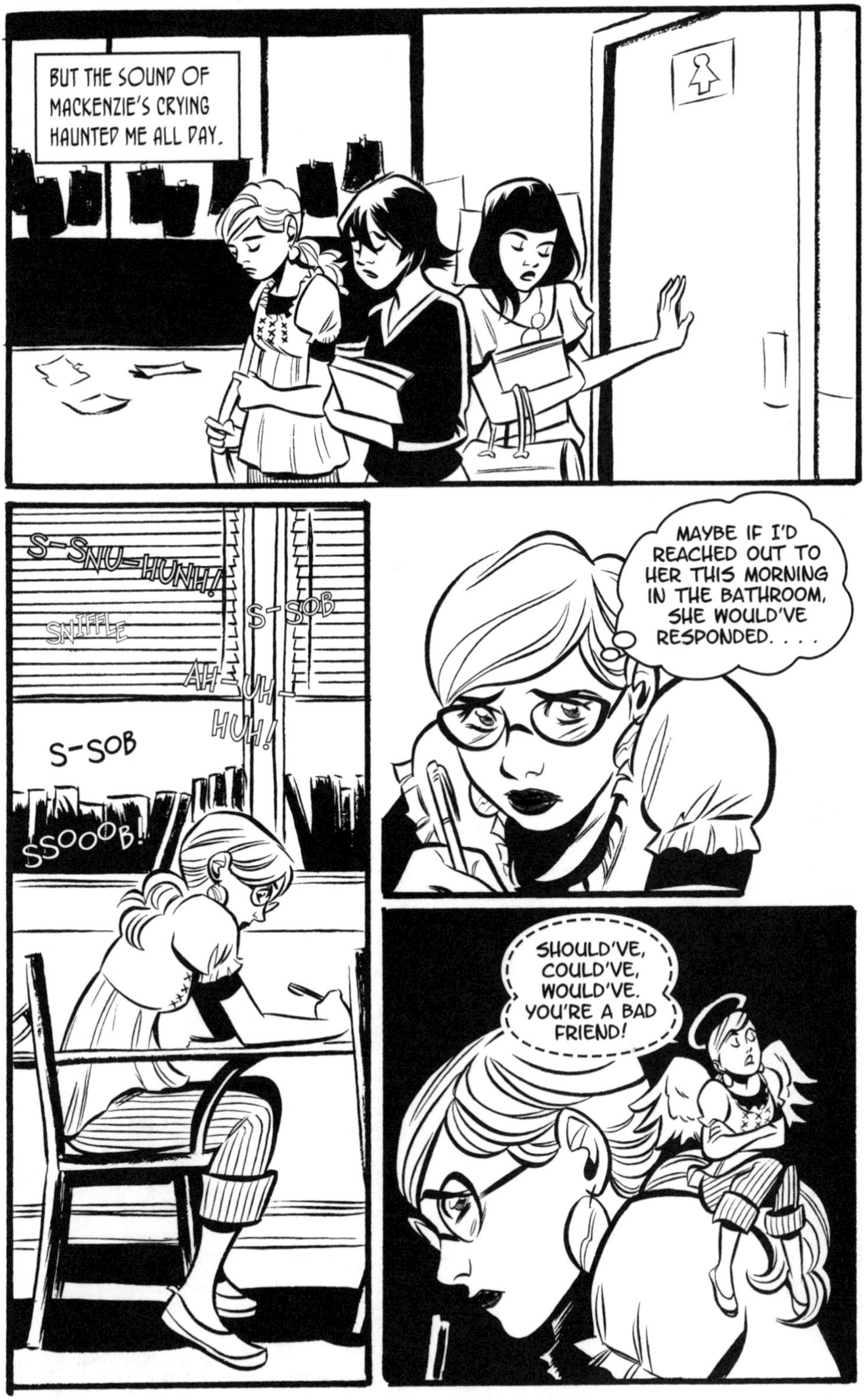
BUT THE SOUND OF MACKENZIE'S CRYING HAUNTED ME ALL DAY.
S-SNU-HUNH!
SNIFFLE
S-SOB
AH-UH-HUH!
S-SOB
SSOOOB!
MAYBE IF I'D REACHED OUT TO HER THIS MORNING IN THE BATHROOM, SHE WOULD'VE RESPONDED. . . .
SHOULD'VE, COULD'VE, WOULD'VE. YOU'RE A BAD FRIEND!

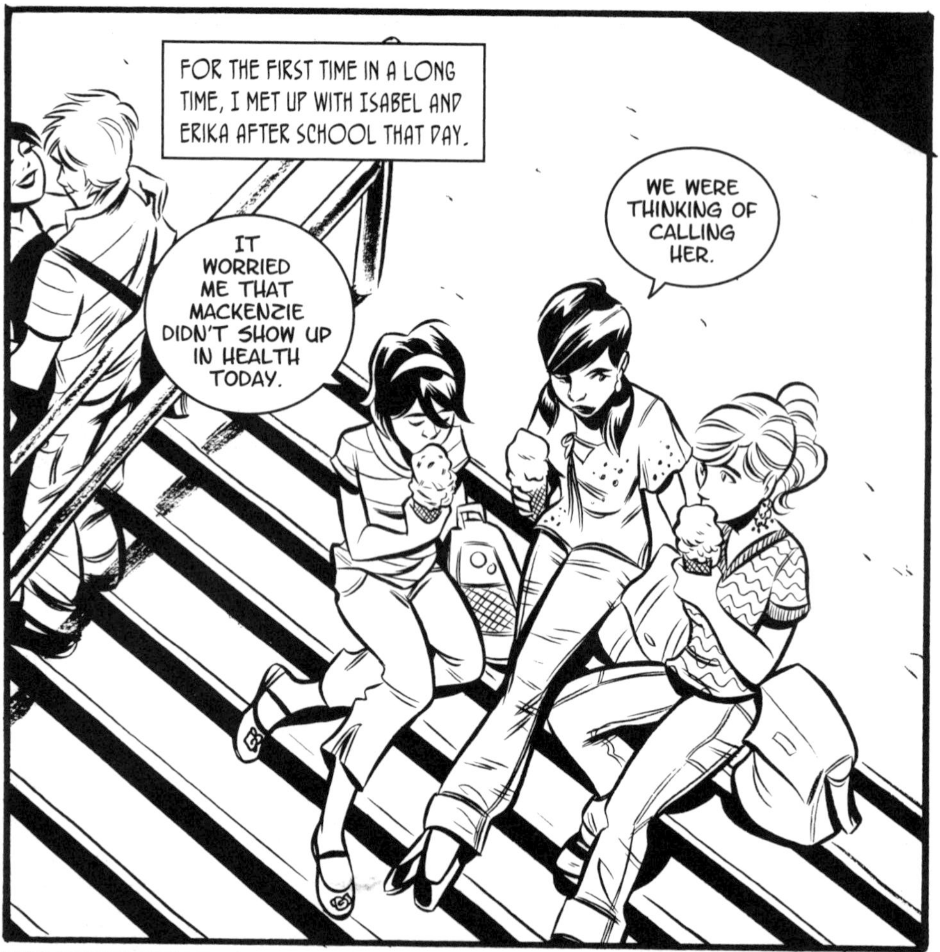
FOR THE FIRST TIME IN A LONG TIME, I MET UP WITH ISABEL AND ERIKA AFTER SCHOOL THAT DAY.
IT WORRIED ME THAT MACKENZIE DIDN'T SHOW UP IN HEALTH TODAY.
WE WERE THINKING OF CALLING HER.

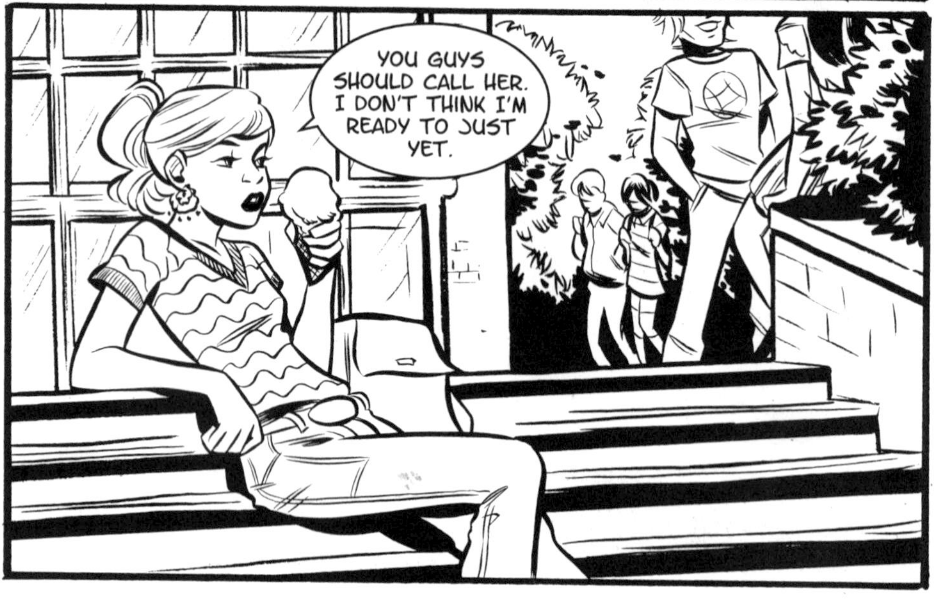
YOU GUYS SHOULD CALL HER. I DON'T THINK I'M READY TO JUST YET.

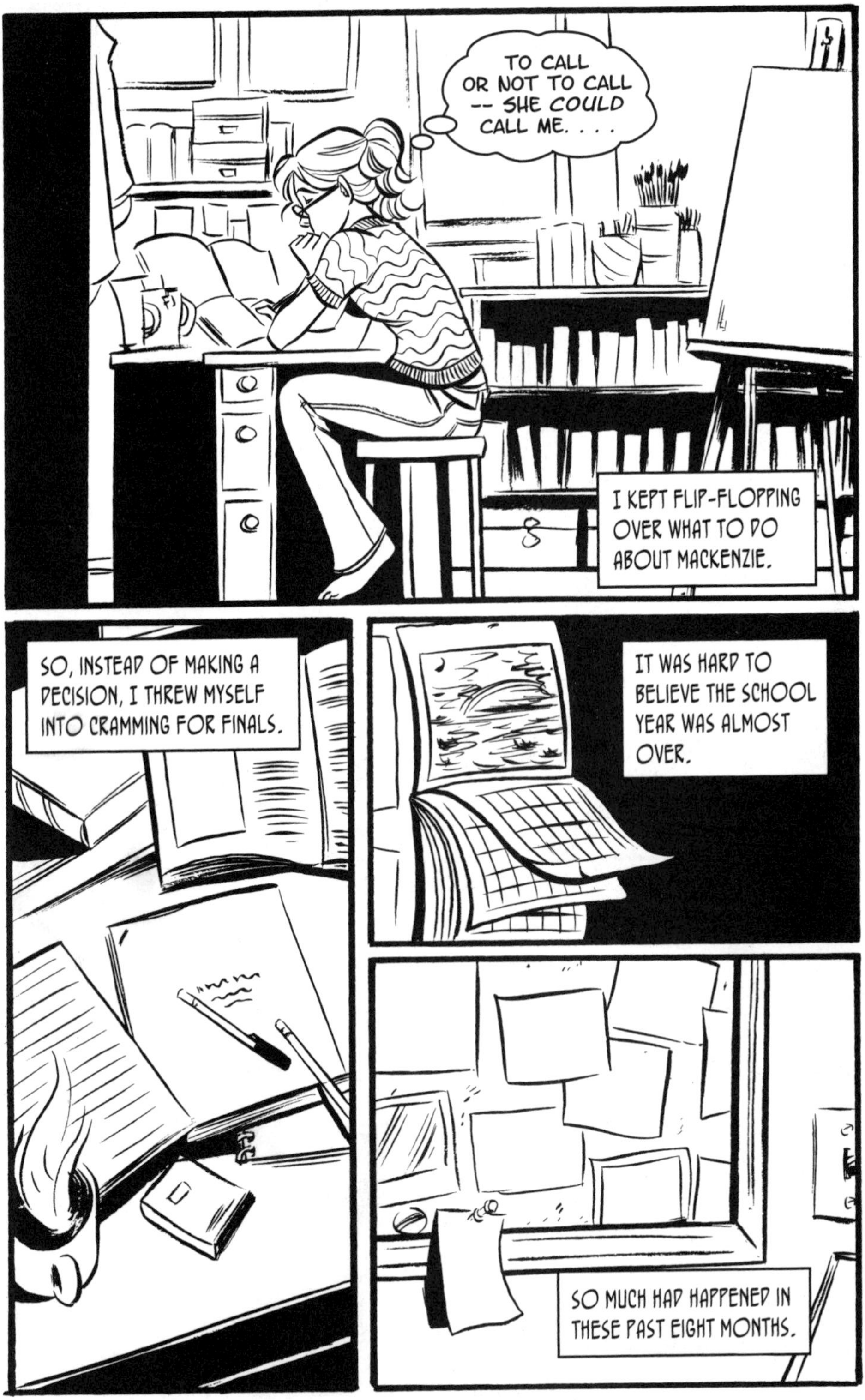
TO CALL OR NOT TO CALL -- SHE COULD CALL ME. . . .
I KEPT FLIP-FLOPPING OVER WHAT TO DO ABOUT MACKENZIE.
SO, INSTEAD OF MAKING A DECISION, I THREW MYSELF INTO CRAMMING FOR FINALS.
IT WAS HARD TO BELIEVE THE SCHOOL YEAR WAS ALMOST OVER.
SO MUCH HAD HAPPENED IN THESE PAST EIGHT MONTHS.

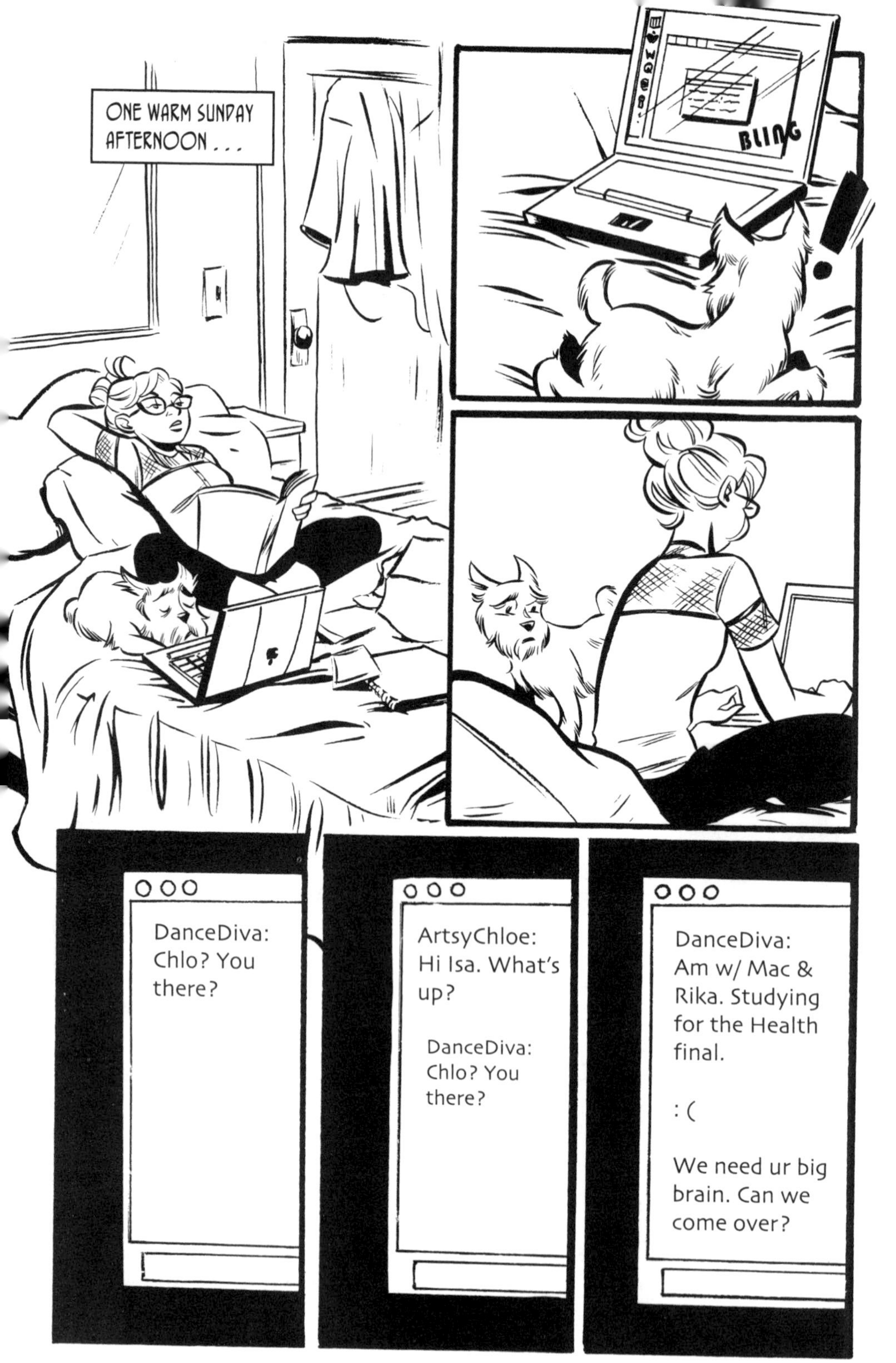
ONE WARM SUNDAY AFTERNOON . . .
BLING
!
DanceDiva: Chlo? You there?
ArtsyChloe: Hi Isa. What's up?
DanceDiva: Chlo? You there?
DanceDiva: Am w/ Mac & Rika. Studying for the Health final.
: (
We need ur big brain. Can we come over?

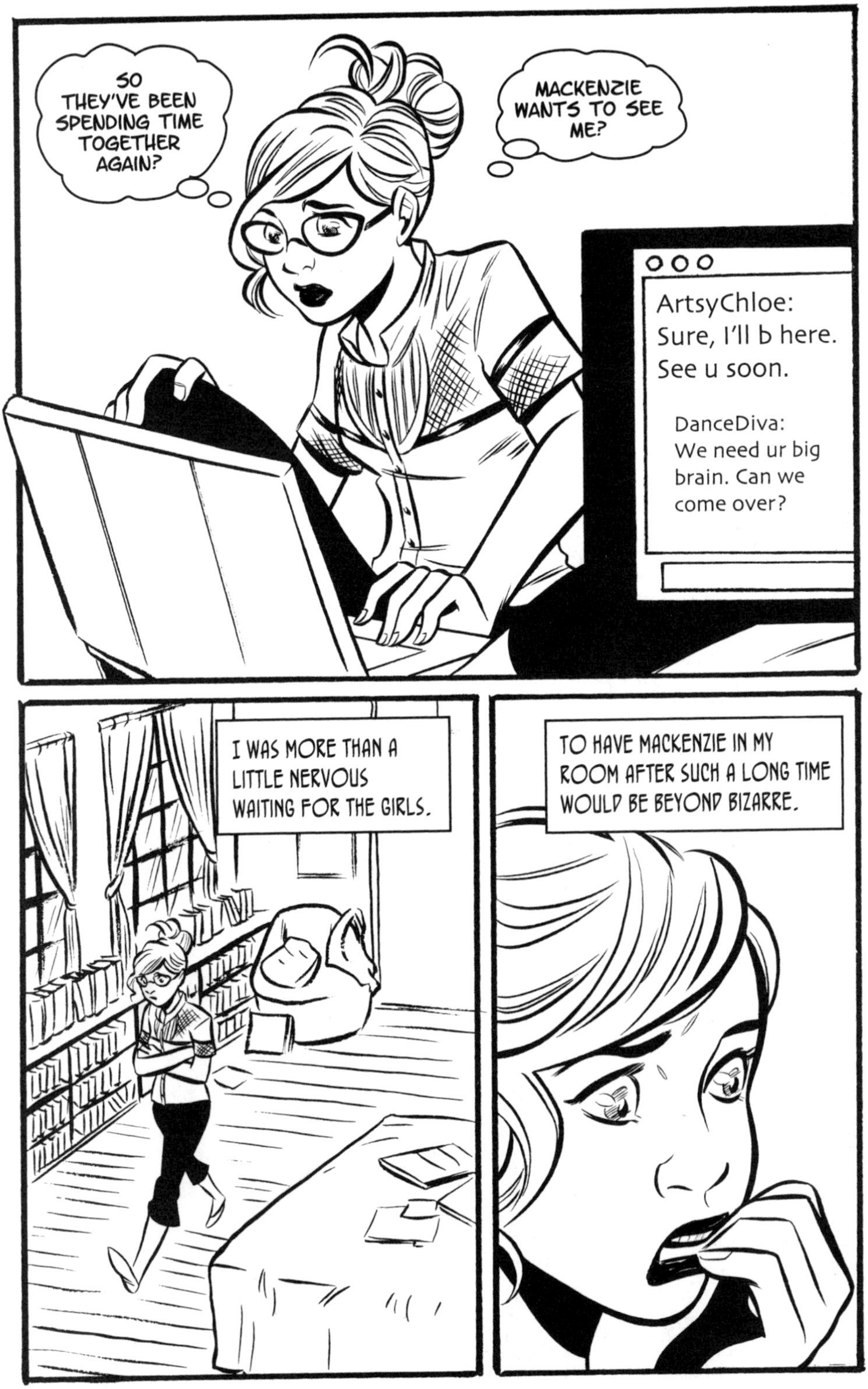
SO THEY'VE BEEN SPENDING TIME TOGETHER AGAIN?
MACKENZIE WANTS TO SEE ME?
ArtsyChloe: Sure, I'll b here. See u soon.
DanceDiva: We need ur big brain. Can we come over?
I WAS MORE THAN A LITTLE NERVOUS WAITING FOR THE GIRLS.
TO HAVE MACKENZIE IN MY ROOM AFTER SUCH A LONG TIME WOULD BE BEYOND BIZARRE.

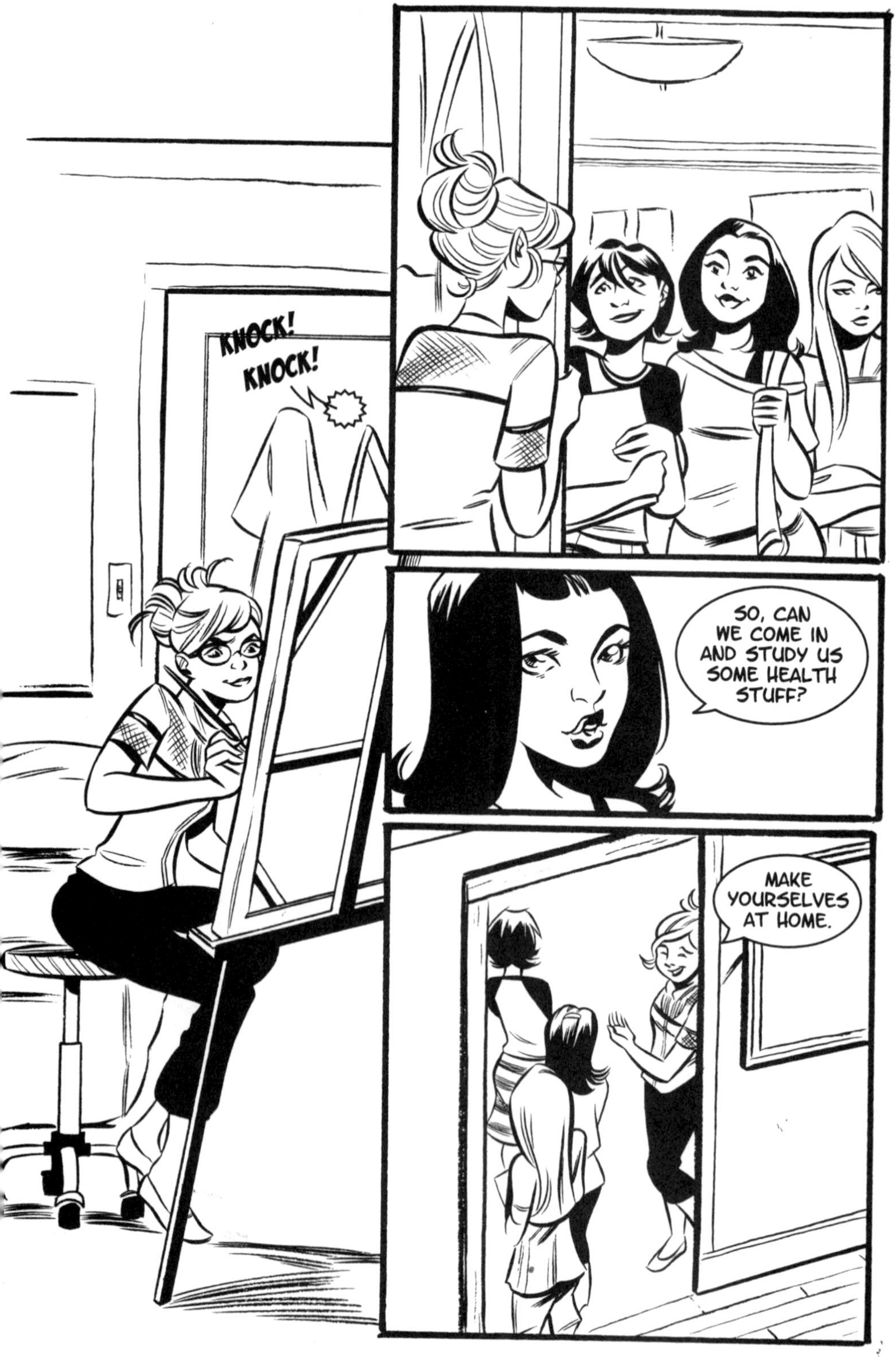
KNOCK! KNOCK!
SO, CAN WE COME IN AND STUDY US SOME HEALTH STUFF?
MAKE YOURSELVES AT HOME.

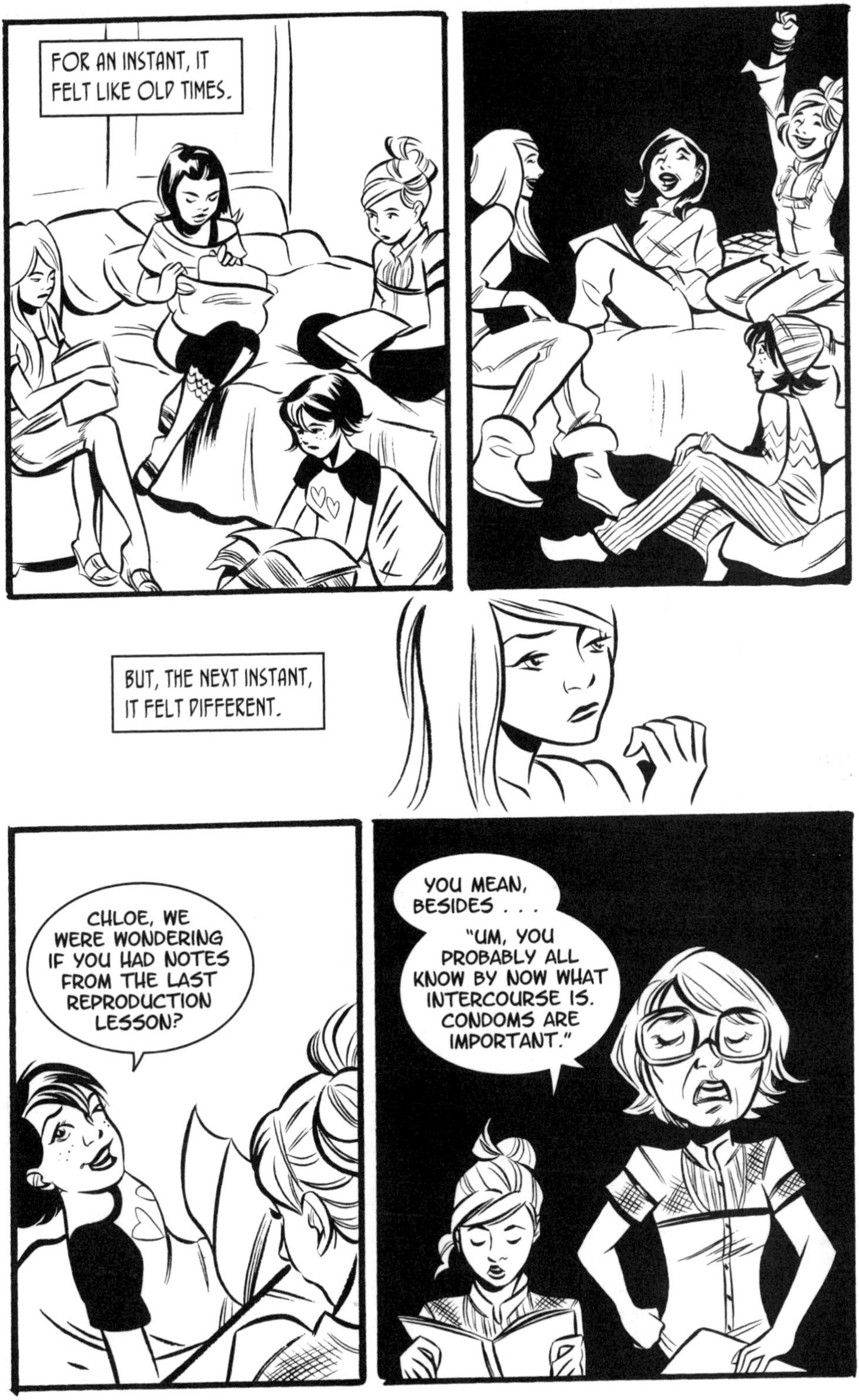
FOR AN INSTANT, IT FELT LIKE OLD TIMES.
BUT, THE NEXT INSTANT, IT FELT DIFFERENT.
CHLOE, WE WERE WONDERING IF YOU HAD NOTES FROM THE LAST REPRODUCTION LESSON?
YOU MEAN, BESIDES . . .
"UM, YOU PROBABLY ALL KNOW BY NOW WHAT INTERCOURSE IS. CONDOMS ARE IMPORTANT."

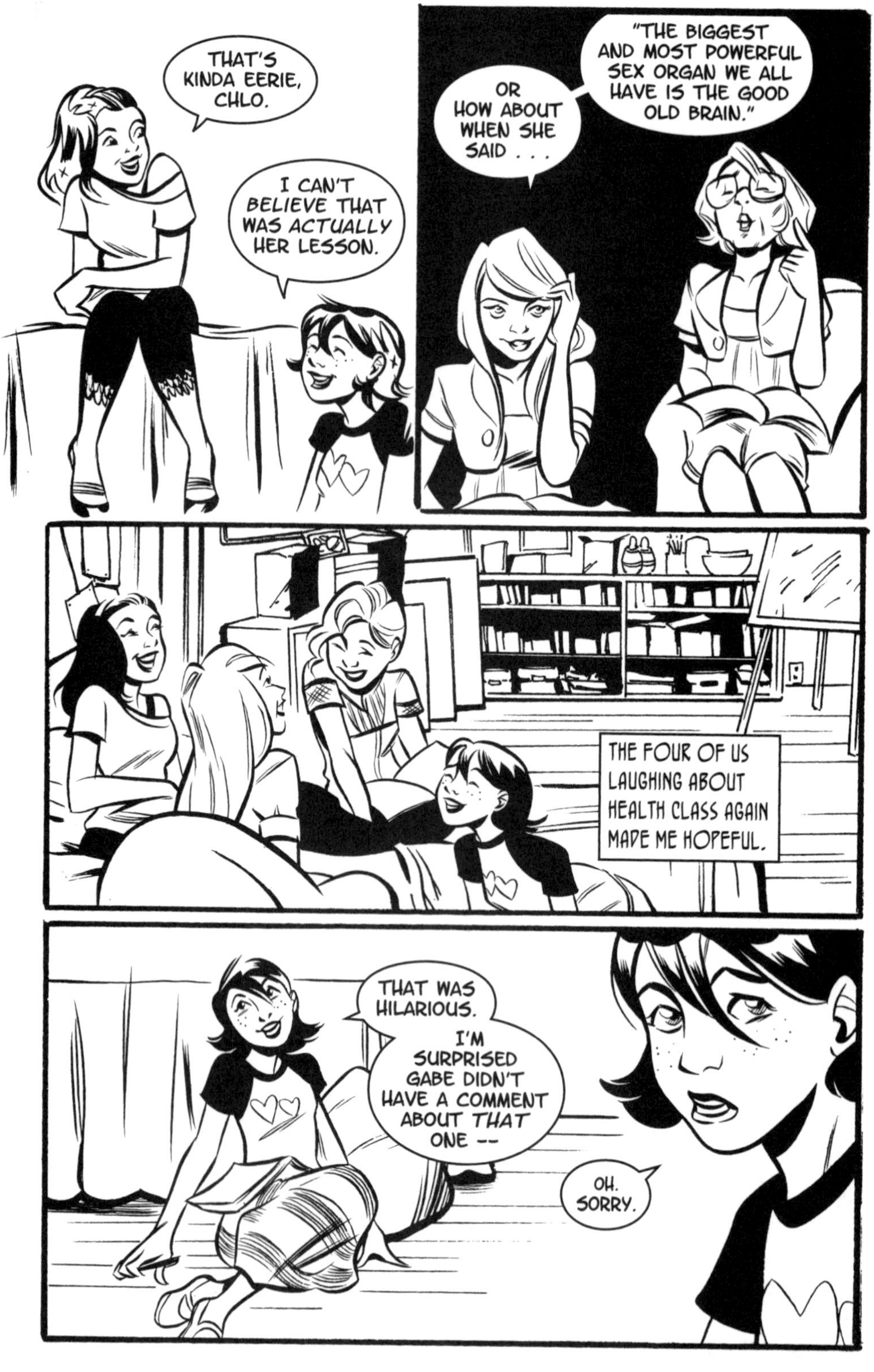
THAT'S KINDA EERIE, CHLO.
I CAN'T BELIEVE THAT WAS ACTUALLY HER LESSON.
OR HOW ABOUT WHEN SHE SAID . . .
"THE BIGGEST AND MOST POWERFUL SEX ORGAN WE ALL HAVE IS THE GOOD OLD BRAIN."
THE FOUR OF US LAUGHING ABOUT HEALTH CLASS AGAIN MADE ME HOPEFUL.
THAT WAS HILARIOUS.
I'M SURPRISED GABE DIDN'T HAVE A COMMENT ABOUT THAT ONE --
OH. SORRY.

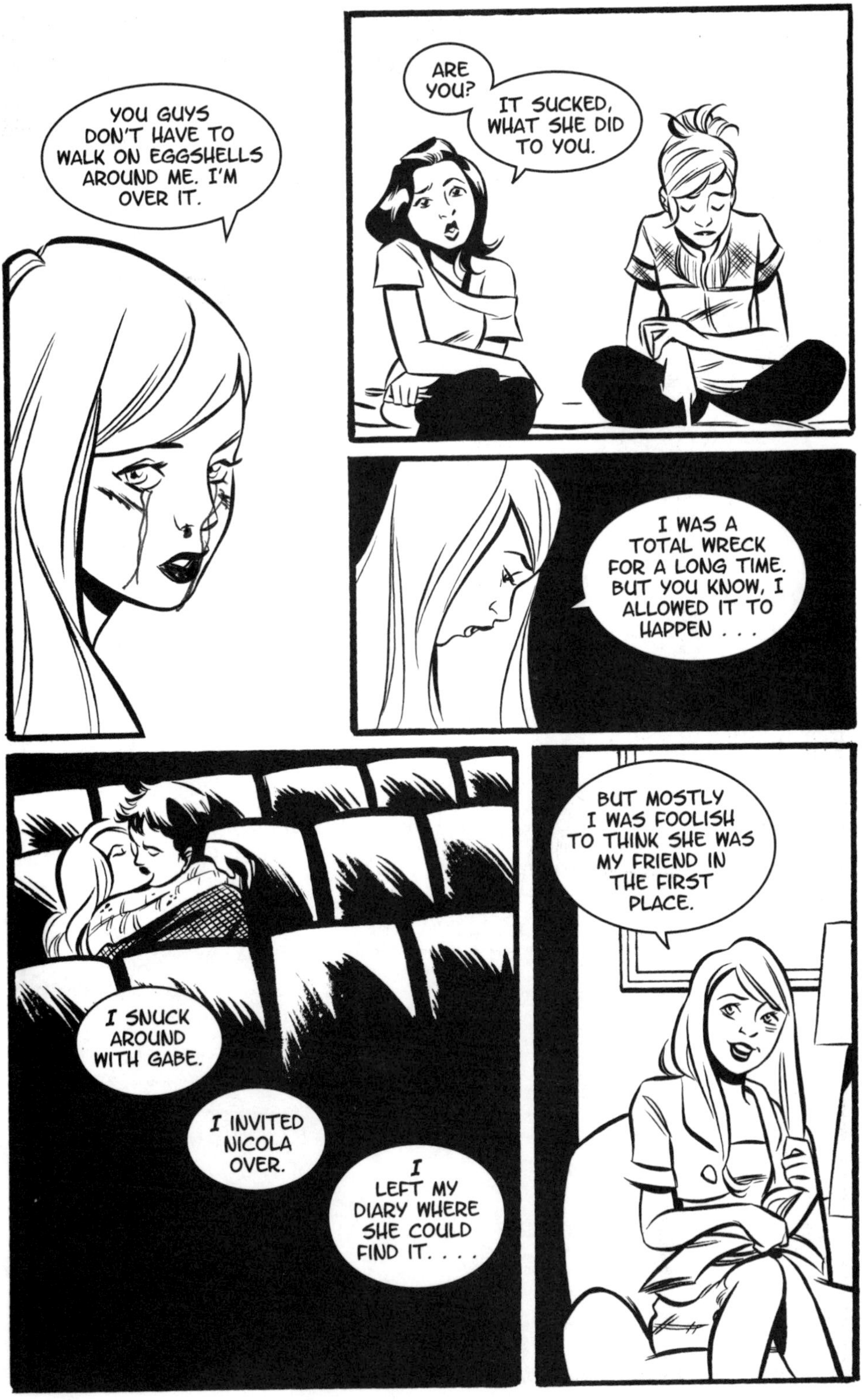

YOU GUYS DON'T HAVE TO WALK ON EGGSHELLS AROUND ME. I'M OVER IT.
ARE YOU?
IT SUCKED, WHAT SHE DID TO YOU.
I WAS A TOTAL WRECK FOR A LONG TIME. BUT YOU KNOW, I ALLOWED IT TO HAPPEN . . .
I SNUCK AROUND WITH GABE.
I INVITED NICOLA OVER.
I LEFT MY DIARY WHERE SHE COULD FIND IT. . . .
BUT MOSTLY I WAS FOOLISH TO THINK SHE WAS MY FRIEND IN THE FIRST PLACE.

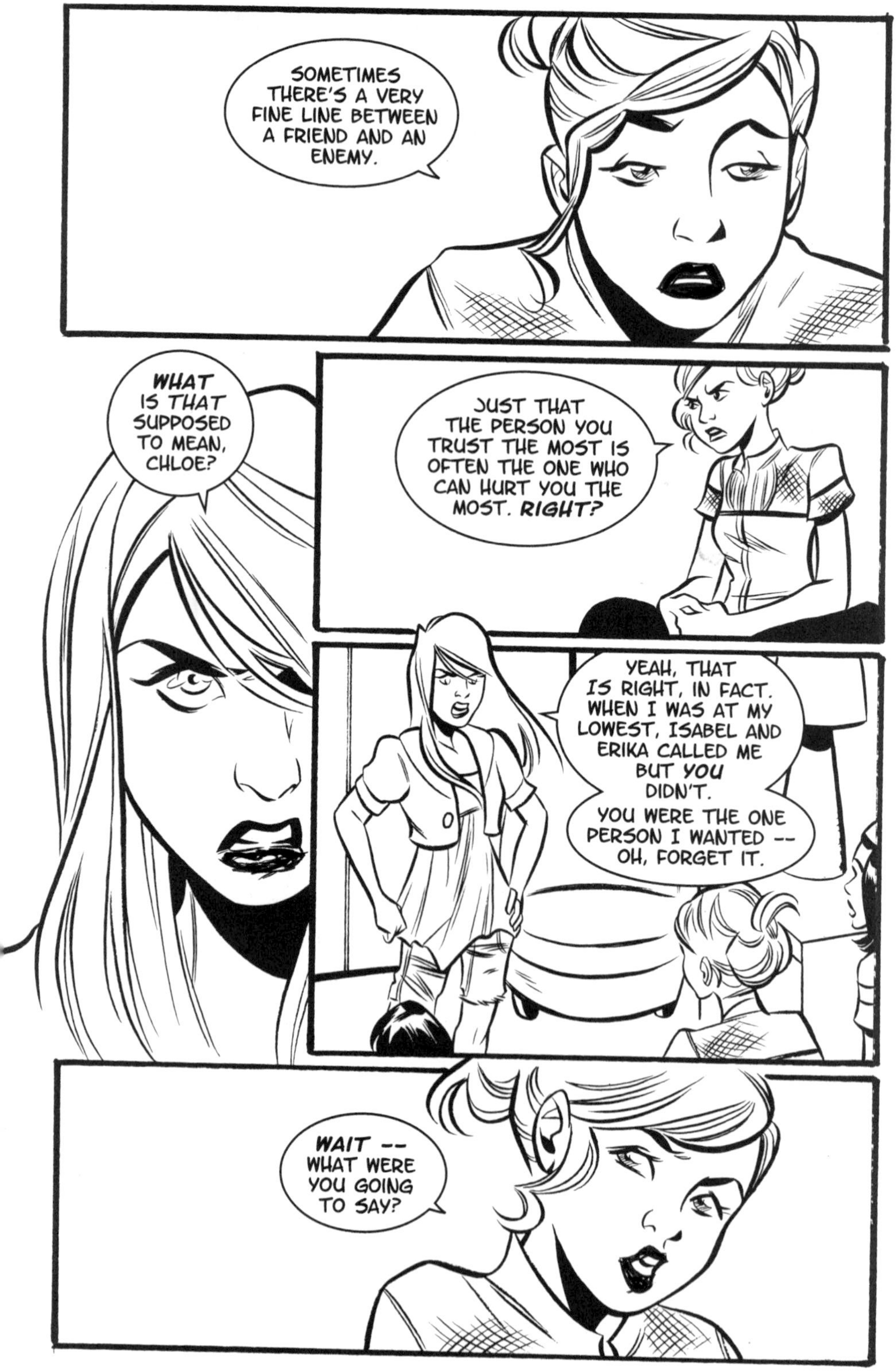
SOMETIMES THERE'S A VERY FINE LINE BETWEEN A FRIEND AND AN ENEMY.
WHAT IS THAT SUPPOSED TO MEAN, CHLOE?
JUST THAT THE PERSON YOU TRUST THE MOST IS OFTEN THE ONE WHO CAN HURT YOU THE MOST. RIGHT?
YEAH, THAT IS RIGHT, IN FACT. WHEN I WAS AT MY LOWEST, ISABEL AND ERIKA CALLED ME BUT YOU DIDN'T.
YOU WERE THE ONE PERSON I WANTED -- OH, FORGET IT.
WAIT -- WHAT WERE YOU GOING TO SAY?

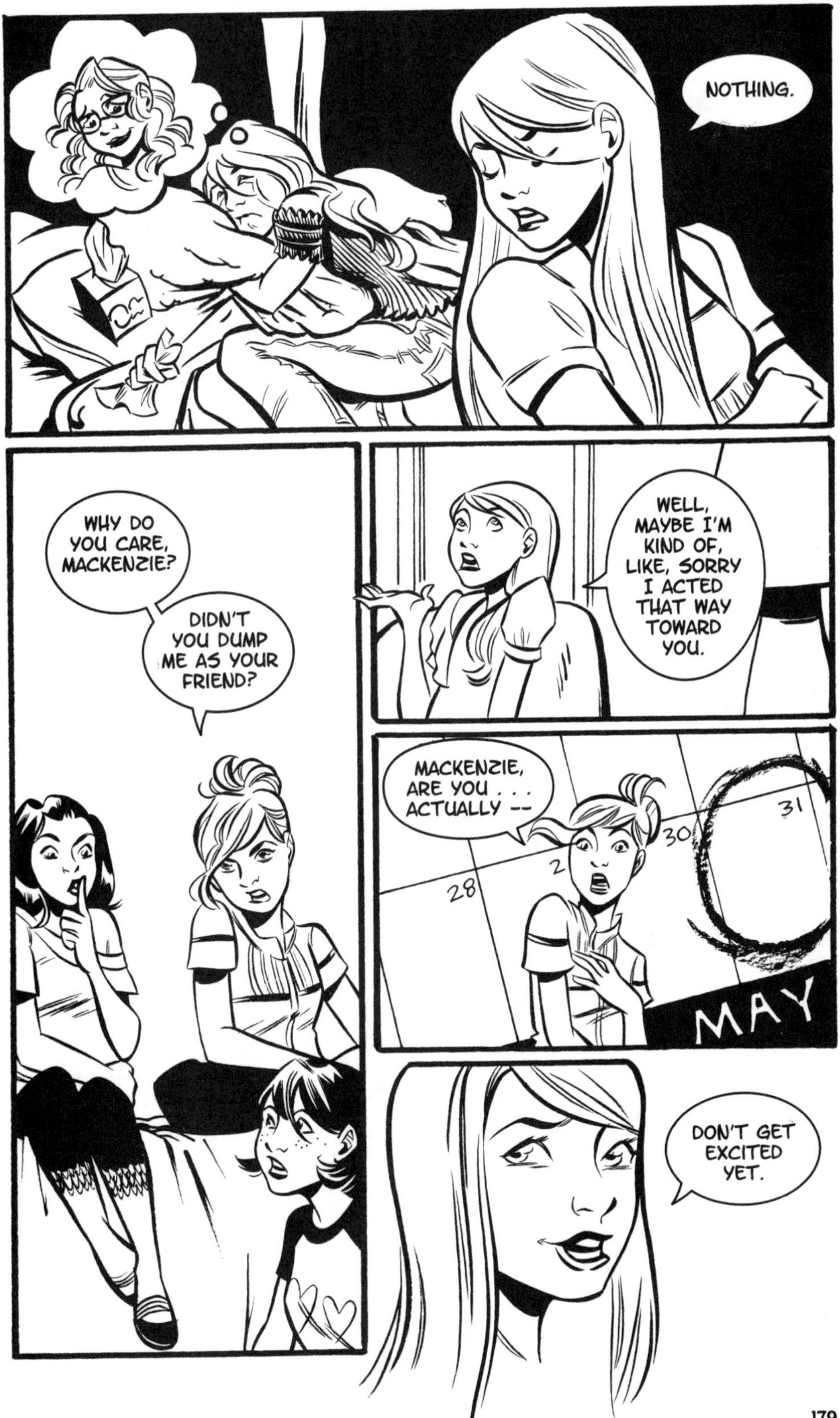
NOTHING.
WHY DO YOU CARE, MACKENZIE?
DIDN'T YOU DUMP ME AS YOUR FRIEND?
WELL, MAYBE I'M KIND OF, LIKE, SORRY I ACTED THAT WAY TOWARD YOU.
MACKENZIE, ARE YOU . . . ACTUALLY --
28
2
30
31
MAY
DON'T GET EXCITED YET.

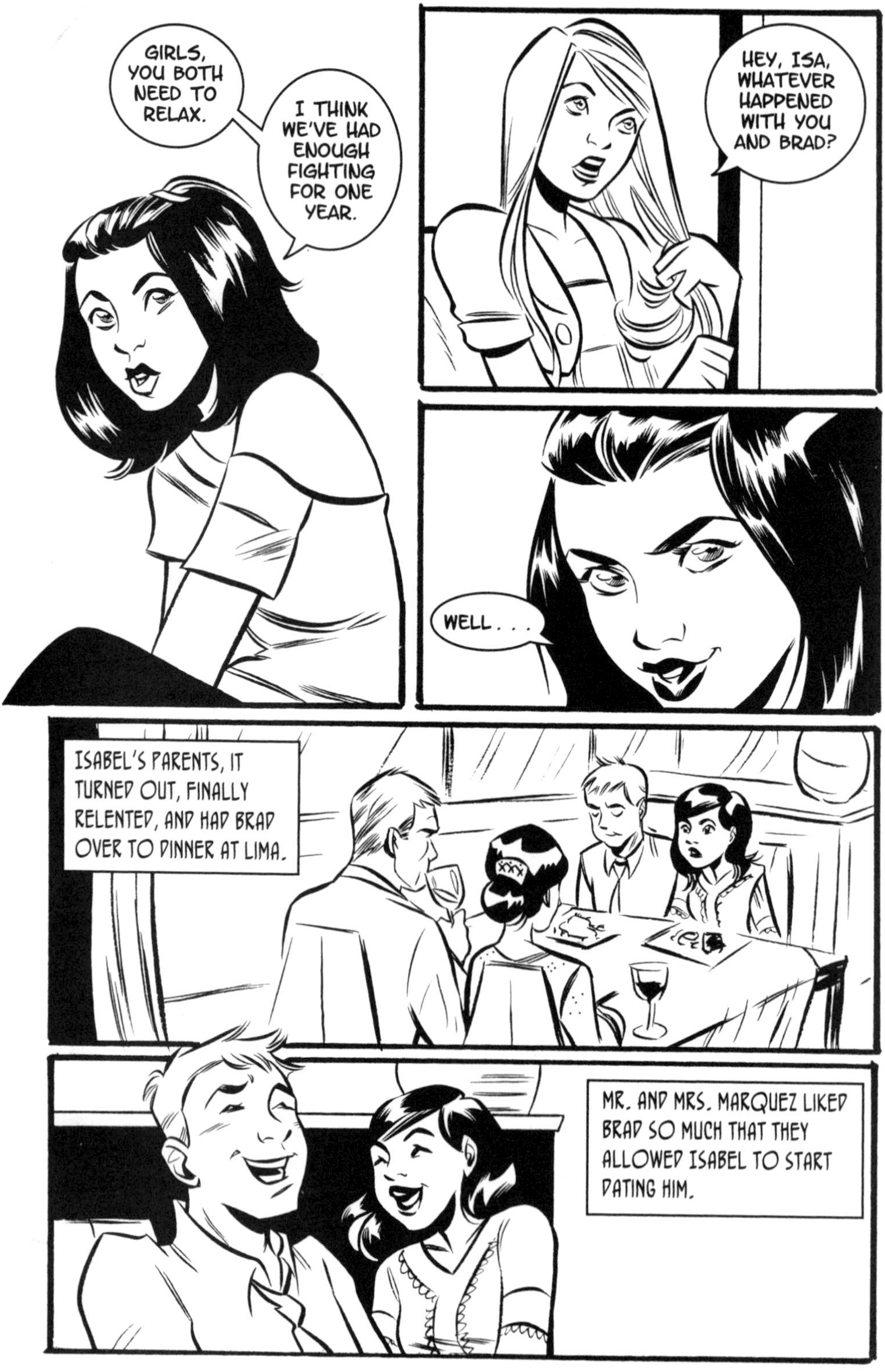
GIRLS, YOU BOTH NEED TO RELAX.
I THINK WE'VE HAD ENOUGH FIGHTING FOR ONE YEAR.
HEY, ISA, WHATEVER HAPPENED WITH YOU AND BRAD?
WELL . . .
ISABEL'S PARENTS, IT TURNED OUT, FINALLY RELENTED, AND HAD BRAD OVER TO DINNER AT LIMA.
MR. AND MRS. MARQUEZ LIKED BRAD SO MUCH THAT THEY ALLOWED ISABEL TO START DATING HIM.

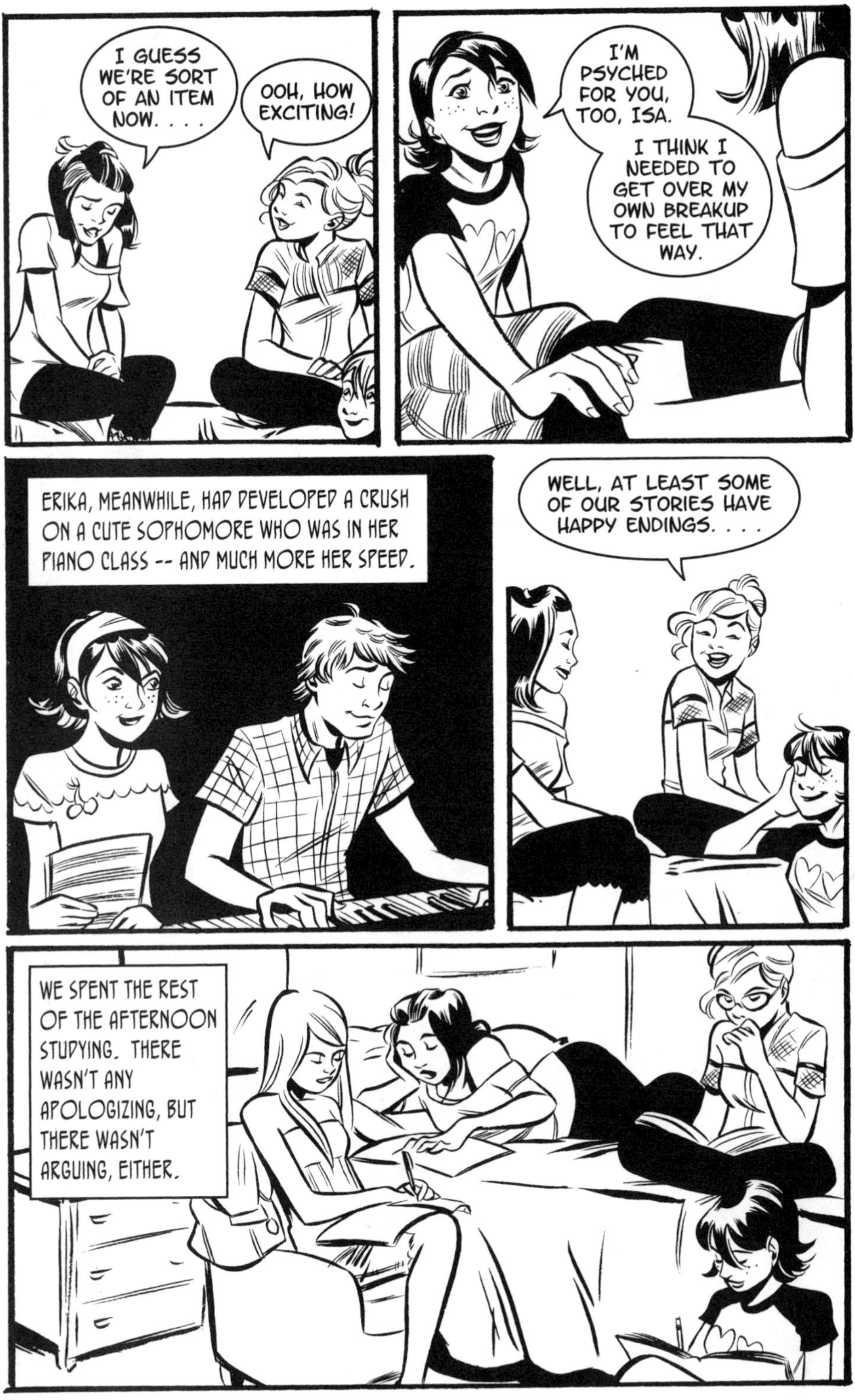
I GUESS WE'RE SORT OF AN ITEM NOW. . . .
OOH, HOW EXCITING!
I'M PSYCHED FOR YOU, TOO, ISA.
I THINK I NEEDED TO GET OVER MY OWN BREAKUP TO FEEL THAT WAY.
ERIKA, MEANWHILE, HAD DEVELOPED A CRUSH ON A CUTE SOPHOMORE WHO WAS IN HER PIANO CLASS -- AND MUCH MORE HER SPEED.
WELL, AT LEAST SOME OF OUR STORIES HAVE HAPPY ENDINGS. . . .
WE SPENT THE REST OF THE AFTERNOON STUDYING. THERE WASN'T ANY APOLOGIZING, BUT THERE WASN'T ARGUING, EITHER.

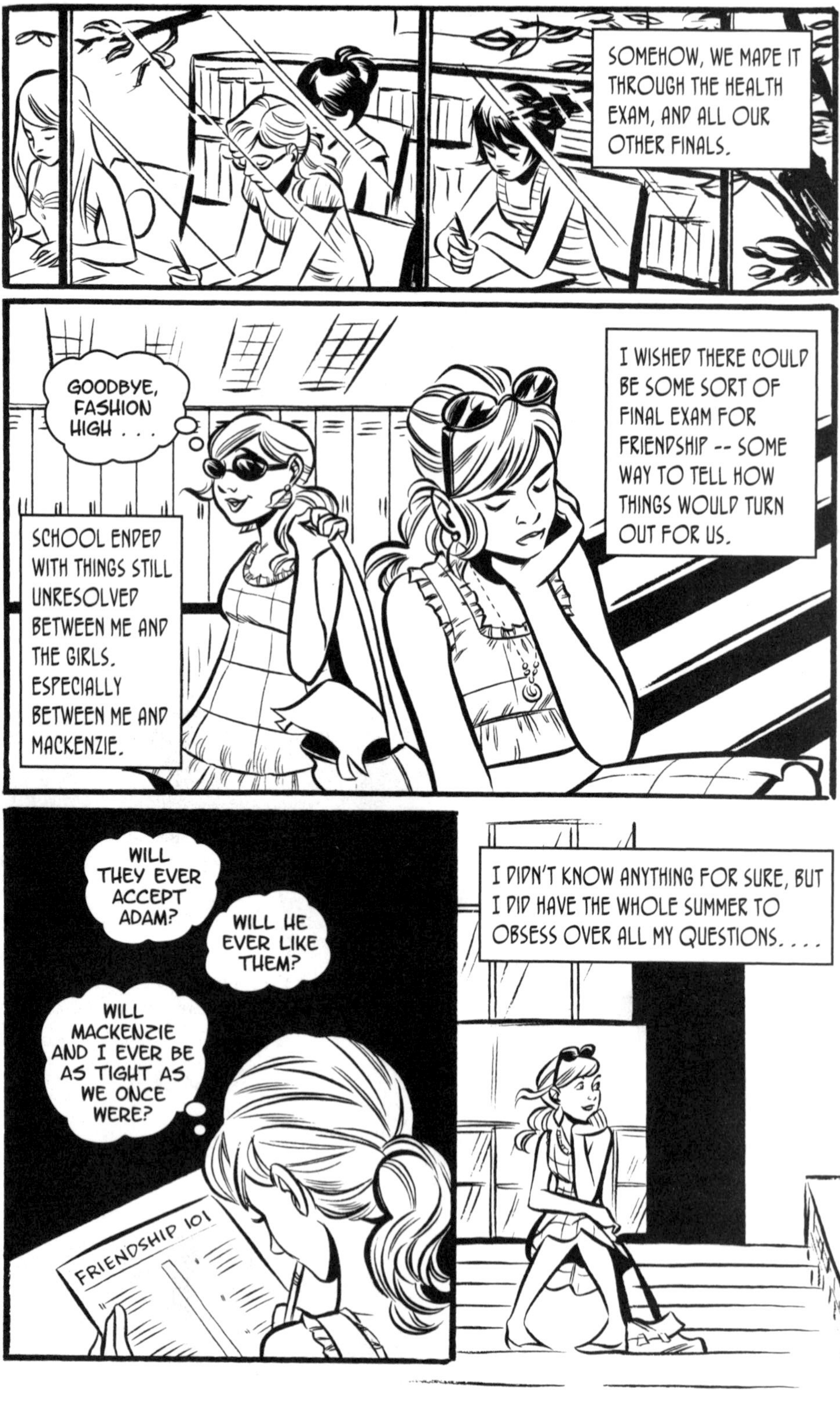
SOMEHOW, WE MADE IT THROUGH THE HEALTH EXAM, AND ALL OUR OTHER FINALS.
GOODBYE, FASHION HIGH . . .
SCHOOL ENDED WITH THINGS STILL UNRESOLVED BETWEEN ME AND THE GIRLS. ESPECIALLY BETWEEN ME AND MACKENZIE.
I WISHED THERE COULD BE SOME SORT OF FINAL EXAM FOR FRIENDSHIP -- SOME WAY TO TELL HOW THINGS WOULD TURN OUT FOR US.
WILL THEY EVER ACCEPT ADAM?
WILL HE EVER LIKE THEM?
WILL MACKENZIE AND I EVER BE AS TIGHT AS WE ONCE WERE?
FRIENDSHIP 101
I DIDN'T KNOW ANYTHING FOR SURE, BUT I DID HAVE THE WHOLE SUMMER TO OBSESS OVER ALL MY QUESTIONS. . . .

Epilogue: Meeting Up

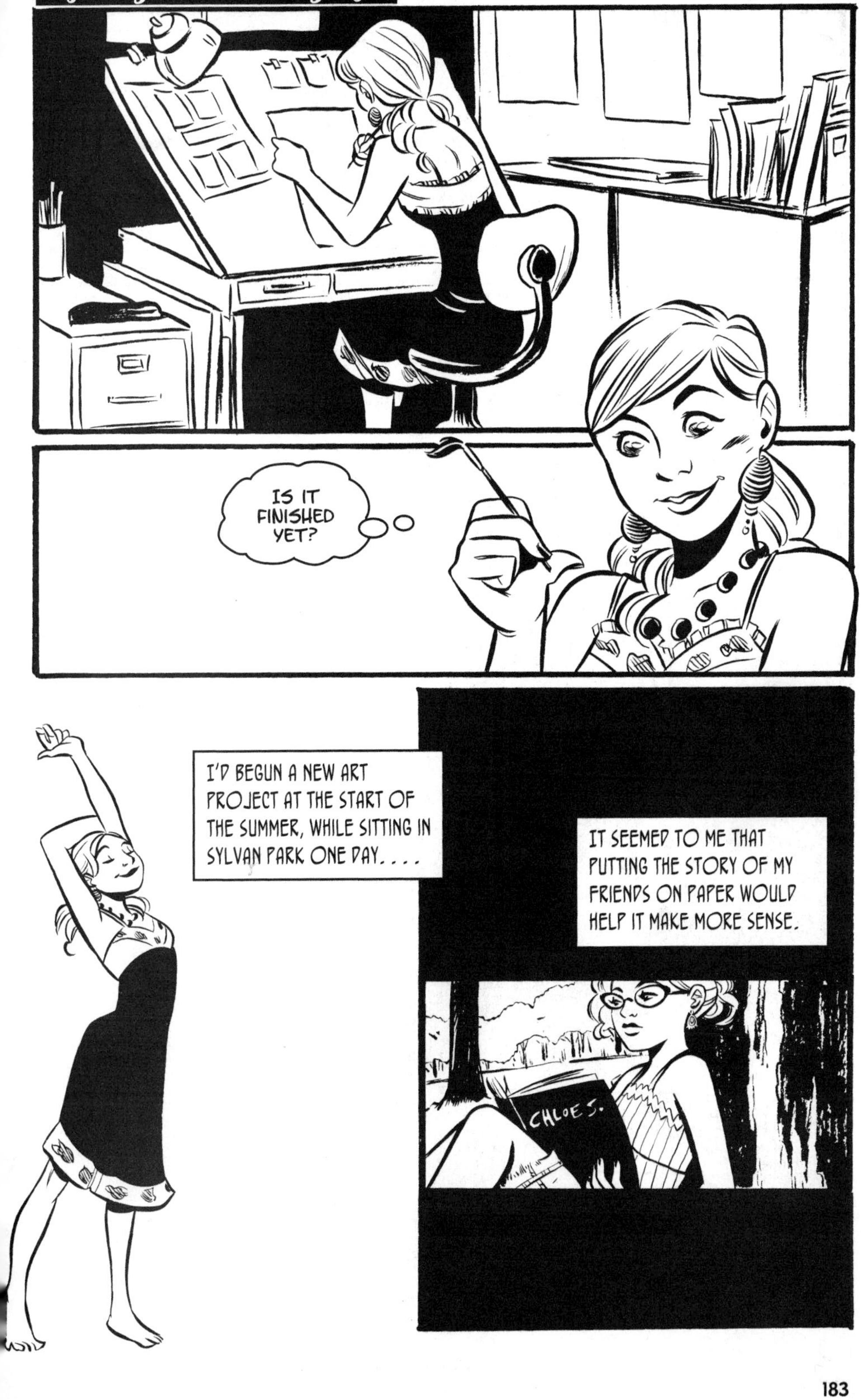
IS IT FINISHED YET?
I'D BEGUN A NEW ART PROJECT AT THE START OF THE SUMMER, WHILE SITTING IN SYLVAN PARK ONE DAY. . . .
IT SEEMED TO ME THAT PUTTING THE STORY OF MY FRIENDS ON PAPER WOULD HELP IT MAKE MORE SENSE.
CHLOE S.

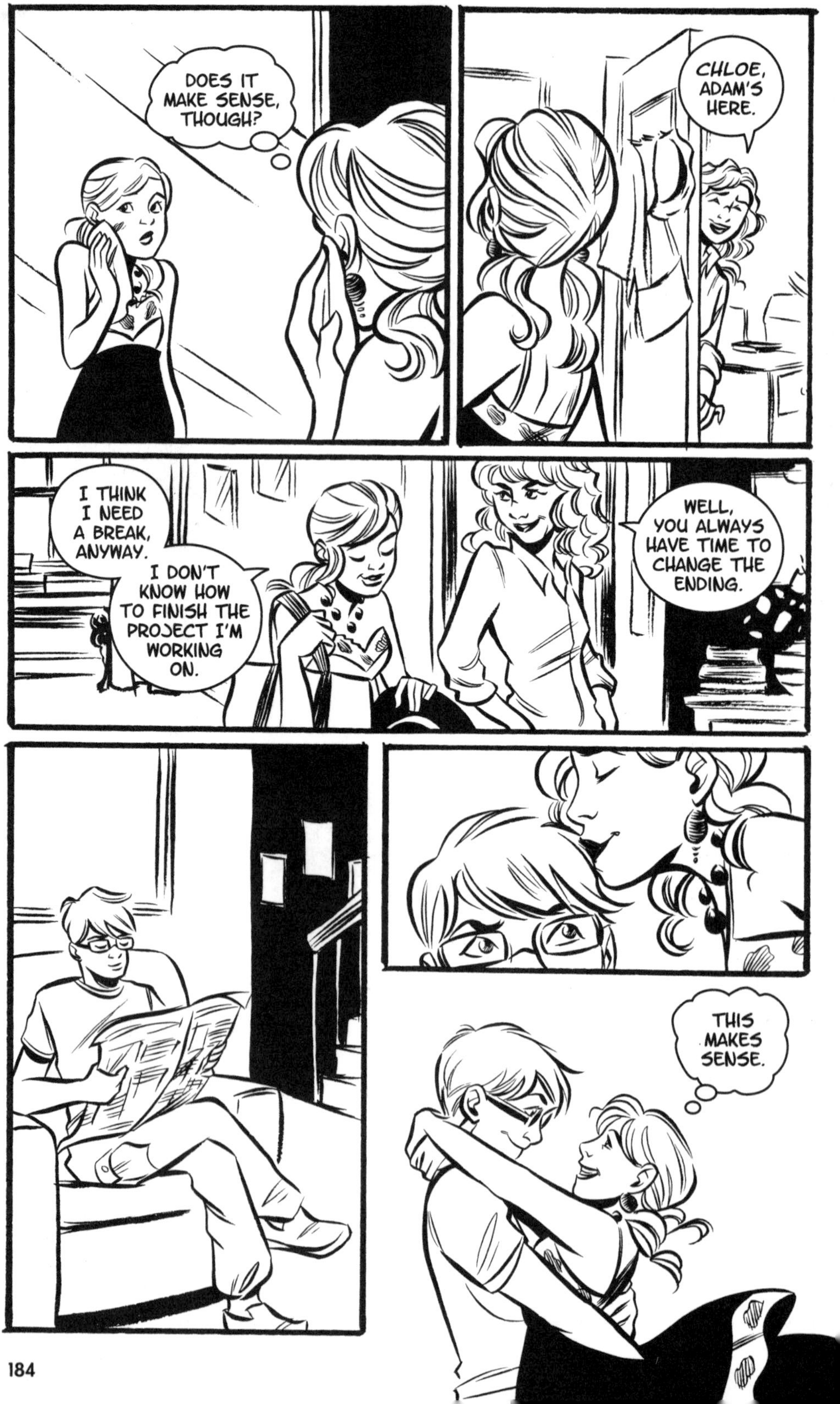
DOES IT MAKE SENSE, THOUGH?
CHLOE, ADAM'S HERE.
I THINK I NEED A BREAK, ANYWAY.
I DON'T KNOW HOW TO FINISH THE PROJECT I'M WORKING ON.
WELL, YOU ALWAYS HAVE TIME TO CHANGE THE ENDING.
THIS MAKES SENSE.

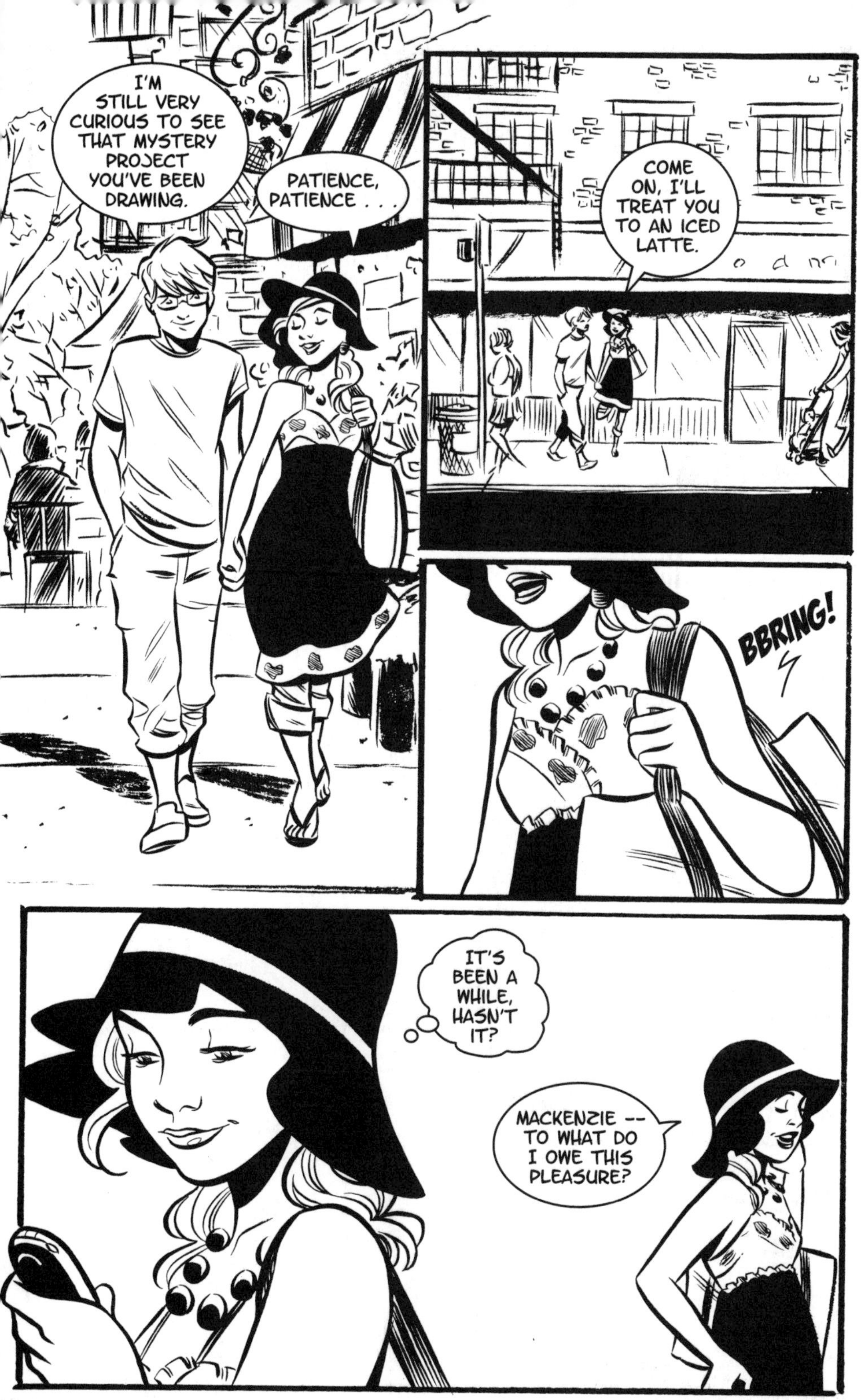
I'M STILL VERY CURIOUS TO SEE THAT MYSTERY PROJECT YOU'VE BEEN DRAWING.
PATIENCE, PATIENCE . . .
COME ON, I'LL TREAT YOU TO AN ICED LATTE.
BBRING!
IT'S BEEN A WHILE, HASN'T IT?
MACKENZIE -- TO WHAT DO I OWE THIS PLEASURE?

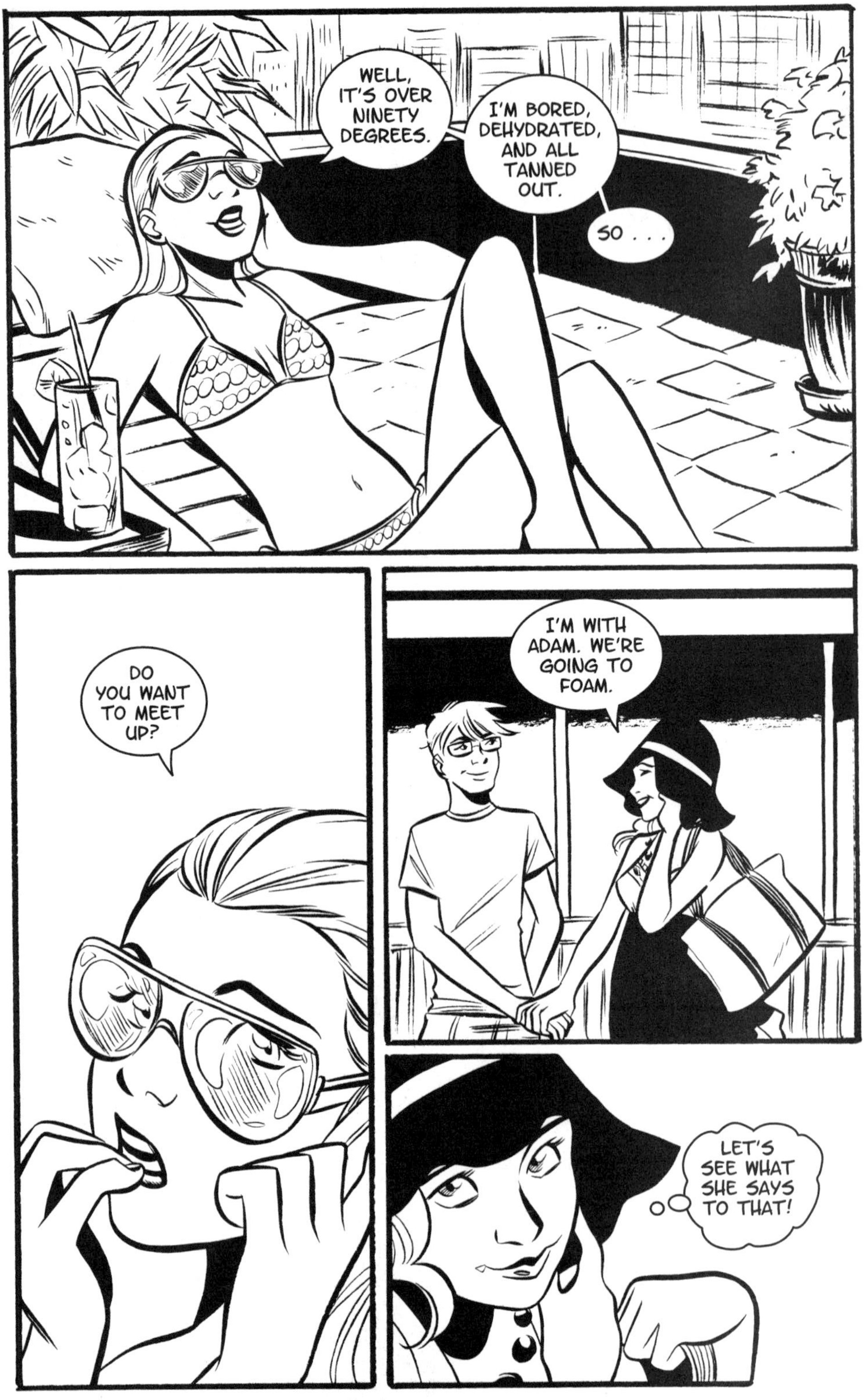
WELL, IT'S OVER NINETY DEGREES.
I'M BORED, DEHYDRATED, AND ALL TANNED OUT.
SO . . .
DO YOU WANT TO MEET UP?
I'M WITH ADAM. WE'RE GOING TO FOAM.
LET'S SEE WHAT SHE SAYS TO THAT!

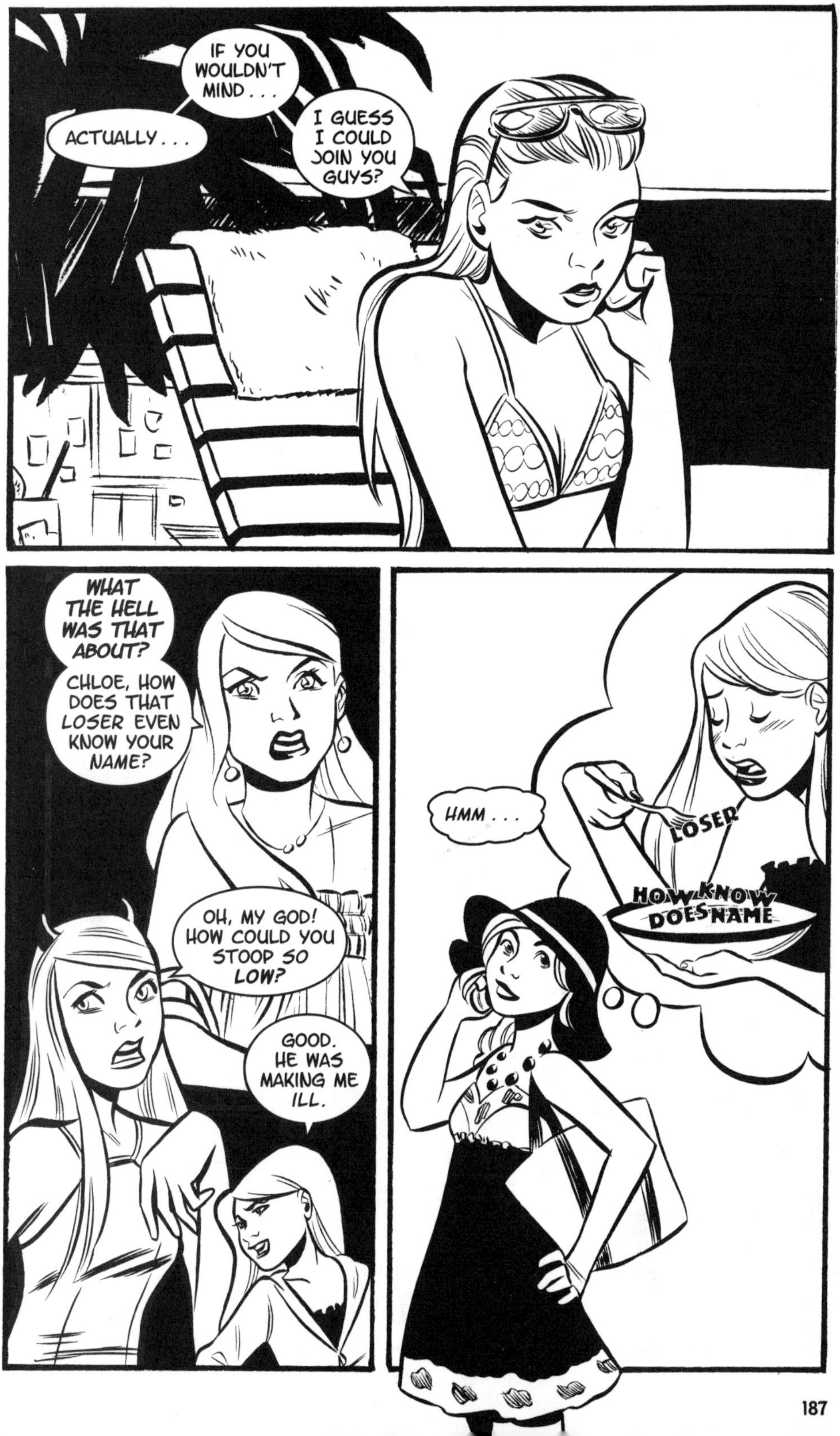
ACTUALLY . . .
IF YOU WOULDN'T MIND . . .
I GUESS I COULD JOIN YOU GUYS?
WHAT THE HELL WAS THAT ABOUT?
CHLOE, HOW DOES THAT LOSER EVEN KNOW YOUR NAME?
OH, MY GOD! HOW COULD YOU STOOP SO LOW?
GOOD. HE WAS MAKING ME ILL.
HMM . . .
LOSER
HOW KNOW
DOES NAME

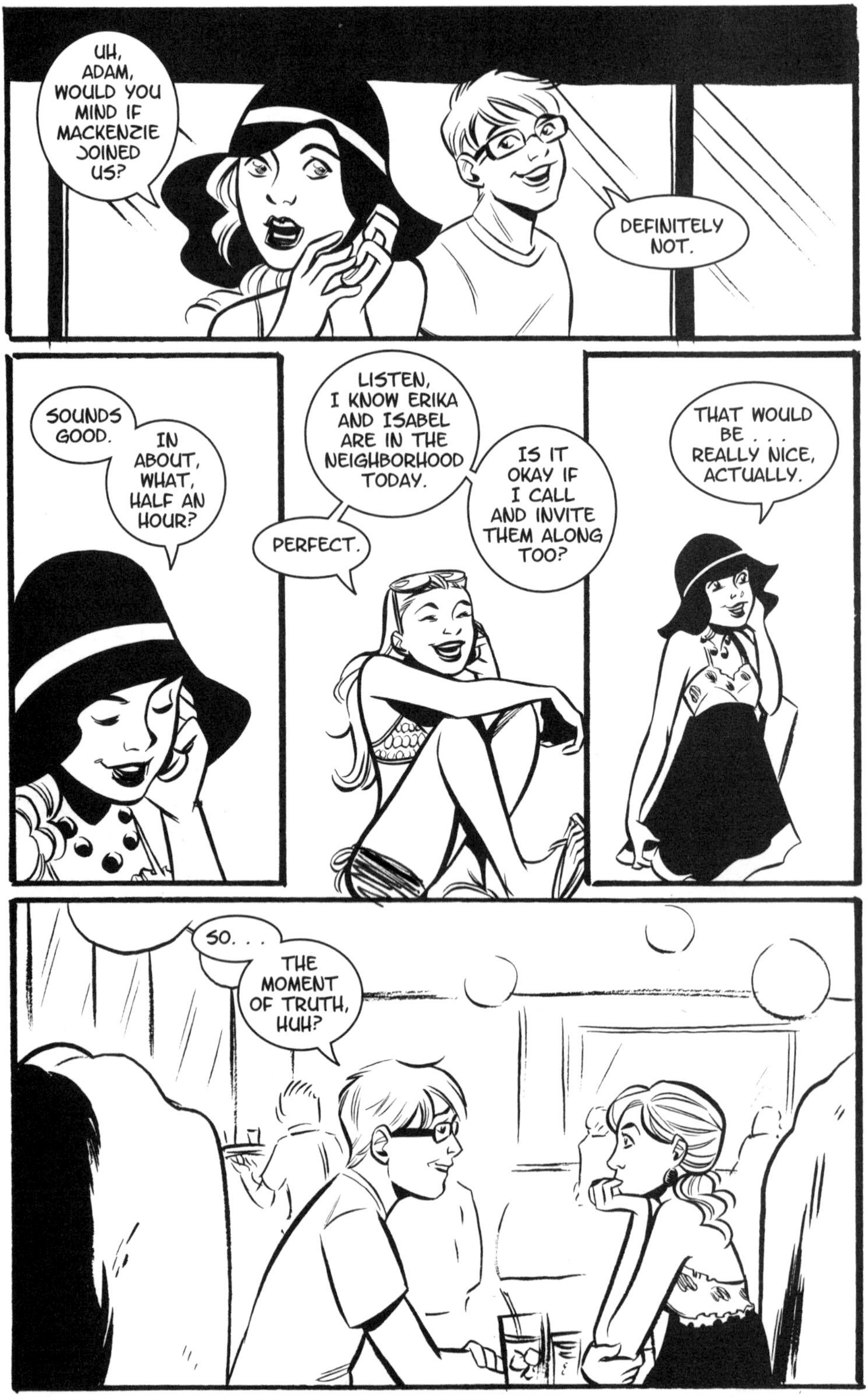
UH, ADAM, WOULD YOU MIND IF MACKENZIE JOINED US?
DEFINITELY NOT.
SOUNDS GOOD.
IN ABOUT, WHAT, HALF AN HOUR?
LISTEN, I KNOW ERIKA AND ISABEL ARE IN THE NEIGHBORHOOD TODAY.
PERFECT.
IS IT OKAY IF I CALL AND INVITE THEM ALONG TOO?
THAT WOULD BE . . . REALLY NICE, ACTUALLY.
SO. . .
THE MOMENT OF TRUTH, HUH?

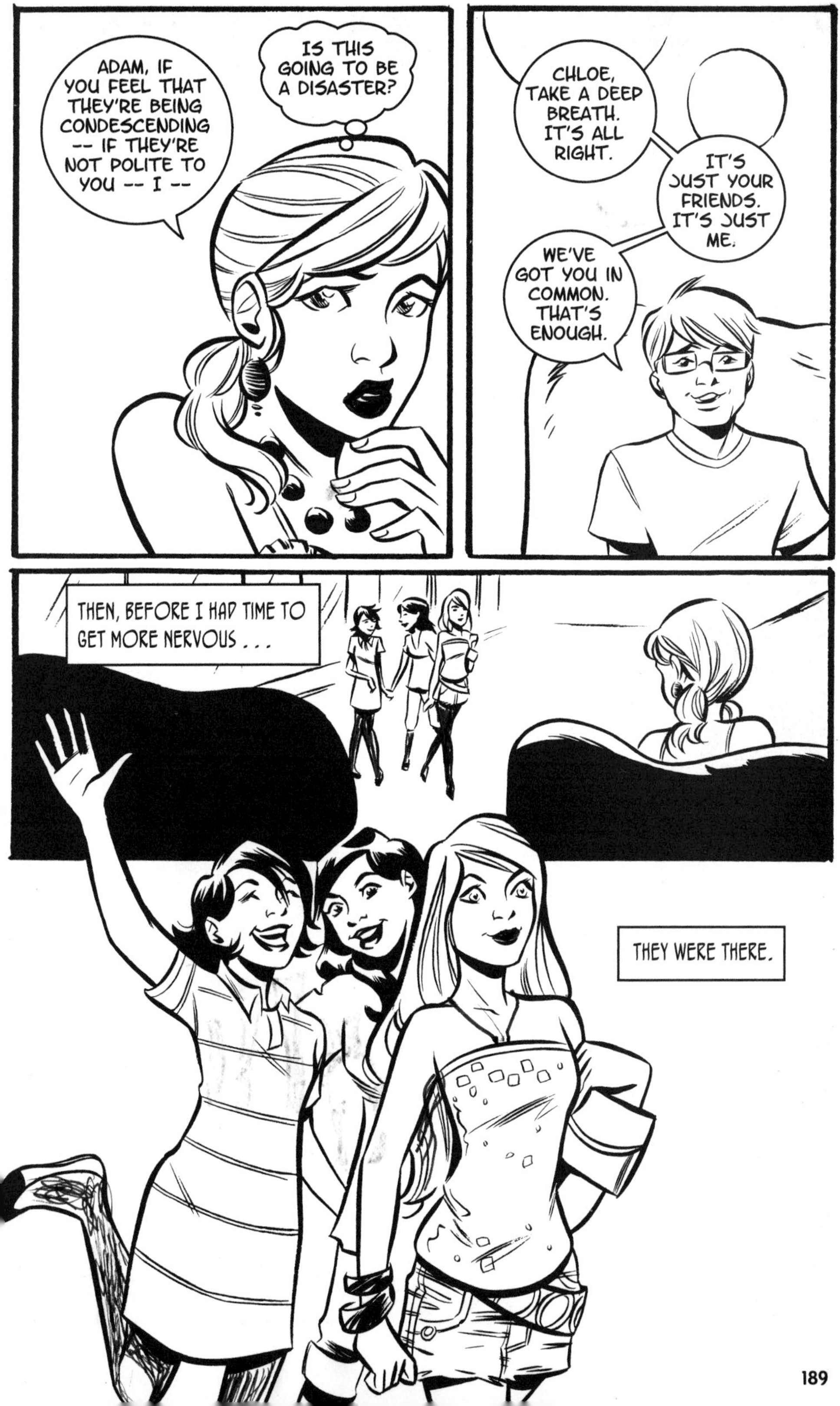
ADAM, IF YOU FEEL THAT THEY'RE BEING CONDESCENDING -- IF THEY'RE NOT POLITE TO YOU -- I --
IS THIS GOING TO BE A DISASTER?
CHLOE, TAKE A DEEP BREATH. IT'S ALL RIGHT.
IT'S JUST YOUR FRIENDS. IT'S JUST ME.
WE'VE GOT YOU IN COMMON. THAT'S ENOUGH.
THEN, BEFORE I HAD TIME TO GET MORE NERVOUS . . .
THEY WERE THERE.

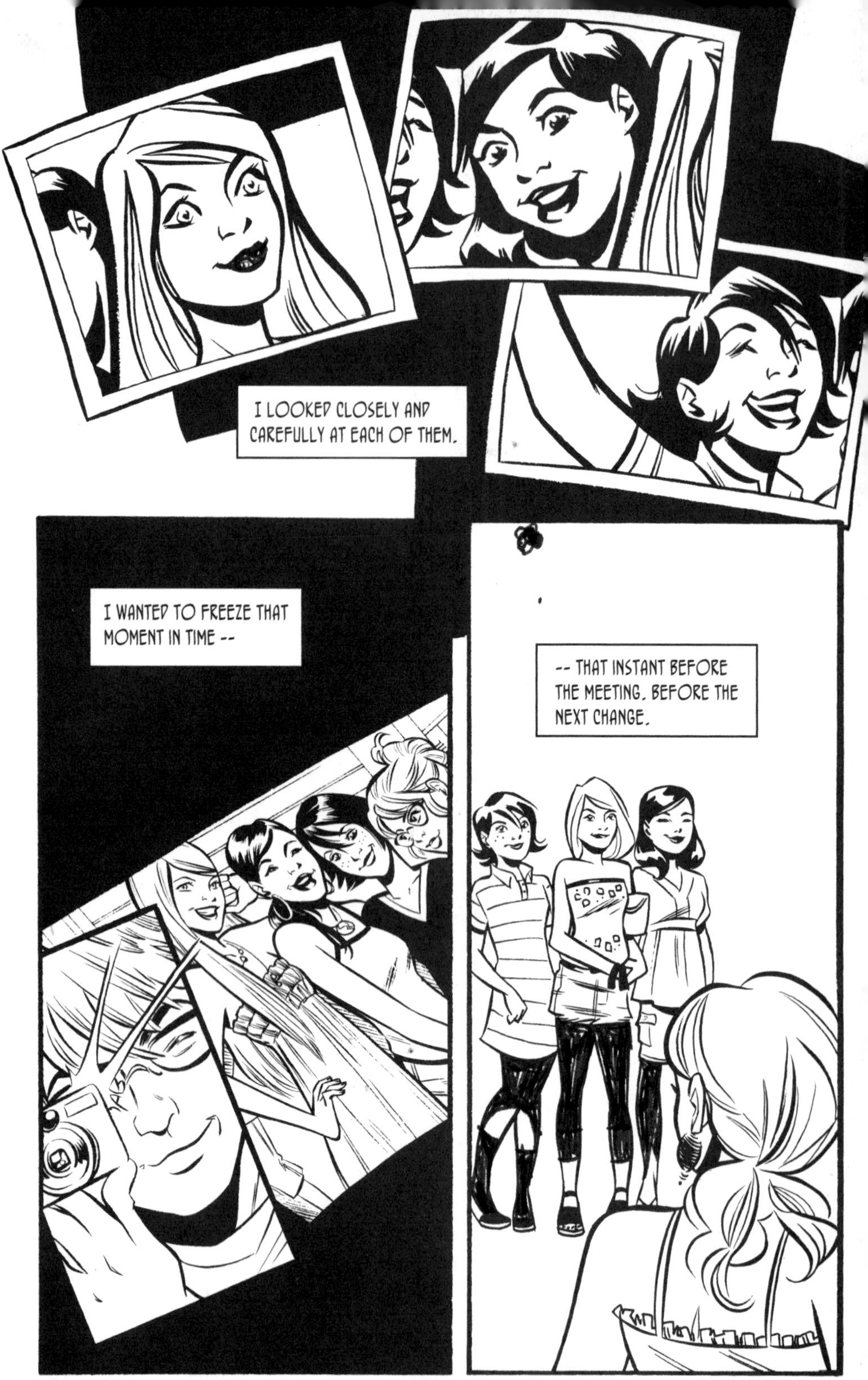
I LOOKED CLOSELY AND CAREFULLY AT EACH OF THEM.
I WANTED TO FREEZE THAT MOMENT IN TIME --
-- THAT INSTANT BEFORE THE MEETING. BEFORE THE NEXT CHANGE.

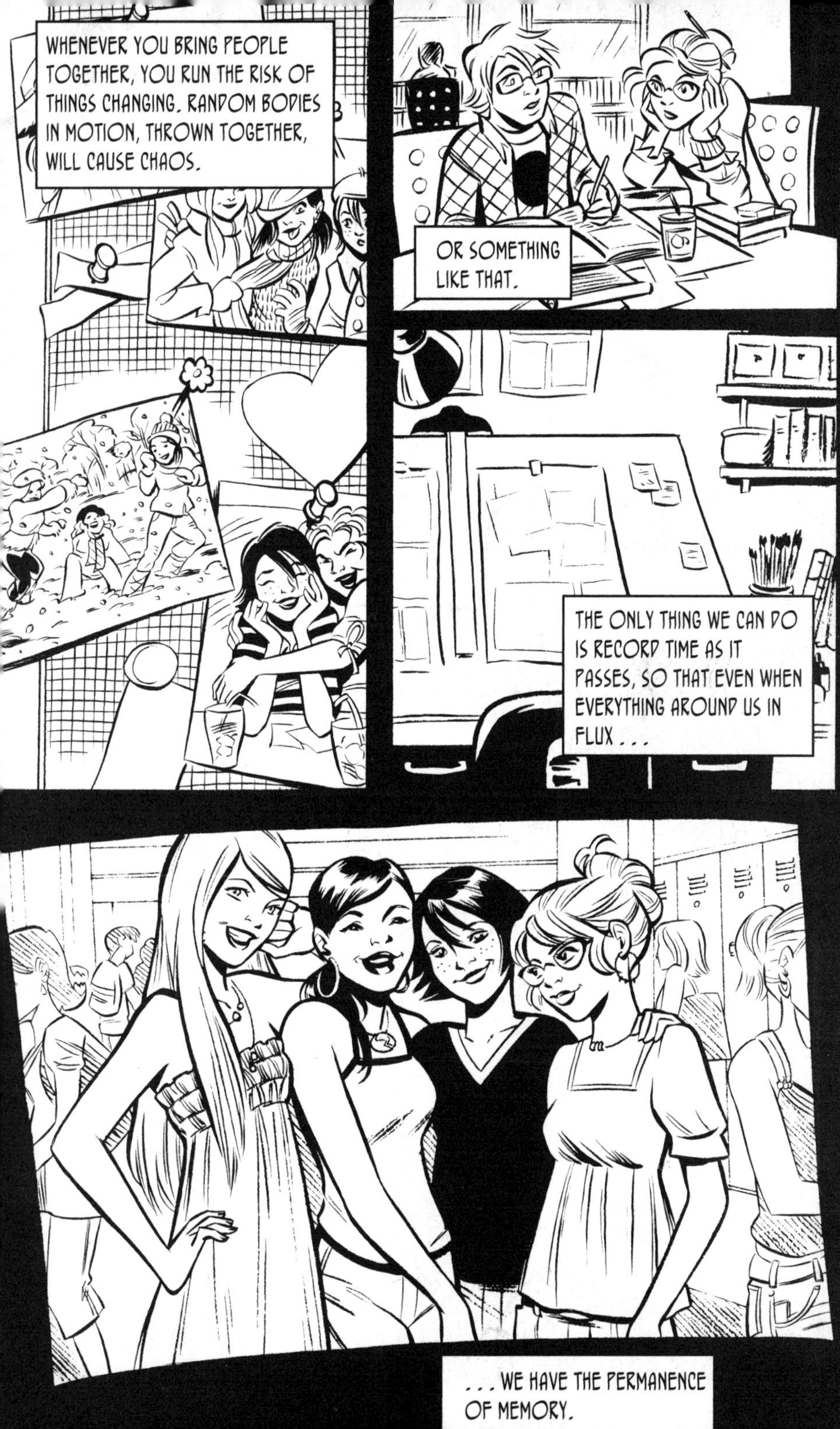
WHENEVER YOU BRING PEOPLE TOGETHER, YOU RUN THE RISK OF THINGS CHANGING. RANDOM BODIES IN MOTION, THROWN TOGETHER, WILL CAUSE CHAOS.
OR SOMETHING LIKE THAT.
THE ONLY THING WE CAN DO IS RECORD TIME AS IT PASSES, SO THAT EVEN WHEN EVERYTHING AROUND US IN FLUX . . .
. . . WE HAVE THE PERMANENCE OF MEMORY.

AIMEE FRIEDMAN is the *New York Times* bestselling author of the novels *South Beach*, *French Kiss*, and *Hollywood Hills*, as well as the romantic comedy *A Novel Idea*. Her work has also appeared in the holiday romance collection *Mistletoe*. Aimee was born and raised in New York City, where she still lives and works as a book editor. She graduated from the Bronx High School of Science (but would have loved attending Fashion High) and has never, as far as she remembers, broken up with her best friends over a boy.

CHRISTINE NORRIE is a Thai-Scot born in West Germany and raised in St. Louis, Missouri. Originally hoping to go into fashion design, she discovered comic books at the age of sixteen and spent six years as a comic shop clerk before moving to New York. Described by *Publishers Weekly* as "a natural storyteller," she has earned two Eisner Nominations, a Russ Manning Nomination, and a 9th Panel and New York City Comic Book Museum Award for her books *Hopeless Savages* and *Cheat*. She currently lives with her husband, daughter, dog, and two cats in a very small apartment in Greenwich Village, New York City.